Caleb

a Novel

CHARLES ALVERSON

LAKE UNION
PUBLISHING

This is a work of fiction. Names, characters, organizations, places, events, and incidents are either products of the author's imagination or are used fictitiously.

Published by Lake Union Publishing, Seattle

www.apub.com

Amazon, the Amazon logo, and Lake Union Publishing are trademarks of Amazon.com Inc. or its affiliates.

ISBN-13: 9781477826232
ISBN-10: 1477826238

Cover design by Olga Grlic

Library of Congress Control Number: 2014941658

Printed in the United States of America

Other Titles from Charles Alverson

The Word

Mad Dog Brewster

Apache Dreaming

Imagine Me

Hooligans

Fighting Back

Goodey's Last Stand: A Joe Goodey Hard Boiled Mystery

Not Sleeping, Just Dead: A Joe Goodey Hard Boiled Mystery

— *1* —

As Boyd Jardine wandered out of Reilly's Tavern, he was drawn to the clamor of voices down by the wharf. A little paddle wheeler towing a barge had just landed, and slaves were being herded, chains clanking, onto the platform where just about everything that came from up or down the river was sold.

Jardine wasn't in the market for another slave. He'd come to Lynche's Landing only to deliver a wagonload of cotton and to get his second-best plow mended. But now his pocket was full of money and his belly half-full of brandy. It didn't hurt to look, did it?

"Step up, step up," the dealer was calling to the shoppers on the boardwalk and idlers on the wharf. "Come see the finest bunch of blacks come down the river this year! Every one a bargain. I've got to sell them all—today! Step up, step up."

Jardine thought they did look pretty good. Especially a high-yellow girl of about thirteen who stood gazing nonchalantly down at him. She had one hand on her hip, and a tear in her sacking shift exposed a small breast. He could smell her from where he stood, and he had to admit it was not a bad smell. Not bad at all.

Jardine was just extending a hand in the direction of the girl when a loud voice called out from behind him, "Careful, Boyd! Nancy would about kill you, and you know it."

He looked around to see Rafe Bentley, his nearest neighbor, laughing and showing his big yellow teeth. Sitting beside him in the buggy, Mrs. Bentley was not smiling.

"Hello, Rafe," Jardine said. "Mrs. Bentley." He raised his straw hat at the sour, angular woman and moved down the platform, not knowing where he was heading, except away from that yellow girl.

His slightly stumbling progress took him past a worn-down old man, more gray-skinned than black, and brought him to the spot where a large, younger man stood turned slightly away from the rest. This one not only wore leg irons like the others, but his hands were cuffed in steel, a sure sign, Jardine reckoned, of a problematic black.

Motivated by no more than curiosity, Jardine looked more closely. The slave was tall, well muscled, and considerably over two hundred pounds. His hands were big and knotted from hard labor, but the most interesting thing about him was his face. There was nothing special about his features—a broad nose cut by an old scar, thick lips, and a strong jaw holding big, regular teeth. But there was something in his eyes that Jardine—even in his pleasantly half-drunken state—thought he recognized, although he couldn't say exactly what it was.

Raising a hand, Jardine gestured for the black man to turn around.

Instead, the slave looked at him directly and said with a dimly recognizable accent, "You don't want to buy me. I'll kill the man who buys me."

Jardine was as dumbfounded as if Jackie, his best mule, had suddenly started spouting Shakespeare. It had to be the brandy, he thought.

"What!" Jardine nearly screamed. "What did you say?"

But the slave's face had closed up like a fist. He looked not down at Jardine but over his head.

Noting the disturbance, the slave dealer worked his way down the platform, pushing his wares out of his way as he went. When he got to Jardine, there was no surprise in his expression. Without thinking, he aimed an open-handed cuff at the big slave's head. He might as well have struck one of the pillars of the wharf for all the notice it got him. But then, remembering why he was on that platform, the dealer adjusted his expression and addressed himself to Jardine.

"High spirits, sir," he said. "They do say it's the sign of a good slave. That is, if a man knows how to handle him."

"I'll handle him, all right," Jardine said. "If I had my pistol on me, I'd shoot him dead."

"That could be an expensive luxury, sir," the dealer said. "This here's a thousand-dollar slave."

"A thousand dollars!" Jardine scoffed. "He looks like dog meat to me."

The dealer grabbed the chain connecting the big man's leg irons to his handcuffs, pulling him off balance and turning him around. "Look at them muscles," he crowed.

"Look at them whip cuts," countered Jardine. The man's broad back was crosshatched with evidence of severe whippings, some old but others still oozing pus.

"Some people," observed the dealer, "think a whip is the answer to everything. For you, sir, I'll make it eight hundred dollars. He's promised to a man down in Baton Rouge who is going to cut my heart out, but I can see that you are the man to tame this blackamoor."

Jardine thought for a long moment. "Five hundred fifty dollars," he said, digging in his pocket.

— 2 —

After getting the bill of sale, Jardine told the dealer's man to strike the leg irons off the slave.

"You sure?" asked the man. "This is a bad one."

"Just get them off," said Jardine.

The dealer's man led the slave to Jardine's wagon. Jardine secured the slave to the tailgate by the chain linking his steel cuffs. Then he asked the slave, "What did you say to me back there?"

The man didn't answer.

"You'll want to talk by-and-by," Jardine told him as he untied the reins and jumped up on the driver's bench.

The slave walked—or ran—every inch of the twelve miles to Three Rivers. When he fell, Jardine—who was not a sadist and kept glancing over his shoulder—stopped the wagon and gave him time to get up. But then he whipped up the donkeys and proceeded along, exactly as if the man were not half staggering, half loping behind, eating red dust and coughing and spitting it back up. Some of the people they passed on the beaten clay road looked with some interest at Jardine driving a mostly empty wagon with a slave stumbling behind it. But in Kershaw County, people minded their own business. If they were white, Jardine raised his straw hat, showed his teeth, and shouted out, "Good day." If they were black, he just didn't see them.

While they were waiting for the mule ferry on the Wateree River, Jardine looked over his new purchase. There were some new skinless patches on his knees and chest and long red streaks where the cuffs had raked his wrists, but nothing serious. Jardine took a long drink of cool water from the earthenware jar in the wagon. Then he filled another gourd and held it up to the slave.

"What did you say to me back there?"

When, once again, the man failed to answer, Jardine poured the water on the ground and went back to waiting for the ferry. The loudest sound was the deep, gasping breaths of the slave.

From the long veranda of Three Rivers plantation, Nancy Jardine, twenty-two years old, more striking than pretty, and just beginning to show her third month of pregnancy, saw the cloud of dust moving down the road from the turnpike. She reached for the brass telescope in its holder on a fluted wooden pillar and put it to her eye. As she had anticipated, it was Jardine. But she hadn't expected to see a black man shambling behind his wagon. The man fell, and Jardine stopped the wagon. Nancy watched until he slowly got up and stood head down. When the wagon started up again, she closed the telescope, saying under her breath, "Boyd, you damned fool."

When Nancy got down to the cotton barn, Jardine was already off the wagon and—with Big Mose standing close by—had broken the chain between the slave's cuffs and nailed each half to the barn door. The man stood between them, spread-eagle and facing the door. With the slim buggy whip in his right hand, Jardine again asked, "What did you say to me back there?"

The new slave, completely red with dust caked on sweat, turned his head to the side, closed his eyes, leaned heavily against the barn door, and gasped. He didn't say a word.

As he stepped back and raised the whip, Jardine sensed Nancy standing behind him. He knew that no matter what he said she wouldn't go away. He felt surrounded by silent adversaries. Bringing the light whip down harder than he'd intended, Jardine heard in rapid sequence the crack of the whip on the man's back, his stifled grunt, and the thump of his big chest hitting the barn door. He saw a spurt of blood as the rawhide broke open a recent welt. He also heard a disapproving intake of breath from Nancy.

Pride barely satisfied, Jardine threw the whip to Mose.

"Get him down and have Dulcie see to those scrapes. Bed him down in the long shed. I'll have a look at him in a few days." Turning around, he feigned surprise at seeing his young wife.

"Hello, darling," he said. "What are you doing down here in all this dirt?"

"I just wanted to welcome you home, dear," she said with a double-edged smile. "Come," she added, taking his slim but masculine hand. "I've got a pitcher of lemonade on the veranda and a real treat—ice. Hurry before it all melts!"

On the veranda in the relative cool of a late June afternoon, Jardine took the glass of lemonade from his wife, sat down on a wicker chair, and pulled her into his lap.

"My God," he said, "that baby must weigh a ton already."

"Thank you!" Nancy laughed.

They talked of this and that: Nancy's busy day, the price of cotton, seeing the Bentleys in town. Nancy did not ask about her husband's new acquisition and would not. It was not her way. But they both knew that the subject would come up eventually.

"I didn't mean to buy him, Nance," Jardine said suddenly. "I had to."

"I know, dear," she said, running a small hand through his thick blond curls.

"You don't know," he protested. "You don't know what he said to me." Jardine waited for her to ask, but he knew better. "He threatened to kill me."

"If you'd run me all those miles behind a wagon and then whipped me, I'd do more than threaten to kill you," she said frankly.

"No, Nance," he said in a pleading voice, almost like a small boy. "He threatened to kill me *before* I bought him."

"Why?"

"He thought I wanted to buy him."

"But you didn't?"

"No!"

Nancy considered this for a moment. "But you bought him."

"I had to," he said.

Nancy slipped her arms around her husband's neck and enveloped him with her small body. "Well, one thing's for sure, darling," she said. "You seem to have got yourself an unusual slave."

"Another thing, Nance," he said, his voice muffled by her long chestnut hair. "He talks funny."

— 3 —

The next morning, while Boyd was out in the fields supervising the slaves, Nancy walked down to the long shed. Taking the stick out of the hasp, she walked into the gloom and waited for her eyes to adjust. Then she saw the new slave sitting on a bale of hay in one corner. A hoop of iron around his neck was secured to a long chain hanging from a thick beam. She could see him watching her. When she got closer but was still well outside the length of the chain, she could see that he had been liberally smeared with Dulcie's homemade salve. It was a villainous blue color with an awful smell, but it seemed to work. On the stamped earth floor was an empty earthenware bowl with a wooden spoon in it. The smell of dirt and sweat was strong in the still air, but she was used to that.

"How are you feeling?" she asked.

The big slave looked at her expressionlessly. There seemed to be no menace in him.

"You'll have to talk some time," she told him. "You live here now. That's not going to change in a hurry. Besides, my husband says you talk funny. I want to hear."

Something changed in the man's eyes. "You talk funny, too," he said.

"I know. I'm from Charleston. My husband says I talk like I've got a mouth full of hot mashed potatoes. Where are you from?"

"Boston." With his flat, nasal accent it sounded like *Baahstun*.

"Massachusetts?"

"It's the only one I know," he said. His tone did not invite further inquiry.

"Tell me," she said. "Why did you threaten to kill my husband if he bought you?"

He paused for a long moment before answering. "I was going to escape from the barge last night. I was desperate."

"Escape to where?"

"I don't know."

"Let me tell you something," she began, but then stopped. "What's your name?"

"Caleb," he said with a touch of surliness.

"Well, Caleb," she continued, "in this part of the county alone, there are five packs of dogs with nothing to do all day but track down escaped slaves. And they don't just track them down. They rip them apart. You may not think it, but my husband did you a favor by buying you, rather than leaving you to escape. If you had succeeded and were still alive now, you wouldn't be for long. Does freedom mean that much to you?"

"Yes." He looked directly into her eyes in a way she'd never seen a slave do. It embarrassed her.

"I can't stop you from running away, Caleb," she said softly. "I can only advise you strongly against it. And I'll give you another piece of advice." She paused until she saw acquiescence in his eyes. "My husband will put you out in the fields, so you won't be seeing much of me, but if our paths do cross, and I speak to you, you would be well advised not to answer me so sharply. My husband won't like it. The people here call me Miss Nancy."

After a long pause he said, "All right—Miss Nancy."

"Good. And my husband likes to be called Master. He insists on it. He will have it."

"Yes . . . Miss Nancy."

She turned to leave but then turned back. "Are you being fed enough, Caleb? Is there anything you need?"

"No, Miss Nancy," Caleb said. "Dulcie is a good woman."

After a few days in the long shed, a good rest, and a lot of Dulcie's cooking, Caleb began to get bored. When Jardine looked in one evening, Caleb got up on his feet—not hurriedly, but quickly enough to be noticed approvingly.

"You feelin' better?"

"Yes, Master." There was nothing sullen in his voice or manner.

That surprised Jardine. He'd expected a long process of education. He didn't know whether to feel sorry or glad. Jardine liked a challenge.

"You got anything more to say to me?"

"No, Master."

"Ready to go to work?"

"Yes, Master."

"Okay. We start work early. Big Mose will turn you loose and show you where you sleep. But remember—my whip is always close by."

— 4 —

Caleb turned out to be a good worker, but the other slaves didn't like him. He was too alien, with his keen, confident gaze and self-contained nature. Caleb never seemed to relax totally. He didn't help break the monotony of long days in the field with coarse humor and old songs. But he worked hard, silently and willingly, which won the others' respect. At first they mocked Caleb's strange, foreign way of talking, but even that didn't last long. Perhaps because he took so little notice of it. Caleb shared a hut with Big Mose, but since Mose was coupled with Dulcie, he had the space to himself most of the time.

Jardine was a slave owner who liked to know everything that was happening on his plantation. One day, about a month after buying Caleb, he opened the door to Caleb's hut and peered into the darkness. The corner Mose occupied now and then was a tangle of blankets and clothing. But the far corner that Caleb had taken over told another story. Caleb's corn-husk mattress had been elevated on a platform of empty boxes, and the ragged sacking sheet and thick blanket had been pulled together with precision. A feed-sack pillow stuffed with clover sat squarely at the head of the improvised bed. An oil lamp with a tin reflector was nailed to the wooden wall, along with a cast-off wooden box that served as a cupboard for Caleb's few possessions.

Jardine poked at the pillow with the swagger stick he carried and revealed something beneath it. Leaning down, Jardine picked up a book. It was coverless, tattered, and water stained, but, by God, a book. Jardine riffled through the pages. He was no expert, but it seemed to be some kind of story set in England in the last century. The people in it were called Bennet. He shoved the book carelessly into the side pocket of his jacket.

Two days later, Jardine rode out into the fields where the blacks were chopping the denuded cotton stalks and signaled Big Mose to give them a rest. As usual, Caleb went off by himself to sit by one of the small rivers that gave the plantation its name. Jardine rode over to where he sat.

Caleb got to his feet—not gladly, but quickly enough. Jardine leaned over the pommel of his saddle.

"Caleb, you missing anything?"

Caleb looked up at him. "Yes, Master."

"And what would that be?" Jardine asked with a sly smile.

"A book, Master."

"A book?" Jardine pretended amazement. "What would you be doing with a book?"

"I got it on the barge. Traded my dinner to a boy for it."

"You went without dinner for a *book*?"

"Yes, Master."

A sudden, astonishing thought came to Jardine. "Caleb," he demanded. "Can you read?"

"Yes, Master."

"And write?"

"Yes, Master."

Jardine reckoned he might as well go the whole hog. "And cipher?"

"Yes, Master."

Jardine thought for a long moment. "How much is six and seven?"

"Thirteen."

"Ninety-one take away eighteen?"

"Seventy-three."

"Eight times forty-three?"

This took a few moments longer. "Three hundred and forty-four."

Jardine paused to calculate that last one in his head and decided to take Caleb's word for it. He moved on to the supreme test.

"Uh . . . two hundred and fifty-six divided by thirteen?"

Caleb had to think a long time about that. "I'm not sure, Master," Caleb said, "but I think it's nineteen and a bit."

Jardine didn't say anything else. He just pulled on the reins and spurred his horse away from the brook. He called to Big Mose, "Get 'em back to work!" and rode toward the house. When he was behind a big line of live oaks, Jardine reined in his horse. Pulling out his little notebook and a pencil, he calculated the long division he had given the slave.

Nineteen point six nine, he worked out, before getting mixed up carrying the naught.

"Son of a bitch!" Jardine exclaimed and spurred the roan toward the house.

Jardine found Nancy in the big food larder doing an inventory of the bottled goods.

"Nancy!" he exclaimed. "You'll never guess what's happened."

"I probably won't, dear," she said calmly.

"I've only bought myself a genius for five hundred and fifty dollars!"

"You told me you paid four hundred and fifty for Caleb," she reminded him.

"Never mind that," Jardine said. "Do you know what that boy can do?"

Nancy kept a straight face. "Play the banjo?"

"No! Goddamn it, Nancy, I'm serious. Caleb can read. I found a book in his hut. Look!" He waved the tattered book at her. "And write. And cipher like a goddamn bookkeeper! Long division! In his head!" He pulled out his notebook and shoved it before Nancy's eyes. "I checked. Look!"

Nancy took the notebook from his hand and confirmed his figures.

"In his head?" she asked.

"Yes! Did you ever hear anything like it?"

"And you've got him chopping cotton," Nancy said, the devil dancing in her soft gray eyes.

"Well, how was I to know?" Jardine demanded. "These damned slaves never tell you anything except things you don't want to hear."

— 5 —

Caleb didn't hear anything more from Jardine for over a week—though he did find the book where Nancy had shoved it back under his pillow. But then one evening at just about sundown, Dulcie came to the door of Caleb's hut and said, "Marse wants to see you in the horse barn." Caleb shoved the book under his mattress and left the hut.

Jardine was waiting for him, whacking the side of his boot with the swagger stick. He liked to think it made him look like an army officer. "Caleb," he said.

"Yes, Master?" It made Jardine a little nervous that this new slave didn't call him *Marse* or *Massa* like the other slaves, though he didn't really feel that he could complain about it.

"Where did you learn to read and write and all that?"

"When I was a boy, Mr. Staunton had a tutor for Brent, and he taught me, too."

"Mr. Staunton? Brent?" Jardine asked angrily. "Who are they?"

Caleb was a quick learner. "Old Master and Young Master," he said.

"That's better. Where the hell were they?"

"Boston, Master."

"Boston?" Jardine exclaimed. "No wonder you're so god-damned uppity. I spent most of a year in Boston myself. At Harvard College."

"Yes, Master."

Jardine was a little disappointed at Caleb's lack of response to this bit of information, but he plowed on. "Caleb, I'm thinking of moving you up to the house. I'm too busy to look after the accounts book, the business side of the plantation, and all that. Do you think you could do that?"

"Yes, Master."

"Well, if I bring you up to the house, don't think you'll be sitting on the seat of your pants all the time. No, you'll do anything Miss Nancy tells you to do and generally make yourself useful. You'll live over the coach house with Andrew, my coachman, and eat with the house slaves. That sound good?"

"Yes, Master."

"All right," Jardine said. "Get back to your hut. I'll let you know what I decide."

"Thank you, Master." Caleb turned and started to walk away from the barn, but Jardine stopped him.

"Caleb! How long you been a slave?"

"All my life, Master."

"No, I mean down here. Down south."

"Almost five years."

"And you never told anyone that you could read and write and that?"

"No, Master."

"Why the hell not? Do you like working in the fields?"

"No, Master."

"Then why not?"

Caleb thought carefully before he answered. "I didn't plan to stay a slave."

Jardine didn't like the sound of that, but it wasn't enough of a challenge to stir things up—not just yet. "Well, you'd better get used to it," he said. "Go back to your hut."

"Yes, Master." Caleb turned to leave, but again Jardine stopped him.

"Wait! You're not teaching any of the rest of my people to read and write, are you?"

"No, Master."

"Well, don't. There're more than enough book-learned slaves around here to suit me. You remember that."

"Yes, Master."

$$— \; 6 \; —$$

Before the week was out, Caleb was working in the plantation office at the back of the house.

Now that he was no longer working in the fields, Caleb was able to get a clearer picture of the Three Rivers plantation and its people. The house itself, a substantial three-story wood-framed building, was about fifty years old. A veranda wrapped around three of its sides, and fluted wooden pillars flanked its big front door. The house was set in about three hundred acres of prime cotton land, which was worked by some twenty slaves. The field slaves, their wives, and a dozen children lived in whitewashed wooden huts scattered around a cookhouse. A series of barns containing livestock and farm equipment separated the huts from the house. The six house girls ate in the kitchen but slept in an annex at the back of the house.

Caleb moved his few belongings into the loft above the coach house. Miss Nancy gave him some of Jardine's father's cast-off clothing, which had been in storage since the old man died four years before. As Caleb began to settle into the routine of the house, his biggest challenge was getting the books in order. Since taking over the plantation upon his father's death, Jardine's method had been to throw all the paperwork into a big box. He'd figured he would find the time to get it organized one of these days.

Caleb set to work, and within a month the books were in order. For the first time, Jardine knew whether Three Rivers was making money and why. Caleb told him that he was paying too much for seed and manure, that he had money in the bank in Charleston not drawing any interest, and that Jed Carter down Oaksley way owed him money that was long overdue.

"You know, Nance," Jardine said in bed one night, "I was right. That boy is a goddamned—"

"Don't swear, Boyd."

"Well, he *is* a marvel," Jardine said defensively, "and we might never have known it. What did we ever do without him?"

"We managed," said Nancy mildly.

"Don't you like him?" Jardine demanded suspiciously. "Is he causing you problems here in the house? I'll—"

"Far from it, Boyd," Nancy said firmly. "Caleb's turned out to be very useful around the house. I just don't think he's the second coming of Jesus Christ, that's all."

"Now who's swearing?" said Jardine triumphantly.

Caleb was more than just useful, Nancy had discovered over the past weeks. He was an extremely well-trained house servant. Unlike Cassie, the house girl, he knew how to lay the table perfectly, with every piece of silver and crystal in order and the damask table napkins folded at each place like little caps. He knew which wine to serve and when, how to make beer, which spice went with which meat, and much of the other household minutiae that Nancy would have learned from her mother had she not been orphaned so young. Instead—though she hoped he didn't realize it—Nancy was learning from Caleb. In her sewing room, she kept a big lined-paper book that was filling up with the useful information she'd gleaned.

Jardine didn't notice the difference, but Mrs. Rafe Bentley, on one of her visits to Three Rivers, commented, "My dear, I must compliment you on your table arrangements. I haven't seen anything to match them this side of New Orleans. And how do you get your silver gleaming so?"

"Hickory ash, household soda, and hard work," Nancy was able to tell her, thanks to Caleb.

One day as they were going over the household accounts, Miss Nancy asked him, "Caleb, we haven't talked about this, but what you said to my husband that day on the wharf, the day he bought you—did you mean it?"

"Yes, Miss Nancy," Caleb said without looking up from the account book.

"Do you still mean it?"

"No, Miss Nancy."

"But you still want to be free, Caleb?"

"Yes, Miss Nancy. I always have. I always will."

— 7 —

When Nancy was about eight months pregnant, she cut herself on a bit of old wire in the bottling room, and blood poisoning set in. Helplessly, Jardine watched her turn pale and then as yellow as old lard. Her girlish gaiety faded away, and she seemed to sink into the big old bed as if she would disappear into the mattress. The poison spread up her left arm until it was dark gray streaked with virulent yellow all the way to the elbow. A fever raged in her that cold compresses and herbal medicines did little to fight.

"I'm all right, darling, really," she told Jardine. "Just tired. I'll be better tomorrow." But he had seen too much blood poisoning to believe her.

Outside, Jardine told Caleb, "I'm going to ride to Wisshatchie for Dr. Hollander. I'll be back late tonight. You and Cassie look after Miss Nancy, you hear? If anything happens to her, I'll—" Jardine stopped. He knew he was wasting time. Jumping on the big roan, he spurred away from the house toward the turnpike. Caleb turned back and walked into the house feeling helpless.

Boyd Jardine always was a strong believer in luck, but that day his luck ran out. Rainfall had been heavy recently, and when he got to the Ossingamee River, he saw that it was in flood. The mule ferry had turned over and sunk. Time after time, he forced the roan to plunge into the fast-running river only to have it lose the fight against the water and begin to be swept downstream. Finally, tethering his exhausted, heaving, and lathering horse to a rowan-berry bush, Jardine sat down and cried like a boy of seven, not a man of twenty-nine.

Back at Three Rivers, the shadows of evening were falling when Cassie came running into the little office, where Caleb was trying to make a stubborn column of figures add up twice in a row.

"You better come," she gasped. "Miss Nancy . . . she's worse . . . she's . . ."

"What can I do?" Caleb demanded. "Master's coming with the doctor."

"You just better come," she insisted. "You better."

When Caleb got up to the big bedroom at the front of the house, he saw that Cassie was right. Miss Nancy was totally yellow now, and she seemed to have shrunk to the point where only the pitifully small bump of her pregnancy stood out underneath the covers. In contrast to the bright white pillowcase, her face looked like one of the little yellow apples that grew out near the horse barn. It was dwarfed by her rich chestnut hair, which fanned out across the pillow.

"Caleb," she said, "is my husband—"

"He'll be back, Miss Nancy," Caleb said helplessly. "It won't be long now."

"I'm so weak, Caleb," she said faintly. "I feel so weak."

"Can I get you anything, Miss Nancy?" Caleb asked, wanting more than anything to escape from that room, with its terrible odor of decaying flesh.

"No," she whispered. "Yes, get me a sip of water. From the nightstand. Please."

Caleb filled a china teacup from the earthenware crock and held it toward Miss Nancy. "Please," she said. "I can't—"

Sitting down on the bedside chair, Caleb supported her head with his left hand while he put the cup to her cracked lips. Her skin felt hot to his touch and her neck limp and boneless. He poured a trickle of water carefully into her open mouth until she started to cough.

"Enough," she croaked. "That's better. That's much better. Thank you." Caleb eased her head back into the groove of the pillow.

Caleb started to get up, but she stopped him with a hand that felt as though it were on fire. "Please," she said. "Please stay. Sit, sit." She tried to raise her head. "Cassie," she said to the house slave, who was hovering behind Caleb wringing her hands and praying, "I think I could eat something. Could you make me some soup?"

"Yes, Missy, right away!" Cassie said and fled through the bedroom doorway.

When she was gone, Nancy looked up at Caleb, who had sat back down on the bedside chair. "Caleb," she said faintly but evenly, "I think I'm dying."

"Miss Nancy—"

"Please listen. I'm so weak, but I feel no pain. I think I'm beyond pain now, Caleb. I don't think I can hold on until Mr. Jardine gets back with the doctor."

"You can do it, Miss Nancy."

"I don't think so, Caleb," she said. "Poor Boyd. You will look after him for me, won't you?"

"Miss Nancy," Caleb couldn't think of anything to say.

"He's not a bad man, Caleb. Be patient. Help him. He'll need it." Her small right hand still gripped his wrist. There was no strength in it.

"I'll do what I can," he said.

"Thank you," she said, so faintly that Caleb could barely hear her. "I'm so sorry . . ." Her voice faded away.

"Miss Nancy—"

". . . about the baby . . . my baby . . . I just know it's a boy. Boyd so wanted a son . . . and I so wanted to . . . to give . . ."

Her fingers released his wrist, and her hand fell limply to the mattress.

— 8 —

"Miss Nancy?"

Her eyelids, the yellow of old ivory, had closed, and her sharp little chin seemed to be tucked into the frilly top of her white lace nightgown. Her left arm, which lay on the bedcover, was almost black. Caleb picked up her right arm to feel for a pulse, but there was none. He tried pressing two fingers to her childlike throat. Nothing. Finally, in desperation, he went to the dresser, picked up the silver-filigree hand mirror, and pressed it to her slack lips. Again, he put the mirror to her mouth. Nothing. Miss Nancy was dead. There was no way out of it.

Caleb was leaving the room to go tell Cassie, when he looked back at Nancy's slim body with its incongruously distended stomach. There was a baby in there, he thought. Perhaps a live baby.

Caleb left the room and met Cassie as she was coming up the stairs with a tray covered with a white cloth.

He made up his mind. "Take that back downstairs, Cassie," he said. "Miss Nancy doesn't want it."

"But—"

"You do as I say. And keep that fire on. Put a pot of water on the stove. As soon as it boils, you bring me a big bowl of it and put it down by the door. Don't you come back in here until I tell you. Understand?"

Cassie looked at him with big eyes, nodded, and went back down the stairs two at a time.

Caleb returned to the bedroom. Miss Nancy's body lay still on the big bed. Only the bump stood out; it seemed to be getting bigger. Caleb couldn't look at anything else. Going to the window, he stared into the distance toward the turnpike, hoping to see a cloud of dust coming from that way. But there was none, and soon he wouldn't be able to see. Caleb lit a big oil lamp with a leaded-glass shade that looked like a church window. He put it on the bedside table and again looked down at Miss Nancy. He shook his head. Looking was not going to get the job done.

Going into the master's dressing room, he picked up the ivory-handled straight razor from the marble washstand. Caleb felt the edge and gave the razor a few hard whacks on the leather strop hanging on the wall. He tested it again. Plenty sharp. Caleb took a large towel from a pile on a shelf near the washing bowl. He carried it and the razor out into the bedroom and put them on the bedside table. Caleb felt an urge to go back to the window, but he shook it off. Reaching down, he grabbed the bedding and threw it on the floor, completely revealing Miss Nancy in the nightgown that had crept up above her knees. She looked like a child, a little yellow child with a swollen belly.

Steeling himself, Caleb reached down, gripped the hem of her nightgown, and gently worked it up until it was over the bump of her pregnancy. He deliberately kept his eyes on the nightgown, but when at last he had to look down and saw the small triangle of rich brown hair where her legs met, he felt nothing but anxiety. The blue-veined skin stretched tautly over her belly like an over-inflated balloon. Now how did Mr. Regan show them?

His mind flashed back ten years to Boston, when Brent's tutor, a failed medical school student at Harvard College, had interrupted their ancient history lessons with demonstrations of some of the basic surgical techniques he had learned before being asked to leave.

"Now, boys," he'd said, "there will be times when your patient will not be able to get that baby out by herself. She just can't. What are you going to do, Brent?"

The thin blond boy of thirteen looked blank. "Go for help?"

"There ain't no help," Regan said scornfully. "There's just you and that woman and that baby inside her. And they're both going to die if you don't do something and do it quick. I've told you all this, damn it. Don't you boys ever listen? I'm giving you the benefit of my considerable education. Do you want to study that dusty old Greek history, or do you want to learn something useful?" Without waiting for an answer, he snapped, "Caleb?"

Wide-eyed, Caleb stared at the tutor. Finally, he guessed, "Ces . . . cesarium something?"

"Right!" said Regan. "Cesarean section. At least one of you dunderheads is paying attention—some of the time." He looked scornfully at Brent. "How the hell," he asked the boy, "can you actually own this nappy-headed boy if he's so much smarter than you?"

Brent didn't answer. He just gave Caleb a dirty look that let him know he would pay for his lucky guess.

"Okay," said Regan. "Pay attention. I'm only going to do this once. I only have one fig." Reaching over to the fruit bowl, he grasped a ripe Smyrna fig and held it out to the boys. He tightened his grip on the fruit until it seemed that its tight purple skin would burst. "Now, this is your pregnant woman's belly. In there is a baby, and it has to come out. And it has to come out in a hurry. The poor little bastard could suffocate in there. Either of you boys happen to have a scalpel on you?" When they both looked baffled, he sighed. "Hand me that penknife, Brent."

Taking the little pearl-handled knife in his hand, Regan brought the thin blade up to the fig until it nearly touched. "Now, boys," he said, "you have to imagine that this fig has a belly button right about here." He touched the fruit delicately with the tip of the blade. "Now, don't go plunging in there. You'll just mess that poor woman up, and that baby will still be in there snug as anything. No, you go due south of that umbilicus—old Snodgrass says about a hand's width—and you go in, there!"

The boys watched with fascination as the thin blade cut into the purple skin and a little spurt of juice welled out. Brent closed his eyes.

"Now, don't be fainthearted, boys. When you cut, *cut.* You're not hurting that woman; you're helping her. As old Snodgrass says, the man with a scalpel in his hand is God. He can do no wrong. Anyway, you just press down on that scalpel hard and c-u-u-u-t"—he drew the word out as the blade plunged in and cut vertically—"through the abdominal and uterine walls. You won't hurt the baby. He's well tucked in down there. You have to give him a nice big cleft to escape through." The fig gushed its rich green many-seeded insides, and both boys closed their eyes.

Putting the penknife down on the desk blotter, Regan reached his delicate fingers down into the depths of the slashed fig and pretended to take out a tiny baby. Then he extended the pulpy mass of the ruined fruit toward his charges. "Care for a bit of fig, boys?"

— *9* —

For the first time, Caleb wished that he'd paid more attention to Mr. Regan's lesson. He laid his left hand on Miss Nancy's swollen, cooling stomach so that his little finger just grazed her slightly protruding navel. Then he brought the straight-edged razor down so that its rounded tip touched the knuckle of his left thumb. Taking a deep breath, he began to push on the razor. At first it only dented the elastic skin, but Caleb took another breath, pushed strongly, and then felt the sharp German steel begin to cut through the abdominal flesh.

"Forgive me, Miss Nancy," Caleb mumbled as he saw blood begin to seep sluggishly from the wound he was making. Biting his lip, he pushed harder and sensed that something resistant, but not hard, was giving way beneath the blade. Finally, he had a slit of ten or twelve inches running from about five inches below her belly button down nearly to the pubic hair. Caleb looked carefully at what he had done.

Ain't no baby coming out of that little hole, he told himself. Caleb had butchered plenty of pigs in the last five years, and he tried to forget that he was not only cutting up a human being, but a white woman and the wife of his master. Swiftly and more determinedly but delicately, he cut both ways from his first vertical slash until he'd created a considerable opening.

"Come on, baby," Caleb said under his breath, but he knew that baby wasn't going anyplace without a lot of help.

Steeling himself, he reached down and pulled back the flaps of skin and tissue that he had created with the razor, looking desperately for any sign of life in there. His fingers felt like tent pegs, huge and insensitive, but he kept groping with them, gently pulling apart anything that got in their way and peering through the dim light of the lamp. Finally, in the morass of pink flesh, gray innards, and pooled blood, he saw the baby tucked up like a young frog. He got his two hands around it. It was the smallest thing that Caleb had ever handled, but he lifted it out of Miss Nancy's dead body as if it weighed a thousand pounds and was made of crystal glass. The umbilical cord uncoiled and followed the bloody, slime-covered baby. Mr. Regan had told them about that. He told them that the baby ate and breathed through the cord until it was born.

Caleb saw that the baby was male. Ignoring the cord, Caleb looked for signs of life in the pale yellow baby. His eyes were clamped shut and his mouth hung open. Caleb knew you were supposed to spank the baby to jolt it into independent life, and the baby felt solid enough in his big hands, but he didn't dare. Seeing that the baby's head and face were covered with a sort of translucent weblike substance, Caleb took a corner of the satin bedsheet and wiped the baby's entire face clear.

Suddenly, with a contortion that went right up Caleb's arms, the baby threw back his head and took a deep breath. The breath came back out in a sharp but feeble cry, and Caleb knew that he had a live baby in his hands. Caleb set the baby on the bed and reached for the towel on the bedside table. He had started to wrap the baby in it when he remembered the umbilical cord. He slashed it with the razor a few inches from the baby's body and finished wrapping him in the soft towel. Striding swiftly to the bedroom door, he opened it and shouted, "Cassie! You bring that hot water up here. Right now!"

When Cassie came up the stairs, panting and slopping hot water along the way, Caleb was blocking the partially open bedroom door.

"Put the water down, Cassie," he said, "and take this." He held out the towel-wrapped baby. Before she could react, he asked, "Are any of the women nursing?"

Cassie's attention was so riveted on that baby that she couldn't answer for a moment.

"Well?" demanded Caleb.

"Yes, Massa," Cassie said in her confusion. "Sukey got a baby. Two or three months."

"Clean this baby up," Caleb said, "and take him to Sukey."

Cassie stood there dumbly with the baby in her arms. "How . . . how Miss Nancy?" she finally asked.

"Not good, Cassie," Caleb said as gently as he could. "Very bad. Now take that baby to Sukey."

The girl walked down the stairs carefully. Caleb picked up the basin of hot water and went back into the bedroom, locking the door behind him. He wrapped Miss Nancy in the bedding and placed her on the floor near the big front window.

He removed the sheets from the bed and used a towel and the hot water to scrub the bloodstain on the mattress to a faint pink. Then he turned the mattress and swiftly remade the bed with clean sheets from the linen closet. He went back to where Miss Nancy lay in her nest of bedding. She was still smeared with blood from the navel down. He wanted to clean her up, but could not bring himself to do the touching involved. Instead, he put a fresh nightgown on his mistress and placed her in the clean bed, arranging her as neatly as he could, with one hand laid on top of the other over her diminished stomach. He fanned her dark hair out over the satin pillow. She looked as though she were in a deep sleep of exhaustion.

Looking around the bedroom, Caleb saw the bloody straight razor on the bed table, quickly washed it, and returned it to Jardine's dressing room. Another glance around the room told him he could do no more. Leaving the lamp on by the bed, Caleb carried the bloody bedding and towels downstairs to the laundry room and plunged them into a vat of cold water. Rolling up his sleeves, he worked at the bedding until the water turned pink. He changed the water again and again until it came out clear.

By this time, it was well after midnight, and still there was no sign of Jardine. Cassie, after reporting that the baby was suckling well with Sukey, curled up on the horsehair sofa in the big reception room and went to sleep. Caleb realized that he was hungry, but he felt too tired to bother eating. He sat down in a big chair to wait and fell asleep.

— *10* —

The sound of carriage wheels and shouting out front woke them both. "Cassie," Caleb said, shaking her to alertness, "go get the baby." Then he walked out of the front door to the veranda.

Jardine had just sprung rubber-legged from Dr. Hollander's buggy. Hollander, a big man with muttonchops and tiny round spectacles, threw his reins to Big Mose. Jardine's roan was tied behind the buggy.

"How is she, Caleb?" Jardine demanded. His clothes were wet and smeared with mud. He'd lost his hat and his thick blond hair hung down in a filthy tangle.

Caleb could not speak. He just stood looking at his master with dumb misery. He shook his head.

"Damn you!" Jardine snarled, ran up the wooden steps past Caleb, and disappeared into the house.

Getting heavily out of his buggy with his bag in his hand, the doctor looked closely at Caleb. "Dead?" he asked.

"Yes, sir." Caleb said helplessly.

"The baby?"

"Alive, sir," Caleb said, "but—"

At that moment, Cassie arrived with the baby, wrapped in a quilt. After opening the quilt and doing a quick but thorough examination of the baby, the doctor turned to Caleb.

"Let's get up there."

In the master bedroom, they found Jardine on his knees on the bed with Miss Nancy in his arms. He was sobbing and talking to her as if he could coax her back to life. In his arms she was like a large rag doll. Jardine kept running his fingers down both sides of her face, hoping that the stimulation would somehow wake her and bring her back to him. He kissed her flaccid face passionately. He was aware of no one else in the world.

With a motion of his head, Dr. Hollander sent Caleb from the room. "Tell the girl to bring the baby," he whispered.

When the door shut behind Caleb, the doctor walked up behind Jardine and put his hand on his shoulder. Jardine shook it off as a horse would a bothersome fly.

"Come on, Boyd," Hollander said. "She's at peace. You can do no more."

"Leave me alone!" Jardine cried without turning his head. He pulled his dead wife to his chest, as if trying to start her heart with the beat of his own. "Go away!"

The doctor put his bag down on a fluted marble table. He got out a small bottle and a tiny beaker the size of a shot glass. Then he poured thick liquid from the bottle into the beaker. Leaving it on the table, the doctor went back to Jardine.

"Boyd," he said, putting a hand on each of Jardine's shoulders, "there's a baby. The baby lived. You have a son."

"I don't care!" The words flashed out before Jardine could think. After a moment, Jardine released his grip on his dead wife and allowed Hollander to pull him to his feet. Hollander walked to the door and opened it, revealing Cassie with the baby. Caleb stood well behind her, wishing that he were invisible. Jardine stood staring at Cassie and his baby as if he didn't understand what he was seeing.

"A son?" he asked.

"That's right," Hollander said, gesturing for Cassie to stay where she was. "Have a look. He's a fine boy."

Jardine took one stiff-legged step forward. Then another. Cassie, in tears, held the baby out toward him. With another look back at his wife, Jardine stared down at the baby but did not take it. "What's his name?" he asked dumbly.

"That's up to you," Hollander said, picking up the tiny beaker. "Here, drink this," he said.

"What is it?" Jardine demanded. "It won't make me sleep?" He looked again at the bed behind him. "I can't—"

"Drink," the doctor commanded, extending the beaker. "You have to. It will make you feel better."

Jardine, eyes half-closed, gave a small shrug and took the beaker. He got most of it down before turning, stumbling onto the bed, and going back down on his knees. He gathered his wife back up in his arms.

Hollander motioned Cassie out of the room and gestured for Caleb to wait there. He then sat down in a blackwood chair. In a few minutes, Jardine was asleep, lying on his dead wife's breast. His thinly stubbled face was almost like a child's.

Opening the door, the doctor motioned Caleb into the room and directed him to carry Jardine across the hall to a guest bedroom.

"Undress him," the doctor ordered, "and get him into bed. He'll sleep for hours. Then go down and get something to eat."

"Yes, Doctor," Caleb said.

— *11* —

Caleb had eaten and was sitting half-asleep at the long rough table in the back kitchen when Cassie told him that the doctor wanted him upstairs. When he walked heavily into the master's bedroom, Caleb saw that the doctor had stripped the bedding off Miss Nancy right to the bottom of the big bed. And he'd pulled up her nightgown to reveal the awful gashes Caleb had made to her abdomen, which was covered in dried blood. In the early morning light, Miss Nancy's skin had begun to turn gray. She looked like the deadest thing that Caleb had ever seen. He wanted to look away but could not.

"Close the door and lock it," Hollander ordered. Caleb did as he was told, then turned back to the doctor, who asked abruptly, "What's your name?"

"Caleb, sir."

"Caleb, did you do this?"

"Yes, sir," Caleb said.

"Clearly she was dead," Hollander said, "or you would have had a hell of a lot more blood."

"Yes, sir."

"But where on earth did you learn how to do a cesarean section? And what did you do it with?"

Caleb explained how he'd learned the procedure and showed him Jardine's straight razor.

"If that don't beat all," said the amazed doctor. "A slave surgeon." He shook his head. "You know," he added, "that if she'd been alive you'd have killed her. You cut right through the dorsal aorta."

"If Miss Nancy'd been alive," Caleb said, "I wouldn't have tried it."

"You know, you saved the baby," said the doctor. "By the time we got here, he'd have been long dead. You did a good job."

"Thank you, sir."

Dr. Hollander shook his head violently. "But we can't stand here talking shop. I want you to understand one thing, Caleb."

"Sir?"

"This didn't happen. If anybody asks, Cassie helped deliver that baby, and then Miss Nancy died. It happened like that. Do you understand?"

"Yes, sir."

"Well, you make sure that Cassie understands it, too. It's vital. And do you have a coffin here or a carpenter to make one?"

"Yes, sir," Caleb said. "A man came through here just last month, selling coffins. Master bought two of them. They're up in the attic." Caleb remembered what a joke Jardine had thought it to be, buying coffins when there wasn't anyone even sick on the plantation.

"Good. Well, get one of them down and get it cleaned up. We have to get this poor girl in the ground as soon as your master wakes up. Now, get moving."

Jardine slept for nearly five hours. By the time he woke, sober, pale, and quiet, Nancy was lying in the newly bought coffin in the big reception room. While Jardine was dressing, Doc Hollander told Caleb, "If you want to say good-bye to your mistress, you'd better go do it."

Caleb walked into the reception room, which was empty except for the open coffin standing on sawhorses in the middle of the room. The coffin lid stood propped behind the front door. It seemed like every flower on the property had been picked, and Miss Nancy, dressed in the white *peau de soie* dress in which she had been married, was covered with flowers to just above her waist. Her hands lay crossed on a bed of pure white roses.

From the side of the coffin, Caleb looked down on the face of the woman who had shown him so much kindness in the months he'd been at the plantation. Though Dulcie had done her best with powder, Miss Nancy's face was still gray-yellow, showing the ordeal she had been through. She looked like an exhausted little girl.

"I'm sorry, Miss Nancy," he said. "I did the best I could." He couldn't think of anything else to say. Turning, he walked through the door to the back of the house.

Big Mose and Hector had dug a grave beneath a big horse-chestnut tree in the family plot, which was halfway up a slope. It was a very small funeral. Only Jardine, the doctor, and the slaves were there. Big Mose and Hector stood ready to lower Miss Nancy into the grave. Caleb stood behind Jardine, who had not seemed to notice him when he came shakily downstairs. Sukey held the newborn baby to her breast. Since the nearest minister was close to thirty miles away, Doc Hollander thought it was up to him to say a few words.

Dr. Hollander moved to the foot of the grave, where a crude cross leaned against a tree stump, ready for erecting. Holding his big beaver-skin hat in both hands, he glanced down at the closed coffin lying on planks over the grave.

"We all knew Miss Nancy as a kind, warm, compassionate, and loving young woman, and we will miss her more than we can know at this time. But Miss Nancy is with God now, and she feels no pain. She is looking down on us from a better place, secure in the

knowledge that we will take good care of the son she left behind, the finest gift she could have given this world." He looked up at the assembled slaves and Jardine. "If you loved Miss Nancy, show her you honor her memory by living the best lives you can." Taking a small black Bible from his coat pocket, he read the twenty-third psalm in a warm and mournful voice. Several of the women began to sob. Finishing the reading, Hollander closed the Bible and signaled the men to lower the coffin.

As Big Mose and Hector struggled with the ropes, Jardine seemed to wake up and notice what was happening.

"Stop!" he cried. "Don't! Wait! You can't—" He stumbled toward the two men who were slowly lowering the coffin, but Caleb stepped forward and took a firm grip on his arms. Jardine spun around, broke free, and looked at Caleb angrily.

"You! What are you doing here?" Jardine demanded. "You killed her, you black bastard! Get away! Get out of my sight!"

When Dr. Hollander moved forward to grab hold of Jardine, Caleb backed away from the gravesite. "I'm sorry, Master," he said as he turned around and walked down the hill toward the house.

Hollander turned Jardine back toward the grave, and the last thing Caleb heard as he walked away was the hollow thud of earth striking the lid of the coffin.

— *12* —

That day, ordered by Jardine, Caleb moved back into the hut he'd shared with Big Mose. Early the next morning, he went to work in the fields. He was more isolated from the other slaves than ever. Though the outside world was told that Cassie helped deliver the baby just before Miss Nancy died, the slaves knew that no one had been in that locked bedroom with the mistress but Caleb. Miss Nancy had died, and Caleb had walked out of there with a living baby. There was talk of magic—white and black. But nobody talked about it to Caleb. They were warier than ever of this funny-talking outsider and left him strictly alone beyond the plainest necessary communication.

Caleb had been back in the fields for just over a month and had not seen Jardine even once. The house slaves said that he wasn't at Three Rivers much, that he spent all his time in Cassatt or another town in the area. He even went as far afield as Camden, the county seat, and when he came back he was so drunk that he had to be carried from the buggy and put into bed. Each time, as soon as he recovered, he was off again. Once he came back with a red-haired woman who the house slaves said was from Charleston. But after a few noisy days, he was gone again, and so was she. The baby, named Boyd after his father, remained with Sukey and had no idea that he wasn't as black as the other baby who shared her swollen breasts.

In the meantime, life stood still at Three Rivers. The slaves did the minimum work necessary, tended their own little gardens, fished in the rivers and the lake, and waited for the plantation to snap out of its dreamlike state. For Caleb, this was a good time. While he'd been up at the big house, Miss Nancy had lent him several books from the library of old Mr. Jardine, and he now spent his free hours reading and wondering if he was ever going to escape. He thought about lighting out while Jardine was away or drunk, but what Miss Nancy had said about the dog packs stuck in his mind. One day, a group of whites had ridden onto the plantation, many hounds snapping around the heels of their horses, demanding to know whether anyone had seen two slaves who had disappeared from a farm a dozen miles away on the other side of the turnpike. All the Three Rivers people had been forced to line up while an angry little man wearing a black hat stalked up and down the row, hitting a whip against his boot and peering closely at their faces.

Finally, late one afternoon, Jardine came home again, and this time Dr. Hollander was with him. They disappeared into the house, but within an hour, the doctor was outside again and heading toward the slave quarter. He found Caleb reading beneath a lime tree.

"What are you reading, Caleb?" the doctor called. He stopped and leaned against the rail fence.

Caleb got up and closed the book. "Something about the Roman Empire, sir," he said, holding up the book.

The doctor looked at the title page and whistled. "You understand this stuff?" he asked.

"Some of it," Caleb said. "I mostly skip the big words."

"I would, too," laughed the doctor. "And a lot of the small ones, too." Then his tone changed. "How are you doing, Caleb?"

"I'm all right, sir."

"You know that your master is home again?"

"Yes, sir."

"He's in a bad way, Caleb," the doctor said. "If your master keeps on this way, he's going to drink himself to death. Or dash his brains out falling from his horse. He's out of control."

Caleb just looked at him.

"He needs you up at the house," the doctor said. "Cassie and those fool house girls can't do a thing with him. The place is going to wrack and ruin. Do you want to come back and work in the house, Caleb?"

"Yes, sir," Caleb said. "Does the master want me back there?"

"Well," Hollander said, "he doesn't know it yet, but yes, he does."

"Does he still blame me for Miss Nancy's death?"

"Caleb," the doctor said, "he knows you didn't kill Miss Nancy. He thinks *he* did, but he's got to blame somebody else. Do you understand that?"

"No, sir."

"I've read about it in books," Hollander said, "but that doesn't mean I understand it, either. Where are your things, Caleb?"

"In that hut over there, sir," Caleb said, indicating his quarters.

"Well, get them," the doctor said. "This is moving day."

At Dr. Hollander's suggestion, Caleb moved into a small room at the top of the house in order to be close by when needed.

— *13* —

Thanks to the medication Dr. Hollander gave him, Boyd Jardine slept for two days and two nights. When he awoke, the doctor had gone back to town, and Caleb was standing by his bed with a bowl of hot water and a towel. A breakfast tray was on the bedside table. Jardine started to rise up angrily, but then fell weakly back onto the pillow.

"Bring me whiskey," he demanded.

"There's none in the house, Master," Caleb said. "Dr. Hollander took it."

Jardine considered this for a moment. "Then get me some wine."

"The wine cellar is locked," Caleb told him. Before Jardine could protest, he added, "And the key is lost. We've looked everywhere."

"Isn't there *anything* to drink?" Jardine asked plaintively.

"Lime juice and water, Master," Caleb said with a straight face.

Jardine thought again and absentmindedly stroked his jaw, encountering nearly a week's growth of stubble. "Give me that, then, and get me my shaving things," he ordered. "And get the hell out of here!"

"Yes, Master."

In the following weeks, Three Rivers returned to normal—or as normal as it would ever be without Miss Nancy. When he got his strength back, Jardine went back to work with a fury, driving the slaves—who had come to appreciate the pace of the slowed-down plantation—with a sharp tongue and a heavy hand. From dawn to dusk he was out on the big roan making sure that the winter crops were in and that the cotton fields were being prepared for spring. The slaves knew that the easy days were over. Jardine drove himself even harder than he drove the slaves and came back to the house every night exhausted but tense, his dark-rimmed eyes snapping with repressed anger.

Under Caleb's direction, the house began to function again. Cassie and the house girls learned that he was at least as exacting as Miss Nancy had been and much less likely to accept an excuse for slipshod behavior. They hated him in the kitchen, but they did what he said. The bakery, the brewery, and the household garden all returned to a productive state. Sukey and little Boyd moved into the house. Her own baby remained in the quarter, to be visited every day.

When Jardine threatened to have the wine-cellar door broken down, Caleb miraculously found the keys, and Jardine once again began drinking too much. Almost every night he fell asleep at the dinner table and had to be carried up to bed. But the more Jardine drank, the more determinedly Caleb, waiting on the table, watered down every glass after the third one.

One evening, when the burgundy had not struck him with the lethal force he was expecting, Jardine raised his fifth glass of wine to the oil lamp and peered into its pale depths.

"What is this, Caleb?" he asked.

"Rosé, Master," Caleb said.

"Rosé?" Jardine exclaimed. "What do you know about rosé?"

"Old Master drank it in Boston and when we were in France."

"France? What the devil were you doing in France?"

"Old Master took us there when I was fifteen and young Master was thirteen," Caleb said. "Old Master believed in travel. He said it was educational."

"Oh, he did, did he?" Jardine mocked. "And I suppose he took you to England and Germany and Italy and all those places, did he?"

"Yes, Master."

"*Yes*, Master," Jardine mimicked. "You're a lying black bastard, Caleb."

"No, Master."

Angrily, Jardine raised the riding crop that lay by his right arm, but then he thought better of it. "All right, Caleb," he said heavily, "tell me about . . . tell me about Paris."

"What about it, Master?"

"*All* about it," Jardine said angrily. He could not quite appreciate the irony of this black—a creature he could sell or even kill if he chose to—claiming to have been to all the places he himself had never had a chance to go.

Caleb, still standing by the table, began telling Jardine about the Paris he'd seen as a fifteen-year-old.

"What are you doing?" Jardine snapped.

"Telling, Master," the confused slave said.

"Well, I don't like being talked down at," Jardine slurred. "Either I'm going to have to stand up, or you're going to have to sit down."

Caleb remained poised.

"And I'm not about to stand up," Jardine said finally, "so sit you down there by the sideboard and tell me all about Paris—if you can."

Dragging the images from his memory, Caleb described the Paris he had known ten years before: the gas-lit, cobbled streets, the beautiful but filthy River Seine, the village of Montmartre, and the gaudily dressed prostitutes lurking half in light and half in dark.

Jardine, who'd managed to get drunk despite the diluted wine, exclaimed, "And I'll bet you liked looking at those white whores, didn't you?"

"Not just white girls, Master," Caleb, who was enjoying telling his tale, said. "Black girls, too."

"Slaves?"

"No, Master, free blacks from Martinique, Haiti, all parts of Africa."

"Damn me," Jardine said. "I didn't know that was allowed. I suppose you felt a bit like a free black yourself, didn't you?"

"Yes, Master."

"I knew it!" Jardine said. "And I'll bet you sneaked off with some of those girls."

"I was only fifteen years old, Master."

"All the same, if you'd spoken French, you would have tried."

"But I did speak French—a little. Brent and I had lessons before we went to France."

"You're a damned liar, Caleb! If you speak French, say me a little of it. Go ahead!" Jardine said.

Caleb thought for a long moment, pulling the words from the depths of his brain. Finally, he said, *"Oui, Maître, je parle français, mais seulement un peu."*

"And what's that supposed to mean?"

"Yes, Master, I speak French, but only a little."

"That's enough," Jardine said gruffly, jumping up and throwing down his linen napkin. "Get this table cleaned up." As interesting as listening to Caleb had been, Jardine still felt aggrieved that a slave had been to all the places he would have gone had he not been called home at the end of his first year at Harvard because his father was ill. And to top it off, Caleb—a slave!—spoke French. That was too much!

But from time to time, Jardine would demand that Caleb tell him more about his European travels with Mr. Staunton and Brent.

But Caleb didn't raise the subject himself, and he was always ready to break off when Jardine showed signs of boredom or weariness.

— *14* —

As the months passed, Jardine began to recover. He spent less and less time up at the old graveyard staring at the rosewood marble tombstone he had imported for Miss Nancy's grave. And, as Caleb got a better grip on the running of the plantation, Jardine traveled farther away and stayed away for longer periods of time.

One Saturday he rode over to Surrattsville for some quarter-horse racing and didn't come back until Sunday evening. He had half a dozen strangers with him whom he'd met at the races. Caleb set Cassie to work getting a ham out of the larder and ordered the house girls to prepare the guest rooms while he served drinks in the big reception room. Within an hour, Caleb and Sissie, one of the house girls, were serving a cold supper in the dining room.

The wine flowed freely, and even after the food had been removed, no one showed much sign of wanting to leave the big oval table. Stories about the weekend's races and those of days past continued. Caleb was unimpressed with Jardine's guests. They were flamboyant city dwellers with pale faces and cheap but showy clothes. The women were pretty in a shallow way, but they showed too many teeth and too much breast in gowns that would have been more suitable for a hotel lobby than a plantation dinner. They looked like flashy flowers on the edge of fading. One of the wives, a sallow woman in her thirties with powdered white breasts and fantastic red hair, kept trying to catch Caleb's eye with a suggestive smile. He determinedly kept his eyes down, avoiding her gaze. Finally, realizing that she was wasting her time, the woman thrust her wine glass at Caleb and snapped, "You, boy, fill me up!" The guests laughed.

More than a little drunk and enjoying himself, Jardine called to Caleb, "Bring the brandy! And if you ladies don't mind, we'll smoke our cigars in here. Caleb, bring a box of the Havanas and some cigarillos for the ladies."

In a few moments, Jardine and his guests were all puffing away and talking with more enthusiasm and noise than sense. Caleb stood in the corner of the dining room in case he was needed and ignored the redhead as she pointedly plunged a half-smoked cigarillo into a full glass of brandy.

The conversation turned to plantation life versus life in the cities, such as New Orleans and Mobile, and then to the difficulties of getting and training good servants.

"I'll say this for you, Jardine," shouted the husband of the redhead. "You've got yourself a good slave here." He pointed his cigar at Caleb. "If I was you, I'd have some chains on his ankles to make sure of keeping him. I don't think I've ever seen a supper served with such style, even by white help over in Mobile."

"Caleb's a useful boy," Jardine allowed, knocking back the rest of his brandy and holding up his glass to Caleb for a refill. "And what's more, he's been to Paris and even speaks more than a little bit of that French." Caleb retreated to the corner again.

"That's ridiculous," cried the redhead.

"Mr. Jardine," trilled a corpulent blonde wearing paste diamonds on her near-naked bosom, "you simply cannot expect us to believe that."

"Jardine, old fellow," said one of the guests, "you might as well tell us your pigs can fly as claim that this slave can *parlez* the *français*. Really, I think it must be the brandy talking."

Jardine was suddenly angry. His face turned pale. "Oh, yes?" he challenged. "I'll show you." He waved an imperious arm. "Caleb, get your black ass over here!"

His guests laughed drunkenly and nudged each other.

"This will be good," said a little man with a dyed black mustache and brown teeth.

"Master," said the slave, coming to a halt next to Jardine at the head of the table, half facing the guests lounging around the table.

"Caleb, my man," Jardine said drunkenly, "give these people some of your best French."

Caleb stood there without speaking.

"Go ahead," Jardine insisted. "Just a little. You know, like you did for me that night when you were describing Paris."

"Are you sure it wasn't Chinese, Jardine?" called one of the men at the other end of the table.

"You just wait," Jardine said. "You'll see. Go ahead, Caleb." Caleb stood dumbly, looking straight ahead. The people around the table were silent with anticipation, but none expected him to speak French. Two of the women exchanged knowing looks.

Jardine looked up with annoyance. "What's the matter, boy? Speak up. These people want to hear some French, and I will have it. You turn, face them, and talk, boy."

Caleb turned to fully face the guests. They gaped like huge fish. His eyes were directed at a point above their heads. His mouth remained shut, not stubbornly, but definitely. There was nothing sulky in his manner.

Finally, the redhead broke the silence with a nervous laugh like a nail being ripped from wood.

"That's all right, Jardine," said a man with a stain of wine down the frilly white front of his shirt. "The boy is nervous. Another time will do. Let's have another sip of that excellent brandy of yours."

Jardine leaped up from his chair with clenched teeth. Spots of color showed on his pale face, and his eyes glittered. "No, it's not all right, damn you," he cried. He reached down into his high-topped boot and withdrew his riding crop. He raised the whip and brought it down sharply on the edge of the table, making the glasses jump and startling his guests. He walked around Caleb and faced him, raising the whip again.

"You see this, boy?" he asked with deadly calm.

"Yes, Master."

"Are you going to talk some French to these people?"

"No, Master."

"Damn you," Jardine shouted and lashed Caleb across the left shoulder of his white jacket. The riding crop struck with a muffled crack, leaving a thin black mark on his jacket, but Caleb did not cringe or waver. The guests' eyes grew round as they exchanged looks. One of the women tittered nervously. "Talk!" insisted Jardine, bringing the crop down on Caleb's right collarbone. Caleb remained unyielding and silent, his eyes looking at neither Jardine nor his guests.

"Do you defy me?" Jardine asked, his voice rising.

"No, Master."

"Then talk, you damned black rascal, before I kill you."

Jardine raised the riding crop to the full length of his arm and brought it down on Caleb's left shoulder again. "You—will—talk—French!" With each slow, deliberate word, Jardine brought the riding crop down harder on Caleb's shoulders and chest, alternating between the right and left sides of his body. Still, Caleb remained immobile, staring straight ahead, his face impassive. His body rocked involuntarily with each blow. The crop caught one of the epaulets of his jacket and ripped it off.

His face now crimson, Jardine paused, panting almost hysterically, and raised the slim whip. He had forgotten all about his houseguests. "Talk!" he bellowed with the full power of his lungs, slashing the crop down across Caleb's left cheek. A line of blood suddenly appeared on his face, and the recoil of Jardine's crop sent a thin red spray over his guests as they scrambled from the table.

"What the hell!" shouted the man with the black mustache. The women clustered together like a flock of pastel hens. They all stared at Caleb's face as blood welled from the cut and dropped from his jaw to his black-streaked white jacket. Though his left eye blinked involuntarily to rid itself of the blood that had splashed into it, Caleb remained as steady as a rock, staring straight ahead.

Jardine, still enraged, raised the crop again and brought it down sharply across Caleb's other cheek. This sent a spray of blood onto Caleb's right shoulder, but he still did not react. Jardine lifted the crop yet again, but when his arm was as far back as it could go, he suddenly stopped and seemed to become aware of the people behind him. Lowering the whip, he turned around to look at them. Two of the women were clearly shocked, but the redhead stared avidly. Her white teeth showed between vivid lips, and her dark eyes were glittering. The men looked on with an almost sporting interest.

"Get out!" Jardine said. "Get out of my house!"

"What?" a few of the guests said in unison, before they all broke out in a gabble of outraged protest as the women caught up their purses. And when Jardine gave them a deadly look and took a step forward with the raised crop, all six of the guests stampeded toward the door, casting wild eyes back toward the madman with the whip. Jardine followed them, stood like a statue in the doorway as they scrambled for their coats, hats, and bags, and then followed them outside. He remained on the veranda until the horses were gathered and hooked up to the brougham and then watched as his guests vanished into the night and the last angry shouts of the men could no longer be heard.

When Jardine turned to reenter the house, he was surprised to find the riding crop still in his hand. He ran a finger down its length, examined the blood that had rubbed off on his finger, then wiped it on one leg of his trousers.

Inside, Caleb, still in his smeared and bloody jacket, was supervising the house girls as they cleared the table and washed the dishes. He did not look up as Jardine appeared in the door and stood watching them with an expressionless face. Jardine turned, strode across the hallway to the door of his study, and disappeared into it. The heavy door closed behind him.

— *15* —

Dulcie smeared her healing ointment onto the cuts on Caleb's face, and nothing further was said about the incident for almost a week. Caleb went on running the house and waiting on Jardine at dinner. There were no more guests. Jardine drank noticeably less wine and did not ask Caleb to bring out the brandy decanter. Nor did he ask for any more stories about European travel. Communication between master and slave was kept to a minimum of brusque orders and silent compliance.

Finally, as he was finishing his coffee one night, Jardine said, "Caleb, why wouldn't you talk French to those people last Sunday night?" His voice held genuine puzzlement.

Caleb stopped placing dirty dishes on the big silver tray and looked at Jardine. "I am not a performing bear, Master," he said.

"Nobody said you were," Jardine said angrily.

Caleb said nothing.

"Damn it, man," Jardine persisted, "is it too much to speak a few words of French when I want you to?"

"I have done it, Master," the slave said soberly. "Many times."

Jardine thought this over. "Well, sure, but"—his face grew red—"how many goddamned slaves in this county can speak a damned word of French or German?"

Caleb did not answer.

"All right," Jardine said defensively, "so those people were a bunch of drunken white trash, but . . ." He didn't know what to say. Suddenly he lashed out at Caleb again. "Damn you! I *own* you, Caleb. You're my property. I could sell you down in Georgia, way where they know how to handle difficult slaves. I could even *kill* you—if I wanted to."

After a long silence, Caleb said, "Yes, Master." He looked directly into Jardine's eyes, not defiantly, but unwaveringly.

"Well, then." Jardine picked up his napkin and then threw it back down on the table. "Oh, get the hell out of here and leave me alone."

It was as close to an apology as Caleb would get, but it marked a clear change between master and slave. Gradually, the two men developed a new relationship.

Jardine was not the kind of man who sought out his neighbors. And the neighbors, after a few rebuffs, respected his bereavement by leaving him alone. For his part, Caleb found the gap between himself and the other slaves too great to bridge. Aside from his position in the house and his role as Jardine's unofficial steward, Caleb's education, background, and accent made him as alien to the field hands as a Martian—and a bit harder to comprehend because he was blacker than most of them. Isolated from their natural peers, master and slave found themselves thrown into a forced intimacy neither expected.

Jardine began once more to ask Caleb about his travels abroad with Mr. Staunton and Brent. Cautiously, but needing the human communication as much as Jardine did, Caleb resumed relating his youthful experiences and observations. As before, Caleb usually stopped before Jardine got bored or restless. These long sessions, usually held in the evening following dinner, always took the form of questions and answers, with Caleb volunteering very little more than what he was asked.

"Tell me about the food in Germany, Caleb," Jardine would demand with just enough edge to his voice to retain his dignity. "Is it true that they eat mostly sauerkraut?"

And Caleb would dredge his memories for details, keeping his answers as impersonal as a travel lecture. Gradually, naturally, the talks gravitated to the study, with Jardine sitting on the big leather couch and Caleb perched on a straight chair before him. As he listened—and responded with more questions—Jardine would sip at a glass of whiskey, but it never occurred to him to offer Caleb any. Nor did Caleb expect it. There came a time each evening—usually when Jardine became so interested in Caleb's narration that he started to forget himself—that he would abruptly get up and say something like, "All right, Caleb, you'd better get the house locked down for the night."

The house girls, on their visits to the quarter, would tell the other slaves of these mysterious sessions behind the closed door of Massa's study. For a time, the sessions became the dominant topic of speculation in the quarter, with as many opinions as to what the men were talking about in the study as there were slaves. This only widened the gulf between Caleb and the others. But although the slaves didn't like him any better, they felt a grudging awe for him that kept insolence in check. His eyes didn't miss much that was going on at Three Rivers, but he dealt with problems and infractions himself, without taking them to Jardine.

As Caleb related tales of his travels, Jardine began to ask questions about his life in Boston. They realized they'd both been in Boston during Jardine's brief stay at Harvard. However, Jardine's experience was mostly in Cambridge near the college and in sordid areas of Boston that the staid Mr. Staunton hardly knew existed. Caleb told Jardine as much about their life in Kenmore Square as he felt he could without violating Mr. Staunton's privacy. Even after all this time and all that had happened, he felt protective of that good man.

One night Jardine burst out, "Well, Christ, Caleb, it sounds to me like you were practically a second son to Staunton—not much of a slave at all. How the devil did he come to own you, anyway? I thought slavery was banned there."

"It was, Master," Caleb said. "My mother was a runaway slave, but she died not long after going to work in Mr. Staunton's house when I was just about five years old. Nobody knew what to do with me, so Mr. Staunton, a kindly man, agreed to keep me as an indentured servant and companion for Brent until I was twenty-one, and then set me free. He had a housekeeper, Mrs. Finlay, who was very good to me and trained me well. I was very happy."

"Then, how the hell did he come to sell you down here? That's hard to believe."

"He didn't," Caleb said carefully.

"Then what happened?" Jardine asked.

"Five years ago, last June," Caleb said, "Mr. Staunton died."

"And?" Jardine asked. "Who owned you then?"

"Young Master."

"You mean Brent, the boy you were raised up with?"

Caleb nodded.

Jardine took another sip. "And *he* sold you?"

Caleb nodded again.

"Son of a bitch!" Jardine exclaimed. "How many years were you together?"

"Fifteen years, Master. Nearly."

"Fifteen years! All that time together, practically your whole lives, and this Brent sold you? He actually sold you?"

"Yes, Master," Caleb said. "Mr. Staunton left the house but not much cash money. It wasn't legal, of course, but before I knew it, money changed hands, and I was in chains headed out of Boston. There was nothing I could do about it. Brent had gambling debts. He didn't know that I would be sold on down here."

"Well, maybe," Jardine said. "But to sell his childhood companion like that. That's awfully cold, Caleb. Don't you feel . . . resentment?" Jardine suddenly sensed that that this exchange was getting into dangerous water.

"Not anymore, Master," the slave said. "It's been a long time."

— *16* —

One evening, as Jardine was refilling his glass with whiskey, he noticed Caleb gazing at his father's books on the shelves of the study.

"You still big on reading, Caleb?" he asked.

"Yes, Master."

"Well, you help yourself," Jardine said with an expansive gesture. "Read any of them you like. Not here, of course. Take 'em up to that room of yours. Mind you take care of them. Daddy was a great reader, and I always thought I might look at some of them. But I never seem to get around to it. Now, I suppose it's too late. You go ahead. It's either you or the paper beetles, and I think you might make more of them."

After that, Jardine would occasionally ask Caleb what he was reading and why. On long winter evenings this often led to Caleb sitting in front of the fire in the study and reading to Jardine from his father's books.

"Christ, Caleb," Jardine would say, "I never knew there was so much in those damned books. Read me some more."

As spring blossomed, Jardine became restless again, and he took to disappearing for days at a time, secure in the knowledge that Caleb would keep the plantation running. The house girls were pretty well trained by now, so Caleb was able to spend some part of each day out with the slaves getting the fields ready for the spring planting. Big Mose knew what do to, and Caleb did not interfere with his authority. But he liked to know what was going on.

One day Caleb rode out on the wagon that took lunch to the slaves in the fields. "Any problems?" he asked Mose.

"No," said Mose, "except those two darkies Massa borryed from the Bentleys ain't worth shit. But we doin' all right." Caleb turned to go back to the wagon, but Mose added, "Tell me something."

Caleb turned back. He and Mose hadn't exchanged more than a dozen words of personal conversation since he'd moved into the house. "Yeah?"

"What are you doing?"

"Same as you. Working for Master."

"You know what I mean. You're educated. I've seen you with those books, doing that writin' in that flimsy thing you carry around. Cassie and the house girls tell us things. We know you ain't no ordinary slave. You can't be plannin' on staying here—not after Boston and Paris and God knows where."

"You're right, Mose," Caleb said. "I'd be away from here if I could. But my face is just as black as yours, and there are three big states between this farm and a place where a black man can walk down a city street without some white face wondering why the hell he isn't wearing a dog collar—and doing something about it. I might have it better than you people in the fields, but I'm still a slave. In five minutes, Master could have me back sweating for you in the cotton, or he could sell me away to somewhere a hell of a lot worse than this place."

"He could," Mose agreed.

"So, I'm just doing my job," Caleb said, "and trying not to worry about things I can't change right now." He turned toward the wagon again. "Right now, I'm going to go see what those house girls are up to while my back is turned."

— *17* —

On one of his increasingly extended trips away, Jardine came back with a new slave in the back of the buckboard. When Caleb came out to greet him, she was climbing out of the wagon. She stared at Caleb uncertainly. Unlike the girl on the platform the day Jardine bought Caleb, this was no teenager. Nor was she high yellow. She was a full-grown woman, looked to be twenty-three or twenty-four, and her skin suggested satin lightly tinted with tea: definitely not white but not approaching black, either. Her nose was a thin blade hinting strongly at Indian blood, and her peculiar blue-gray eyes could have come from anywhere. The woman's body was mature, but not overripe. If she were a peach, Caleb thought, you'd want to get your teeth into her right away.

Caleb could see that Jardine wanted to help her down but did not dare to do it. "Caleb," he said as casually as he could, "this is Missy. She'll be working in the house with the girls. I believe she's got some skills. You find out about that." With a look back at Missy that was meant to be casual and masterly, he strode into the house, leaving Caleb to unload the wagon and then get the boy to take it around to the barn.

"You got things?" Caleb asked Missy.

"Just this," she said, holding up a worn bag sewn from an old coat her former mistress had thrown out.

"All right," Caleb said blankly. "Just grab a hold of that bag of flour and follow me."

When Caleb entered the back kitchen with Missy, the house girls bunched in a defensive semicircle and looked at her as if she were a stray cat in a hen house.

"This is Missy," he told them, echoing Jardine's words. "She's going to be working with you girls in the house."

"We don't need no more help!" said Drusilla, one of the house girls. She often acted as unofficial spokesgirl for the rest. She respected Caleb, but she wasn't afraid of him. She had a tongue on her.

"Well, you've got it," Caleb said, adding sharply, "and we might need more help here in the house if I decide to send some of you girls back out to the fields." He looked directly at Drusilla, who was just as black as Caleb and nearly as tall. She dropped her eyes first. "After you-all get the wagon unloaded, show Missy where you sleep."

Missy turned out to be a good worker. She'd obviously been trained well and knew most of the household tasks. Though the other girls openly shunned her, preferring to work together and leave Missy to do the single-handed jobs, Caleb had no criticism to offer about her willingness or skills. Jardine didn't even mention her again until Missy had been at Three Rivers for nearly a week.

One morning after breakfast as he was getting ready to ride to the fields, Jardine asked with studied casualness, "That new girl, Caleb, how's she settling in?"

"All right, Master." Caleb told Jardine only what he thought he ought to know.

"No trouble with the other girls? She's a good worker?"

Caleb ignored the first question. "She knows her job, Master," Caleb said, "and she seems willing enough."

"That's good," Jardine said absently. "That's good. Where's my riding crop?"

"Here, Master." He picked the crop up from the floor beside Jardine's place at the table and extended it toward Jardine. For a brief moment both had their hands on the slim whip and had the same thought, but neither voiced it.

— *18* —

After Missy had been at Three Rivers for nearly a month, Jardine told Caleb that she might help him by waiting on the table. Missy spent the afternoons—when the girls were usually off—learning some of the finer points of table service from Caleb.

"I hope you're paying attention," Caleb told her. "If you mess up Master's dinner, you're going to be back sweeping floors and folding sheets."

"I won't mess up," she told him coolly. "I learns fast."

And she did. Under Caleb's close supervision, Missy soon became a skilled table servant, quick but not hurried, unobtrusive but always there when needed. She developed the sixth sense a waiter needs to anticipate, rather than just react to demands.

Jardine was very pleased, and Caleb didn't mind having the work taken off his hands. But he watched Missy very carefully—not out of jealousy or fear for his position, but because he had learned that if you don't control things, things will sure as hell control you. Before long, Jardine suggested casually that it seemed a waste of Caleb's time to watch Missy serve breakfast and lunch. The girl had the routine down perfectly. Caleb agreed and retreated during Jardine's daytime meals to the little windowless storeroom that he had turned into his private office. There he read some of the old books that had quietly migrated from Jardine's study. By very convenient coincidence, the door to that storeroom stuck badly. If any of the house girls forgot to knock—a practice that Caleb encouraged without much success—he had plenty of time to stick his book out of sight before the door was fully open. Thanks to Missy, Caleb was making good progress through the collection of books.

A couple of weeks later, Jardine suggested that it might be more convenient if Missy moved from the annex she shared with the other house girls into an empty room at the top of the house. It was at the opposite end of the rough and uncarpeted corridor leading to Caleb's room, but it was reached by a different stairway from the back of the house, and a door had long ago been installed in the middle of the corridor, isolating the room. Caleb had never known the door to be unlocked.

The house girls cleaned and refurbished the long-vacant little room, but they didn't do it cheerfully. You could hear their non-verbal but expressive grumbling halfway down the back stairs. Aware of the legitimacy of their grievance, once the girls had made Missy's room livable, Caleb gave them a basket of food from the kitchen, and allowed Andrew to drive them up to the lake in the wagon. Being realists, the girls accepted this as scant compensation for indignity above and beyond the call of duty. As they left, Drusilla and Caleb exchanged a look that couldn't be put into a thousand words.

Missy moved into the little room with the big bed and very quickly transformed it. Raiding the castoffs in the attic with a free hand, without realizing it she turned the room into a fair approximation of a harem. As a finishing touch, a band of red crepe around the oil lamp created an atmosphere of cozy decadence.

The day Missy moved into her new room, Jardine left for a long weekend at the Bentley's place six miles away. This was possibly the last thing that he wanted to do at that particular time, but Jardine had learned as a boy that what Mrs. Rafe Bentley wanted, Mrs.

Rafe Bentley got. And what she wanted that particular weekend was for Jardine to meet her second cousin from down Savannah way. So he would meet her second cousin. With a sigh and a blank look at Caleb that was returned just as blankly, Jardine got up on the best gig and headed for the Bentley's plantation.

With Jardine gone, Three Rivers went slack. Not as slack as it would have gone without Caleb there, but if there was one thing slaves knew, it was how to make the most of an opportunity. Instinctively, Caleb knew that it would be futile to take too much notice. Anticipating the inevitable, he told Cook and the house girls that if they got things in good shape by Friday afternoon, they needn't be seen again until after Saturday lunch. It would not have done his authority any good to have to go looking for them in the quarter Saturday morning. He hoped he wouldn't have to go looking for them Saturday afternoon. He was counting on Drusilla to see that he didn't.

— *19* —

Of course, Missy didn't go with the girls when they fled in a chattering, excited group. Nobody asked her. She said to Caleb, "I expect you'll be eating in the kitchen."

"You expect wrong," Caleb told her. "I'll be eating in the dining room, and you'll be serving me. I have to make sure that your skills aren't slipping."

"My skills are doin' all right," she said. "Who's goin' to cook?"

"I'm going to cook," Caleb said, "and you're going to help. But first, set the dining room for one."

"One?" Missy raised her carefully plucked eyebrows.

"One."

When Missy returned from the dining room, Caleb had his jacket off, an apron on, and the big cast-iron range roaring. On top was a big pan of water just beginning to bubble. "Go out back," he told Missy, "choose one of the white hens—a fat one—kill her, pluck her, clean her, and bring her in here."

She looked at him with her eyes narrowed. "You crazy?"

"No," said Caleb. "I thought you said your skills were good."

"My skills, Mr. Caleb," she said tartly, "don't include killing no chickens."

"No?" said Caleb, pretending to be amazed. "What did you do for your last master?"

"Mistress," Missy corrected. "I was a lady's maid—and a good one."

"Then why'd she sell you?"

"She didn't. Massa did. They got in a big fight. She cut a whole bunch of his clothes up, so Massa sold me. Broke her heart."

"I'm sure," said Caleb. "Well, I can't make up for your lack of education all at once. I'll go get the chicken. Do you think you can wash and peel those potatoes on the table and put them in that pot when it boils?"

"I'll try."

"Try hard."

When Caleb came back with the gutted chicken, the potatoes were in the bubbling pot. He looked in to make sure they had been well peeled. "Looks okay," he said. "Can you section a chicken, Miss Lady's Maid?"

"I can try."

"Not on my dinner, you can't." Caleb threw the chicken onto the big carving board and reached for a knife. "Go out back to the little garden and bring back half a dozen onions and a big handful of greens. Do you think you can do that?"

"I'll try," Missy said shortly and left the kitchen.

"Wash those greens two or three times and put them in a pot of water way at the back on the stove," Caleb said upon her return. "And chop those onions sort of middling. Then I'm going to show you something." He slapped the last piece of chicken in flour and put it into the big frying pan full of sizzling lard.

"What?"

"You'll see."

By the time she'd finished those tasks, Caleb had the potatoes off the fire and cooling in a vat of water. He had a bowl of eggs, a jug of olive oil, and salt and pepper on the big table. "Now watch closely," he said. Breaking half a dozen eggs into a big bowl, he whipped them into a froth with a big rattan whisk and added salt and pepper. He dipped a forefinger in the mix and tasted it.

"What are you doin'?" Missy asked.

"The easy part. But keep your eyes open. The hard part's coming up." Keeping the whisking steady with his left hand, he picked up the jug of oil and poured a thin but steady stream into the bowl. The egg mixture began to thicken and smooth immediately.

"What are you making?" Missy demanded.

"Mayonnaise," Caleb said, still whisking and pouring with delicate precision. "Get me a head of garlic from the larder."

"What for?"

"Because I say so."

By the time Missy got back, the mayonnaise was coming to a final thickness. "Clean two cloves," Caleb told her, "put them in that mortar, and crush them real fine. And hurry it up. The chicken is almost done."

"Garlic makes my fingers stink," she complained.

"It's a good stink," Caleb said. "You ought to try shoveling shit."

Missy wrinkled her nose at him but obeyed.

— *20* —

Twenty minutes later, Caleb was sitting at the head of the big dining table and unfolding his napkin. He had quickly washed his hands and face, and was wearing his good jacket. Missy, wearing her serving apron, came in from the kitchen carrying a platter of deep-brown fried chicken and placed it in front of him on the table between a big bowl of potato salad and a smaller one of boiled greens.

"That looks excellent, Missy," Caleb said. *"Mes compliments au chef."*

"Who?"

"Never mind. Now, back in the stillroom you'll find a bottle of white wine cooling in a bucket of water. Open it and bring it in here. I'm hungry."

Caleb was biting into a chicken leg when she returned with the bottle and started to pour the wine.

"Haven't you forgotten something?" he asked coldly.

"What?" She couldn't keep the irritation out of her voice.

"Wine," said Caleb, "especially cold white wine, is never served from an unwrapped bottle. Wrap it in a white napkin. That's part of your skills, girl."

Sullenly, Missy wrapped the bottle and poured a little into Caleb's glass. She stopped and pulled the bottle back.

"That's good," he said. He took a sip of the wine and rolled it around in his mouth. "That's good, too," Caleb said. "You may pour me a glass."

Missy filled his glass, put the wine back in the silver bucket on the sideboard, and turned around to face Caleb.

"Do you know what your trouble is?" she asked.

"Tell me," Caleb said, raising an eyebrow.

"You think you're white!" Missy said angrily before wheeling around and stalking back into the kitchen.

At just about that moment, Jardine was sitting at an elaborately set table in the garden of Bellevue, the Bentleys' plantation. Martha Bentley had a thing about eating outside in the summer that no amount of flying insects could discourage. Around the table, half a dozen black boys wearing white gloves disturbed the air with palmetto leaves. This had the effect of moving the insects from guest to guest.

To Jardine's left was SallyAnne Carter, Martha Bentley's much-praised second cousin from Savannah. On his other side was Colonel Braddock, who'd been stone deaf since a cannon went off too close to his head at the Battle of Buena Vista. Jardine recognized this seating arrangement as a pretty good tactic, as it meant that he would have to talk to SallyAnne. But he also saw that Martha had made a rare mistake by putting SallyAnne at his side. Full face, with her high cheekbones and vivid color, SallyAnne was pretty enough. But in profile, her slightly hooked nose made her look a bit like a young turkey. Jardine suspected that if she ever stopped smiling—which she hadn't yet—she would look like a very depressed young turkey.

When Jardine had arrived earlier that day, Martha Bentley had looked searchingly at his left sleeve. *Oh, damn.* He realized that he'd left his black armband on the bureau in his dressing room. Not that he cared whether Mrs. Bentley thought he was making enough display of mourning Nancy. If he'd cared enough about her opinion, he might have reminded her that true grief was in the heart, not on the sleeve. But the armband might have been a useful barrier between himself and SallyAnne, who was now leaning toward Jardine and giving him a good look at her slightly freckled cleavage.

"I believe you live not very far from here, Mr. Jardine," she said.

He allowed that he had a small place on the other side of the turnpike and had to suggest that she might like to come over for a visit while she was in the neighborhood.

"Oh, I'd love that," she said. "What do you grow?"

"Cotton, Miss Carter," he said. "That's mostly all people in these parts grow. There are a few putting in some acreage of tobacco these days, but I don't think it's got any future. This always was cotton country and always will be." Jardine was nearly boring himself into a coma.

"How's the boy, Jardine?" Doc Hollander called from the other end of the table, saving Jardine.

"Just fine, Doctor," Jardine called. "Getting bigger every day. Soon I'll have to get him out in the field behind a plow."

"Give him a few more months," said the doctor good-naturedly. "I'll get over to see him one of these days."

"You do that."

In truth, as much as Jardine loved the boy, he couldn't yet see him without feeling a stab of fresh grief at the loss of Nancy. The price he'd paid for a son was too high. Not that he'd been allowed to forget him. Dulcie was always coming to Jardine with little reports about how he was getting along with Sukey. You could sum these reports up with two words: all right. He'd lost that yellow color, gained some weight, and—according to Dulcie—was a good eater and a fair to middling sleeper.

"Oh, Mr. Jardine," SallyAnne asked, "how old is your baby?"

"Four months soon," Jardine said.

"How precious! And what's he called?"

"Boyd, I suppose," Jardine said. "Like me." Realizing how strange and offhand that sounded, he added quickly, "He hasn't got an official name yet."

"We'll have to take care of that soon, Mr. Jardine," said Pastor Buchanan, the Baptist minister, from across the table.

"We surely will, Pastor," Jardine said.

After lunch, while a croquet match was raging, Martha Bentley trapped Jardine in the gazebo.

"Oh, Boyd," she said, "I understand you've got a new slave. Someone said it was a girl."

"Yes, ma'am," Jardine replied coolly. "I bought her over in Lynche's Landing last month. My man Caleb has been getting a bit lonely, and I think maybe I've found a wife for him."

"Caleb," said Mrs. Bentley thoughtfully. "I've heard quite a bit about that darkie. When are we going to get a look at him?"

"And his bride!" laughed Rafe Bentley, who had just walked in.

"Why, next Friday, ma'am," Jardine said. "That is, if you and your company will accept my invitation to visit Three Rivers."

— *21* —

That night at Three Rivers, Caleb was in his room reading by the oil lamp when he heard soft tapping at his door. Marking his place with a bit of paper, he got up and opened the door.

It was Missy. She stood in the hall wearing a long white nightgown. Her hair, loosened from its usual neat bun, hung down to her shoulders.

"Where'd you come from?" Caleb asked.

"Down there." With a sideways movement of her head she indicated the room at the other end of the narrow corridor. Caleb looked and saw that the tall door was open. He'd never seen it open before. When he looked back at Missy, she was smiling and holding up a key attached to a ribbon tied around her neck.

"Master knows you have that key?" Caleb said.

"Nobody knows about this key but me."

"And me."

"And you."

"What do you want?" Caleb asked.

"You," she said simply.

"Well," Caleb said, grabbing her by her slim wrist, "you'd better get in out of that hall." He knew that nobody could possibly see her, but it still made him nervous. He pulled her into his room and wedged the door shut behind her.

Missy was looking around Caleb's room. It was lined with wooden boards, whitewashed, and as austere as a soldier's barracks. The only thing unusual about it was the small shelf of books Caleb had put up next to the head of the bed. There wasn't much else to catch Missy's eye.

"You read those?" she asked.

"No," said Caleb, "if I wake up in the middle of the night hungry, I eat them. It's a long way to the kitchen. Can you read?"

"What do I need to read for?"

"You'd be surprised. The whole world is in those books."

"They look a bit small to me," Missy said.

Caleb changed the subject. "You know," he said directly, "you coming down here is foolishness. We can't be starting anything. You know Master didn't bring you out here for me."

"I know," she said simply. "That door is never going to be open again after tonight. But it is now." She leaned forward and kissed him softly. "I want you to be the first."

"Ever?" Caleb emphasized the question with his eyebrows.

Missy showed fine little teeth in a smile that carried all the way to her eyes. "First here," she said.

"Come on," said Caleb, grabbing her wrist again.

"There's no hurry."

"The hell there isn't."

"Blow the lamp out," she said.

"Why?"

"Just do. Please."

"Down?"

"No, out. Please."

It was near light when Caleb woke up. Something was fluttering at his chin and nose.

"Hey!" Then he woke up completely and felt the warm, soft full contact of her naked body pressed against his.

"What are you doing?"

"Butterfly kiss," she said, blinking rapidly so that her long lashes brushed his cheekbone. "Like it?"

"It's different, all right," Caleb said.

Morning light streamed in through the little window high up on the wall of Caleb's room. The early sun colored a patch on the opposite wall.

"It's going to be a good day," Caleb said, looking up. "A hot one."

"Aren't you going to tell me how good I was?" Missy asked.

"You know."

"But I still like to hear. A girl likes to hear it."

"Okay," Caleb said, wrapping her in his powerful arms. "You are the sun, stars, and moon, and when I feel your skin against mine I explode with volcanic passion. I am your own Vesuvius."

"I don't understand that, but it's pretty," Missy said. "That you or the books?"

"A little of each," said Caleb, kissing her hungrily, "but the more I think on it, the more me it gets."

"You ain't thinking," said Missy, kissing him back.

Full light found her still locked in his arms.

"Let's just stay like this all day," Missy suggested.

"Sure, we'll have Cassie bring us breakfast in bed. How many eggs you want with your grits?"

"You're not romantic."

"Not anymore, I guess," Caleb admitted, "but you catch me later. You'll get romance. But right now, I want to see."

"See?" Missy pretended that she didn't know what he was talking about.

"See!" said Caleb emphatically, taking a handful of the blankets covering them both.

"Wait a minute!"

"Minute's up!" Caleb pulled the blankets down, revealing her totally naked body. There were no surprises. The breasts were full but still stood high, the nipples well defined. Her torso tapered to a slim waist before flaring to impressive but still girlish hips. The pubic hair under her tight stomach was the color of smoked honey, and it coiled in a tight triangle that had obviously been trimmed.

"What you think?" Missy asked in a slightly tight voice. "You want to buy me?"

"I'm thinking," Caleb said, reaching out a hand. "Let me just—"

"Let you just nothing," Missy said, stopping his hand. "I want to show you somethin.'"

"What?"

"Somethin,'" said Missy. "You just keep your big hand to yourself and your bright eyes on the area between my bellybutton and my bush."

"Okay," said Caleb, "but—"

Before his eyes, the hard, smooth muscles of her stomach seemed to melt until what had been firm, taut flesh was now flaccid. Missy's body had aged ten years in two seconds.

"What the hell!" Caleb said before he could stop himself.

"Pretty, huh?" Missy's voice was bitter as she pulled the blanket back up. "Had me a baby when I was thirteen, another at sixteen, and one more last year. That will do things to your belly, you believe me."

Caleb put his arm around her shoulders, and she didn't pull away. "Where are they?" he asked.

Missy shrugged. "Who knows? White men don't want a girl like me to come complete with no family. They took them away, one after the other, before I could even nurse them. Don't want to mess up my pretty breasts, you know. Got to keep 'em firm. Massa likes them firm."

Caleb felt a tear fall on his chest and pulled her tight to him. He held her until she stopped shaking. "But," he whispered, "how do you do that thing with your stomach?"

"Muscle control," she told him. "Old mammy down New Orleans way showed me how, but I had to study long and so hard. I can hold it twenty minutes now, but it's getting harder." Her voice grew confidential. "No white man ever seen the real me."

"It's a good trick," Caleb said. "Had me fooled."

"Has them all fooled," Missy said. "Now it's my turn."

"To what?" Caleb asked suspiciously.

"To see! Strip that blanket, boy!"

Reluctantly, Caleb pulled the blanket down until he was naked to the knees. Missy looked at him appraisingly.

"Well," she said, "I can see that you ain't had no babies yet. Good, wide hips, though—child-bearin' hips."

"Thank you," Caleb said.

"But whatever do you do with that thing?" Missy reached down and flicked his limp penis with a forefinger.

"I'll show you!" Caleb said, raising his body and rolling over on top of her. He could feel himself getting hard.

This time the sex was slow, almost loving. Caleb collapsed on top of Missy, exhausted.

"My," Missy said after a while, tangling her fingers in his kinky hair. "You were a hungry boy. What do you usually do?"

"What do you mean?"

"For a woman, sex, pussy?"

"There's a girl down in the quarter. She meets me now and again in one of the barns."

"I hope she's clean," said Missy.

"I hope *you're* clean," Caleb replied.

"Don't you worry 'bout that. Massa took me to a doctor in Cassatt, and that white doctor gave me a clean bill of health. Massa don't want no diseases."

"Me neither." A little later, Caleb looked at the sunlight on his bedroom wall. "Hey, girl, we have to get moving."

"Do we have to?"

"You know we do. No telling who's going to be wandering up here to the house."

"They're all drunk and asleep in the quarter."

"Don't count on that—not if you want to stay sweet with Master."

"Oh, all right." Missy started to move, but Caleb stopped her.

"First we got to get some things straight."

"Such as?"

"First," Caleb said, "this is the one and only time this is going to happen. From now on, I don't know you, and you don't know me. We work together. That's all. No foolin' around. We have to act as if white eyes are on us all the time. I don't want you even to look at me with any old secrets. A lot depends on this."

"You don't have to tell me," Missy answered sharply. "I got more to lose than you do."

"You think so? Master suspects you, maybe he beats you and throws you away like an old shoe that stepped in dog shit—"

"Thank you!"

"But what do you think he's going to do to some trusty slave who just happens to be messing with his little bit while he's away?"

"He likes you," Missy declared.

"Master likes his hound dogs," Caleb said, "but if they get into his chicken house, he whips the shit out of them. He hangs them up for the buzzards. That isn't going to happen to me."

"I know, I know," said Missy. "But think of somethin', Caleb."

"What's that?"

"In a couple of years, maybe less, Massa's going to get tired of me. Or he's going to get himself a nice little wife. She'll know. They always do. But can't we wait until then, and then maybe I can be your woman?"

Caleb looked at her sharply. "You love me?"

Her eyes were intelligent and honest. "No, but—"

"Well, you're a good, smart girl and all that, Missy. And a damned wonder in bed, but I don't love you, either. And if you last as long with Master as I think you will, I'm not going to be around then. I'm going to be free!"

"How?"

"I don't know, but as sure as you got two pretty titties, I'm going to be free. Even if it costs me my life."

"Oh, yes, a free dead man," Missy scoffed. "That sounds just fine and dandy."

"Don't you want to be free?" Caleb asked her with wonder.

Missy thought for a moment. "You know what my freedom is? A roof over my head, a warm, dry bed, enough to eat, and work that's not too hard. That's my freedom. Oh, and a good man and a couple of babies. I'll take that."

"Okay," said Caleb, "you do it your way. But you mind what I said. You hear?"

"I hear."

"Good. Now you get your sweet butt down the hall, lock that door, and don't ever open it again. Understood?"

"Understood," said Missy a bit sulkily.

"Do you recall where you found that key and exactly *how* it was when you found it?"

"I remember," said Missy. "I'm not stupid."

"I know you're not, but this is important. Too important. You get that key back there, and Master better not suspect that it ever left its hidey-hole. Or we are both in trouble."

"Okay, okay," Missy said impatiently. "I'm going."

"No, wait," Caleb insisted. "Maybe Master doesn't suspect, but he's a white man and a slave owner, and they think a certain way."

"So?"

"So," Caleb said earnestly, "we have to trust each other. If Master suspects, he's going to get tricky and try to turn us against each other."

"What you mean?" Missy asked.

"I mean, he's likely to come to you and say, *Missy, you might as well fess up. Caleb done told me he had you. Make it easy on yourself, girl.* Well, don't you believe it. And I won't either. Master can beat me to death before I tell him the truth, because he's gonna beat me to death if I *do* tell the truth. And that applies to you, too. You never had that key, you never opened that door, you never were in here. You admit nothing. You stick to your story—our story. Even if he looks at you funny, you just ignore it. Act natural. You're innocent. You didn't do anything. You understand?"

"I understand."

"Good," Caleb said. "Now get."

Missy slipped on her nightgown, and Caleb followed her to the door of his room. As she was going through the doorway, he grabbed her wrist. "One last thing."

"Another one?"

"Yeah. What's your name?"

"Missy."

"I mean your *real* name."

Missy turned back toward him, looking serious. "Melissa," she said.

"That's a very pretty name," Caleb said. "Very pretty. Master knows that?"

"He never asked."

"Well, I did," Caleb said. "And it's our secret. Okay?"

"Okay," she said softly, and Caleb released her wrist.

When Caleb heard the door in the corridor close, he quickly walked to it and listened as Missy turned the key in the lock with a raspy sound. Then he examined the rough wooden floor on his side of the door for minute scrapes that would show that it had been opened. He saw nothing except disturbed dust. Walking back past his door to the tall, thin window at the end of the corridor, he turned and saw that in the slant of morning light there were two sets of footprints on the dusty floor leading to the door. Wrapping the head of a broom with a cloth, he swept the rough floor lightly, covering the footprints with an even layer of dust as he walked backward to the door of his room. Looking back down the corridor, he saw an undisturbed layer of dust right up to the partition door. He reckoned that would do. He'd have to tell Missy to do the same on her side of the door.

— *23* —

Caleb was standing out front when Jardine returned from the Bentleys' late Sunday afternoon. Missy was nowhere to be seen.

"How's it going, Caleb?" Jardine asked, throwing him the reins. "Any problems? Any excitement?"

"No, Master. Things pretty much as usual. Nobody did much work. We had a good vacation."

"That's more than I can say," Jardine replied.

"Would Master like a cup of tea?"

"Later. I have some things to do. Where's Missy?"

"Gone to church meeting down in the quarter, Master. That old preacher is visiting again."

"Pious is she?"

"It looks like, Master. Will there be anything else?"

"Take Bruno to the stable and tell William to rub him down well. I gave him a bit of a workout on the turnpike. That old boy can run. Any of the house girls around?"

"Yes, Master. Drusilla."

"Not worshipping God, eh?"

"No, Master."

"I'll have to watch that one. Well, tell her to heat me up some water—very hot. I've got six miles of red dust on me. I can taste it."

Upstairs, Jardine went to his room and looked behind his tie rack. The big brass key still hung where he had left it, caught at a small angle by a slightly proud nail at the bottom. As far as he could see, it had not been moved. Pocketing the key, he went down to the kitchen, where Drusilla was tending the old boiler. It was already starting to steam.

"I want that water boiling, Drusilla," he called as he passed her.

"Yes, Massa," she replied without looking up.

Walking through the kitchen and back offices, Jardine came to the back staircase and climbed up it. He opened the door to Missy's room and was amazed at the change in it. From a spare room full of junk, it had become a cozy and feminine bedroom. The rough wooden walls were concealed with hangings that he recognized as old bedspreads from his mother's day. The small window was covered with a red scarf so that the room was bathed in a roseate light from the late-afternoon sun. On the floor was a rich Persian rug. For a moment Jardine's temper flared—where the hell did she get that? But then he remembered: it was the rug Uncle Giles set on fire one Christmas. Underneath that chest in the corner would be a large burnt patch. How like his mother not to throw that rug out. The double bed was tidily made and covered by a counterpane that had once been a rich royal blue. It was now faded but not displeasing. Jardine reflected that he had not only gotten himself a good-looking girl but one with style and taste.

He closed the lockless door and looked down the hall toward the tall, narrow door that divided the passage. The afternoon light streaming in illuminated the dust motes in the air. The floor was newly swept and mopped. Swiftly moving to the door, he took out the brass key and tried it in the lock. At first it would not move, but gradually, with a small grating sound, it turned, and Jardine slowly pushed the door open. The old, dry hinges creaked. On the dusty floor on the other side were footprints that led from the other staircase to Caleb's room at the end of the hall. He would have to have a talk with Caleb about the housekeeping. Satisfied, he pulled the door shut, locked it with some difficulty, and returned the key to his pocket.

After dinner, Jardine called Caleb into his study. He did not order him to sit down. This was business. "Are you satisfied that Missy can meet my standards in the dining room?" he asked Caleb.

"Yes, Master. She still needs watching on some of the small matters, but she's learning fast. She pays attention and she doesn't make the same mistake twice. I think she'll make a good dinner server. And soon."

"That's good, because we've got half a dozen guests coming to stay for two nights next Friday, and I want things to go smoothly. There are some people who think a house can't be run without a woman. I want to show them different."

"Yes, Master." Caleb waited to see if that was all.

"Oh, Caleb," Jardine asked, "what did you do while I was away?"

"Pretty much like the rest, Master," Caleb said. "Not much. I did some reading and caught up on the bookkeeping. I think it's in pretty good order now."

"I'll be checking it," Jardine said briskly. "That will be all."

"Yes, Master." Caleb started to leave the study.

"One other thing," Jardine said.

Caleb turned back. "Master?"

"Missy," Jardine said, and Caleb caught his breath. Blood rushed to his head.

"Master?"

"What do you think of her?"

"She's smart. Hard worker. Pretty willing and makes a good appearance."

"Do you find her easy to work with?"

"No problems so far, Master."

Jardine paused. This was damned tricky. Caleb was a slave. So was Missy. But they were human beings. "Damn it, Caleb. Sit down for a minute. Over there next to the sideboard. You know I don't like you hovering over me like that."

Caleb sat down. "Yes, Master?"

Jardine didn't really know where to start, but he had to start somewhere.

"You know Mrs. Bentley," he began, then stopped.

"No, Master."

"Yes, you do. She was all over the place last year after—you know what I'm talking about. And, well, after next weekend, you'll know her one hell of a lot better, damn it, so just listen."

"Master?"

"She's going to come here with about a million eyes looking for all kinds of things that I am doing wrong. Do you know what I mean?"

"No, Master." Caleb was not going to help him.

"Don't play dumb with me, Caleb," Jardine warned. "The Bentleys are bringing a party with them, including this cousin of hers from Savannah who—well, never mind. But I want to show them that Three Rivers is a showplace, the best-run farm this side of the turnpike. Or on either side, for that matter. I'm counting on you, Caleb, in the next few days to make sure that it is. I want you to run the raggedy asses off of those house girls to make sure it is. And anybody else on this damned place. You understand *that*?"

"Yes, Master."

"And I want you to see that Cook serves up the best food those folks have ever had. I'm having a whole raft of good things sent over from Camden and the ice to keep them fresh. You're always running on about how things are done in Boston and Paris and those places. Well, I want them done better at Three Rivers next weekend. That clear?"

"Yes, Master."

"I want . . ." Jardine faltered. "You know damn well what I want. And I better get it."

"Yes, Master."

"Is that all you can damn say? *Yes, Master?*"

"No, Master."

"Oh, get the hell out of here." Caleb got to his feet. "And tell that Drusilla girl that if that bath water isn't scalding, she'll be out in the field tomorrow morning, working for a change."

"Yes, Master." Caleb turned to leave the study.

"Hold on!"

Caleb stopped at the door. "Master?"

"This is important. Mrs. Bentley has got some funny ideas. And one of these just might be that you and Missy are—well—a couple. That Missy came here to be your . . . to be with you. Do you understand what I am talking about?"

"Yes, Master. I think so." Caleb's face was perfectly straight.

"Well, if that's what Mrs. Bentley wants to think," Jardine said, "that's fine with me. That's what she'll find. We want Mrs. Bentley to be happy, don't we?"

"Yes, Master."

"Good! You have a little talk with Missy and explain what I mean. Just for next weekend. You think you can do that?"

"Yes, Master."

"All right, you can go. I want my bath in ten minutes, my supper in an hour, and I don't want to see your black face again until tomorrow. Missy can serve me. Is that clear?"

"Yes, Master."

"Go!" But before Caleb could get through the door, Jardine stopped him again. "Caleb!"

"Yes, Master?"

"Get something done about the corridor outside your room. It's disgusting."

"Yes, Master."

— *24* —

Jardine watched with approval as Missy served his evening meal. Caleb was right. The girl seemed like a fast learner and was very willing. She did not have Caleb's style. That could not be expected. But she served quietly and efficiently and made no serious mistakes that he could see. She would do.

For the moment he was not sorry that he'd bought her, though he'd been arguing with himself over the wisdom of doing so. She was certainly a lot better to look at than Caleb. He hadn't been wrong about her trim figure, though there was nothing immodest about the way she carried herself.

When she brought him his coffee and brandy and stood waiting quietly to see if Jardine wanted anything else, he said, "Missy?"

"Yes, Massa?"

"Do you like it here?"

"It's just fine, Massa."

"And your room is okay? You found the furnishings and things you need?"

"Yes, Massa. It's very comfortable."

"Well, that's good," said Jardine. "After you get this cleaned up, you're finished for tonight. I might come up later to see what you've done with your room, to see if there is anything else that you need."

"Yes, Massa."

The following Friday afternoon, the Bentley party arrived in two carriages. Aside from Miss SallyAnne and the Bentleys, there was Pastor Buchanan, who, it seemed to Jardine, spent more time visiting the neighbors than he did running his church, and Mrs. Mayflower, Bentley's widowed and elderly aunt, who also lived at Bellevue.

Jardine was on the broad front steps of the house when they rolled up. Caleb, Missy, Drusilla, and the other house girls were lined up behind him, all looking very spruce in their best outfits. Drusilla held little Boyd. Jardine figured that, of all the house girls, she was the one least likely to drop him. Just before the guests were scheduled to arrive, Jardine had had her go and get the baby from his wet nurse. Though he'd meant to see the child during the week before, Jardine had not got around to it. Now that he looked down at the red-faced infant, Jardine wondered why he did not feel a great surge of paternal pride rather than just pain and regret. He supposed that would come later on.

The women made a beeline for the baby, relieving Jardine of any need for an elaborate welcome. He did not yet feel comfortable in the role of host without Nancy. Jardine noticed that Martha Bentley, despite her eagerness to see little Boyd, favored Caleb and Missy with a penetrating, if brief, scrutiny. Standing slightly aside from the house girls, the two certainly seemed to make up a small unit of their own, though there was no overt show of feelings between them. Caleb, Jardine thought, had done a good job of telling the girl how to behave.

The weekend went smoothly enough. Jardine played the gracious host, but avoided paying SallyAnne Carter any special attentions that would encourage her to start daydreaming about being mistress of Three Rivers. She wasn't a stupid girl, and once she'd put Jardine in the "interesting but not interested" category, she relaxed and enjoyed the country life she so seldom experienced down in Savannah.

At dinner on Saturday night, she leaned across the table and asked, "Mr. Jardine, do you really think there will be a war? I've been reading the Atlanta papers, and it looks very serious to me."

"War?" asked Jardine. He hoped that his long pause made it appear that he was gathering his thoughts rather than wondering what the hell she was talking about. "I don't think so, Miss Carter. The Yankees will hardly want to fight over the issues in question." He rushed on before she could ask him specifically what he thought those issues were. "Of course, we are rather out of the way down here and seldom see the big city newspapers."

"I brought some with me," SallyAnne said, "to read on the train. I could leave them with you if you would be interested."

"That would be most kind of you," Jardine said smoothly, thinking that Miss Carter would make some man a good wife. Some other man.

After dinner, when Mrs. Mayflower and SallyAnne were taking turns trying to pound out a tune on Three Rivers' Steinway piano, Martha Bentley motioned for Jardine to step out onto the veranda with her.

"You don't like her, do you, Boyd?" Mrs. Bentley asked bluntly once they were out of earshot of the big parlor. She was famous for her uncommon directness.

"No, not that way, Martha," Jardine said. No point trying to let her down easy. She'd see right through him.

"That's a shame. I promised her mother I would see what I could do, and you looked like a sitting duck to me."

"Thank you," Jardine said.

"Well," she said candidly and only a little defensively, "I thought that, without Nancy, by now you would be wallowing in bachelor squalor and might snap up any presentable girl of good family and reputation. She's a virgin, you know."

"I'm sure she is." Jardine said. "And not bad looking, either."

"Don't praise my horse, Boyd Jardine," she said sharply, "unless you are in a buyin' mood. I saw you eyeing SallyAnne's bosom with that 'just looking' expression on your face. I've got other prospects, you know, and I'll place her before this visit's out."

"I'm sure you will, Martha," said Jardine. "You're a formidable woman."

"Yes, I am," she agreed. "And I know that you don't need advice from me on how to run Three Rivers or your own life—"

"But you're going to give me some," Jardine cut in.

"Yes, I am," she said. "Now, you may think you're fooling me with this new girl of yours. What's her name?"

"Missy."

"Yes. She doesn't look much like a Missy to me, and unless I am losing my touch, you haven't got her matched up with that fancy buck darkie of yours in there, either."

"They're very fond of each other," Jardine said, "considering the short time she has been with us."

"Yes," Mrs. Bentley said, "and I am the Queen of Australia. Boyd, I am a pretty good judge of chemistry, and there's about as much going on between those two darkies as there is between you and SallyAnne."

"I admire Miss Carter," he said languidly.

"Well, that majordomo of yours *admires* your Missy, too. They make a good serving team, but you did not bring that doxy—"

"Strong language, Martha."

"—here to warm his lonely bed."

"You embarrass me," Jardine said, without feeling the least bit embarrassed.

"So, I ask myself," she plowed on, "if Missy is not warming—"

"Caleb."

"—Caleb's bed, whose bed is she warming? That's what I ask myself." She looked him directly in the eye.

"I appreciate your concern, Martha—"

"Save that for your Sunday sermon, Boyd," she said with exasperation. "I've known you since you were still peeing on your shoes—"

"Martha!"

"—and I know you are relatively discreet. I just want to make sure that you stay that way. You know how things get around in this neighborhood. I would not want folks to get the wrong—or the right—idea about what is going on at Three Rivers. I want to keep on visiting here. I like your food."

"Thank you."

"You remember what happened to Jed Kimball after Rebekah died?"

"I heard some rumors," Jardine said.

"Rumors, hell. It was a screaming scandal. Before Becky was a month in her grave, Jed had himself a yellow girl in his bed and not only in his bed, but also at his table. She took to styling herself Miz Kimball, until some right-thinking people took her to Hollerton Junction and put her on a southbound train."

"And Jed shot himself."

"He did that," Martha Bentley said, snapping her mouth shut on the words like the trap on a gallows. "He was lucky that someone didn't save him the trouble. Another word to the wise, Boyd: don't shit where you eat."

"Martha, you shock me."

"That's not all I'll do to you if I hear *rumors*."

"Do you have any other tidbits of advice before we rejoin the party?" Jardine asked, offering her his arm.

"Yes. Keep an eye on that Caleb. I can't quite put my finger on it, but I think that fellow might just be a bit too good to be believed."

"I'll bear that in mind," said Jardine as they went back into the house.

— *25* —

On Sunday evening, after the fanfare of the Bentley party's departure had died down, Caleb and the house girls were tidying up. Jardine retired to his study with the Atlanta newspapers that SallyAnne had given him. Opening the big broadsheet, Jardine stared at the mass of information competing for his attention. Never much of a reader, he found the type swimming in front of his eyes.

"Caleb!" The slave appeared in the doorway to the study. "Have you got things under control out there?"

"The girls are just going to the quarter, Master. I'm putting out the lamps."

"Well, hurry it up and then get yourself in here. These damned newssheets are giving me a headache."

In a few minutes, Caleb was seated in his usual chair next to the sideboard that held the oil lamp. Half in shadow, Jardine lay limply in his father's old leather armchair. The newspaper was the first Caleb had seen in over a year. At his last owner's a slave being seen next to a newspaper would have been reason for a flogging. Caleb's eyes devoured the columns of type like molasses candy.

"Well?" said Jardine impatiently. "Are you reading that to me or just to yourself?"

"There's so much of it, Master. What would you like me to read to you about?"

"Oh, anything that catches your eye. You must have had some practice with that sort of thing back in Boston. Is there anything in there about cotton prices?"

For the next half hour, Caleb read aloud at random from the big pages of the newspaper. Court cases, stock reports, cotton prices dropping.

"Christ, wouldn't you know it," Jardine moaned. "Pretty soon we won't be able to give the stuff away. Go on, go on. I can take it."

Caleb went on, letting the neat formations of type pour into his brain, not always quite sure whether he was still reading aloud. But as long as Jardine wasn't complaining, he just kept reading. After a while, Caleb looked up and saw that Jardine was asleep in the big chair, his mouth hanging open. At that, Caleb stopped reading for Jardine and continued reading for himself.

On an inside page, he found an article about negotiations for admission to the Union of two new states, Kansas and Nebraska. The issue was whether they would be admitted as slave states or free states. Though he hadn't seen a map in some time, Caleb had a vague idea where those territories were. In his mind's eye, he tried to trace a route from Three Rivers to either of those places where a man might find and keep freedom. He made a mental note to try to find a fairly recent map of the United States in old Mr. Jardine's library.

It was well after midnight when Caleb found himself falling asleep over the gray expanse of the newspapers. Jardine was still snoring quietly in the chair. Folding the precious newspapers, he stacked them on the sideboard, laid a quilt over his sleeping master, blew out the lamp, and went up to bed with visions of headlines and little black type still before his eyes.

— 26 —

A few weeks later, Jardine told Caleb, "There are going to be some changes around here. Get Jabeth up here to turn the big guestroom at the end of the hall into a nursery with a sleeping area for a nurse. He'll find a lot of nursery furniture up in the attic. I want it finished by the end of the week. It's about time little Boyd joined civilized society. Any questions?"

"No, Master."

"You should have," Jardine countered. "You should be wondering who that nurse will be."

"I am wondering, Master."

"Well, it's Missy." Jardine studied Caleb's face keenly, but could discern nothing that gave away emotion or thought. "Is that going to be a problem for you?"

"Missy has learned fast and has become very useful in the dining room. It won't be easy to replace her," Caleb said in a businesslike tone.

"You'll manage," Jardine said. "Promote one of the house girls. Have you got a prospect?"

"Yes, Master."

"I thought you might have."

After lunch, Caleb went into the kitchen, where Drusilla and the other house girls were tidying up.

"Drusilla," he said, "I want to talk to you when you've finished here. In my office." Caleb walked into the hallway leading to his little office.

After a few minutes, Drusilla appeared in the doorway. She didn't say anything.

"Come in," Caleb said, indicating the chair by the side of his desk. She sat down, still silent but seemingly at ease. While waiting to see if Drusilla would speak first, Caleb openly studied her. She was tall for a woman, slim but not bony. Drusilla's flesh looked as though it would be resilient to the touch. Beneath her loose cotton dress her small, high breasts seemed to resist gravity. Her face was handsome, with high, wide cheekbones, a fleshy but well-shaped nose, and appraising eyes below hair wrapped in a cloth. The lobe of her left ear had been mutilated, but had long since healed. Her eyes gazed at him without expression.

Finally Caleb asked, "Do you like your work, Drusilla?"

"It's better than the fields," she said shortly. "You going to send me back?"

"Why would you think that?" Caleb asked her.

"You don't like me," Drusilla said. "Never have."

"And why's that?"

"Because I don't kiss your black ass like Missy and the other girls," Drusilla said flatly.

"And you don't like me," Caleb told her.

"That's right."

"Why?"

"You don't think you're one of us. You've got your bags all packed. With your educated reading and writing and Yankeefied ways, you think you're going to be gone from here while we're staying. In your head, you're already on your way."

"On my way where?"

"North, where else? Where you belong. You think. Far away from us nappy-headed slaves in the field. Do you know what the people call you down in the quarter?

"No."

"Mr. Yankee White Nigger," she spat out.

"You too?"

"Why not?" she asked defiantly.

"Am I mean to you here in the house?" Caleb asked.

"Mean?" The question seemed to puzzle her. "I do my job. I earn my bread. You got no call to be mean. Without me, those girls run you ragged. You don't know anything about this house. You got here yesterday; you leaving tomorrow. Good-bye." Her lips curved down in an ugly sneer.

"It's a shame you don't like me, Drusilla," Caleb said. "I was going to offer you Missy's job."

"You tired of Missy?" she said.

Caleb ignored the question. "Missy's got another job. She won't be working with me anymore. I'm going to need a new girl to train in the dining room. Can you recommend one of the girls for the job?"

"Yes," said Drusilla immediately. "Me!"

"But you don't like me."

"I don't have to like you," Drusilla said. "I'll do the job well. I know it already. I've watched what you and Missy do. It's easy."

"Oh, is it?" Caleb could not help but show his amusement. "Maybe you don't need me in the dining room, then?"

"Yes, I do," Drusilla said. "For a while. I still can learn."

"Your modesty amazes me, Drusilla," Caleb said. "If I give you the job, can one of the other girls take your place?"

"Teazie is okay," Drusilla said. "I'll kick her fat ass, and she'll do just fine. With an eye on her now and then."

"And I suppose you've got another girl picked out to join the house girls?" Caleb asked.

"Yes. There be a girl in the laundry. Thin and not much to look at, but she got promise."

"You've got it all figured out, haven't you?" Caleb asked with wonder.

"Yes."

"Anything else?" he asked.

"Yes. If you want me for your bed, too, there are two things."

"You think I might?"

"Yes."

"And what are these things?"

"First, you have to let Mammy Doc down in the quarter look at you. I'm not catching anything that Missy might have."

"You think that might be a problem?" Caleb asked, trying to pin her down with his stare.

Drusilla did not flinch. "Yes, it might."

"I see. And the other thing?"

"You have to teach me to read and write."

"Anything else?"

"No." She looked at him directly but without defiance.

"Well," said Caleb, trying to be businesslike, "I'll consider what you said and let you know. You can go to the other girls now."

Drusilla rose from the chair gracefully and walked out of the tiny room without looking back.

Caleb tried to believe that he hadn't made up his mind about Drusilla, but he knew that it had been made up for him.

— *27* —

It did not take Caleb long to work his way through the newspapers Miss SallyAnne left at Three Rivers. First he read the portions that he thought would be of interest to Jardine aloud. After the first few lines, if Jardine wasn't interested, he would call out, "Skip that," and Caleb would move on to another article. Then, in his own room, Caleb would devour the newspapers line by line. Jardine was surprised to find that he missed the newspapers once they were all read. That night after dinner, he said to Caleb, "Well, where's the newspaper?"

"All finished, Master."

"All?"

"Yes, Master."

"Well, let's try reading them again," Jardine suggested, but it didn't work. He soon got bored, and on his next trip to Cassatt, Jardine ordered a copy of the *Charleston Courier* sent once a week. Both Jardine and Caleb waited eagerly for it to arrive and then made it last as long as they could. Soon, Jardine was having Caleb reading almost the entire newspaper to him. He would sit in his armchair sipping brandy as Caleb read.

"Don't think I couldn't read this paper to myself," Jardine told Caleb more than once. "I could. But what is the point of keeping a literate slave around the place if you don't use him?" It wasn't really a question, and Caleb felt no need to answer him.

As they devoured the papers, one topic began to dominate: the growing conflict between the government in Washington and the slave states. War went from being a remote speculation to a recurring subject and then to an almost definite prospect.

"All this talk about war," Jardine said after Caleb had read an editorial on the conflict of aims between the two regions, "is beginning to sound serious. Well, I don't want any part of it. From what Colonel Braddock says about that affair he got involved in down in Mexico, it's not a hell of a lot of fun. Do you think it will come, Caleb?"

"I don't know, Master, but it sure sounds like people are talking themselves into it."

"Well, I'm against it," said Jardine, pouring himself another glass of brandy. "I may not have been up north very long, but I was there long enough to know that those Yankees are crazy sons of bitches and there is one hell of a lot of them. I like Three Rivers just fine as it is, and I don't think any old war would improve it."

Caleb did not say anything.

"How about you, Caleb?" Jardine asked, half taunting. "You think that if the Yankees came down here and kicked our raggedy asses, they'd set you free?" When Caleb did not answer, Jardine added, "Maybe give you Three Rivers, and you could hire old Boyd Jardine to work for you. *Yes, Master Caleb, no, Master Caleb, right away, Master Caleb.* How'd you like that? I bet you would."

When Caleb did not answer, Jardine started to say something else but then thought better of it. "Read me some more of that paper, Caleb. Anything but that damned stuff about war."

The combination of the warm evening and the brandy soon had Jardine yawning and fighting off sleep. "That's enough reading for tonight, Caleb," he said. "I'm going to bed."

"Yes, Master." Caleb folded the newspaper, put it in its place on the sideboard, and got to his feet. He was about to leave the study when Jardine stopped him.

"You still got that idea in your head about being free, Caleb?" Jardine asked.

"Yes, Master."

"You think you'd be better off than you are at Three Rivers?" Jardine asked. "I treat you well here, don't I?"

"Yes, Master."

"Well, why then? You got a big bag of gold coins hidden somewhere so you can pay for the roof over your head, the food in your belly, and the clothes on your back?"

"No, Master."

"Well, tell me this: What would you do if I said tomorrow, *Okay, Caleb, you're a free man*, and gave you a piece of paper to prove it?"

Caleb thought for a moment. "I don't know, Master. Probably go back to Boston."

"You think they love niggers up there?" Jardine asked incredulously. "You think someone's going to take poor Caleb in and look after him? Because he has a piece of paper saying he's a free, free man?"

"No, Master."

"Well, you bet they won't. The world's not like that. There's a saying I learned up there at Harvard. It goes like this: *Nothing for nothing*. And that's what they'd give you. Nothing! Damn it, Caleb, you're going to close the house up now and then go to bed, right?"

"Yes, Master."

"Well, just suppose Caleb was just a little bit hungry. What would Caleb do?"

Before Caleb could open his mouth to answer, Jardine continued. "I'll tell you what he would do. He'd go back in that kitchen, cut him a couple of big slices off of a ham, and grab a big chunk of fresh-baked bread and maybe even a jug of that new batch of beer brewed last week. Does that sound possible, Caleb?"

"Yes, Master."

"You bet it does," Jardine said triumphantly. "Damn, it sounds all right to *me*. Now tell me this, Caleb," Jardine continued more seriously, "do you know any house in goddamned Boston where you could do that?"

"No, Master."

"*No* is right," Jardine crowed. "I think I've made my point. Now, get me a candle, Caleb. I'm going to bed."

"Yes, Master."

Later, lying in bed with his lamp blown out, Caleb thought about what Jardine had said. It was true that he hadn't thought much beyond the very idea of freedom. And he knew that when it came, if it came, he would be exchanging a solid known—in fact, a not-so-bad present—for a totally unknown future. But there was something deep inside Caleb that could not settle for anything less than freedom.

In his own larger, more luxurious bed below, Jardine was bothered by no such thoughts. The combination of brandy and fatigue allowed him to fall into a deep and dreamless sleep.

— *28* —

A few weeks later, Jardine went for a visit to Charleston with the Bentleys and a party of other local people.

"I don't know how you can leave that darkie in sole charge of Three Rivers for this long. I couldn't sleep at night." Jardine was sitting with Martha Bentley on the top deck of a paddle wheeler as it churned down the Wateree River through the black night.

"That's because you don't know Caleb," Jardine said.

"Nor would I want to," she responded. "I wouldn't have a bumptious slave like that on the place. That boy thinks he's white. Who knows what on earth he is up to?"

What Caleb was up to was a complete turnout of the house. With the exception of Jardine's bedroom and study, everything came out, including the contents of the kitchen, larder, brewery, bakery, and dry stores. The field slaves were brought up from the quarter to do the carrying.

"I swear," said Big Mose, struggling with one end of the vast sofa from the big reception room, "that Caleb is worse than Marse Boyd ever could be. I was goin' fishin' this afternoon."

"Plenty of time for fishing when we get finished, Mose," said Caleb, carrying a big leather chair down the broad front steps. "Plenty of time, plenty of beer, and plenty of barbecue. But right now there's plenty of work to do. Let's get it done." The grumbling continued but so did the work, and nobody worked harder than Caleb.

Coming down from the attic, which had been cleared for the first time in over twenty years, Caleb nearly bumped into Missy. Since Missy had moved into the nursery with little Boyd, now called Birdie by everyone but his father, Caleb had spent little time alone with her. He wasn't particularly happy to see her now, but she stood in his way without moving.

"How are you doing, Caleb?" she asked.

"Just fine," Caleb said.

"And how's Drusilla getting on with her new job and *otherwise*?" Missy's big smile was cold.

"She's learning the dining room right smartly," Caleb said. "As for the *otherwise*, that's a personal matter, Missy, and nothing for you to concern yourself with. I'd have thought that you had enough to do in the nursery."

"Oh, I do," said Missy. "You know, Caleb, you really ought to visit us in the nursery once in a way while Marse Boyd is away. Birdie has got so used to the presence of a man, and he does miss it."

"I might do that, Missy," Caleb said, "and I might bring Drusilla along with me. She likes babies."

"Is that necessary?" Missy asked. "I thought maybe, just for old time's sake—"

"You thought wrong," Caleb said abruptly. "If you've got any wayward thoughts, you can just forget them. Things are the way they are, and they're going to stay that way. You understand me?" His face was hard.

Missy weakened. "I miss you, Caleb. He's not the man you are," she said softly.

"You'd better be getting back to your nursery, Missy, and get ready," Caleb said. "We'll be coming there before long to clear it, and you better be all packed up."

"You afraid of Drusilla, Caleb?" Missy's catlike smile was back.

"No, but you ought to be. If she finds out you're even thinkin' of messing around where you don't belong, that girl is likely to rip your heart out."

"She's obviously got your heart where she wants it," Missy replied.

"Go to your nursery, Missy," Caleb said sternly and stared at her until she did.

A little later, Caleb was in the dining room with one of the house girls, packing up the linens, when Drusilla came in with a determined look on her face.

"Get out," she told the house girl.

But before the frightened girl could move, Caleb said quietly, "You keep on packing, girl. I'll be right back." He motioned with his head for Drusilla to follow him out through the big double doors to the garden. When they got out of earshot, he stood looking calmly at Drusilla until she spoke.

"I hear you been talking to that Missy."

"That's right."

"What about?"

"That's my business," said Caleb, "but I'll tell you that it's nothing for you to worry about. If it was, you'd be the first to hear about it—from me."

"I don't want you talking to her."

"I talk to everyone on this farm, Drusilla," Caleb told her calmly, "including Missy. There's not a damned thing you can do about it but trust me to tell you the truth. And I am. You have nothing to worry about."

"You sure?" Drusilla looked at him with narrowed eyes.

"As sure as sure can be," Caleb said. "Let us understand each other. You're in the dining room because I chose you to be. You are in my bed because you chose to be. You can stay in or leave either, or both. They do not depend on each other. Now, you had better think about that. In the meantime, I want you to go back in that dining room and apologize to that little girl. You about frightened her to death. When I'm working with someone, you have no right to order them about. Is that clear?"

"That's clear," Drusilla said, but she avoided his eyes. She turned without another word and walked back into the dining room.

— *29* —

When Jardine came back from Charleston, he wasn't alone. With him were two women: a pretty young woman with masses of curly blonde hair and an older woman dressed all in black with a face like a closed barn door. Strapped on the back of the buggy was a big trunk. When Jardine had helped the two women down, Caleb came forward. The rest of the house staff stood on the veranda, wondering who the visitors were.

"Caleb," said Jardine, "Miss Lacey and her aunt Mrs. Brooks are visiting for a while. Get some bedrooms ready."

"They are ready, Master," Caleb said, signaling for two of the boys to come forward to get the visitors' luggage.

Jardine gave Caleb a quizzical look and then said, "This is Caleb, Lacey. I think I told you about him."

"Yes, you did." Her smile was wide, but her voice was cut glass. "And how did you get along, Caleb," she asked, "with your master away?"

"Just fine, Miss Lacey," said Caleb.

The visitor let her gaze traverse the front of the house as if to say, *We'll see about that.*

"And where, Boyd," she asked in a completely different tone of voice, "is that precious baby of yours?"

Jardine's eyes scanned the veranda, but Missy was already coming forward with Birdie in her arms. She dropped the two women a curtsy as Caleb had taught her and the other house girls, and held the baby up like a bouquet of fresh flowers for them to admire.

The women made all the appropriate noises, but Caleb noticed that the younger woman was paying at least as much attention to Missy. Her violet-blue eyes ran over the pretty young slave without missing a thing. This, Caleb thought, was not a good thing. At least, not for Missy.

After Caleb and Drusilla had settled the ladies in the guestrooms at the front of the house so that they could freshen up after the dusty trip from the river, Jardine motioned Caleb into his study and closed the door behind them.

"What the hell have you been doing here, Caleb?"

"Just a bit of cleaning up."

"Just a bit?" Jardine said. "The old place looks like new. Except for this study." He looked around.

"And your room," Caleb said. "I thought we'd leave those two until you came back."

"You thought right," Jardine said, "but how did you know I'd be bringing guests back?"

"I didn't, Master. I just thought that with you being away it was a good time to get some work done. I know how you hate upset."

"Upset," said Jardine. "Yes, that's the word for it. Well, Caleb, so far you are doing fine, but I want things to go smoothly while Miss Lacey and her aunt are here. Do you understand?"

"Yes, Master."

"It's very important."

"Yes, Master."

"By the way, Caleb," Jardine said, as the slave was leaving the room. "When you unpack my bags, you'll find a batch of newspapers from Charleston. I saved them for you."

"Thank you, Master."

Dinner, which was augmented by the Bentleys, Pastor Buchanan, and young Jim Braddock, who was home on leave and proudly wore his gray uniform from the Citadel, went well. Everyone—even Martha Bentley—seemed impressed with the way that Caleb and Drusilla served the meal: smoothly, swiftly, and unobtrusively.

"Damn, Jardine," Rafe Bentley said between the salad and the fish course. "I'm going to get you over to Bellevue to see what you can do about smartenin' up our house darkies. I can't do a thing with them."

"That would cost you a bundle, Rafe. Skills like mine don't come cheap."

"Is it true, Boyd," Martha Bentley asked, ignoring the fact that Caleb was serving her at that very moment, "that your Caleb can read and write?"

"Some, Martha, some," Jardine said. He was not eager to discuss the subject. Caleb kept his face blank but could not help thinking of the new stack of newspapers under his bed, including a month-old copy of the *New York Times*.

As he helped Drusilla serve dinner, Caleb noticed that Miss Lacey's eyes kept going back to the large oil portrait of Jardine and the late mistress of Three Rivers that hung in a heavy gilt frame. Once, while they'd polished the silver, Miss Nancy had told Caleb that it was painted the year before by a wandering artist. He'd turned up at their door and offered to paint their portrait in exchange for the cost of materials, room and board, and fifty dollars cash if the likeness was satisfactory. Jardine had wanted to turn the fellow away, but it was getting dark and storm clouds were gathering. The artist was emaciated and wearing only a thin coat and no hat.

"Tell you what," the artist had said with a Tennessee accent. "Let me stay tonight, and I'll do a free preliminary sketch. If you don't like it, I'll go in the morning and you can keep the sketch or burn it as you like."

Miss Nancy, her eyes shining, told Caleb how after dinner that night, the sketch had burst into life under the artist's hand. With a few quick strokes, her face and Jardine's had appeared on the sketch pad. There was no question of the artist leaving the next morning. In fact, he was at Three Rivers for over two weeks and left only after framing and hanging his work. He'd planned to come back this year to do another painting—this one of Miss Nancy, Jardine, and their child.

— *30* —

Miss Lacey and her aunt's visit went pleasantly enough, with picnics, excursions, visits to the neighbors, and all of the pleasant—if limited—activities available in rural South Carolina. Not once did Miss Lacey ask to see the slave quarter. As a Charleston belle, her only experience was with house slaves up close and stevedores and other street laborers at a distance. She made sure that she visited the nursery at least once a day, where she held little Boyd as if he were a lifelike doll. She studied Missy without seeming to notice her; to Miss Lacey, the nurse was just a pair of brown hands to pass her the baby and a small problem to deal with.

The day before Miss Lacey and Mrs. Brooks were scheduled to return to Charleston, Jardine called Caleb into his study. His face was serious.

"Caleb," said Jardine, "we've got a problem."

Caleb said nothing.

"I'm going to take Miss Lacey and her aunt back to Charleston. There are going to be some changes around here. Miss Lacey's coming here to live at Three Rivers as mistress." Jardine paused as if he expected some reaction from Caleb.

"Congratulations, Master."

"Thank you, Caleb," Jardine said absentmindedly. "But, as I said, there are going to be some changes around here."

"Master?"

"Damn it, Caleb, Missy has to go. Miss Lacey just won't have her on the place. She's going to bring her own nurse for little Boyd back from Charleston."

Caleb knew what he was saying, but he looked at Jardine blankly.

"Don't you pull that dumb act on me," Jardine flared. "You know what I mean. While I was in Camden the other day, I arranged for somebody to pick her up next Thursday. You tell her—and give her this." Jardine handed Caleb a gold twenty-dollar coin. "And you make sure that she's ready to go on Thursday morning. But don't tell her until late the day before. Understood?"

"Understood, Master."

"Drusilla will be going along with us to take care of little Boyd. Let her know. Tell her to pack for three weeks."

"Yes, Master."

"The wedding will be held down there," Jardine continued. "Miss Lacey has a whole passel of relations who can't be expected to trek all the way up here. And we haven't got room for them, anyway. Repaint the master bedroom and Miss Nancy's dressing room by the time we get back." He paused, then added, "That's it," dismissing Caleb.

"Very good, Master." Caleb turned to leave.

"One other thing," Jardine said.

Caleb turned back.

"Put that oil painting of Miss Nancy and me up in the attic. Wrap it up carefully in some blankets."

"Yes, Master," Caleb said. "Will that be all?"

"Of course that's all," Jardine said angrily. "I'd tell you if there was more, wouldn't I? Now get out of here and do as I say."

No sooner had Jardine's carriage disappeared toward the turnpike, the dust cloud from its wheels still visible in the distance, than Caleb went up to the nursery.

"Hello, stranger," Missy said, looking up from the baby clothes she was folding. "Drusilla's hardly out of sight and you're already visiting me. You are a bad boy."

"I've got something to tell you, Missy," Caleb said soberly.

"Really?" Missy opened her eyes wide in mock surprise. "What can that be?" Then she laughed harshly. "Save your breath, Caleb. What day are they coming?"

"Thursday."

"What are you doing telling me so soon, fool?" she laughed. "Don't you know that I might do something rash? Like burn down the damned house! When were you supposed to tell me?"

"Wednesday night."

"Well, well." Missy taunted. "Caleb, the perfect slave, done gone ahead and disobeyed orders, and his master hardly gone a minute. Maybe you will be free one of these days. You're learning. Why you telling me so soon?"

"I thought it was fair."

She laughed. "You're going to have to forget about fair if you're going to be a black white man, honey. They don't know nothing about fair. You might as well give it to me." She held out her hand, and Caleb put the gold coin into it.

Missy admired the coin. "Caleb," she said, "your Master Boyd may be a low-down, cowardly, gutless man-boy, but he's not too stingy. I didn't expect more than ten." She tucked the coin safely into a secret pocket in the waistband of her skirt. "You know why they took that baby with them?"

"I think so," said Caleb.

"That's right," Missy smiled scornfully. "Because your Master Boyd was afraid I might poison little Birdie. After months of taking care of that precious little baby, I'm supposed to turn around and kill him just because his daddy is fool enough to marry that bundle of golden locks and flounces. Because that's what thrown-away slave women do. Every time." She laughed. "If that were true, this state would be littered with little crosses so you couldn't hardly walk. I love that baby, and now I'll never see him again."

Caleb did not know what to say.

Missy had been talking more to herself than to Caleb. Then she looked up at him. "Caleb, will you do me a favor?"

"That depends on what it is," Caleb said carefully.

"Oh, don't worry. I'm not trying to get into your bed while Drusilla is away. Will you let me serve you in the dining room until the man comes for me?"

"Yes, Missy," Caleb said seriously, "you can do that."

So, every night that remained, Missy set the table for one. And after she and Caleb prepared his meal, he sat in solitary splendor and ate while she served him with quiet efficiency.

Finally, on Missy's last night at Three Rivers, she broke her silence while serving. "Tell me honestly, Caleb, am I better at serving than Drusilla?"

Caleb thought for a long moment. "I have to admit, girl," he said, "you are better."

Missy said no more, but she went back to the empty nursery to sleep with some consolation and a little less worry about what the future would bring.

— *31* —

The next morning, earlier than they'd expected, the slave trader's man came. He was a little man, verging on old age, in a rusty black hat and a long duster that nearly reached his ankles. He had the benign face of a lay reader or a Bible salesman, but the manacles and leg irons in the back of his wagon were real enough. Beside them on a pile of sacks sat a toothless old woman in a red kerchief. Missy and Caleb, who was carrying her bag, came out of the house just as the wagon reined up. Missy was wearing her oldest sacking dress, but inside her bag was a fine selection of Miss Nancy's clothes that Jardine had ordered packed away and forgotten.

"That her?" he asked Caleb, consulting a crumpled list he pulled from his coat pocket. "That Missy?"

"It is, sir," Caleb replied. "Can we give you some breakfast before you go on?"

"I wish you could," the man said, "but I've got three more darkies to pick up and a boat to catch before noon. I'm already running behind. Get up there, girl, with mammy," he said to Missy. "We'll just forget about the irons. You don't look to me like you want to do any running this morning."

"Sure don't, uncle," Missy said as Caleb helped her up to the back of the wagon with her bag and a sack of food he'd put together from the kitchen. Missy might be traveling a couple of days before she was sold. Caleb went to the front of the wagon and offered the man another small sack.

"Some biscuits and ham and things from our kitchen, sir," he said, "just in case you don't have time to eat this morning. And a bottle of beer."

"Thank you, son," said the slaver. "Very thoughtful. Thank your master for me." He looked narrowly at Caleb. "Say, where is your master?"

"Charleston, sir," Caleb said.

The slave trader's man thought that over. "Well," he said, "this isn't getting the job done. We're off." He cracked his whip over the heads of the horses, and they shambled to a leisurely trot.

"Best care, Missy," Caleb called out as the wagon turned toward the drive.

"You, too, Caleb," Missy said. "And tell Drusilla something for me."

"What's that?"

"That wedding silver from Memphis could use a touch of polish."

"I'll do that." Caleb stood and watched the wagon until it was out of sight. Missy did not wave.

Jardine came back one morning a bit more than a week later. With him were Drusilla, little Boyd, and a new nurse, a horse-faced woman in her forties, but no Miss Lacey. Caleb came racing down from the master bedroom, where he was supervising the painting, to find Jardine jumping down from the buggy. Jardine's face was set.

"Don't say a word, Caleb," he said when he saw the slave. "Don't say a goddamned word. Just get this rig unpacked." Jardine stalked into the house and disappeared into his study.

Caleb exchanged looks with Drusilla and then said hello to the nurse. "I'm Caleb," he told her. "Drusilla will show you where the nursery is so that you can get the baby settled. Then, come on down to the kitchen and meet the house people."

When they got into the kitchen, Caleb asked Drusilla, "What happened?"

"I don't rightly know," she said. "Of course, I didn't see much of them on the boat because I was minding the baby. But Miss Lacey came in once a day to see Birdie, and she seemed happy enough. Once we were in Charleston, we got to Miss Lacey's daddy's house, a big old place, and things started moving toward the wedding. But then two or three days later, Mr. Boyd, his face near as black as yours, said, 'Pack up; we going home.' So I did. Nobody told me anything. When we got to the boat, Rose—that's the nurse—was waiting there, and so was Master. No sign of Miss Lacey, her daddy, or anybody even to wave us good-bye. All the way back up the river, Mr. Boyd sat up to all hours drinking but not talking. Of course, I didn't dare ask him anything."

"I suppose we'll find out if he wants us to know," Caleb said.

"When did Missy go?" Drusilla asked him.

"Last Thursday."

"Any problems?"

"What do you mean, 'any problems'?" Caleb asked angrily. "Master says a slave goes, a slave goes. You've been around long enough to know that. What are you trying to ask?"

"How'd you feel about her leaving?"

"You know slaves don't have feelings," said Caleb. "If you gotta know, I think we lost a good nurse for nothing, but maybe this Rose will be a better one. You got any more questions?"

"No, I guess not," said Drusilla.

"Good," Caleb said, "because I've got to go upstairs and get that bedroom put together again. You get the dining room ready for Master's lunch."

"He won't eat," Drusilla predicted.

"That's not the question," Caleb said. "You get it ready even if he *never* eats again."

Drusilla was right; Jardine did not come out of his study until late that day. When he did, he was drunk.

"Where's my goddamn dinner?" he demanded, though it was nearly midnight.

"It's coming out of the kitchen right now," said Caleb.

"Well, hurry it up." Jardine sat down at his place at the end of the long table and looked around with bleary irritation for something to yell about. He spotted the oil painting of himself and Nancy on the wall.

"Caleb!" he bellowed.

Caleb came out of the kitchen with a tray. "Master?"

"I thought I told you to take that painting down and store it in the attic."

"I did, Master."

"Well, what's it doing back up?"

"I had it put up again this afternoon," Caleb said.

"Why?"

"Because I thought you would want it. Do you want me to take it down again?"

Jardine looked confused. "No," he said at last. "Just leave it be. And give me my damned dinner."

Jardine fell asleep several times over his dinner and ate almost nothing, but when Caleb tried to get him to go to bed, he resisted angrily. "Who's the goddamned slave here, you or me?" When Caleb did not answer, Jardine said, "That's right. And don't you ever forget it," before lurching back to his study and slamming the door. On his way to bed, Caleb listened at the study door and heard Jardine mumbling to himself, bottle and glass clinking.

In the morning, Caleb found Jardine sprawled on the big horsehide sofa in his study with his mouth open. A nearly empty bottle lay on the floor in a pool of drying whiskey. Caleb threw a blanket over Jardine, mopped up the whiskey, closed the study door, and went about his business. It was late afternoon before Jardine appeared. He was ghostly white, and for a half hour he was only able to say two words: "My head!" But after drinking a whole lot of water—which got him slightly drunk again—and taking some headache powders Miss Lacey had left behind, Jardine went up for a bath. When he came back down, he was ravenously hungry and somewhat like his former self.

Jardine ate the delayed breakfast Caleb served him in silence. But as he stirred his second cup of coffee, Jardine looked up at Caleb.

"I'll bet you're just busting with curiosity, aren't you?"

Caleb surprised him by saying, "Yes, Master."

"Well," Jardine said, "you can just go ahead and bust."

But later that evening, after Caleb had given him a report on affairs at Three Rivers during his absence, Jardine said, "Sit down, Caleb. I hate to give you the satisfaction, but I have to tell somebody what happened in Charleston, or I think I'll explode." Caleb sat on his usual chair at the end of the sideboard.

"A couple of things first," Jardine said. "I'm telling you only because there is no one *else* to tell. You can just imagine what Martha Bentley would say. She'd *I told you so* me into an early grave and never leave off reminding me that that turkey-faced cousin of hers *and* her ten thousand dollars a year is marrying a tobacco farmer up in Lancaster. Second thing is, I don't want any comments from you. You are just a pair of ears for this purpose. Understood? And third and just as important, I don't want you telling anyone on this place—not even Drusilla. If I get one hint, one sniff, one *anything* that you have, I'll sell you down Hampton County way where they use darkies like you for gator bait. Agreed?" He looked sternly at Caleb.

"Agreed, Master."

"All right," Jardine said, and he sat silently for a while staring at his desk. Finally, he started. "Well, you know, Caleb, things were okay when we left here. Oh, I was sorry to have to get rid of a good girl like Missy, but I could sort of understand Miss Lacey's point of view. What women don't know, they can figure out, and if she was going to be little Boyd's new mama, I reckoned she had a right to pick his nurse. That aside, things were pretty fine until we got to Charleston. In fact, they were pretty fine in Charleston. Miss Lacey's papa has a big old house near the cathedral, and we settled in there in some state and comfort. That importing business of his must be doing all right. We had no complaints, or at least I didn't."

Jardine cut a cigar and lit it off the lamp on his desk. "Then, Caleb," he continued, "we started meeting relations. That Miss Lacey has more cousins, aunts, uncles than anyone you have ever met, and I think I howdied every damn one of them. Nice enough, but I think there's some Creole blood there somewhere. A couple of her old uncles were near as black as you are, Caleb, but a man would risk his life by pointing that out. Needless to say, I did not bother. Anyway, the first couple of days were nothing but a blur of socials and preparations for the wedding, though my end of that was pretty much limited to buying new formal wear and the biggest diamond ring Charleston had to offer. I didn't even have to choose a best man. Miss Lacey's squirt of a little brother was going to be that. The rails were greased for sure.

"But then came the train accident, and I was the star of it. The third day we were in Charleston, Miss Lacey's daddy invited me down to see their business premises. Well, he gave me the grand tour, which was long enough to suit me, and then we went up to his office that looks out over Hamlin Sound. He gave me a nice glass of whiskey and a Havana cigar about a foot long. Everything was pretty mellow all right. Then, off came the velvet gloves, and I found out what the real arrangement was. Old Daddy Clayton pretty quickly forgot about his role of gracious host, and the hard businessman began to show through. He started talking about *certain alterations* that would have to be made before the wedding on Sunday. And then I really started listening. That whiskey stopped tasting so good, and the cigar was like a piece of old rope soaked in tar.

"I won't burden you with the gory details, but getting rid of Missy was just the opening act in this little drama. Though Miss Lacey was apparently too shy to say so, she had a whole parcel of other modest changes she wanted made around Three Rivers before she would consent to become the second Mrs. Jardine. I'll give you the short list. For starters, you had to go, Drusilla had to go, and some lame dog of a second cousin had to come in as overseer. *And* I had to agree to let Miss Lacey spend six months of each year with her dear mama in Charleston and transport mama to Three Rivers for the other six. There were a whole lot more, not least to do with little Boyd. Apparently, like the portrait of Nancy and me, he was to be discreetly farmed out somewhere because Miss Lacey did not fancy raising someone else's brat. You can imagine my reaction to that, but these were just the pick of the litter. I listened politely. Being just as businesslike as Pa Clayton, I said that they sounded like very interesting proposals. I asked could he put them on paper so that I'd be able to study them. Would you believe it, Caleb, he opened a drawer and handed me a sheet of paper with his proposals—I call them demands—all neatly laid out on it.

"He all but handed me a pen along with them. I told him I needed to study Miss Lacey's suggestions, shook his hand, thanked him for the tour, whiskey, and cigar, and got the hell out of there. First, I ordered Drusilla to pack up little Boyd and be ready to fly. Second was the steamship office for tickets. Third was that jeweler's where I sold back the ring—at a considerable loss, I might add. Fourth was a slave dealer to pick up old Dobbin, the boy's new nurse. Fifth and final was a short but interesting interview with Miss Lacey and her mama. I told them, with regrets, that I would have to reject their terms and the marriage was off. Then I invited them to drop by Three Rivers any time they were in the neighborhood. I grabbed Drusilla and little Boyd and got the hell out of there before any of her hot-blooded kin could decide I'd insulted somebody and call me out."

Jardine finished his narrative and looked up at Caleb. "So, there you have it, Caleb," he said. "A tale of adventure, romance, and sheer stupidity. I'm back here without a wife, without a damned good nurse who I sold into God knows what situation, out of pocket more money than I like to talk about, but—I hope—a little wiser. You got anything to say about all that?"

"No, Master."

"And a damned good thing," Jardine said menacingly. "You just try to forget it, and I'll try to remember it next time I am tempted by a pretty face and a lot of curly blonde hair."

When Caleb was about to leave, Jardine remembered something. "Did Missy have anything to say when she left?" he asked.

"Just good-bye, Master, and thanks for the twenty dollars."

Jardine thought for a moment. "I guess I deserve that, Caleb," he said quietly.

For all of his hurry to get away from Charleston, Jardine did not neglect to bring back another stack of newspapers, which Caleb slowly read to him. One theme was repeated so often that it became clear to both of them.

"Damn me, Caleb," Jardine exclaimed, "if there isn't going to be a war. Get me the atlas, the big one with the red cover." Jardine laid the big book open on his cleared desk and put his finger on it about where Three Rivers was. "I suppose," he said sarcastically, "that you are an expert at map reading."

"No, Master," Caleb said, but as they studied the detailed map, it became clear that he knew his way around it at least as well as Jardine did.

"As any fool can see, when the national government stops fooling around and comes down here to start putting down the rebellion, Three Rivers is going to be smack dab in their way," said Jardine. "And since it's not likely to move, what are we going to do?"

Neither of them had the answer to that.

— *32* —

A few days later, after continuing to read the papers and talking to neighbors and strangers he met on trips to local towns, Jardine again called Caleb to his study.

"You still got your heart set on being free, Caleb?" he asked.

"Yes, Master."

"All right. I've been thinking. I reckon when this coming war starts, owning slaves is going to be an even worse proposition than it is now. If the Yanks don't come through here and free you, one night you'll take advantage of the confusion and just head north."

Caleb did not deny that.

"Okay," Jardine said. "I've decided that if you are so bound and determined to go up north and take your chances, I'll sell you your freedom for the same price I paid for you. Do you have five hundred and fifty dollars, Caleb?"

"No, Master," Caleb said, though it was hardly necessary.

"You got five hundred and fifty red cents?"

Caleb just shook his head.

"Well," Jardine said, "I'm not about to give you your freedom for nothing, and I'm not going to sell you to some other poor devil because you'd just disappear, wouldn't you?"

"I'd try, Master," Caleb said.

"So that leaves one other possibility. You have to—or rather, we have to—come up with some way that you can make that money. You got any ideas?"

"No, Master."

"Well, you'd better do some thinking, and so will I."

When Jardine came back from his next trip to town, he was buzzing with excitement. Now, he thought, where the hell are they? Going into the horse barn, he began opening boxes, searching through one and then turning to another. Soon the floor was littered with worn-out harnesses and other odds and ends.

After a while, the smallest house girl knocked breathlessly on the door of Caleb's little office. "Massa's in the big horse barn," she blurted, "and he wants you. Right away."

Putting away the account books, Caleb went out the back door and was soon at the horse barn. He found Jardine deep in a big steamer trunk, throwing things out of it.

"Aha!" he shouted in triumph and came out with a pair of worn boxing gloves. Then another pair. Caleb looked at him stupidly.

"Caleb, you ever do any fighting? I mean in the ring—prizefighting?"

"No, Master," Caleb said. "Brent and I were given boxing lessons when we were boys, but the only real fighting I've done was rough-and-ready with no rules."

"That might come in handy," Jardine said. "I learned to box at the Citadel and then did a lot of it at Harvard when I should have been studying. Let's see how much I remember." He threw a pair of gloves to Caleb. "Strip down to just your trousers," he said, "and put those on."

"Why, Master?"

"Because I said so, damn you. Who's the master here? Get them on!"

While Caleb was stripping off his shirt and pulling on the gloves, Jardine used a hoe handle to line off an improvised ring in the dirt just outside the stalls. Then he also stripped off his jacket and shirt and called in Old William to lace up his gloves. Then William tied Caleb's laces. When they were ready, Jardine sent William back to work and faced Caleb.

"For the next few minutes, I want you to try to forget that you are a slave," said Jardine. "We are just two boxers trying to knock each other's heads off. You got that?"

"I think so, Master," Caleb said.

Jardine squared up to him, and Caleb desperately tried to remember what the boxing teacher had taught him and Brent all those years ago. While he was thinking, Jardine's glove came through Caleb's upraised hands and hit him in the face. It was not a hard blow, but it stung Caleb into alertness.

"For Christ's sake," Jardine complained, "are you going to sleep? We're supposed to be boxing." He threw another right, but Caleb picked this one off. "That's more like it," Jardine said, dancing around. "Now, come on, let's box!"

As he faced Jardine, Caleb remembered something the old boxer had said: *Boys, half of the art of boxing is not getting hit. You manage that long enough and eventually the other feller will get tired and be ripe for the picking.* That philosophy began to drift back into Caleb's consciousness, and he soon found that he could fend off Jardine's enthusiastic but clumsy punches with ease. He was beginning to enjoy watching his red-faced, sweating master vainly throw punch after punch. Very few of them came anywhere near Caleb.

"Come on, damn you," Jardine puffed. "Hit me! You're supposed to be a boxer, not a dummy."

Desperately, Caleb tried to do as he was told and launched a roundhouse right at Jardine's bobbing head. The feeble punch came no closer than a foot.

"That's a little better," Jardine called. "Keep it up. Keep it up! Come on, try to hit me." He launched a vicious right cross at Caleb's head but succeeded only in hitting his glove.

Caleb shifted his weight from foot to foot and warded off Jardine's punches, but the ones he threw came nowhere near Jardine. It wasn't that Jardine was so elusive. It was as though something was staying Caleb's arm, taking the strength and direction out of his punches before he could launch them.

Finally, Jardine stopped what he hoped was very stylish bobbing and stood there, red-faced and gasping. "Christ," he said, "I can't keep this up. I'm going to die of exhaustion or old age before you lay a glove on me." He lowered his gloved and trembling hands to his sides. He stuck his chin up at Caleb. "Now, come on, you big black bastard. Hit me! That's an order!"

Caleb raised his hands to do as he was told, but nothing happened. Jardine was an easy and inviting target, but Caleb simply could not will his muscles to move. He lowered his hands again. "I can't, Master," he said.

"Why the hell not?"

"I don't know," Caleb said, "but I think I might kill you. I can't take that chance."

Jardine looked at the massive muscles on the slave before him and wondered if what Caleb said might be true.

"Are you some kind of Quaker?" he asked.

"No, Master. I just can't hit you."

"We'll see if you can hit at all," Jardine said. "You just stay here. Don't move an inch. I'll be right back."

— *33* —

Storming out of the horse barn, Jardine strode over to the big barn where slaves were cleaning out a large accumulation of manure. He studied the three men as they worked. He considered Big Mose. He was the right size, but he was also pushing sixty years of age and was too valuable to damage in the event Caleb could actually fight. Finally, he shouted, "You, Caesar, come here."

The slave dropped his pitchfork and walked over to Jardine doubtfully. He was about twenty years old and muscular but both thinner and taller than Caleb. "Massa?"

"You want to earn a quarter?" Jardine asked.

"Yassa."

"Then follow me." Jardine turned on his heel and marched back to the horse barn with Caesar following close behind, wondering what Master Boyd was up to. But he looked forward to having that quarter.

When they got into the horse barn, and he saw Caleb waiting there wearing boxing gloves, Caesar was even more confused. He stopped and shifted his wondering gaze back and forth from the master to the house slave. Caleb paid no attention to him.

Jardine turned back to him. "Caesar, you do any boxing? You know, fist fighting?"

"Nawsa, not much. Us boys, we mostly wrestle. Don't need no 'quipment for that. Nobody gets hurt."

"Let's see your muscles."

Sheepishly, Caesar raised his arms until his fists were alongside his head and flexed. His biceps were well developed, and his young body was lean and hard.

"You'll do," said Jardine. "What do you think, Caleb?"

"He'll do, Master," Caleb said.

"All right, Caesar," Jardine said. "Here's what we're doing. You're boxing with Caleb here. You'll wear these gloves I've got on, and you have to stay within these lines I've scraped in the dirt. You're going to fight as many three-minute rounds as it takes, and I'll give you a quarter for every round you last. If you can beat Caleb, I'll give you another two dollars. How's that sound?"

"That's fine, Massa," Caesar said. He applied his limited mathematical skills to how much he could earn, but he stopped cold when he came to two dollars. He'd never had two dollars together in his whole life. And although he had nothing in particular against Caleb—the two had never exchanged two words—he had no natural liking for the privileged house slave with the peculiar way of talking, either. This might be fun as well as profitable. At the very least, he'd have a quarter.

"Quarter anyway, Massa?" he asked just to be sure.

"Quarter anyway," Jardine assured him, reaching into the pocket of his trousers and fishing out a coin. "Here, put that in your pocket. You're a rich man already. A professional fighter."

Liking the sound of that, Caesar eagerly took the coin and tucked it away.

"Now," Jardine ordered, "strip off that shirt and put on these gloves. Time to stop talking and start fighting."

As he watched Jardine tie the boxing gloves onto Caesar, Caleb realized that the young man had no idea what he was getting into.

His only assets were strength, youth, and speed. Caleb knew that these were not enough.

Finally, the gloves were on, and Jardine backed out of the improvised ring. "Okay, boys," he said, peering at his pocket watch. "When I say go, you go. When I say stop, you stop. Got that?"

"Yes, Massa."

"Yes, Master."

"Well, then," Jardine said. "Go!"

Caleb stepped forward rapidly while Caesar was still thinking and struck a sharp right just where Caesar's left arm met his shoulder. The blow rang out in the silent barn. Suddenly, Caesar wasn't thinking anymore; he was reacting. But instead of darting back, Caleb stayed in close and hit him again in exactly the same place on his other arm. The punches didn't hurt, but they were a reminder to Caesar of why he was in that barn.

Caesar shook himself like a big thin dog and launched a roundhouse right that might have murdered Caleb if it had landed anywhere near him. But by that time, Caleb had backed off and was bobbing and weaving in a pattern that he vaguely remembered from his brief training.

"Now you're going!" shouted Jardine. "Show me something."

What Caleb showed him was a lot of speed and mobility, but not much power and absolutely no savagery. For two full rounds he treated Caesar like a giant, slightly mobile target while he revived his dormant boxing education. He tried out a bit of everything the old pug had taught him and Brent. And at the end of each combination, he hit Caesar with a sharp, painful punch to a different part of his body.

By the third round, Caesar was enraged, confused, and desperate to come to grips with this stinging whirlwind. Forgetting about the easy money he was earning and anything he might have learned from studying what Caleb was doing, Caesar charged at Caleb. All that effort got him was a flurry of sharp punches as he passed. Then he gave up boxing entirely, reverting to what wrestling he knew. But before he could get a grip on Caleb, a quick jab to each kidney drove Caesar back in confusion, opening him up for a knockout punch.

But Caleb did not deliver it. Instead, he followed his retreating opponent, delivering harassing, stinging, and humiliating punches, which did no real damage.

"Come on, Caleb," Jardine cried, consulting his watch. "Finish him! You're costing me money."

As if responding to a cue, Caleb stopped dancing, weaving, and dodging, and strode like a panther directly into Caesar's path, his eyes focused on the younger man's chin. At first, daunted by Caleb's glinting eyes and determined expression, Caesar fell back and covered up, his dark eyes peeking over his gloves. Then, gathering both strength and heart, Caesar launched himself with weakening legs straight at Caleb, like a bull tiring of sport and going in for the kill.

Stepping slightly to one side, Caleb delivered a straight right to the point of Caesar's chin. Caesar's momentum still carried him forward, and Caleb stepped aside and followed up with a left hook, which landed just below Caesar's right ear. Caesar dropped to the dirt floor, and Caleb stepped back and lowered his hands.

"Damn!" Jardine shouted, jumping into the ring. "You can fight. But why did you take three rounds? You could have finished him off in one."

"That depends on what you want, Master," Caleb said. "Caesar working or Caesar lying in his bed with a broken jaw."

Jardine shook his head. "Get a bucket of water and wake that boy up," he said. "He's got work to do."

"He won't be worth much this morning," Caleb observed. He knelt down and shook the boy's shoulder gently. "Caesar," he said softly, "come on, boy, it's all over. Up you go." He helped the groggy youth to his feet.

"Wha . . . happen?" Caesar asked.

"You slipped," Caleb told him.

"All over?"

"Yes, it's all over, Caesar," Caleb said. "You did well."

"Quarter," Caesar suddenly shouted and dug into the waist-band of his ragged trousers. He found the coin and relaxed. "How many?" he demanded.

"Rounds?"

"Quarters!"

Caleb glanced at Jardine, who was trying to look as though his part of the transaction was over. Caesar looked at them with a half-afraid, half-belligerent expression that showed that he expected Jardine to cheat him. Neither man spoke.

"Oh, all right," Jardine said testily, digging into his pocket and giving Caesar another three quarters. "Now, get back to work. And don't you talk about this."

Caesar stumbled back to the big barn, still slightly groggy but clinking the coins together happily. Both Jardine and Caleb knew that the first thing he would do was show Big Mose and the other slaves the money and tell them everything that had happened. The big barn would not get cleaned out that morning.

"This boxing is an expensive business," Jardine complained.

"It could have been worse, Master," Caleb said. "Caesar could have lasted five rounds or even beaten me."

"Not if you know what's good for you, he couldn't have," Jardine said. "Now, get yourself cleaned up and come to my study. We got some talking to do."

— 34 —

A little while later, Jardine was sitting behind his desk, excitedly showing Caleb a poster he'd picked up in Camden. It announced a big fight show that month featuring a visiting white heavyweight. The program would also feature bouts between slaves whose masters entered them.

"There's a prize, Caleb," Jardine explained. "Maybe five or ten dollars for the winner of each bout."

"Even if I win, Master—and there ain't going to be many Caesars in *that* ring—it's going to take the rest of my life to get enough to buy my freedom," said Caleb as he examined the poster.

"Now, that's where you're wrong, Caleb," Jardine said eagerly. "The five or ten dollars is nothing. That's beer money. The real payoff is in the side bets. Suppose Barney Kingston from over Cassatt way puts that big black of his, Pompey, in the ring. Barney's going to want to back his boy with some real money—fifty, a hundred, maybe more. They tell me that thousands change hands on a busy day. We can do it, Caleb," Jardine continued. "You fight, I bet, and we both win. What do you say? Do you want to be free or don't you?"

"I want to, Master," Caleb said seriously.

"Well, then?"

Caleb just looked at him, but Jardine knew what he was thinking. "Here's the deal, Caleb," Jardine said. "You can have all the prize money, and I'll give you a percentage of the wager money I win."

Caleb continued to look closely at his master.

"Don't you trust me, Caleb?" Jardine asked.

"Yes, Master."

"Well, then?"

"Mr. Staunton always said that the terms of a deal ought to be settled in advance," Caleb said.

"Oh, he did, did he?" Jardine said. "And did he happen to say what percentage for Caleb would be fair?"

"No, Master."

Jardine looked at his slave long and hard. Finally, he spoke. "Are you sure that he didn't mention something about a fifty-fifty split of *all* winnings?"

"That does sound familiar, Master," Caleb admitted.

"Did he say anything about Caleb getting any money for beating Caesar today?"

"I believe, Master, that he suggested that three dollars might be fair."

Jardine wasn't happy about it, but he paid up.

When Drusilla heard about Caleb's intention to purchase his freedom by prizefighting, she was skeptical. "Marse Boyd's going to feed you to the chopping machine," she predicted, "and you're likely to end up with a whole lot of lumps and no money—and no freedom."

"That's if I don't win," Caleb said. "What do you know about these fights?"

"Nothing. But from what I hear, they nothing but dogfights for black men so that white men can get drunk and hoot and holler and brag. *My nigger can beat your nigger.* That's all they saying."

"Well this one can't think of no other way to buy his freedom, so he'll just have to take his chances."

"It's *any other way*," Drusilla corrected him. "If you're going to be my teacher, you better sharpen up your language. You talk like those people down in the quarter."

"I talk better English than Master Boyd," Caleb said defensively.

"That's not saying much. Now, let's get back to my lessons. I want to learn to read before I'm too old to see the page."

"Why do you want to learn to read and write, Dru," Caleb asked, "if you're not looking to be free?"

"You never know what's going to happen, and I never heard of it hurting anybody to learn something," she answered. "Now, let's get to work. I'm getting sleepy."

For the next three weeks, Caleb trained in the horse barn every moment he could spare. From memory, he dredged up as much as he could of what the old fighter had said about training and what he'd seen in that Boston gymnasium. Taking a piece of clothesline, he made himself a skipping rope and ignored the giggles of the children from the quarter who gathered to watch him and wonder.

Caesar hung around the horse barn so much in hopes of duplicating his big-money day that Jardine finally hired him for fifty cents a week to serve as Caleb's sparring partner. Twice a day, the boy put on the gloves and did his best to hit Caleb while he practiced what he could remember of the old Irishman's defensive techniques. It finally got so that Caleb could go a three-minute round without being hit once, no matter how hard Caesar tried. Caleb saved his own punches for the bales of hay he strung up with a rope in the middle of the barn, and he went through several of those. Jardine complained that he was going to destroy next winter's food for the horses, but he was secretly pleased with Caleb's progress. It was his idea that Caleb should sit for an hour each day with his hands soaking in buckets of brine. He'd heard somewhere that it hardened the hands. When nobody was looking, Caesar did the same.

35

Finally, the Saturday of the first boxing match arrived. Early that morning Caleb loaded up the wagon with all the things Jardine thought they would need: the boxing gloves, tape for Caleb's hands, water, sponges, an old bathrobe of Jardine's, and some towels. Drusilla insisted that Caleb take some arnica and a roll of bandages from the first-aid kit.

"I'm not going to war, woman," Caleb complained, but it didn't do him any good.

Finally, when the sun was just peeking over the horizon, they were ready to go. Caesar hung around the wagon, hoping that Jardine would take him along and maybe even let him fight. He was very disappointed when the wagon, with Caleb riding in the back, started toward the turnpike without him.

"Don't be downhearted, boy," called Big Mose. "You lookin' for a fight, I'll box you." He windmilled his big fists in front of his chest and grinned broadly. "I'll box your ears. But you'll have to pay me fifty cents. No? Well, then, I guess we better get to work."

A crowd of men and boys was already gathering by the time the wagon reached Camden. There was a feeling of holiday in the air, and small boys hung around the bunting-decked platform in the town square that was serving as the boxing ring. They flexed their muscles, made a lot of noise, and chased each other as they pretended to be prizefighters.

Dotted around at a fair distance from the platform were more than half a dozen wagons much like Jardine's, each with a slave, sometimes two, and a bag or crate of boxing paraphernalia in the back. The owners and the slaves looked at the competition with what they hoped was cool confidence and indifference.

Leaving Caleb to look after the wagon, Jardine jumped down and walked over to greet Barney Kingston, who had indeed brought Pompey, a burly man who seemed nearly as wide as he was tall and who was dressed in a red velvet suit made from a slightly faded pair of old curtains. On his head he wore a straw hat with a band reading VOTE FOR BUCHANAN. He was enjoying all the attention.

"Howdy, Barney," Jardine said genially. "Your boy looks good."

"Well, Boyd," Kingston drawled lazily, "he is pretty fit. I can't say that yours looks up to much."

On orders from Jardine, Caleb was wearing old clothes that were two sizes too big. He was hunched over in the back of Jardine's wagon looking at the pair of old canvas boots on his feet. A shapeless felt hat hid most of his face.

"Well," said Jardine dismissively, "he's new. I brought him along this morning mostly to get him used to crowds. We may not even fight unless we find something that looks easy. But I've got another young fellow at Three Rivers who looks very promising. You've heard of my Caesar?"

"Can't say I have," said Kingston. "Drink?"

"Why not?" said Jardine and followed him into a nearby hotel.

When Jardine returned to the wagon, he was very excited. "It's all arranged, Caleb," he crowed. "You're going to fight that fool Pompey this morning. Three rounds for a purse of five dollars. But better than that, Kingston took my side bet of fifty dollars and gave me two to one odds. That means that you get—"

"Fifty-two dollars and fifty cents, Master," Caleb said. "That is, if I win."

Jardine looked stunned. "You mean there's some doubt?"

"There's always some doubt, Master," said Caleb. He wished that he'd had a better look at Pompey.

The big crowd in the square was getting impatient waiting in the weak morning sunshine for the show to begin. But there was as yet no sign of the professionals. Some of the planters were talking about going ahead and matching their slaves, when a cheer came up from the fringes of the crowd, and a big open landau rolled into the square. All four seats were full, and one of them was occupied by a black man dressed just like the three white men in the other seats. An excited buzz swept through the crowd. The cheers soon turned to muttering. Local people just weren't used to sights like that.

The driver of the landau, a beefy man in his late forties, jumped down and then sprang into the ring like a boy. Cupping his hands around his mouth, he bellowed, "Good morning, ladies"—he peered around at the crowd—"or rather, good morning, gentlemen and boys, to our prizefighting spectacular. Allow me to introduce myself. I am Hannibal Hogan, former heavyweight champion of the world, and it is great to be here in"—he glanced at one of the banners—"Camden!"

He looked again at the crowd now pressing in on the platform. "The boxing matches will begin in just a little while, but first let me introduce to you my associates, who will be displaying their pugilistic skills for you today." The other three men had come down from the landau and had climbed into the ring behind Hogan. They stood nonchalantly flexing their muscles beneath their smart suits. The two whites were in their early twenties and wore derby hats. The black, who was a little older, was hatless, and his hair was cropped so short that he looked bald. Between the two larger men, he looked almost like a boy. He looked around with seeming indifference, ignoring the murmurs of hostility from some of the crowd.

"First," shouted the ringmaster, "is the middleweight champion of the Seaboard states, who will this morning defend the title he won only last month by knocking out Killer Caruso in the very first round! Mr. Tom Flynn, the New Jersey Mauler!"

Flynn, a stocky man with tightly curled blond hair and a thick mustache, stepped forward and struck a fighting pose. The crowd roared.

"And," Hogan bellowed, "challenging Mr. Flynn for his title this very morning here in Camden is a young boxer who I predict will in a very short time bestride the prizefighting world like a colossus, the Hamtramck Hercules, Harry Benson!"

Benson, a dark-haired man sporting bushy eyebrows and a goatee, sprang forward like a young panther. He squared up to Flynn so closely and so pugnaciously that some of the crowd thought the men were going to fight right there and then. Their bunched fists nearly touched.

"You may believe, folks," Hogan told the crowd, "that there is no love lost between these two prize pugilists. Show these good people, Tom, what Harry did to you in your last encounter."

Tom Flynn opened his mouth in a broad but derisive grin, showing two teeth missing from his upper jaw. At the same time, he feigned a vicious punch at Benson's head, and Benson moved in closer.

"Easy, gentlemen, easy," Hogan told them soothingly. "You'll get your chance in just a little while to show these good people which of you is the better man. In the meantime—"

Then a voice came from the back of the crowd: "What's the nigger doing up there?"

"I'm glad you asked that question, sir," Hogan shouted. "The man you see in this ring is no ordinary nigger. This one"—he gestured toward the black man who was still standing in a relaxed manner behind him—"is not only *free*, but also of royal blood. This, my friends, is Prince Zulu, come to these shores to witness the best boxing in the world and display the skills which make him the middleweight champion of South Africa."

The black prince directed a low, foreign-looking bow toward the crowd. Half of them applauded and the other half booed.

"Later this very morning," Hogan continued, "Prince Zulu will give an exhibition of his boxing skills. That is, if any of you gentlemen have a black contender whom you will allow to take the risk of climbing into the ring with his majesty for a winner-takes-all prize of one hundred dollars in gold!"

The tumult after this announcement was so great that it took Hogan five minutes to be heard again. "And now," he shouted, his voice beginning to sound hoarse, "if gentlemen with boxers to match will come up to ringside to make arrangements, the boxing spectacular will begin shortly."

Jardine looked at Caleb with doubt in his eyes. "Do you believe that?" he asked. "Free *and* a prince—*and* a boxing champion. I never heard of anything like that. Did you, Caleb?"

"No, Master," Caleb said.

Beginning the day's activities were half a dozen short bouts between local slaves. Caleb and Pompey were scheduled to be the last of these. Sitting in the wagon, Caleb had a good view of the action in the ring.

Hogan shepherded the first pair of slaves, who were stripped to the waist and wearing boxing gloves, into the center of the ring and announced to the crowd, "Each match will be three equal rounds of three minutes. If there is no knockout, the referee— that's me—will make a decision. My decision will be final, and the winner will collect a purse of five silver dollars.

"Now," he said, pushing the slaves apart, "go to your corners and come out fighting." This was quickly followed by the ting of a bell struck by Prince Zulu, who was serving as timekeeper. The boxers shambled toward each other.

The first five matches were more circus than sport. With little thought for matchmaking, the unskilled blacks were paired haphazardly. They punched blindly away, hoping to connect. Inside the first round it became clear how each bout would end, and the only real question became whether the bouts would last the full three rounds. Only two did. In the other three matches, the loser wisely decided that being "knocked out" was preferable to taking further punishment. If these losers had thought more about what would happen when they got home, they might have put on a better show.

But the crowd enjoyed themselves enormously, laughing and whooping and shouting encouragement to their favorites. At the end of each bout, Hogan raised the right hand of the winner, who received five silver dollars in a showy clink of coins. Outside the ring, the owners of the winners proudly showed off their champions. The losers skulked back to their wagons.

It was clear from the beginning that the sixth match would be different. Jardine wanted to remain in Caleb's corner, but Hogan pointed out that Caleb would have a better chance with an experienced second. As Harry Benson tied the sweaty gloves on Caleb's hands, he asked in a low voice, "Ever fight before?"

"Not in the ring, sir," Caleb replied.

"Well," said Benson with a glance over his shoulder at Pompey in the opposite corner, "my advice would be to box him for a round. Don't get anywhere near those young hams he calls hands. You can start fighting him in round two—if there is one." He slapped Caleb's gloves. "Go!" he said, jumping from the ring.

When Prince Zulu hit the bell, Caleb moved forward. If he hadn't, the match might never have started. Pompey, stripped to his red velvet trousers, took just one step and stopped. He was as immobile as the traditional carved wooden statue of an Indian in front of a tobacco shop. And nearly as hard. With no waist to speak of, Pompey's body looked like a black side of beef. Even before he'd moved a muscle, he was already glistening with sweat. He held his gloved hands before him like battering rams.

Mindful of Benson's advice, Caleb advanced cautiously. Pompey did not move. The two slaves looked at each other for a long moment.

A voice called out from the crowd, "Come on! At least ask him to dance, won't you?" The crowd roared with laughter.

Feeling foolish just standing there, Caleb darted in and landed a slapped right high up on the side of Pompey's face. Pompey did not move, and Caleb felt as if he'd just struck the side of a prize bull.

Encouraged by Pompey's apparent unwillingness to carry the fight to him, Caleb decided to take the opportunity to try out all of the punches he'd practiced in the horse barn. He pretended that Pompey was a bale of hay and, moving as swiftly as he could, hit the stolid slave with six different punches in about ten seconds. The bored crowd roared, and Caleb was beginning to think that this was fun when suddenly Pompey's right arm, which had seemed as stationary as a hitching rail, flew out with surprising speed and struck Caleb a glancing blow on the jaw.

Reeling back, not hurt but stunned, Caleb saw that Pompey was lurching after him, his thick arms pumping like pistons. "Get him, Pompey!" a hoarse voice called out, and the mass of men and boys shouted their approval. Caleb got his gloves back up just in time to deflect two massive blows. He was wondering what to do next when the bell sounded.

"Was that three minutes?" Caleb asked Benson as the second mopped at his face with a sponge.

"It was long enough," Benson said. "I told you. Stay away from him. Move around; use your legs. Make him chase you all over the ring. It don't matter what the crowd thinks. You stand and fight, and that monster will kill you." The bell sounded. Caleb got up, his legs trembling slightly.

Caleb acted on Benson's advice throughout the entire second round. Getting up on his toes, he circled around Pompey as fast as he could, throwing punches whenever he saw an opening, but never staying in one place long enough for Pompey to retaliate. Caleb landed all the punches, but they were glancing blows that didn't seem to affect Pompey at all. To anyone watching, it would have looked like a game of tag, with Caleb always "it." Caleb could feel his legs getting weary, but the only effect the exertion of the fight seemed to have on Pompey was to make his gasping breaths louder and his little eyes seem smaller. Caleb was glad to hear the bell sounding the end of the second round.

"Nice going," said Benson, and he sponged Caleb down. "You're getting smart. He gave Caleb a sip of water. "Spit it out." Massaging Caleb's shoulder muscles, he said, "This is it. I want you to start out with about a minute of the same as last round. Dance the hell out of him. Don't even try to hit him. Are you listening?"

Caleb nodded.

"Okay, then stop dead in your tracks and wait for him to come to you. Keep your chin down and your eyes on his. As soon as he gets within range, let him have everything you've got. Never mind his punches. You have to hurt him or he'll kill you. Once you hurt him, finish him off." The bell rang.

Again, Caleb followed instructions, dancing around Pompey like a child around a maypole. The hot and sweaty crowd hooted. "If you catch him," someone called, "you can kiss him!" Others demanded that Caleb stand and fight. Caleb thought of looking for Jardine among the multitude but had no time.

Finally, after what seemed much longer than a minute, Caleb stopped dancing. He stopped running. He picked a spot pretty near the middle of the ring and just stood there eyeing Pompey. It took a moment for the stocky man to realize that the chase was over, but once he did, Pompey stumbled toward Caleb with his arms pumping and a determined look in his eyes.

The moment Pompey came in range, Caleb put a stiff right through his guard and landed a punch right between Pompey's eyes. Caleb felt the jolt all the way up his arm but did not hesitate. He lashed a left at Pompey's nose, felt the cartilage break under his knuckles, and saw a spurt of redder-than-red blood. He followed quickly with a right high on Pompey's left cheek. The punch skidded into Pompey's eye socket, closing his eye.

Caleb was also being hit. Pompey's pistoning fists were pummeling him badly, but he tried not to think about it. Hearing the crowd roaring for blood, he leaned forward and continued to punch until he felt that his arms would fall off. Pompey, his face covered with blood from the nose down and trying to blink the sweat from his good eye, did not back up. But neither was he moving forward. Something in his eyes said that he knew he was in trouble. He tried to cover up.

Ignoring his growing exhaustion, Caleb continued to punch at the hurt and bewildered man. He'd just landed a squishy left to Pompey's right cheek when—as if from far away—he heard the bell, and Hogan was in the ring raising his right hand. Caleb looked around for his master and saw Jardine jumping up and down beside a morose Barney Kingston. While someone led Pompey back to his corner, Hogan made a great show of counting five silver dollars into Caleb's still-gloved hands.

"You're a lucky boy," Hogan told him. "Another round and that animal would have killed you."

36

When Caleb got back to where Jardine was waiting, Barney Kingston had disappeared, and Jardine was contentedly patting the pocket of his jacket holding their winnings.

"Well done, Caleb," he exulted. "Well done! I knew we could take that great pile of pudding. Barney's mad as a hornet. How do you feel?"

"I don't know, Master. I still can't believe I've been and done it, but my body tells me I have." Caleb looked around in wonder.

"Well," Jardine said, "that money in your hand is real enough. You'd better let me put it with the rest of our winnings."

Caleb had forgotten all about the silver dollars clutched in his right hand. He opened his hand, looked at the coins, and then handed them over to Jardine.

"Whew!" Jardine exclaimed. "My nose can believe you've been doing something pretty strenuous. You stink like a polecat. They tell me that there's a horse trough set up on the other side of the ring. You go take a dip in it and then go sit in the wagon. I've got some business to talk."

Pompey was still at the trough when Caleb got there. Another of Kingston's slaves was gently pouring water over his battered face. His left eye was totally closed, and his nose had swollen to twice its normal size. He was totally impassive and did not seem to even register Caleb's existence. But the other slave, a wizened man in his fifties with sparse white hair like dabs of cotton, did. He looked at Caleb and said, "You think you tough, boy? You'll find out who's tough next time Pompey gets a hold on you."

Caleb said nothing. He poured the refreshingly cool—if none-too-clean—water over his head and body. He had begun to ache so completely that he imagined Pompey had delivered a punch to every square inch of his body.

"You hear me, boy?"

"I hear you," said Caleb, still pouring.

"Least you could do," the slave continued, "is give Pompey a couple of those dollars you just won. He deserves that. Could have killed you if he'd a mind to."

"Can't," said Caleb. "Master's got it." He was suddenly grateful that Jardine had insisted on holding the winnings.

"All of it?"

"Yep."

"So what you got to show for your winning, boy?" the slave demanded.

"Same as Pompey," Caleb said. "Hurts."

Caleb went back to the wagon and dug into the bag of food Drusilla had packed. His jaw ached as he chewed the ham and oven biscuits, but he chewed them all the same. And he drank thirstily from the jug of beer at the bottom of the bag. It wasn't cold, but it was good.

In the meantime, the grudge match between Tom Flynn and Harry Benson was about to begin. Taking up a speaking trumpet, Hogan bellowed, "Due to the very personal nature of the fistic encounter you are about to witness, there will be no set rounds. There will be no bell to save either boxer should he be hurt. No sir, good people of Camden, South Carolina, these two young champions will fight nonstop until one or the other of them is on the floor bloody, battered, and beaten. Are you ready for the fight?"

The crowd roared, and the two white boxers leaped into the ring. Without another word from Hogan, they set upon each other. The fight was fast, loud, and spectacular, and Caleb was sitting on the back of the wagon enjoying it when he felt a tug on the leg of his trousers. He looked down and saw Prince Zulu looking up at him.

"How you feeling, sport?" the prince asked him.

"Better," Caleb answered. "That Pompey is a hittin' fool."

"You can hit some yourself," Prince Zulu said and then paused and looked at Caleb curiously. "What kind of funny accent is that?"

"Boston, Massachusetts," Caleb said. "I was raised there. Only been down south going on six years."

"Well, you're lucky you haven't been lynched yet for talking like that."

"Speaking of talking," Caleb said, "that doesn't sound much like a Zulu accent you got."

The prince showed a set of big white teeth. "Would you believe that only three years ago I arrived from Zululand without a word of English?" he asked.

"No, I wouldn't," Caleb said.

"Well, thousands and thousands do," the prince said. "You tired?"

"Some. Why?"

"How'd you like to make twenty-five dollars?"

"How?"

"Fighting." He indicated Flynn and Benson on the distant platform. "When they're done I'm supposed to fight some local black boy, winner take all, for a hundred dollars."

"A hundred dollars?" Caleb asked. "You just said twenty-five."

"There ain't no hundred dollars," the prince said. "There never was. For a hundred dollars I would be willing—even delighted—to knock your head off. But for the generous prize of twenty-five, you will have the honor of dancing around in the ring with me while I *pretend* to knock your head off."

"A fake?" Caleb asked.

"Sure," said the prince. "A fake. Do you suppose that Tom and Harry are really fighting up there?"

"They're not?"

"Hell, no. Harry won last week in Fargis, and today it's Tom's turn. As soon, of course, as they stop playing the fool and giving these yokels their money's worth." He pulled a gold watch from his waistcoat pocket. "In about six minutes, Tom is going to stop taking a beating, pick himself up off the mat at the count of nine and a half, and put Harry away in a ferocious and bloody display of pure pugilistic mayhem."

"Bloody?"

"Phony," said the Zulu. "From inside Tom's special gloves. Only not always. Tom lost those teeth last month when he forgot to slip a punch. He wasn't half-sore."

"Do you ever fight for real?" Caleb asked.

"Only when there's big money. For instance, when some local tough can get backers to bet big on him. Then either Tom or Harry will take the local champion to the cleaners."

"What about you?"

"Me?" the prince looked amazed. "Fight a white man? I want to go on wearing my balls. I'm used to them. And I wouldn't look good hanging from a tree." He looked around to make sure that they were not being overheard. "That's why I'm scoutin' you for a bit of an exhibition. How about it?"

"What do I have to do?"

"Just follow my lead," said the prince. "I'll take care of everything. But one important thing: when I choose you from this mob, don't be in too big a hurry to accept. Make me coax you. Make some of these crackers threaten your life if you don't get your black ass in the ring. But once you're in there, I want you to put on a show. Get mad at me. Take a punch at me. We gotta generate some excitement. Do you think you can do that?"

"I suppose so," Caleb said. "Where's the twenty-five bucks?"

"In my pocket."

"I'd feel better," Caleb said, "if it was in *my* pocket."

Prince Zulu looked at him carefully. "I'm beginning," he said, "to believe you *are* from Boston." He reached into his pocket and pulled out a twenty-dollar gold coin and a tiny five-dollar piece. He stealthily gave them to Caleb. "Don't cross me."

"I'll be sitting right here," Caleb said.

"One thing," Prince Zulu said. "You better tell that proud master of yours not to bet any money on you. The odds will be good, but you believe me, he better not take them or you'll be in trouble."

"Thanks," said Caleb. "I didn't think of that."

"That's why I'm free," Prince Zulu said, "and you're not." He continued on his way.

Just as the prince had predicted, Tom Flynn, battered near to the point of surrender, made a miraculous recovery and completely turned the tables on Harry Benson. The crowd roared with a single voice and pressed forward to see the goateed young giant switch from predator to victim. Benson's sneering face turned white with fear and panic as Flynn set him back on his heels with a sneak punch and then stalked him mercilessly around the ring. As the Zulu had also foreseen, a heavy blow to Benson's face drew copious blood, which dripped to the surface of the platform. Stunned, Benson could do nothing but cover up as the blond fighter pummeled him into abject surrender. Finally, Benson was lying on the platform, apparently unconscious. Elated by his triumphant reversal of fortune, Flynn gave his unconscious opponent a final kick in the ribs. Some close to ringside would have sworn they heard the comatose vanquished cry out, "Damn it, Tom!" But he did not move, and Hogan raised Flynn's gory glove in total victory, while his men circulated among the crowd settling bets.

Benson was still being dragged from the ring when Jardine returned to the wagon, wiping beer from his mustache. "Time we got started back," he told Caleb, "if we're going to get home before dark."

"But, Master," Caleb said, "Prince Zulu is going to fight."

"I've seen about enough fighting for one day," Jardine said. "And we've made some good money. Besides, if that darkie is either a prince or a Zulu, I'm the governor of Georgia. Don't believe everything you hear, Caleb."

"Fact is," Caleb said, "he is going to fight *me*."

"You?" Jardine asked incredulously. "What for?"

"Twenty-five dollars." Caleb pulled the gold coins from his pocket and covertly showed them to Jardine.

"You didn't ask me," Jardine said accusingly.

"You weren't here. Twenty-five dollars. That makes a hundred and thirty for the day. For just a few minutes in the ring." He handed Jardine the coins.

"Well, I never," said Jardine, but just then Hogan began shouting through the speaking trumpet from the platform. Standing behind him was a confident-looking Prince Zulu, stripped and ready to fight.

"And now, citizens," Hogan shouted, "in our final event, Prince Zulu, middleweight champion of all South Africa, will challenge any local darkie to go three rounds for the handsome purse of one hundred dollars in purest gold coin of the realm. Winner takes all!" Hogan held up a small leather purse that clinked when he shook it.

Jardine was mouthing "one hundred dollars?" when Caleb begged him hurriedly, "Don't bet on me, Master, whatever you do." Jardine nodded his understanding.

By then, Hogan was peering out into the crowd looking for a challenger. "How about you, uncle?" he shouted to a middle-aged black man sweeping the porch of a local shop. The slave looked startled, dropped his broom, and dashed inside the shop while the white crowd hooted.

"Well, then," Hogan demanded, "how about one of the brave warriors we saw fight earlier?" He shaded his eyes. "Where are they?" Finally, he pointed a stubby forefinger directly at Caleb, who was still sitting on the tailgate of the wagon. "You, boy! What's your name?"

Caleb did his best to look startled. "Me, sir?" he cried. "Caleb, sir!"

"Well, Caleb," Hogan said. "You're some dandy fighter. How'd you like to make a hundred dollars for your master?"

"Me, sir?"

"Yes, you! Get up here!"

Caleb hesitated, looked at Jardine, and turned as if to go the opposite way. But the crowd between Jardine's wagon and the platform began to take an interest.

"Get up there, boy," cried an old man. Other voices picked up the theme.

"What's the matter, Jardine? Your darkie chicken?"

"I'd fight him myself," sneered a boy in a striped shirt, "only I'd get my hands dirty."

Jardine held up his hand. "You got something to say to my slave, Jimmy Witherspoon?" he said derisively. "You say it to me. I'll whip your ass." The boy lost interest in Caleb.

Jardine looked up at Caleb on the wagon. "You want to fight, Caleb?" he asked.

"I'll fight, Master."

"All right then," Jardine said. "Get on up there!"

The crowd made a wide corridor for Caleb to walk up to the platform.

"Knock his black head off, boy," shouted a farmer with a red face.

"Kick his royal Zulu butt!"

"You can do it, Caleb."

Hogan reached down and helped pull Caleb into the ring. Once he was on the platform, it was clear to the crowd that Caleb—a natural heavyweight who was well muscled by years of hard work—loomed over the compact form of Prince Zulu. Caleb recognized this fact, too. Seeming to gain confidence, he reached out a big hand and patted Prince Zulu on the head. As the crowd sniggered, the prince angrily knocked Caleb's hand away and turned to walk to his corner. Getting in the spirit of things, Caleb sneaked along behind him, grabbed Zulu around the waist, and held him high above the platform like a struggling child.

"Good, good," Prince Zulu whispered to Caleb. "Now, put me down, and then block my right."

When Caleb at last put him down, the prince swung a round-house right at Caleb's head that the slave blocked with ease. Then Caleb held his big jaw down temptingly and prodded it with his forefinger, daring him to swing at it. But Hogan got between the two fighters and pushed Prince Zulu to his corner, where he listened to the prince's angry complaints. Hogan finally returned to the middle of the ring and once again raised his speaking trumpet.

"My friends, Prince Zulu has never been so insulted in all his stay in our wonderful country."

The crowd hooted and laughed, and somebody shouted, "Go get him, Caleb! I'll give you two bits for one of his ears."

"Accordingly," Hogan shouted, silencing the crowd, "Prince Zulu has personally authorized me to state on his behalf that he is offering odds of five to one that he can defeat Caleb over three regulation rounds of boxing. Anyone who wants to accept his bet, please see my men at the apron of the ring."

As a number of the crowd surged forward, Hogan led Caleb to a corner of the ring and began to lace up his gloves. "Did Zulu tell you what to do, son?" he asked Caleb.

"More or less, sir."

"It's not difficult," Hogan said, finishing the laces. "Just fun him for the first round, beat him up in the second, and then take a beating in the third. He won't hurt you. But make sure you are down well before the last bell. Put on a show. Got it?"

"I think so."

Hogan went to the middle of the ring and hushed the crowd with a calming motion of both hands, like pushing down on a feather bed. When he spoke again, his voice was loud but soothing. "Friends, because of an unfortunate happening in Littleton just a few weeks ago, which left a local darkie in the hospital struggling for his life, I want to make sure that Caleb here is fighting of his own free will." He turned toward Caleb. "Do you understand, son, that you could get hurt here?"

"I'm not afraid," Caleb said loudly. "Your old prince don't look so tough to me." The crowd roared its approval.

"Okay, lad," Hogan said. "On your head be it. Let the fight commence!"

At the sound of the bell, Prince Zulu came tearing out of his corner and, before Caleb was even fully standing, launched a murderous blow at Caleb's jaw. It landed with a terrific sound, but Caleb felt almost nothing. He cocked his head at Prince Zulu as if to say "is that the best you can do" and pushed the prince away as if he were a troublesome small boy.

"Put him away, Caleb," cried a voice from the crowd.

"Hell, *throw* him away."

For the next two minutes, Caleb, drawing on his defensive skills, made a thoroughgoing fool out of the smaller man. Whatever vicious punch or combination of punches Prince Zulu threw at him, Caleb caught them with his gloves and didn't even try to hit back. As the prince began to appreciate the skill Caleb was showing, he became more desperate in his efforts to hit Caleb. At one point, Prince Zulu swung so hard—and missed—that he threw himself off his feet. Caleb picked him up with exaggerated concern.

From then until the end of the round, the prince was like an infuriated wasp trying to make an impact on the hide of a water buffalo. Caleb held him off with ease, and after each flurry, he reached out and tapped the prince dismissively on the forehead with a big glove, adding insult to injury. At the bell, the crowd was delirious with joy, and Prince Zulu slouched back to his corner, apparently seething with frustration.

"You know, Tom," he told the victor of the last bout as he was sponged down, "it's a good thing we're just having a good time out there. I don't know if I could hurt this yokel. He's really good."

"Well, you have to start hurting him eventually, Cass," Flynn said. "It's in the script." The bell sounded.

Round two started the same way round one ended, with Caleb making a fool of the visiting champion. Then, after the prince threw a vicious roundhouse right that missed so completely that it spun him around, he gave Caleb a slight nod. The next time the prince rushed at Caleb, he found himself met with a straight right that took him right off his feet and dumped him flat on his back. Prince Zulu lay there seemingly stunned.

Hogan strolled to the middle of the ring and didn't start to count all that fast. The crowd was at least two counts ahead of him and baying like the hounds of hell when Hogan got to "six, seven, eight."

But if the bettors in the crowd were counting their winnings, they stopped suddenly when, at the count of nine, Prince Zulu slowly got to his feet and faced Caleb, shaking his head in confusion. He didn't shake it long, because Caleb reached out with a left that sent the Zulu reeling back toward his corner. For the rest of the round, Caleb pursued the middleweight, hitting him at will but failing to put him down. At one point, Prince Zulu was forced into doubling up completely with his gloves and forearms protecting his head. Caleb was just winding up to knock him into the middle of next week when the bell rang. The crowd doubted that the Zulu prince could even make it back for the third round.

As Caleb was resting from the exertion of throwing so many punches, Hogan drifted over to his corner. "You ready, son?"

"Yes, sir," said Caleb.

"It don't have to be a full three-minute round," Hogan told him. "I'll give you the signal."

At the bell for round three, Prince Zulu did not seem keen to leave his corner. He stood there, his glistening face dotted with white lotion to stop the bleeding, and peered uncertainly at the giant slave. Taking his cue, Caleb motioned at him elaborately with both gloves, as if saying, *Come on out and play.*

When Prince Zulu didn't respond, Caleb shrugged his great shoulders and stalked forward. But just as he got within firing range, the prince's gloved fist snaked out and caught him smack between the eyes, making a loud noise but not doing much damage.

Nonetheless, Caleb staggered back, covering up, and Prince Zulu swarmed after him, delivering a blizzard of blows to Caleb's arms, gloves, and shoulders. As sound effects, the punches were very effective, but they hardly hurt Caleb. In fact, it was a welcome rest. But finally, tiring of looking at the inside of his wrists, Caleb opened up just in time to receive a murderous uppercut from Prince Zulu. The glove missed by a hair, but its stiff laces raked the side of Caleb's face with a sharp sting. Caleb didn't think it was overdoing things to fall straight back as if the uppercut had landed.

Caleb lay there with legs and arms tucked up like a beached turtle, while Prince Zulu loomed over him. The crowd urged him to get up and save their bets, and Hogan, figuring it was all over, swiftly counted, "four, five, six, seven, eight—"

But Caleb surprised both fighter and referee, and delighted the Camden crowd, by struggling to his feet at the very last second. With a shake of his head that sent a spray of sweat and saliva all over the packed ringside, Caleb clumsily began lumbering toward Prince Zulu, throwing a windmill of tired punches as he advanced.

Retreating slowly to his corner, Prince Zulu warded off the showy but feeble punches and wondered what this country boy was up to. A wiser man would have taken that last count and been on his way home with twenty-five dollars. With his back against the improvised ropes, Zulu saw that as Caleb threw each punch, his head was wide open. After faking a panicky look left and right, the prince wound up and threw a straight right at the middle of Caleb's forehead. The Zulu felt the painful jolt right up to his shoulder socket.

The punch stopped Caleb as effectively as a freight train. Looking stunned, he dropped his gloved hands, spun around, and fell like a sack of grain toward the middle of the ring. The impact of his dead weight shook the platform, and a groan went up from the crowd. Caleb lay with his nose mashed against the boards and his head throbbing, listening to Hogan count him out. He did not even twitch. As Hogan and Tom Flynn carried Caleb from the ring, a disappointed member of the crowd spat in his face.

— *37* —

"Are you sure you're all right?" Jardine asked Caleb back at the wagon. After lying still for a long time in case anyone in the disappointed crowd was watching, Caleb managed to sit up at the back of the wagon with his legs hanging down. He kept his head bowed.

"Yes, Master," he said. "The prince didn't hit me very hard. Most of the noise came from those special gloves they have. There's something inside them."

"Is he *really* a prince?" Jardine asked.

"I don't know," Caleb said.

After a while, Jardine said there wasn't much point in them starting back for Three Rivers that late in the afternoon. He'd met some friends, so he decided to spend the evening with them and get an early start the next morning.

"You can sleep in the loft over the hotel stable," Jardine told him, digging into his pocket. "Get the horses settled. Make sure they rub them down and give them a good feed, and then find something to eat." He handed Caleb a silver dollar. "Don't get yourself in any trouble, and be at the hotel at seven in the morning."

Caleb took the horses over to the hotel stable and followed Jardine's instructions. When he was sure that the horses were being looked after properly, he climbed the ladder to the loft, threw a blanket from the wagon over a pile of loose hay, and lay himself down on it. The prince may not have hurt him much, but two fights in one day—one of them for real—had left Caleb feeling exhausted and bruised.

It was fully dark when Caleb woke. The stable was deserted except for the night man, an old one-armed black man who lived in a little shack between the horse stalls. Caleb asked him how to get to the black side of town and then set out walking, his floppy hat pulled well down over his eyes to thwart recognition. When the paving began to break up and the street lights became sparse and dim, Caleb knew he was getting closer. Following the sound of voices, laughter, and the plinking of a banjo, he came to a shack with a large hand-painted sign that read RIBS. Through the opaque cloth over the windows, he could see dim lights and dark shadows.

Just then the door to the shack flew open, and a man stumbled out, nearly falling over. Before the door could close again, Caleb slipped in. He found himself in a bare room with four or five occupied tables and a long rough counter with several stools. Sinking onto a stool, he asked a fat man in an apron that had once been white, "How much for ribs?"

"Fo' bits."

"What do I get with them?"

"Greens, beans, my special sauce."

"Okay. Beer?"

"Ten cents."

"Okay."

When the big plate of spareribs got there, they were meaty and black with sauce, just the way Caleb liked them. The greens were too salty and the beans overcooked, but Caleb dug in like a starving man, washing down big bites with swigs of beer.

"Another," he called, plunking down the bottle on the bare counter.

The fat man opened another beer. "What you been doing, brother? Digging ditches?"

"Naw," said a voice behind Caleb, "he's been beating up Zulu princes. Gimme a plate of those and a bottle of that. Easy on the sauce." Prince Zulu dropped onto the stool next to Caleb. "How's your head, champ?"

"It might stay on," said Caleb. "You still here?"

"I think so," said the prince.

"I thought you'd be long gone," Caleb said. "That crowd didn't look happy."

"The crowd never looks happy at the end of the day," the prince said. "Hogan and the boys lit out for Hopetown soon as the set was struck, but I decided to stay here. Those Hopetown boys are mean. I'll meet the show tomorrow on the way to Montgomery. Besides," he added loudly for the benefit of the proprietor, "I wanted to get outside of some of Charlie's ribs. My gut is almost healed from the last time."

They ate in silence for some time. Caleb sucked the last bone clean and pushed his plate away. A little later, Prince Zulu did the same. "Good as ever, Charlie," he called. "You'll make some man a fine wife. Two more beers for me and the champ here." The cook plunked the bottles down with a growl and took away their plates. "It's not the food that brings me here," Prince Zulu said, wiping his hands on a large white handkerchief. "It's the personality of the cook."

"You really a Zulu prince?" Caleb asked him, taking a drink of beer.

"Well, I might be a Zulu and I might be a prince," the other said. "Can you prove otherwise?"

"Nope," said Caleb. "What's your name when it's not Prince Zulu?"

"Cass," said the other, extending a surprisingly small hand. "Cass Clay."

Caleb shook it, saying, "Caleb . . . Staunton, I guess."

"You only guess?" Clay asked.

"Well, that was my owner's name up in Boston, but since I was sold south, I don't much like to use it. Just call me Caleb." He told Clay briefly of how he'd come to be sold south instead of being set free. "I was raised near to a brother with Staunton's son," Caleb explained, "but when he died, the boy sold me south rather than freeing me as his father promised."

"Cold. Very cold," Cass said. "But it don't surprise me. I've heard a lot worse."

"What's it like being the only black with the boxing show?" Caleb asked him.

"You get used to it. Like anything else. The closer you get to a big city, the better it gets. Whites in a dump like Camden can't bring themselves to believe that a black man can ever be *really* free. The whole idea goes against the grain. If I wasn't a prince, they'd have probably torn me limb from limb long ago. That and this."

Before Caleb could see where it came from, Clay had a bone-handled straight razor in his hand and had flicked it open.

"Put that away, Cass," Charlie called from the stove. "People be thinking that my pig meat is tough."

Just as suddenly as it had appeared, the razor was gone.

"You use that?" Caleb asked.

"When I have to."

"I'm going to be free," Caleb said.

The other man didn't comment, so Caleb told him how he and Jardine were going to work the country boxing circuit until Caleb had the five hundred fifty dollars he needed to buy himself.

"Hard way to earn money," Clay observed.

"Most of it will come from side bets," Caleb said.

"If you win," Clay said. "And if you can trust your master. Think you can?"

"I think so," Caleb said. "But trust him or not, I'm going to be free."

"Then what?"

"Going north," Caleb said vaguely. "Looks like there's going to be a war."

"I think so, too," said Clay. "And soon. I'm heading north, too. I hear there's a shortage of Zulu princes up there. Maybe I'll see you." He downed the last of his beer and got off his stool, slapping some money down on the counter. "Charlie," he called, "this is for me and my friend, the champ, here. If I hear of you charging him even a penny, I'll come back and put a royal Zulu curse on you."

"Okay, Cass," said the cook without turning from the smoking stove.

"Where are you staying?" Clay asked Caleb.

"Over the stable," Caleb said.

"Free men don't sleep in no hay," Clay said. "There's a little girl over this side of town who promised to bust my nappy head with a skillet if I ever poked it through her door again. I'm going to go find out if she's a woman of her word. Keep punching, partner." He shook Caleb's hand and strode through the door.

— *38* —

Well rested but as stiff as a plank door, Caleb was waiting in the wagon when Jardine walked down the wooden steps of the Camden Hotel at seven o'clock the next morning.

"You look rough," Jardine told Caleb. "About as rough as I feel. I ran into some old boys with a bottle and a deck of cards last night. They insisted that I try both." When he saw alarm in Caleb's eyes, Jardine added quickly, "Oh, don't you go worrying. I've got two pockets, Caleb. One holds *my* money, and the other holds *our* money. I never reached into the second one."

"Besides," he added as he climbed up on the wagon and Caleb slipped into the back, "I won. We didn't need those old boys' deck because the hotel had a brand new one, and I opened it myself. You don't expect a share of my poker winnings, do you?"

"No, Master."

"And," Jardine added as he backed up the horses, "I don't imagine that there's anything left of that dollar I gave you, either."

"No, Master," Caleb said.

"I didn't think so," Jardine said. "Let's go home."

When they got to Three Rivers, Drusilla was bursting with curiosity, but didn't ask a single question. One look at Caleb told her that he hadn't fared too badly, and she knew that he was as eager to tell as she was to hear. That night as they were lying in the double bed that Caleb had brought down from the attic, she went over his body in detail, admiring his fine collection of bruises. Caleb did his best to tell her exactly how each had been earned. She pushed hard on several of them just to hear him cry out.

"That's cheating, isn't it?" Drusilla asked when Caleb had finished telling her about his match with Prince Zulu.

"I suppose so," Caleb said, "but it's cheating white men, and nobody told those fools they had to bet against a professional boxer. I'm not sorry for any of them, especially the one who spat on me."

"The one I feel sorry for is Pompey," Drusilla said. "What did he get out of being beaten up?"

"Nothing."

"I don't suppose you even bought him a beer out of that money Marse Boyd gave you."

"Nope. I didn't see him."

"Did you go looking for him?"

"No."

"You're a hard man, Caleb," Drusilla announced. "Or maybe you're only determined. I bet you've still got that dollar."

"Sure do."

"How much winnings does that add up to?"

"Sixty-five dollars," Caleb said.

"And you didn't buy me anything?"

"No," said Caleb, but he wished he had thought of it. He made a vow he would next time.

"You trust Marse Boyd?" Drusilla asked.

"That's what Cass—Prince Zulu—asked," Caleb said.

"Well?"

"I have to," Caleb said. "I got no choice."

— *39* —

Almost every weekend for the rest of the summer, Jardine and Caleb traveled to the fairs and shows within a thirty-mile radius of Three Rivers in order to take advantage of the boxing craze that was sweeping the county. After a couple weeks of Caesar's begging, Jardine finally let him go along as Caleb's corner man and boy of all work.

Sometimes Caleb fought. Sometimes he didn't. As word got around in the small world of county boxing, Caleb became well-known. He could no longer pose as a shambling oaf who could take on the Pompeys and even be offered odds. Many slave owners took one look at him and went searching for easier matches for their boxers. The fact that he had lost to Prince Zulu was a plus. Caleb couldn't look too good. Some of the more gullible became convinced that Caleb *was* Prince Zulu. Some rash owners even offered their slaves to fight Caleb for nothing, just for the honor involved. Jardine wisely turned down these opportunities. Caesar, on the other hand, declared he would fight anybody for anything and privately began calling himself Prince Caesar.

With careful choice of opponents and judicious betting, Jardine and Caleb's winnings piled up. By the end of August, they had just over seven hundred and fifty dollars in the pouch, and Caleb had salted away twenty-seven dollars of his own. The fair season was ending, and both men knew that there wouldn't be many more opportunities to reach Caleb's target that year. The county fair at Shreevesville looked like a chance to get it over with in one go. Because the fair was a week long, the three men left Three Rivers on Monday morning and didn't plan to return until the following Sunday.

As they said good-bye, Drusilla asked Caleb, "Do you think you'll make it?"

"I have to," Caleb said. "I can't be a slave for another year. Master says this time next year there will be a war on with the North."

"Maybe that will free you," Drusilla said.

"Maybe it won't," Caleb said. "I'm not going to wait to find out." He kissed her. "Got to go now. I'll bring you a pretty."

"You just bring me back Caleb in the same shape he's in now," Drusilla said, "and you can keep your pretties."

When they got to Shreevesville, the county fairground was all set up and beginning to come to life. Compared to the other fairs and shows they'd been to, it was a vast metropolis of tents. At night it came ablaze with lamps and torches. The boxing ring, a custom-built affair that traveled all over the southern states, was in a huge tent at the end of the fair's main thoroughfare. It was there that Jardine and Caleb planted themselves to wait for opportunities to add to their poke. Jardine spotted Barney Kingston at the beer tent and greeted him jovially.

"I'm not sure I'm talking to you," Barney growled, "after what your boy did to my Pompey and how you misrepresented him. You still got those outsized clothes on him?"

"I'll tell you what, Barney," Jardine said, taking a long swig of beer, "we'll give you a rematch, and I won't ask for odds this time."

"You're too goddamned kind, Jardine," Barney said. "That Caleb of yours won't be fighting Pompey no more because Pompey ain't mine. He wasn't worth a damn after that fight, and I sold him."

"You got anybody else?" Jardine asked keenly.

"I might and I might not," said Kingston. "Are you buying the beer?"

The entire day passed without so much as a nibble. Not wanting to seem too eager, Jardine contented himself with talking to acquaintances and buying a few drinks, seldom bringing up the topic of Caleb or boxing. But that night, when illumination spread through the fairgrounds like a prairie fire and the boxing tent became the center of attention, things began to liven up. The boxing show at Shreevesville was a much bigger operation than Hogan's. The poster outside boasted that it featured nine boxers, five white and four black. They all looked like professionals.

Jardine paid admission for the three of them to the boxing tent, and when they got inside, the nine boxers were parading around inside the ring like a pride of lions. The boss, a dwarf-sized man who called himself Colonel Moran, was extolling their virtues from the center of the ring, his foghorn voice amplified by a speaking trumpet.

"Every one a champion, ladies and gentlemen, boys and girls, mothers and sons," Moran chanted, "back here in beautiful Shreevesville to introduce to you the science of pugilism at its highest level." The colonel paused and raked his beady black eyes challengingly across the crowd. "*And* to offer the brave hearts among your menfolk a chance to display their manliness and win a nice piece of money at one and the same time."

Moran lowered the speaking trumpet, and at his signal all of the boxers but one white man suddenly turned toward the ropes and vaulted from the ring like a troupe of prize horses. Left in the ring with Moran was a squat boxer wearing shiny red satin tights and boots dyed the same color. He was of only average height and his legs seemed spindly, but above the waist he suddenly bulged out in a plinth of pure muscle topped with hardly any neck and a round head that looked as hard as a cannonball. He slowly raised his arms like a giant pair of horns, and his biceps bulged alarmingly.

"Folks," said Moran through the speaking trumpet, "I have the honor to introduce to you Professor Stanley Mott, the finest scientific boxer of his or any day. Just to start the evening off with a bang and spread some of my money around, I am going to offer to any gentleman in this audience one hundred dollars in gold just for staying in this ring with Professor Mott for only three short rounds. One hundred Federal dollars, gentlemen, in your hand! You don't even have to hit the professor. In fact, I'd rather you didn't! And he might not hit you. But the professor can hardly show his amazing pugilistic skills without an opponent, now can he?" The colonel looked around the ringside in a friendly manner.

"Now who wants to earn one hundred dollars gold and show his lady friend his courage and skill?" he asked. "How about *you*, sir?" Moran's finger snaked out and pointed at a large country boy wearing a cap and holding tight to a pretty blonde in a ground-sweeping dress. The girl looked up at him inquiringly, but the boy was already moving toward the ring, unbuttoning his collar as he went.

"Now there's a brave young man," announced the colonel. "Give him a hand, everybody."

By the time the applause petered out, the country boy was stripped to the waist and sitting on a stool in one corner of the ring wearing boxing gloves. He'd already started looking not so happy to be there. In the opposite corner, Professor Mott leaned back against the ropes and steadily observed him.

"Remember the rules now, young man," Moran told him and the audience. "All you have to do is stay on your feet for a mere three rounds, and you will walk out of this ring with a hundred dollars to spend on your fair lady. Ready?"

The country boy nodded uncertainly, and the bell sounded. Before the boy could even get to his feet, Mott was in the center of the ring in the classic boxing stance, set and waiting like a terrier outside a mouse hole. The bell rang again insistently, and someone from the crowd bawled, "Kill 'em, Jem!" The boy awkwardly got to his feet, raised his arms protectively, and shambled toward the professor.

Mott waited alertly until their gloves nearly touched, and then sprang into action. As if sparring by himself, he danced all around the boy, throwing a brisk flurry of punches so fast that his gloves were a blur. Mott moved so speedily and so gracefully around the stone-still boy that the audience began to laugh. "Slow down, Jem!" cried a rowdy. "He can't see you!" Color crept up Jem's face, and just then—like a hummingbird hovering in front of an ox— the boxer came to a sudden halt in front of the boy. He leaned his chin tantalizingly close to Jem's boxing gloves and smiled invitingly. Eventually, the impulse got from Jem's brain to his arm, and he launched a roundhouse right. But Mott was suddenly gone, and Jem, thrown off balance by the velocity of his punch, nearly fell to the canvas-covered wooden platform. The crowd laughed, and Jem's girl covered her face.

It's a good thing she did, because Professor Mott, tiring of punching plain air, began to repeat his display, this time using the boy as a target. In a sequence too rapid to calculate, his gloves beat a tattoo on the boy's arms, shoulders, and chest that sounded like distant rain. They weren't painful punches, but they were annoying, frustrating, and embarrassing. Jem couldn't seem to do anything to stop them. If he put his gloves up, the professor beat on his stomach like a drum. If he dropped them, Mott delivered a rapid flurry of punches to the chest and shoulders that brought angry red blotches to his pale trunk. Jem was still thinking of what to do about this when the bell sounded.

Moran had to lead him by the arm to the stool in the corner while Mott returned to his corner and leaned casually on the ropes. He was not even breathing hard.

During the break, Jem got more advice from his friends in the crowd than he really needed. At the bell, he jumped up as if stung by a bee and raced toward the center of the ring, but Mott, without seeming to hurry, got there first. He waited for the boy like a matador would a bull. Paying no attention to the windmilling of Jem's arms, the professor launched a rocket-straight right that met the boy's onrushing chin with a crack.

The boy stopped as if he'd hit a wall. His arms dropped, and his body seemed to sag in sections until his knees hit the canvas and threw his body forward, where he skidded to a halt, face down. The professor stood waiting, but there was nothing to wait for. Moran looked down at the prostrate boy with benign curiosity and then raised Mott's arm without bothering with the count.

"In three seconds of the second round," he announced, "another triumph by Professor Stanley Mott!" As the dazed boy was dragged from the ring, Moran inquired, "Any more challengers, ladies and gentlemen? Step right up!" The only answer was an abundant shaking of heads and a shuffling of feet as potential gladiators sought to rule themselves out as candidates.

"I'm shocked, ladies and gentlemen, that there are no other local champions willing to test the skills of Professor Mott. I'll tell you what I'll do: I'll raise the prize money to *two* hundred dollars and lower the requirement to *two* rounds only. Surely I can do no more than that?" He looked keenly around the crowd. Temptation showed on a lot of faces, but no hand was raised.

"I am disappointed," Moran announced. "I thought better of Shreevesville and its mighty men." He shook his large head sadly, but then, as if struck by inspiration, he said, "Tell you what, unless there are serious objections, I will open Professor Mott's challenge to men of the African race."

A murmur ran through the crowd. "No nigger can face him!" called out a voice.

The colonel's eyebrows raced toward his hairline. "No?" he challenged. "Shall we just see? Are there any slave owners in the crowd willing to determine—for a prize of two hundred dollars, re-member—whether one of their darkies can withstand the fistic tal-ents of Professor Mott for a mere two rounds? Two short rounds."

Jardine and Caleb exchanged looks. Caleb shrugged, and Jardine's arm shot up like a tollgate. "I've got a boy here!" he shouted.

The crowd muttered doubtfully, but Moran jumped in. "*Have* you, sir? Well, send him up here."

"I will!" Jardine said loudly. "Caleb, get yourself up in that ring!"

To Jardine's surprise, Caleb responded in an equally loud but sullen voice, "Nossir! That little feller will kill me!"

At that, the crowd took up hooting and hollering. "Kick his black ass up there!" someone suggested. "I'll do it!" shouted an-other. All eyes were turned toward Jardine as the crowd wondered how he would handle this disobedience. The tent was suddenly hushed.

"Caleb," said Jardine sternly. "Did you hear me?"

"Yes, Marse," Caleb said, not meeting his eye. He stood with his head down and his shoulders hunched.

"Do you see this crop? Do you?" Jardine's voice was relentless as he raised his riding whip.

Caleb raised his eyes reluctantly. "Yes, Marse."

"Well, I am going to wear it out on you if you are not up in that ring in about ten seconds. Now, get moving."

As if on strings, Caleb turned and slouched through the part-ing crowd. Jardine followed a step behind him, slapping the riding crop rhythmically on his open hand. When he got into the ring,

Caleb stripped off his shirt and sat down to allow one of Moran's men to lace up his gloves. When the man had finished, Jardine, who was standing outside the ring on the apron, whispered to Caleb.

"Do you know what you're doing?"

"I think so, Master," Caleb said with his eyes intent upon the lounging Mott.

When Moran finished reminding the crowd of the terms of engagement, the bell sounded. Caleb got up slowly and looked around as if he didn't know where he was.

"For Christ's sake," hissed Jardine. "Here he comes."

As with the white boy he had just dismissed, the professor came at Caleb with a whirring blur of punches. But realizing that he had a round less to prove his point, Mott did not waste the punches on the air. He immediately began a brisk tattoo on Caleb's body. The satisfying thump of leather hitting torso was greeted by cheers from the crowd.

To the professor's surprise, Caleb did not react. Cowering behind his arms and gloves, Caleb soaked up the blows without lowering his arms, ignoring the rattle of punches as if they were flea bites. The professor increased his speed, but the effect was the same. He simply could not lure Caleb either into punching back or lowering his defenses. No matter how fast Mott danced around him, Caleb managed to deny him a vulnerable target. Caleb had yet to throw a single punch.

Realizing that he was in danger of looking silly, Mott redoubled his efforts and danced around Caleb like a mosquito looking for a soft place to sting, trying at the same time to make it look like an exhibition. Half the crowd marveled at his speed; the other half at Caleb's apparent cowardice.

"Come on, fight him, you booger!" shouted a local wit. Others started booing. "Knock him out, Prof!" came from several quarters.

When, reluctantly, Moran rang the bell signaling the end of the first round, Mott, for the first time, sat down on the stool in his corner. "I can't hit the black son of a bitch," he panted. "And he won't fight."

"You better hit him," muttered Moran. "That's my two hundred dollars on the line. Do anything you have to. Just put him down!"

In Caleb's corner, Jardine told him, "You're looking pretty silly out there, Caleb. They all think you're a coward."

"Isn't that what we want, Master?" Caleb asked.

"But don't those punches hurt?"

"Not two hundred dollars' worth," Caleb answered as the bell rang.

In the second round, Professor Mott came out just as fiercely, wasting no time trying to get past Caleb's defenses. Still dancing, he faked a left to the head and followed up with a low right that landed with a painful thump several inches below Caleb's belt. Only by a slight twist of his hips did Caleb escape the full effect of the foul blow.

A gasp went up from the crowd, and Jardine shouted angrily as Caleb, his face reflecting agony, lowered his guard for a fraction of a second. But before Mott could follow up, the slave slowly crumpled to the canvas-covered boards. Mott stood back with satisfaction, and Moran rushed out to begin the count.

"Serves him right, the damned sissy," called a boy from the crowd, but all around him boos started ringing out at the brazen nature of the foul. "Coward!" shouted a woman at Mott, but the professor just stood there with his eyes fixed on his writhing victim.

"Three, four, five," Moran counted.

Jardine started to climb into the ring, but Caleb, through his pain, shook his head in warning.

"Six, seven, eight," Moran continued, not even bothering to rush the count, as he would have if he had been in doubt. The crowd was now yelling angrily, but he ignored them. He had weathered too many irate crowds over the years to be much bothered by this one.

"Nine," Moran started to reach for Mott's hand, but Caleb was suddenly on his feet and back into his defensive shell. The crowd surged forward around the ring, and a score of hands grabbed hold of the apron and began to shake it. The sudden movement nearly threw Moran from his feet.

Racing for his speaking trumpet, Moran raised it to his mouth. "Due to the danger of riot, I declare this bout—"

But now the whole crowd was chanting, "Fight! Fight! Fight!" Their efforts were making the ring rock like the deck of a ship in a storm.

Moran dropped the speaking trumpet, raised both arms in surrender, and shouted, "Fight on, gentlemen!"

Caleb just stood there, but Mott leaped into a frenzy of action as he launched desperate punches at the big man. But nothing he did could get his punches through to Caleb's head, and Mott dared not try another foul punch. He knew that the crowd was too aroused for that.

"Fight, you black bastard!" Mott gritted through his teeth, but Caleb might have been a tree for all the response he got.

Finally, when the round had gone well over three minutes, people in the crowd began to chant, "Time! Time! Time!" Several men held up their timepieces and gesticulated angrily.

Ringing the bell, Moran waded into the ring, waved Mott off, raised Caleb's hand, and shouted, "Due to a foul blow in the second round by Professor Mott, I declare Caleb the winner!"

The crowd exploded with cheers, the ring stopped rocking, and Jardine was quickly over the rope and holding out his hand for the two hundred dollars.

The rest of the evening's card of fights—blacks against blacks, whites against whites—were exciting enough, but none of them could eclipse the spectators' wonder at the cowardice of the slave Caleb and the dirty fighting of the white Professor Mott. Many of the whites felt that it didn't matter if the professor cheated. Awarding the victory—and the prize money—to Caleb, they reckoned, would give *their* blacks the wrong idea.

— *40* —

For the next couple of days, Caleb and Jardine lay low. Caleb, discovering that Professor Mott's punches were not as painless as they had seemed the night before, spent an entire day in a straw bed over the stables with Caesar bringing food and unsought advice.

"Had been me, Caleb," Caesar said, "I'd have walloped that professor, white man or not."

"Sure you would have, Caesar," Caleb said. Even though Mott had got nowhere near his jaw, it hurt Caleb even to eat. He could only lie there and wish that he'd thought to bring a book from Three Rivers. Finally, as much to get rid of Caesar as anything, Caleb sent him out to scour Shreevesville for a newspaper some white visitor might have thrown away. Caesar came back with six, though he had to run half the way back to escape a crowd of white boys who accused him of stealing the papers.

With his stomach full—if still painful—Caleb lay back and read the papers in the light streaming through the high opening where hay was hoisted into the loft. A big headline in a week-old copy of the *New Orleans Picayune* proclaimed, "Politicians Desperately Seek to Avoid Coming Civil War."

Jardine, as befitted a man whose fighter has disgraced himself even while winning two hundred dollars, stayed well away from the hotel and taverns where the boxing crowd congregated. He didn't see the *Picayune* headline, but talk among the locals and visitors from the fair was about little else. Most still thought that war could be avoided and were counting on support from England and other European powers to allay the Yankee taste for confrontation.

Toward the end of the second day, Jardine was walking down the plank sidewalk of Shreevesville's main street when Colonel Moran hailed him. Allowing himself to be dragged into a hotel bar, Jardine sat sipping at a brandy and water while the colonel got to the point.

"The long and the short of it, sir," Moran said at last, "is that I want to buy that Negro of yours. That is, if you can bring yourself to set a reasonable price. I will not try to bamboozle you, sir. That performance he put on the other night was first-rate. That boy has a future in the ring. The professor is not the same man he was before he tangled with your slave."

"But," Jardine protested, "Caleb never touched him."

"Exactly," said the colonel. "He had free access to the boy, but Mott could neither strike a vital place, nor put him down by legitimate blows to the body."

"Yes," Jardine observed, "that low blow your man landed was not very sporting."

"But paid for, sir," Moran reminded him briskly, "handsomely and from *my* pocket. Thanks to your—"

"Caleb."

"Yes, Caleb," the colonel said. "My concession, though not completely unrewarding, is drawing neither the crowds nor the profits I have come to expect from this county fair year after year. But," he said with emphasis, "if I had your Caleb, I could not only redress that little matter, but give poor Stanley a chance to regain some of his self-esteem."

"Well," said Jardine, "I hate to disappoint you, Colonel, but aside from the fact that Caleb is one valuable slave, the boy has his heart set on being free."

"Free!" Colonel Moran reacted as if Jardine had challenged his most precious principles. "Whatever for? If there is one thing I cannot abide, Mr. Jardine, it is a free black. My experience with that species has been too protracted and painful to discuss, but I would rather have no blacks in my show than a single free black. They are nothing but trouble."

"I feel the same way, Colonel," Jardine said.

"And good riddance to them, sir," said the colonel fervently. "But may I take the liberty of inquiring whether your man's activities in the ring have proved as rewarding as you'd hoped?"

"Not quite, Colonel," Jardine said. "The fact is that we are still some three hundred dollars short of our target. And, as you know, Shreevesville is the last event of any size until next spring."

"All too true," agreed the colonel. "Three hundred dollars, you say?" Colonel Moran hunched closer to Jardine. "Perhaps," he said, "we can find a way to come to an accommodation."

The next morning, giant posters all over town and outside Colonel Moran's boxing tent announced:

SPECIAL GALA EVENT!!!
REMATCH BETWEEN PROFESSOR MOTT AND CALEB,
THE SLAVE OF MR. BOYD JARDINE
OF THREE RIVERS PLANTATION.
TONIGHT IN THIS TENT AT 8 PM.

PLUS: SPECIAL INVITATIONAL CHALLENGE
WITH A PRIZE OF $500!!!
COME ONE, COME ALL!

Caleb, who had recovered except for a slight tenderness in the kidney area, asked Jardine, "Are you sure this is going to work, Master?"

"No, frankly, I am not," Jardine answered. "But we've got Moran's three hundred dollars that, with his other two hundred, puts us over our goal. Why? Are you worried?"

"Of course I'm worried, Master," Caleb said. "I can still feel his punches from the other night. I'm glad to have the money, but that professor is a very tough little man."

"And you, Caleb," Jardine said, "are a very tough—and strong— big man, with very little to lose except a reputation as a coward. Of course, if you'd rather I gave Colonel Moran back his money—"

"Oh, no, Master," Caleb said hurriedly. "I'll fight, but I can't help worrying."

That night Moran's big tent was full to bursting by seven thirty, and scores of the disappointed milled around outside in hopes of a miracle that would make more room. Several local bravos engaged in impromptu boxing matches just to get rid of excess energy.

Inside the tent in a concealed compartment, Caleb waited to be called. The butterflies in his stomach had gone and had been replaced by the certainty that he was going to earn the rest of his freedom money that night. That afternoon Moran and Mott had spelled it out for him. Still, Caleb reckoned, the price he was paying for freedom was not too high.

But before Caleb could get to that part of the evening, he had to get through Colonel Moran's bright idea of inviting any *two* local fighters to challenge Mott or Caleb. The winning challengers would share the five-hundred-dollar prize if they could knock down either of Moran's boxers within three rounds. Caleb didn't like the idea of this very much, but he was encouraged by Moran's confidence in him. Mott, the old professional, didn't seem to be bothered at all by the unusual conditions of these bouts.

Moran, of course, saved the rematch until last, but he warned the professor and Caleb not to wear themselves out on the challengers. He wanted them fresh for the main event of the evening. In all, there were eleven sets of challengers, six white and five black, carefully handpicked by the colonel.

Since Mott had the extra bout, he went first. As the crowd yelled encouragement, his opponents, two toughs from the Shreevesville stockyards, smirked at their friends and whispered hurried tactics for defeating the little man. Alas, the tactics were not enough, and the professor danced between the hulking youths, hitting each in turn until, in just over a minute, both were laid out in a rough figure *X* in the middle of the ring.

Then it was Caleb's turn. His opponents were a couple of big but green field hands who had been rounded up and carted into town the minute their owner heard about the five-hundred-dollar prize. Neither had ever had gloves on before, nor did they want to fight. Caleb put them out of their misery within seconds, allowing each youth a half-hearted punch and then tapping each on the chin with a sharp right. Their owner might not be pleased, but the slaves would have something to tell people in the quarter that night.

And so it went. At least partly due to the fact that two unskilled boxers were as much of a menace to each other as they were to the professionals, none of the pairs even came close to winning the five hundred dollars. Moran would have been extremely disappointed—to put it lightly—if they had.

Mott's final pair of opponents—a giant butcher and a wizened little man who worked at one of the stables—were so mismatched that the crowd, which was getting bored seeing challengers hit the floor with such regularity, cheered up and rooted for the locals with renewed fervor. The professor disposed of them quickly by picking up the stable hand, placing him gently into the butcher's arms, and then tapping the larger man lightly but sharply on the chin. Wisely, both stayed down.

Mott and Caleb's hands were jointly raised by Moran, and they were about to go to the back of the tent and rest a bit for the main event, when a white man, a small farmer who worked a few acres outside of town, shouted, "It seems to me that the nigger owes us a fight." The audience around him quieted down. "And I've got one for him. I don't have two fighters, so I can't enter for the five hundred dollars, but I'll put my man up against this Caleb for a stake of two hundred fifty dollars. If my man loses, Mr. Jardine can have him, a fine field hand, free and clear." As the crowd murmured its approval, the farmer put his fingers to his mouth and whistled sharply. Pompey appeared from the crowd of blacks at the back of the tent.

Though it hadn't been that long since Caleb defeated him at that first fair, Pompey had clearly been through some hard times. Besides his uneven gait, Pompey now carried one shoulder low, and his right eye looked to be permanently half-closed. Already stripped to the waist, Pompey was still in splendid physical shape, but there was something slack about the way his powerful arms hung at his sides. His good eye was watching the path to the ring.

"I'm very sorry," Moran began to say, "but the challenge portion of this evening's attractions is now complete. Ladies and gentlemen—"

But the crowd, wrathful at being denied something extra for its money, began to shout and clap and boo. "Let them fight!" came a voice from the rear. "Caleb's afraid of him. Look at him shake!"

The crowd roared its approval for over a minute until Moran, with raised hands, silenced them. "All right," he said with a glance over at Caleb, "but if you want extra, you have to pay extra. My men will pass the hat among you for contributions—generous contributions—to a pot to be awarded to the winning fighter."

Quickly, Moran's roustabouts were up in the stands shaking their hats in front of faces and refusing to move along until nickels, dimes, or quarters had been thrown in. "Pay up," they demanded.

Within minutes, they were back at ringside, their hats sagging with coins.

"Just a damn minute," Jardine protested from behind Caleb on the ring apron. "I'll be damned if I am going to risk my man against that slab of meat. I don't much want him anyway."

"Master," said Caleb. "Please. I'll fight him. Please."

Jardine looked at his slave closely. "I don't know what you're up to, Caleb, but if you lose, the money comes out of your share. You understand that?"

"I understand," Caleb said.

Pompey climbed into the ring, and one of Moran's men worked his corner. The crowd murmured as Pompey stood up even before the bell rang.

Moran gained the center of the ring and announced, "One round to a conclusion, my friends, between Caleb and Pompey. Go to it!" Then came the bell, and Caleb moved forward to meet Pompey, beginning with a series of showy punches. Then he moved in close, tied up the big man, and whispered, "What you want, Pompey?"

"Nothin'," Pompey grunted, "just to get away from that cracker. He treats slaves worse than animals."

"Okay," Caleb said. "You chase me until I catch you. Understand?"

"Understand," Pompey said, pushing Caleb backward hard.

The crowd roared its approval. "Kill him, Pompey!" shouted a red-faced fat woman.

With unexpected energy and agility, Pompey suddenly launched himself at Caleb and began throwing huge punches. Caleb either caught them on his gloves or slipped away, always dancing just outside of Pompey's range. Pompey put all he had into his punches. But the last thing that he wanted was for any of them to connect. Jardine couldn't be worse than that devil Scroggins.

After more than a minute, Pompey was breathing hard. Caleb tied him up again and whispered, "You had about enough of this?"

"Yeah," Pompey panted.

As Caleb pushed away, Pompey—with the crowd shouting him on—launched himself at Caleb again. As Pompey's wild punch missed his head, Caleb delivered a straight right to the slave's jaw. It landed with a loud thud, and Pompey fell. Moran pushed Caleb back and began counting. Pompey twitched at seven, but he stayed down.

"Eight, nine, ten!" Moran grabbed Caleb's hand and raised it. Then, while the crowd was still shouting, Moran pushed him from the ring. Pompey stayed on the floor for a few minutes and then got up and looked around, wondering what to do next.

While Caleb headed to his compartment in the tent, Jardine jumped down from the apron and found Moran's men just finishing bagging the collection of coins. To their disappointment, he took the heavy bag and said, "I'll relieve you of that."

In the stuffy little compartment, Caleb sat down on an old trunk and rested. He knew that he was but an exhibition away from having enough money to buy his freedom, but it was still hard to accept. Freedom had been a distant goal and a dream for so long that to be so close to it now was like finding a rainbow standing still rather than receding ever into the distance. He didn't quite know whether he could believe it.

After fifteen minutes, one of Moran's men came to tell Caleb, "It's time. The colonel wants you in the ring." When Caleb got there, the spectators were settling down on their benches, hawkers were selling snacks, and Mott was lounging in his corner. Once Caleb was in place, Colonel Moran went into a long speech, but neither boxer listened. They knew what was going to happen. In the first round, Caleb would display his defensive skills, daring the professor to land a telling blow and building up the pressure of the crowd and Mott's frustration. The second round would be Caleb's chance to show off his fighting skills as he tried to finish the little man off. At the end of the round, the smaller man would be on the ropes but would be saved by the bell. In the final round, Mott and the crowd would have their revenge. Mott would pursue the black man, punishing him for the first two rounds, and—to everyone's satisfaction save those few who had bet on Caleb—the third round would end with a knockout. Mott's honor and reputation would be vindicated, and the white race would reign triumphant.

The first round went as planned. As hard as Mott tried, he could not penetrate Caleb's defenses. Every punch landed either on his gloves or harmlessly on his shoulders or upper arms. Toward the end of the round, Caleb got the feeling that there was real desperation in Mott's punches, but that didn't make them any more effective. When he went back to his corner at the bell, Jardine said, "Nice going, Caleb. You made a monkey out of him."

As Caleb rested, the crowd was not so pleased. Some whites were beginning to mutter about the indecency of a black man being as slippery and cowardly as to refuse to stand up and fight. Others dared Caleb to hit a white man. When the bell sounded for the second round, all the shouts and cheers were for Mott. If the few blacks at the back of the tent were on Caleb's side, they kept quiet about it.

Caleb leaped forward to show the crowd what he could do in the way of fancy punching, but was suddenly met with Mott's terrific straight right hand, which barely missed the tip of his chin and scraped painfully along his left cheekbone. Before he could recover, Mott hit him with a left that jolted Caleb and then an uppercut that would have ended the fight right there had it landed.

Blindly, Caleb went into a crouch and tried to gather his senses, but the little man pursued him across the ring, landing stinging punches right and left and giving him no time to settle and defend. In Caleb's corner, Jardine—who knew the fight plan—looked angrily at Moran, who was refereeing. Moran merely shrugged and watched as his fighter tore into Caleb. The crowd, loving this turn of events, was on its feet shouting for blood—black blood. But before Mott could do any more serious damage, Caleb managed to shake off his confusion and settle into a consistent defense. Once again, the smaller man's punches mostly landed harmlessly, though Caleb's arms and body were taking a considerable beating. Caleb was beginning to doubt that the second round would ever end, and he glanced desperately over at Jardine, who was wondering about the same thing. The timekeeper seemed to have gone to sleep over the bell. Slipping down from the ring, Jardine went over to the man and, hitching back his coat, showed him the butt of the pistol. Suddenly, the man struck the bell, ending the round.

"What the hell is going on?" Jardine demanded when Caleb had slumped onto his stool in the corner.

"I think," Caleb panted, "that the professor has changed his mind. He couldn't wait for the third round."

"Well," Jardine said through gritted teeth, "all bets are off. I want you to take that little bastard apart in the next round. But don't hurry. I need a little time. Don't put him away until you see me again." Motioning to Caesar to take his place in the corner, Jardine got down from the apron and disappeared into the shadows behind the ring.

"What you gonna do, Caleb?" Caesar asked nervously, looking out onto a sea of excited and angry white faces.

"What do you think, boy?" Caleb said. "I'm going to fight for my life."

In the opposite corner, Moran seemed to be arguing with his fighter. Caleb was grateful for the extra rest. But, finally, Moran threw up his hands in disgust and gave the timekeeper the signal to ring the bell.

Caleb got up warily, willing to let Mott set the pace. It was clear from the beginning that the little man wasn't going to settle for a victory. He wanted to annihilate Caleb. The excited crowd demanded no less. Caleb would have been happy to follow the original script, but that had been torn up. Besides, he had Jardine's instructions.

Waiting carefully in a defensive posture until Mott got within reach, Caleb suddenly lashed out with an open-handed slap that sent the smaller man reeling, leaving him unhurt but confused and embarrassed. The crowd was suddenly on its feet, red-faced with anger and shouting for Mott to kill the black bastard. Mott would have gladly done so had Caleb not gone back into his defensive tactics. Once again, the smaller man stalked Caleb all over the ring, daring him to slug it out. But Caleb refused, doing his best to look frightened. Whistles and jeers came from the crowd, along with a shower of small coins and rubbish. No one in the crowd was still sitting, and the blacks at the back of the tent had begun to slip away to their homes or the wagons of their owners.

The angrier the professor got, the more elusive Caleb became. Finally, his vision obscured with rage, Mott lost all control and began brawling rather than fighting. Forgetting the rules, he had only one object: to destroy the black man. Finally, working Caleb into a corner, Mott unleashed another low blow directly at his crotch. It would have put him down if Caleb had not again managed to twist his body and take the blow directly on the bone of his hip. Caleb felt the shock of the punch vibrate through his bones.

But the effect on Mott was even worse. First, his right arm went numb. Then it began to tingle and burn as if it were on fire. Hardly able to lift his arm, much less punch with it, Mott backed off, and the crowd began to jeer him as well as Caleb. The rain of missiles increased. Moran, though acting as referee, had no idea how to end this fiasco and still save his tent. Looking around wildly, he turned to signal the timekeeper to sound the bell ending the bout, but there was no timekeeper to be seen. Moran tried to get between the boxers, but the look in Caleb's eye sent him away.

From the corner of his eye, Caleb saw that Jardine was back and trying to talk to Caesar over the roar of the crowd. Finally, Caesar slipped from the apron and disappeared. Catching Caleb's eye, Jardine gave him a single emphatic nod and a flick of his head toward the back exit of the tent.

At this, Caleb literally leaped at Mott, brushing aside his defenses and smashing a quick series of punches to the head. Mott reeled, and it was only the contrary motion of Caleb's punches that held him up. Suffering a final crushing blow, Mott fell to the canvas-covered floor. Without waiting to see if Moran would begin the count, Caleb vaulted over the ropes, missed the apron entirely, and hit the packed-earth floor running. Blindly, he followed Jardine's back.

A couple of Moran's roustabouts made feeble efforts to stop them, but then stood back. Suddenly, they were outside, and Pompey and Caesar were sitting on the driving seat of the wagon, both looking nervously in every direction.

"Go!" Jardine shouted as he and Caleb leaped into the back of the wagon. The pistol was in Jardine's right hand. Caleb pushed Caesar aside and snatched the whip. Seizing the reins, he lashed the horses into a trot and then a gallop. Behind them, some men burst out of the tent but could do little but shout after them. Jardine hunched low in the back, ready to fire his pistol if need be. "Head for the turnpike," he shouted to Caleb.

Within fifteen minutes, the horses were trotting along the dark and quiet turnpike, and the four men in the wagon began to relax. Caesar had taken back the reins, and Caleb, Pompey, and Jardine peered backward for signs of pursuers. Caleb imagined that he could still hear the tumult inside the boxing tent.

— *41* —

It was very late when they got back to Three Rivers. Caleb thought he could get to sleep without waking Drusilla, but the minute he touched the bed, she was wide awake. She sat up and lit the candle.

"You succeed?" she asked.

"What do you think?"

She looked at his cheek, which was still smeared with dried blood. "I think somebody been hitting you on the face. What he look like?"

"Like a floor carpet, last time I saw him," Caleb said. "A white floor carpet."

"You been fightin' white men?"

"Just one."

"That's one too many," Drusilla said.

"Well," Caleb said, "he was the last one I'll ever fight."

"You got the money?"

"Master has," Caleb said. "But I've got something else." He reached for his back pocket and pulled out something wrapped in newspaper. He handed it to Drusilla. "Sorry there wasn't time to get it wrapped pretty. We left Shreevesville in kind of a hurry."

Drusilla undid the paper and pulled out a string of dark yellow-brown beads that weren't a bad match for her eyes. Even in the feeble light of the single candle, they glowed richly.

"Man said they were called amber," Caleb said. "It's some kind of stone that washes up on the beach. You like them?"

"I like them," Drusilla said, holding the beads against her breasts. "Going away present?"

"Just a present."

The next morning, Caleb didn't say anything about the money they had won, but he kept close at hand. Finally, as he was passing the door to the study for the sixth time, Jardine called him in.

"You want something, Caleb?" Jardine was trying to hide a smile.

"Yes, Master." Caleb looked at him stolidly.

"Oh, all right," Jardine said. "I was just joking with you. Draw up a chair and sit down." He pointed to a chair in front of his desk.

Caleb looked doubtful.

"Go ahead," said Jardine. "If you're going to be free, you'll have to get used to sitting down with white people again." He paused. "But not too used to it as long as you are here," he added meaningfully.

Once Caleb had sat gingerly on the chair, Jardine reached into a desk drawer and pulled out a thick envelope. He tipped it onto the desk. Silver and gold coins spilled out.

"Last time I counted this," Jardine said as he quickly sorted the money into two heaps, "it added up to twelve hundred and fifty dollars. That makes six hundred and twenty-five dollars each according to our agreement. That sound right to you?"

"Yes, Master."

"So," Jardine continued, "our *other* agreement was that I would let you buy your freedom for the same amount I paid for you—five hundred and fifty dollars—though you have to admit that you are worth more."

Caleb didn't say anything.

"But a deal is a deal," Jardine said, and he lifted a sizeable stack of coins from one pile of money and put it on the other. "That leaves you with your freedom *and* seventy-five dollars on top. Not bad going for one summer, eh?"

"No, Master."

"So that's it," Jardine said. "I'll write you up a piece of paper explaining that Caleb, formerly the slave of Boyd Jardine of Three Rivers, is now a free man and all that means. You can have that later today, if you like."

"That's fine, Master," Caleb said.

"Okay." Jardine put his hand on Caleb's remaining money. "You can have this now, or if you like, I can keep it for you until—"

"I'll take it, Master," Caleb said, "if you don't mind."

Jardine looked surprised, but he pushed the money toward Caleb. "Here you go, Caleb. You're a rich man."

Caleb took the coins and put them in his pocket without counting. But he didn't get up from the chair.

Jardine looked at him. "I guess that's it," he said again, "unless you can think of something else." He looked at Caleb inquiringly.

"There is one thing, Master," Caleb said.

"And what's that?" Jardine asked, beginning to look agitated. When Caleb did not respond, he added, "Well?"

"Pompey, Master."

"What about him?"

"Pompey was a prize, Master," Caleb said shortly but firmly.

"Well," Jardine said, "I didn't really want him, but I suppose he was. What of it?" He tried to stare Caleb down, but the slave sat impassively, refusing to meet his eye. Finally, Jardine spoke again. "So, Caleb," he said, "you think that because you won Pompey in the ring you ought to have half of what he's worth? Is that it?"

"Yes, Master," Caleb answered quickly.

"If that doesn't beat everything," Jardine exclaimed, throwing down the pen he'd unconsciously picked up. "You've got your freedom, you've got another seventy-five dollars on top, and now you want half of Pompey's value."

"Yes, Master."

"Well, how much do you think he's worth?"

"Pompey's mighty strong," Caleb said. "A good worker."

"That farmer in Shreevesville last night didn't seem to think so," Jardine pointed out. "He put Pompey up against a two-hundred-and-fifty-dollar prize. Sounds to me like Pompey is a two-hundred-and-fifty-dollar slave. If that, considering the way you punched him around."

Caleb didn't say anything. He just sat there.

"Well?" Jardine asked. "What do you have to say to that? You know, free blacks own slaves, too. You're going to be free today. How much would you give me for Pompey?"

"I don't want Pompey, Master."

"No," said Jardine, "and you can't afford him, either. But say you did."

"I reckon, Master," Caleb said slowly, "that Pompey would be cheap at four hundred and fifty dollars."

"You do, do you?" Jardine stared at him.

"Yes, Master."

Jardine exhaled sharply. "So, Caleb, you expect me to take two hundred and twenty-five dollars from my pile here and give it to you for a darkie that I don't even want?"

"Pompey's a mighty strong worker. And he can blacksmith some," Caleb said.

"I suppose he can cook and sew, too," Jardine said disgustedly. "You know, Caleb, you ought to take up dealing in slaves. You're a natural." He started sorting through his of pile of coins, counting as he shuffled. Suddenly, he threw some in Caleb's direction. "Two hundred dollars!" he exclaimed. "And not a penny more. Now get out of here. I'll have your paper ready after dinner."

"Thank you, Master," said Caleb, picking up the money.

Later that day, the two again sat opposite each other in Jardine's study. Jardine, ignoring Caleb, was writing with some care on a piece of fine white parchment. Now and again he referred to a big book open on his desk. Finally, finished to his satisfaction, he blotted the parchment, dripped some melted red wax on one corner, and pressed a big bronze seal into the wax. Jardine then set the document to one side to cool.

"There," he said, looking up. "As soon as I get that certified over at the county courthouse, you're a free man, Caleb. What are your plans? I expect you'll be going north. There's not much demand for ex-slaves from Boston here in Kershaw County, and I don't imagine that you're eager to stay."

"No, Master."

"But the question is," Jardine said, "are you in a big hurry to leave?"

Caleb was confused by the question. "I don't rightly know, Master. I've been thinking about being free for so long that it's hard to believe that it's finally happening. It's all sort of sudden like."

"I can believe it is, Caleb," Jardine said. "And I'll tell you something you may not agree with, but I don't think you're ready to be free."

Caleb looked at him skeptically.

"I just don't," Jardine continued. "Oh, once we get this piece of paper stamped, you can tell me to go to hell and just walk out of here free as a bird with your two hundred and seventy-five dollars." He looked sharply at Caleb. "And I expect you've got a few more dollars salted away, don't you?"

"Yes, Master."

"So you're rich and free as a bird and you think you have no problems. Right?"

Caleb just looked at him.

"Wrong!" exclaimed Jardine. "You may not want to hear this, Caleb, but you don't have the first idea of how to act like a free man. Not even a free black man."

Caleb didn't know what to say.

"Get up out of that chair, go out in the hallway, and count to five. Then, knock on the door," Jardine ordered.

"Master?"

"That's not so difficult, is it?" Jardine said. "Do it."

Clumsily, Caleb got up and did as he was told. After he'd counted to five, he knocked on the big mahogany door.

"Come in," Jardine said.

Caleb entered the room hesitantly, but before he could even get near the chair he'd been sitting in, Jardine jumped up and said, "That's what I mean! That's what I mean!"

Caleb stopped as if frozen.

"You walked into this room like a man trying to steal a chicken or a servant looking to clean up—anything but a free man calling on another free man," said Jardine. "Now, let me show you what a free man would have done. Sit down in my chair there. The one behind my desk." When Caleb hesitated, Jardine said, "Go on. It won't bite you. Now you just sit there, and I'm going to show you how it's done."

Once Caleb was seated uncomfortably behind the desk, Jardine walked out into the hall, waited for a moment, and then knocked loudly on the door. After a pause, Caleb said, "Come in." He added quickly, "Master."

Without hesitation, Jardine strode into the study with his head up and his eyes on Caleb. He marched up to the desk with his right hand extended. "Good to see you, Caleb," he said briskly, picked up

Caleb's hand, and shook it. Then he all but threw himself into the chair in front of the desk.

"See what I mean?" he said. "I didn't hesitate, look shiftily around, or waste a single second wondering how I would be received. I knew that as a free man I would not only be accepted, but welcome. Of course," he added, "if *you* behave that way down here, somebody will set the dogs on you. But, believe me, Caleb, when you get up north, folks are going to judge you by how you act. You act like a shifty-eyed darkie, they'll think you're a runaway slave no matter what that piece of paper in your pocket says. Some slavetaker will have you in chains and headed south in his wagon before you can say boo. Now, get out of my chair."

When the two men had changed positions, Jardine leaned his elbows on the desk and said, "Tell you what, Caleb, I'll make you a deal. If you'll stay six months and train me a new Caleb, I'll teach you how to act like a free man so well that people will think you were born free. *And* I'll pay you fifty dollars a month as my household manager! That'll give you more money when you get up north. Things are expensive up there. How does that sound?"

Caleb thought for a moment. "That sounds good, Master."

"You're damned right it sounds good," Jardine said. "It *is* good. Is it a deal?" He held out his hand over his desk.

Caleb got up and shook it. "It's a deal, Master," he said.

"Now that that's agreed, the first thing you have to do is stop calling me Master," said Jardine. "It was fitting and proper when you were my slave, my property, but now that you are my free employee and servant, you'd better call me Mr. Jardine. Go ahead."

"Master?"

"I just told you," Jardine said. "I'm Mr. Jardine now. Give it a try."

"Yes, Mr. Jardine," said Caleb uncertainly.

"That's better," Jardine said. "Damn me if I won't make a free man of you yet or die trying. Now get me a drink. This is dry work."

"Yes, Mr. Jardine," Caleb said with more confidence.

— *42* —

The next afternoon, Big Mose hitched up the wagon, and Jardine and Caleb rode over to the county court in Camden. Jardine insisted that Caleb sit up on the driver's seat with him and kept reminding him, "Don't slouch!"

Bart Conroy, the county recorder, looked at the paper Jardine had drawn up as if it were a lease on the moon.

"What is this, Boyd?" he asked.

"What does it look like?"

Conroy scratched his head. "Looks to me like you're giving this nigger his freedom." To the recorder, Caleb was not even there.

"I'm not giving him anything," Jardine insisted. "I'm selling him his freedom for five hundred and fifty dollars. It says so right there."

"Yes," Conroy said. "I can see that. But is he worth that much?"

"He thinks so," Jardine said. "I think so. What's your problem?"

"Well, nothing, Boyd, but free blacks are scarce in these parts—if you don't count that one-armed blacksmith over near Jeffers Crossroad, and he was free when he came here."

"Well," Jardine said impatiently, "now there'll be two of them if you'll get out your stamp and do your job."

"It'll cost you ten dollars."

"I'll try to live with that," Jardine said. "How many times have I paid you ten dollars for exercising your right arm a little?"

But Conroy was reading the document. "What's his name?" he asked.

"What's it say there, Bart?"

"It says Caleb."

"Then his name is Caleb," Jardine said. "Now for Christ's sake, stamp it."

"Caleb what?" Conroy asked.

Jardine looked questioningly at Caleb. "Caleb anything?"

"Just Caleb, Mr. Jardine."

"You heard the man," Jardine said. "Just Caleb. You want my ten dollars or not?"

"Sorry," said Conroy. "He's got to have at least two names. Ain't a free soul in this county with only one. I can't do it, Boyd."

For a moment, Caleb saw his freedom fading away like early mist on a sunny morning, but then Jardine had an inspiration.

"Tell you what," he said, "make that Caleb Rivers. Caleb T. Rivers. Will that do you?" He was talking to Caleb as much as Conroy. Caleb nodded.

"I suppose so," Conroy said. "What's the *T* stand for?"

"Anything in your damned law say it has to stand for anything?" Jardine demanded. "Just Caleb T. Rivers. Here, I'll write it in." Grabbing a pen from a marble stand on Conroy's desk, he completed the name. "Now sign and stamp the damned thing before I decide to vote Republican next time."

"Oh, you wouldn't do that, Boyd," Conroy said hurriedly. He signed the document with a flourish and then took down from the shelf a wooden box containing a tall device that embossed the county seal over his signature. "Damn, that's pretty," he said.

"Yes," Jardine said. "Ten dollars' worth of pretty." He gave Conroy the money.

Conroy shook his hand. "Don't forget to vote next month," he said. Motioning to Caleb, he asked, "When's he leaving?"

"Soon," Jardine said. "Soon."

When they got back to Three Rivers, Caleb couldn't find Drusilla anywhere. One of the house girls said she thought Drusilla was upstairs, and Caleb found her just finishing moving out of his room and into the little room where Missy had lived.

"Where are you going?" Caleb asked.

"Where are *you* going?"

"Nowhere. Least not for six months."

"And then?"

"North."

"You going to buy me and take me with you?"

"No."

"There's your answer, then," Drusilla said.

"What answer?"

"You're leavin'. I'm stayin'," Drusilla said. "You're free. I'm a slave. I never had much time for girls who sleep with the master—like that Missy."

"I'm not the master!" Caleb exclaimed.

"You workin' on it," Drusilla stated, picking up the last armload of her belongings.

"You want to keep learning to read and write?" Caleb asked.

"I'd like to," Drusilla said, "but Marse Boyd won't like it."

"Mas—Mr. Jardine won't know," Caleb said.

"So you say." Drusilla continued toward the door. "We'll see about that."

Caleb stood aside reluctantly. "You taking them beads?" he asked.

"And why not?" Drusilla asked. "You gave them to me, didn't you?" And she was gone.

"I was just asking," Caleb told the empty room.

Jardine, who was clearly enjoying the process, continued Caleb's education as a free man the very next afternoon. He called Caleb into his study.

"Have a seat, Mr. Rivers."

"Thank you, Mr. Jardine," Caleb said, forcing himself to sit well back, not perched on the edge of the chair like, as Jardine said, "a goddamned bird."

"Well, Mr. Rivers," Jardine continued, "we better talk about your course of study. What do you think a free man has to know besides how to enter a room? By the way, you still do it like a man looking to steal somebody's hat. We have to work on that. But what else do you have to learn?"

"I don't know," Caleb said.

"Let's see," Jardine said, ticking off his fingers. "There's hunting, fishing, dancing, shooting, fencing—oh, lots of things. Let's start at the beginning. Have you done much fox hunting?"

"No, Mas—Mr. Jardine," Caleb confessed. "I used to ride in Boston, but a slave doesn't have a whole lot of time for hunting."

Jardine was amazed. "In this county," he said, "people are born in the saddle and learn to jump before they can feed themselves. That's where we'll start. Tell Mose to have two of my hunters saddled and ready at nine tomorrow morning. You, Mr. Rivers, are going to start learning to be a free black huntsman."

"Yes, Mr. Jardine."

"By the way," Jardine said, "do you have any idea what the *T* between your first name and last name stands for?"

"Three?" Caleb guessed.

"Right! What do you think of it?"

"It's a name," Caleb said.

The next morning, Mose was waiting in front of the stable with the hunters. Rumors had been flying in the quarter about the strange doings of Caleb and Marse Boyd, but up until then there hadn't been any riding involved. When Caleb came out of the house dressed in one of old Mr. Jardine's riding jackets, Mose could not believe his eyes.

"Stop gawking, Mose," Jardine said, "and give Mr. Rivers a leg up on that horse. Haven't you ever seen a free black before?"

Mose did as he was told and stood watching in wonder as the horses trotted through the gate and toward the woods.

After observing for a while to see whether Caleb could ride at all and then deciding that he was surprisingly adept for a city boy, Jardine led him on the route the local hunt usually took when it worked Three Rivers. "Of course," Jardine told him, "we're not likely to raise a fox today, and we have no dogs, but the principle of the thing is about the same. If you see something in your way, jump the hell out of it and try to stay in the saddle. For instance," he said, pointing, "see where that fence meets that line of magnolia bushes?" Caleb said that he did. "Well," Jardine continued, "last winter, when Millie Holborn's big bay ran away with her, she cleared that. She's been bragging on it ever since. Do you want to take your chances?" Without waiting for an answer, Jardine spurred his hunter and lit out in that direction. After a brief hesitation, Caleb followed.

As his horse pounded over the slight decline toward the fence, Jardine had no time to worry about how Caleb was doing. Since Nancy's death, he'd had little taste for hunting and less practice, so he needed to concentrate on his own ride. Besides, a free black's neck was his own responsibility. Nearing the fence and feeling the horse beneath him gathering for the jump, Jardine forgot about everything else. Then, man and horse were flying through the air and landing with a solid thump that jolted every bone in his body. Regaining control of the horse, Jardine glanced over his shoulder, but there was no sign of Caleb. He'd started to rein the hunter around when he looked to the right and saw Caleb sitting on his hunter calmly looking at him.

"How'd you get here?" Jardine demanded with astonishment.

"Same way you did, Mr. Jardine," Caleb said, trying not to look too proud of himself.

"You lied to me," Jardine accused. "You have hunted before."

"No, sir," said Caleb.

"Then, how?"

"Well, Brent and I did do some jumping, though we weren't supposed to," Caleb said. "Mr. Staunton didn't approve. Said it was dangerous."

"Some jumping," Jardine repeated suspiciously. "Like how high?"

"Oh," Caleb said, "five, six, sometimes seven feet. Of course, we came off a lot."

"Seven feet!" Jardine scoffed. "Well, we'll just see about that. Follow me." Jardine kicked his horse into motion, and Caleb followed.

When Jardine and Caleb rode back into the stable yard in the early afternoon, they both looked as though they'd been dragged backward through a hawthorn bush. Jardine had lost one sleeve of his riding jacket, and the right side of his face was deeply scratched from jumping through a hedge rather than over it. Caleb looked even worse. He'd been in two rivers and Thorndike Ditch. His old riding clothes looked like something off a scarecrow.

"Well," said Jardine as he threw his reins to Mose, "I think we can scratch hunting off the list. With the chances you take, much more of that and you won't live long enough to get up north. I'd dearly love to see you ride with the Kershaw hunt, but somehow I don't think that's going to happen."

Caleb was too exhausted from the morning's activity to even answer, so Jardine continued, "Now, get me some lunch. I'm starving."

Drusilla had lunch all laid out by the time Jardine had drenched his head under the pump in the yard and dried his hair. Jardine sat down at the long dining table, and Caleb, who had quickly changed into his own clothes, assumed his usual position behind and to the left of Jardine's chair. He didn't have much to do except to see that Drusilla didn't make any mistakes.

Jardine started to dig in but then stopped and looked up at Drusilla. "Set another place, Dru," he said and then added to Caleb, "You're going to eat lunch with me today, Mr. Rivers. Let's see if you are as good at eating like a free man as you are at jumping." When Caleb hesitated, Jardine snapped, "You heard me. Sit down."

When Drusilla, her face stony, had set another place to Jardine's right, Caleb sat uneasily, his eyes flicking from Jardine to the serving dishes and back. He didn't know what to do first.

"Didn't you eat with the Stauntons," Jardine asked him, "up in Boston?"

"Usually Brent and me ate in the kitchen," said Caleb.

"Brent and *I*," Jardine corrected. "Well," he said, reaching for a dish of potatoes, "the main object of civilized dining is to get your belly full without neglecting table conversation." He helped himself, saying, "That was a splendid run this morning, Mr. Rivers. I especially enjoyed seeing you go head over heels into Little Creek. Potatoes?" He offered Caleb the dish.

"Thank you, Mr. Jardine," Caleb said, taking the potatoes and helping himself. He tried to think of something to say. Finally he said, "It was a very refreshing experience."

"I'll bet," Jardine said. "If I may suggest, Mr. Rivers, that most free people prefer to eat potatoes with a fork?"

"So I've heard, but thank you, Mr. Jardine, for that reminder. I appreciate it."

"No problem, Mr. Rivers," Jardine said. "Do you think you could pass me the meat platter?"

For the next few months, Caleb—when he wasn't working—attended the Boyd Jardine Academy for the Education of Free Blacks. One by one, Jardine tested his skills and, where he could, improved them. When it came to swordsmanship, Jardine, who'd received training at the Citadel, had the advantage with the foil, harrying Caleb from one end of the barn to the other crying, "Gotcha!"

"I can't tell you *how* many times I've killed you today, Mr. Rivers," he told Caleb during a break, "but let me assure you, if this were the real thing, you'd be deader than chivalry."

But when it came to the sabers, Caleb's superior size and strength combined with his natural ferocity gave him the advantage. Forgetting, in the heat of the moment, that Jardine was his former master and present employer, Caleb pressed Jardine until his back was flat against a wall of hay bales.

"Yield!" he demanded, adding as an afterthought, "Sir."

"I think I just might," said Jardine, dropping his blade, "before you separate my head from my body. You know, it's a good thing that Nat Turner didn't have you on his side back in '28."

"More, Mr. Jardine?" Caleb asked.

"I don't think so, Mr. Rivers," Jardine said. "I've sort of got used to being in one piece. If you get any better with that pigsticker, the county will be up in arms claiming I'm raising a free-black insurrection here."

Most of the county didn't pay a whole lot of attention to what Jardine was doing at Three Rivers. But when Martha Bentley heard from Bart Conroy that not only had Jardine allowed Caleb to purchase his freedom, but that the black was still at Three Rivers, she took the first opportunity to pay a call. When she arrived unannounced, Jardine and Caleb were in the big dining room and the Persian carpet was rolled back. Little Boyd was sitting in his high chair to one side chewing on a rusk and watching intently.

"You're just in time, Martha," Jardine said, coming out onto the veranda to greet her. "I'm trying to teach Caleb how to waltz and damn me if I can remember how to do it myself."

"You're teaching him to *what*?" Martha asked.

"Waltz. But we've got no music. Jeff—the fiddler down in the quarter—doesn't know a waltz from a fandango. I believe you're a dab hand yourself at dancing that sort of thing, Martha. Maybe you can give us some pointers." He turned toward the door to the house, calling, "Mr. Rivers! Get yourself out here."

Caleb, who had been lurking in the hall, stepped out on the veranda reluctantly, greeting Mrs. Bentley awkwardly.

"Martha," Jardine said, "I'd like you to meet Mr. Caleb T. Rivers, the newest free black in Kershaw County. Mr. Rivers—Mrs. Rafe Bentley."

Caleb bowed low—but not too low—as Jardine had taught him and said, "Mrs. Bentley, my very great pleasure."

Martha did not extend her hand. Caleb hadn't expected her to. Instead, she looked at him as if he were a monkey in clothes and said with cool politeness, "Mr. Rivers, would you mind if I had a word with Mr. Jardine—alone?"

Caleb bowed again, saying "Mrs. Bentley," and went back into the house.

When the door had closed behind him, Martha wheeled toward Jardine.

"Boyd Jardine, have you gone completely out of your mind?"

"Possibly, Martha," Jardine said. "It's long been rumored in these parts, but what did you have in mind particularly?"

"Can't you guess? It's what you've been doing with that baboon. Rafe told me about you taking him all over creation during the summer beating up on darkies—*and* a white man! That was bad enough. I reckoned I had to make some allowances what with Nancy dying like that and all."

"Very kind of you, Martha," Jardine said. "I appreciate it."

"Even after you spurned my cousin," Martha added.

"Lovely girl," Jardine said.

"That's beside the point," she said angrily. "But now I find that you've not only freed this . . . this . . . but you are teaching him how to *waltz*, for pity's sake. What *else* are you teaching him?" she demanded, not really expecting an answer.

"Oh," said Jardine casually, "not much. Just hunting, table manners, etiquette—what did you think of that bow?—shooting, fencing. Say, Martha, you ought to see that boy with a saber. I'm lucky to be wearing all my limbs."

"Saber!" Martha Bentley looked alarmed. "Shooting? What are you trying to do, Boyd, raise a slave revolt?"

"Slave revolt? Of course not, Martha," Jardine said. "Caleb's as free as I am."

"Well, won't either of you be free or even alive, Boyd, if it gets out what you are doing here at Three Rivers. With war just around the corner, people are not going to be too understanding about you arming and training regiments of free blacks."

"I hadn't considered that angle," said Jardine.

"Well, you had better consider it, and in a hurry," Martha Bentley said, "if you want that darkie of yours to live to enjoy his freedom. And you had better get him out if this county and out of this state."

"I'll bear that in mind," said Jardine. "But we were just going to sit down to lunch. Won't you join us?"

"Us?" said Martha frostily. "Who are *us*? You and that trained monkey?"

"Well, yes," Jardine confessed. "You see, after nearly five years eating with field hands and then here in the kitchen with the house slaves, Caleb's table manners were a little rusty, so I—"

"If you think I am going to sit down anywhere within five miles of a nigger at a dining table, Boyd, you are as crazy as everyone thinks you are."

"That's possible," said Jardine.

"I may be very hungry when I get home, but I'll still be able to say that I never ate lunch with a nigger." Mrs. Bentley turned toward her carriage, but at that moment a child's cry came from inside. Spinning around, she rushed into the room and picked up little Boyd.

Following in her wake, Jardine said, "I forgot. You haven't seen Boyd Junior for some time. What do you think?"

Examining the child as if he were a blue-ribbon winner at a livestock show, she said, "I'm shocked and amazed that you seem to have a healthy and normal boy here."

"Thank you," said Jardine modestly. "We do our best. The house girls all call him Birdie, but I won't have it. I'm thinking ahead when he's forty years old and a local magistrate. How would it look?"

At that moment, Rose, the child's nurse, appeared in the doorway.

"I'm sorry, Martha," Jardine said, "but Junior has to go eat his lunch."

Mrs. Bentley reluctantly surrendered the child and turned back toward the veranda.

"I'll give you credit, Boyd," she said. "You may be losing your mind, but you've turned out to be a half-decent father."

"You're too kind, Martha."

Without another word, Mrs. Bentley climbed back in her gig, ignoring Jardine's efforts to assist her.

"I could at least have made her a sandwich," Jardine said to himself as the gig disappeared up the drive.

— *43* —

That evening, Jardine called Caleb into his study. "Sit down," he said. "We have to talk."

When Caleb was settled, Jardine asked, "Any idea what about?"

"Mrs. Bentley's visit," Caleb said. "She didn't look happy."

"That's putting it mildly. She thinks I'm crazy and that you're a murderous black likely to assassinate the quality folk of Kershaw and nearby counties in their beds. Are you?"

"No," said Caleb without hesitation.

"Thank God for that. But I've been doing some thinking since she was here, and I think Martha is right about one thing. You have to get out of this county, this state, and this region. It's time to go north. Are you ready?"

"I think so."

"Even without knowing how to waltz?" Jardine asked. "You'll never be able to travel in the best circles, Mr. Rivers."

"I'll make do, Mr. Jardine."

"I hope so. How's Caesar coming along training for the dining room?"

"Okay, but slow. The boy has the will to learn, but his energy rushes so far ahead of his abilities that he trips over himself. But with Drusilla managing him, he'll be all right. She's a good woman."

Jardine looked at him with a slight smile. "How's her reading and writing coming along?"

Caleb was startled, but he answered, "Pretty good, especially the reading. Drusilla reads almost as well as I do. She can write, but she's slow."

"And her arithmetic?"

"Very good. She's been doing the accounts now for over a month."

"I know," said Jardine. "And you know that I told you not to go teaching any of my slaves to read and write."

"You didn't mean to include Drusilla," Caleb assured him. "Who's going to read your newspapers to you when I'm gone? Do you know how much it would cost you to buy another slave with her abilities?"

"More than five hundred and fifty dollars, that's for sure," Jardine said. "How soon can you be ready to leave here?"

"Tomorrow morning."

"That soon?" Jardine said with surprise.

"Yes."

"Okay," Jardine said. "Be ready right after breakfast. If we hurry, we can catch the noon boat to Great Falls."

This took Caleb by surprise. "We?"

"Sure. I'm going with you. I'm your ticket to freedom. On your own, you wouldn't even get out of sight of Three Rivers. But we'll talk about that in the morning. On the way. In the meantime, I've thought of one more skill necessary to every free man—black or white. You play much poker, Mr. Rivers?"

"Brent and I used to play some in—"

"I know," Jardine said, "in the kitchen. What did you play for? Matchsticks? Buttons?"

"Mostly," Caleb admitted, "but sometimes Brent had a few pennies."

"Well," Jardine said, "your poker skills are about to face a severe test. Why don't you run upstairs and get some of that fortune you've got hidden away, and we'll play a few hands?"

"I don't know, Mr. Jardine. I'm going to need all the money I've got."

"You're going to need *more* than you've got, Mr. Rivers," Jardine said. "And this is your last chance to get it. Why, I'm famous as the poorest poker player in the county. Ask anybody. Ask Rafe Bentley. Go get your money, Mr. Rivers."

When Caleb got back, Jardine had cleared the round leather-topped table and placed several oil lamps around it. He was sitting at the table behind a stack of gold coins, shuffling a deck of cards. "You're just in time, Mr. Rivers," he said. "Five-card draw, jacks or better to open. Nothing wild. Just real poker."

"That sounds good, Mr. Jardine," Caleb said, sitting down opposite him and putting his money on the table. He held out his hand. "If you don't mind, I'll just cut those cards a little."

Handing Caleb the deck, Jardine said, "You're learning, Mr. Rivers. You're learning."

An hour later, Jardine was beginning to regret suggesting this final addition to the skills Caleb would need in his new life as a free man. After winning a few small hands, Jardine found the tide had begun to turn. Caleb, playing very tight poker and drawing strong hands, was beginning to win. He was just over a hundred dollars up. This had not been Jardine's idea. He hadn't planned to take much of Caleb's money, but he had hoped that Caleb would leave with a healthy respect for the white man's skill at cards. It wasn't working out that way.

"Well," Jardine said, shuffling the deck, "it's getting late, and I imagine you have some packing to do and some good-byes to say, so shall we make this the last hand, Mr. Rivers?"

"That'll be just fine, Mr. Jardine," Caleb said. "Same limit?"

"Oh," Jardine said nonchalantly, "since this is the final hand, why don't we just say table stakes. You know what that means don't you?"

"Well, I believe it means that you can bet all the money you have on the table."

"Exactly, Mr. Rivers," Jardine said. "You're catching on. Are you ready?"

"Ready."

Jardine dealt the cards, and when he picked up his hand he found that he had two kings, the queen of hearts, and a six and seven of clubs.

"I'll open," Caleb said, pushing fifty dollars out to the center of the table.

"Will you?" said Jardine, glad to see some of his money back on the table. "Well, I'll see your fifty and raise you twenty-five. Just to keep you honest."

After Caleb had pushed out the twenty-five, Jardine asked him, "Cards?"

"Oh," said Caleb as casually as possible, "I think I'll just play these, if you don't mind."

"Not at all," said Jardine. But he did mind. To keep all five cards meant that Caleb must have at least a straight, and that hand would beat Jardine even if he drew a third king. "I think I'll take two cards." He discarded the two low clubs, hoping that Caleb would think that he had trips and was going for a full house or four of a kind.

Dealing himself two cards, Jardine looked at them—another king and the four of diamonds. He tried to look pleased but not too pleased. "Shall we say another fifty dollars?" he said, pushing his bet to the middle of the table. This was just to lure Caleb out of his depth.

To Jardine's surprise, without hesitation, Caleb said, "Oh, let's make it two hundred," and threw the coins into the pot carelessly. He looked at Jardine calmly.

Forgetting his imaginary full house or four of a kind, Jardine stared at his hand of three kings, queen high, and then at Caleb. Christ! Another two hundred dollars! He saw that Caleb's left hand was already reaching for his pile of money to increase his bet. Jardine reached out for his own money but then stayed his hand and threw his cards face down into the pot. "Go ahead, take it," he said, trying to keep bitterness out of his voice.

"I will, sir, thank you," Caleb said, reaching toward the pot, but Jardine stopped him with a motion.

"I'll just trouble you for sight of your openers for that last hand, Mr. Rivers."

"Of course, Mr. Jardine," Caleb said. He flipped over his hand, revealing two aces, the other king, and two small cards.

"You black bastard!" Jardine exclaimed involuntarily. "You bluffed me with a lousy pair."

"That's what Brent always used to say." Caleb raked in his winnings.

When Caleb was upstairs packing, Drusilla knocked on his door.

"I've come to say good-bye," she said.

"Come in."

"That's not much," she said, looking at the few belongings Caleb was packing into a worn carpetbag that Jardine had given him.

"There's not much I want to remind me of this life," Caleb said.

"Is it that bad? Seems to me like you and Marse Boyd 'most like brothers these days. Ridin', eatin' at the same table, foolin' around with those silly swords."

"That's only because I bought my freedom, and I'm leaving," Caleb said. "Otherwise, I'd be just like any other slave—a piece of property."

"Like me?"

"Like you," Caleb said.

"You so sure it's going to be better up north?" she asked. "I've heard stories that they don't exactly love niggers up there, despite all this abo . . . abo . . ."

"Abolition."

"Abolition talk. They say that folks are killed every day, just for being black."

"They say that," Caleb agreed, "but if I can't be free down here, I guess I'll have to try being free up there. If I die, I'll die free."

"Is it that important?"

"I guess so."

Drusilla didn't say anything.

"Oh," Caleb said. "You be glad to hear that Mr. Jardine's going to keep you in my job. At least until Caesar gets a grip on it."

"Then I haven't much to worry about," Drusilla said. "That boy will have a beard as long and gray as Uncle Ebenezer's before he get a grip on very much."

"That's not what Caesar thinks. He thinks he's only *that*"—Caleb snapped his fingers—"far from running this plantation all by his self."

"I'll cure him of that by letting him serve Marse Boyd and his guests dinner just one time. He'll be out choppin' cotton *so* fast."

"You're a hard woman," Caleb said, smiling.

"It's a hard life."

"Another thing," Caleb said. "Mr. Jardine knows that I've been teaching you to read and write."

"I know," Drusilla said. "The hardest thing to keep at Three Rivers is a secret. What he say?"

"Well, he wasn't exactly pleased," Caleb said, "but when I pointed out that you could read his papers to him nearly as well as I can, he cheered up a little bit. But I don't think he'd like it much if you spread it around."

"Even to Caesar?"

"You'll have to ask him that yourself," Caleb said. He snapped the carpetbag shut. "That's it."

Drusilla held out her hand. "Well, good-bye, Caleb," she said.

Caleb took Drusilla's hand and pulled her close. "You sure you wouldn't like to stay the night, just for old time's sake?"

"I'm sure," Drusilla said, breaking free. "I'll remember you, all right, without no little Calebs tugging at my skirt to remind me."

"You know I've always been careful."

"No," she said. "*I've* always been careful. And I'm staying that way. Good-bye, Caleb," she repeated.

"Well, okay," Caleb said, "but aren't you a little bit curious what it's like to sleep with a free man?"

"No," Drusilla said, opening the door, "but if I ever am, I'm sure that this won't be my last chance."

"You know best," Caleb said, "but not even a little good-bye kiss?"

"I guess I can manage that," she said, kissing him lightly and then dancing away when Caleb tried to grab her. "You free niggers sure get up to some tricks."

"We sure do," said Caleb as he watched her walk down the narrow hall.

Caleb got up early, heated water for a bath, and dressed carefully in the best of old Master Jardine's clothes that Gabe, the tailor in the quarter, had cut down for him. Looking in the cracked mirror, he thought he was a pretty good example of a free black. He was downstairs supervising Caesar as he laid the breakfast table when Jardine came down.

Jardine took one look at him and exclaimed, "Caleb, what the hell do you think you're playing at?"

"Mr. Jardine?" Caleb said.

"If you think I am going to travel with you looking like a black Beau Brummell, you're crazy."

"Bo who?" Caleb asked.

"Never mind," Jardine said. "There has to be something I know that you don't. You remember those old clothes you wore the first time I took you to Cassatt and you fought Pompey? Where are they?"

"I threw them in a pile in the barn," Caleb said.

"After we eat," Jardine said. "You go throw them on yourself. You're supposed to be traveling with me as my slave, not an entry in the Easter Parade. You think some good old boys wouldn't throw you in the river looking like that? And me, too?"

Caleb knew he was right, but looked down at his clothes regretfully.

"You pack those," Jardine ordered, "and you can put them on again where it's not an insult for a nigger to wear shined shoes. Now, let's get moving. That boat isn't going to wait for you even if you are free. And neither am I."

In less than an hour, Drusilla, Caesar, and the house girls were out front to wave Jardine and Caleb good-bye. Behind them in the doorway, Birdie's nurse held the child up so that he could see. Caleb sat in the back of the wagon wearing the outsized old clothes, which had not improved by being thrown in a heap. Drusilla managed to keep a straight face, but Caesar and the house girls kept covering their mouths and giggling.

"Take a last look, Caleb," Jardine said. "You won't be seeing Three Rivers no more. That is, unless you come back some day wearing a Yankee uniform."

Caleb took a look. Now that he was leaving, it didn't seem quite so bad.

Jardine cracked the whip over the team's heads. "I'll be back in a week or three, Drusilla. You try to keep that Caesar under control. If he acts up, you tell me." Caesar didn't look happy. Everybody waved as the wagon rolled down the drive.

As they neared the Three Rivers gates, Caleb heard a noise. Big Mose and the cotton crew were shouting and waving their hats. He raised his own floppy hat and waved it back.

— *44* —

Jardine and Caleb got to the river landing with time to spare. After they stabled the horses and boarded the steamboat to Great Falls, Jardine met some county people he knew and retired to the cabin, escaping the thin mist that had begun to fall. Caleb, shuffling in shoes several sizes too big, joined half a dozen slaves who were huddled amid bales of cotton and hay, a couple of cows, and a big pen of chickens. Two of the men held a piece of canvas over their heads, and the water that gathered on it kept running down Caleb's neck.

Through a window looking into the cabin, Caleb could see Jardine and the other white men sitting around a table playing cards. He thought of the money in the belt around his waist, and he knew that he could increase it if he were in that game. But he didn't have to wonder what they would say if he went back there and asked if he could sit in.

An old man who looked at least ninety years old asked Caleb pleasantly, "Who do you belong to, boy?" Caleb felt like telling him, *I belong to me, Caleb T. Rivers, that's who*, but he knew he couldn't.

"Mr. Jardine of Three Rivers," he told the old man.

"Is he a good massa?"

"He all right," said Caleb. Just then, two of the white deck-hands, without a word to the slaves, began shifting the cargo to get ready for the next landing. The black passengers scattered like pigeons. Caleb moved with the rest, but he did not do it gladly. He wondered idly where a free black would have ridden, but he thought he knew.

In Great Falls, they had a couple of hours to wait for the train. Jardine, who had won more money than he had lost to Caleb the night before, was feeling good. "I like the way you walk in those shoes, Caleb," he said.

"Thankee, Massa," Caleb said with an exaggerated slur. "Mos' kind." In a quieter voice he asked, "How was the game?"

"Like taking candy from a baby," Jardine said. "Those old boys are paying for our trip. I hope you're grateful."

"Sure is, Massa."

"Don't overdo it," Jardine advised him. "I'm going over to the hotel to get something to eat. You find something and meet me right here"—he glanced up at the clock on the town hall—"at six o'clock."

"Yassa."

Jardine started to turn toward the hotel but saw that Caleb wasn't moving. "Well?" he asked.

Caleb just looked at him and held out his hand.

"What?" Jardine exclaimed. "Why, you," but he dug into his pocket and pulled out two quarters, dropping them carelessly into Caleb's hand. Caleb didn't move an inch. "What are you waiting for?" he demanded.

"I hear food comes costly hereabouts," Caleb said.

"Why, you rascal," Jardine said. "If I still owned you, I'd sell you for dog meat." But he reached back into his pocket and pulled out another quarter. "Will this do you?"

"Yassa." Caleb pocketed the coins, touched the water-soaked brim of his hat, and turned away.

"Six o'clock," Jardine called after him, "and don't stuff yourself on that caviar."

Caleb stopped a black man leading two horses and asked where he could buy something to eat. The hostler directed Caleb down an alley and told him to keep walking until he came to a bend in the river, then look for a house with a big red tin sign. After trudging through the mud for ten minutes, Caleb found the house. It was a rickety affair with a sharply sloped roof and an entrance through a lean-to. Inside, an old woman looked up at him from a big cast-iron range.

"You got a toilet here, ma'am?" Caleb asked, badly in need of one after the long boat ride.

"You eatin'?"

"Yes, ma'am."

"Lemme see your money."

Caleb showed her the coins.

"We got the backyard," she said, waving her ladle toward the other door. "It go right down to the river, and I suggest you do jus' the same."

When Caleb returned, he found that the food was a lot better than the facilities. After the old woman piled a second helping of fried fish on Caleb's plate, cut him another big chunk of bread, and filled his cup with chicory coffee, she said, "You're not from these parts."

"No, ma'am," Caleb said. "Down river a piece. Kershaw County."

"What you doing up here?"

"Catching a train. My master's over at the hotel eating."

"Poor him," she said. "All the darkies works at the hotel come *here* to eat. That cook over there can't even boil water without scorchin' it. Where you going?"

"North," said Caleb. "Can you keep a secret?"

"If I couldn't, there be some niggers around here in a heap of trouble," she said. "What is it? I hope it's a good one."

Caleb leaned toward her. "I'm going to be free." He wasn't sure why he didn't tell her that he already was free.

"Hmm," she said. "You think you'll like it?"

"Of course," said Caleb indignantly. "Who wouldn't?"

"Well," said the old woman, "I been free these fifty years and more, and I haven't noticed all that much satisfaction from it. I have to keep this place goin' fifteen to sixteen hours a day just to stay alive. And that includes Sundays. If I didn't have a niece who comes in Sunday morning and Wednesday evening, I wouldn't even get to church."

"You've never been tempted to leave?" Caleb asked.

"For where, son?" she asked. "For where? You want more fish? I got some apple pie."

"Just the pie, ma'am," Caleb said, "and some more of that terrible coffee."

The old woman slapped his shoulder with her wiping cloth. "Mouthy as you are," she predicted, "you goin' to last about six minutes up north."

Jardine came out of the hotel to find Caleb waiting at the bottom of the steps. "Well," he said, spitting to get a bad taste out of his mouth, "I hope you got your belly full."

"Yassa," Caleb said, "but they ran out of caviar."

At the train station, Jardine bought two tickets to Charlotte, North Carolina. When he walked Caleb to his car, it turned out to be a boxcar with narrow benches running lengthwise on each side. On the benches were black passengers who were trying to sleep away the journey. Others sprawled on the plank floor, using bags for pillows and coats for covers.

"Well," Jardine said, "it's not exactly first class, but it's only a few hours until we change."

"I'll manage," Caleb told him.

"I'm three or four cars on up ahead," Jardine said. "I'll check on you later. Sweet dreams, Caleb."

Caleb just grunted. When Jardine left, he tried to make himself comfortable on a bench that sloped too much for comfort whether he sat up or lay down.

Caleb finally lay down on the bench and, wrapping himself around his bag and using his arm for a pillow, managed to drop off into a light sleep. Sometime later he sensed, without really waking, that the train had stopped, but he clung tenaciously to sleep. Then he felt a cool breeze as the boxcar door was thrown open with a crash. He tried to ignore it until he was shocked fully awake by a hard blow to the back.

"Get up, you," shouted a harsh voice. Half a dozen white men were walking up and down the car, shoving and kicking the sleepers into consciousness. One of them swung an oil lantern. A frightened child cried out, and her mother hushed her. The black passengers fearfully forced themselves fully awake and waited for what was to happen next.

The invaders had separated and were questioning the passengers in the car. One, a big man with a full black beard and a flat-topped hat, pushed Caleb roughly. "You, who are you?"

"Caleb, suh." Caleb thought immediately of the freedom paper and money in the belt deep under his clothes. He couldn't show one without revealing the other.

"From where?"

"Three Rivers, suh, Kershaw County."

"What are you doing so far from home?"

"Travelin', suh. With my master."

"Oh, yeah?"

The bearded man shouted over his shoulder, "I think we've got one, Jim." He asked Caleb gruffly, "You got papers?"

"No, suh. Massa—"

By then the man called Jim was also looking down at Caleb. He snatched the floppy hat from Caleb's head and, grabbing a handful of hair, yanked his head back. "Let's get a look at you."

Caleb tried to look terrified. It wasn't hard.

"Look at that scar, Morgan," Jim said. "Didn't one of those runaways have a scar on his face?"

"Damned if he didn't," said Morgan. "Get up, boy!"

"But, suh—"

Morgan kicked Caleb hard in the leg. "Get up, damn you," he exclaimed. "I'm not here to argue with niggers. You're getting off this train."

He reached down to pull Caleb to his feet, but Caleb let his weight go dead. Morgan pulled his arm back to take a swing at him, when a voice came from the open boxcar door.

"Is my nigger giving you trouble, gentlemen?" asked Jardine. He climbed into the boxcar.

"This your slave?" demanded Morgan.

"Sure is," Jardine said lightly.

"Can you prove it?"

"Do I have to?" Jardine asked him. "How are you doin', Caleb?"

"All right, Master," Caleb said. "So far."

"We've got warrants," blustered Morgan. "Looking for runaways." He moved aside to let one of his companions by with a scared-looking black boy who was very much under his control. But Jardine stepped in their path.

"May I see those papers?" Jardine asked and hitched back his coat to reveal the butt of his revolver sticking out of the waistband of his trousers.

"Who are you?" asked Morgan, who seemed to be the boss.

"Boyd Jardine of Three Rivers Plantation, Kershaw County," Jardine said. "At your service. You seem to have mistaken my slave for one of your runaways. You could be making the same mistake with this boy. Now may I see those warrants?" The man with the black boy in tow made as if to push past him, but Jardine said softly, "I wouldn't if I was you." The man looked at Morgan.

"Now, those warrants," said Jardine.

Angrily, Morgan reached into an inner pocket of his coat and shoved a small sheaf of papers into Jardine's hands. Jardine peered at them in the semidarkness. "Could I have that lamp over here, please?" he asked. Grudgingly, Morgan snatched the lamp from the man holding it and held it overhead. Jardine shuffled through the papers unhurriedly.

"This train don't stop here long, Mister," Morgan protested.

"Won't be long now," Jardine said soothingly. "Which one of these are you claiming this boy is?"

Morgan grabbed one of the papers out of Jardine's hand and growled, "This one."

Jardine studied the paper carefully. "What's your name, boy?" he asked.

"Marcus, Massa. Marcus Beauclerk," the boy said shakily.

"How tall are you?" Jardine asked him.

"Don't rightly know," the boy said. "Tall enough, I guess."

Jardine told the boy, "Turn your head, Marcus, so I can see your right ear."

Reluctantly, the boy did so. Jardine could see that the top portion of the boy's right ear was missing.

"Looks like you're a long ways from home, Marcus," Jardine said, after looking at the rest of the details on the warrant.

"Yessir," Marcus said, dejectedly.

"They're probably missing you," Jardine added.

Up ahead the train whistle hooted.

"This train's leaving," said Morgan. "We've got to get off."

"I won't stand in your way," Jardine said. "Seems to me that you have the right man here."

"Why, thank you very much," Morgan said. He signaled to the man holding Marcus, who firmed up his grip on the boy's collar.

"Damn you," he snarled at Jardine, snatching the papers from his hand. "Nobody minds their own business these days. Come on, boys!" The one with Marcus in hand followed the others to the door of the boxcar and jumped out. Morgan followed them. At the door, he stopped and looked balefully at Jardine. "We might meet again someday, Mister," he said.

"My pleasure," said Jardine, following him to the door. "If you are ever in the neighborhood of Three Rivers, feel free to drop in. I'm sure that Caleb will be glad to renew your acquaintance. Won't you, Caleb?" Caleb didn't say anything.

Morgan jumped down from the car with an oath, and Jardine, making sure that they were leaving, followed. He called to the men as they walked away, "Do you think you could help me close the door?" But they didn't answer, and Caleb and another man were already closing it from the inside.

Jardine walked forward to his car and stood on the step until, with another blast of the whistle, the train began moving. Then he stepped up into a passenger car with a genial wave at the men who were disappearing up the track with their quarry.

When the train stopped at Charlotte, Jardine collected Caleb from the boxcar.

"Did you get any sleep?" Jardine asked.

"Yes," said Caleb.

Jardine looked at him out of the corner of his eye. "Ain't no use going all surly and sullen on me, Caleb," he said. "I suppose you think I should have taken the boy off of those slave catchers and toted him up north."

"I guess not," said Caleb.

"You *know* not," Jardine said. "That boy was the bona fide property of some folks who had every right to have him back. That's the law. You know that."

"Suppose so," said Caleb.

"You ought to be grateful that I came along when I did. Otherwise, you'd be chained to that Marcus and headed south in even less comfort than you're traveling north. Those catchers aren't too particular. They wouldn't give a damn about that piece of paper I gave you."

"I know," Caleb said finally. "And I am grateful. I just—"

"I know, and I'd probably feel the same way in your position," said Jardine. "But you have to look out for yourself, Caleb. We're not there yet. Now, let's find some food. My innards are starting to eat themselves." He gave Caleb a dollar and turned away to make sure that he knew that he wasn't going to get any more.

Jardine disappeared into the station hotel, and Caleb searched for something to eat. He saw a black boy sitting on a steamer trunk and gnawing on a chicken leg.

"Where'd you get that?"

"Round back of the station," the boy said, still chewing. "Old woman called Mary got a whole basket of it."

"Any good?"

"Sure is," said the boy. "Better than starving to death. A lot better."

Caleb found Mary, an old woman with one glazed-over eye, and bought fifty cents' worth of chicken wrapped up in newspaper. He was walking back to the front of the station and eating when he encountered Jardine, who looked very disgruntled.

"You wouldn't believe what they're trying to pass off as food in there. I'd rather starve to death." He looked closely at the bundle in Caleb's hand. "What have you got there?"

"Fried chicken," Caleb said.

"Any good?"

"Not bad," said Caleb, still eating. "Friend of mine called Mary cooked it."

"Oh, you've got a friend here, have you?" Jardine asked. "How much have you got?"

"Quite a bit," Caleb said. Then, as if the thought had just occurred to him, he asked, "Would you like some?"

Jardine looked shiftily around the station. "Not here," he said, "but just slow down on that eating and follow me." Jardine led Caleb down the platform to an area where cargo was stacked high. Pressed between bales of cotton and boxes of machinery, he grabbed the package from Caleb's hand, reached into it, and began chewing hungrily on a chicken breast.

"I'll bet," he said through a mouth full of chicken, "you weren't even going to give me any. You're a selfish bastard, Rivers."

Caleb just kept eating. But when they'd finished the chicken, he asked Jardine, "I don't suppose you could get us a couple of bottles of beer from that hotel."

"You don't want much," Jardine said, but he returned with the beer just as their train was called.

The rest of Caleb and Jardine's trip north passed without incident, but it wasn't easy. At one point in southern Virginia, there was a forty-mile break in the railway line, and they had to switch to a stagecoach. The coach driver was against carrying Caleb at all. "People don't like traveling with niggers," he said. But Jardine slipped him an extra dollar, and Caleb was granted the privilege of clinging to the trunk at the back of the coach while Jardine rode inside with a very nice-looking young lady returning to her home in Richmond. This was not so bad until it started raining. Then it was hell. When they got to where the railway line recommenced, Caleb was shaking with cold, and his arms—frozen in their death grip on the trunk—would not straighten out for half an hour.

When Jardine came out of a nearby inn where he'd shared dinner and a bottle of wine with the young lady, he found Caleb huddled around a campfire, trying to thaw out by drinking some nasty-tasting moonshine. "Nothing like freedom, eh, Caleb?" he said. Caleb did not answer.

"Slaves aren't what they used to be," Jardine remarked to the young lady. "Sometimes I don't know why I bother."

Finally, when their final train pulled into New York City, Jardine collected Caleb from yet another boxcar, and they stood on the deserted platform in the grayness of early morning.

"Well, Mr. Rivers," said Jardine, "I guess this is it. I'm going to get me a hotel room and catch up on some sleep before I see a few of the sights and then head back. What are you going to do?"

"I don't rightly know," Caleb said. "Find some work, I guess."

"Think you might go back up to Boston?"

"I could," Caleb said, "but after six years I don't hardly know anybody up there. I think I'll hang around here and see what I can do. Might be some opportunities."

"Might be," Jardine said. "But if you get tired of the delights of this place"—he looked around at the cold, dirty, and misty railway platform—"there's always a job for you at Three Rivers. We'll just forget about that piece of paper I gave you."

"And my five hundred and fifty dollars?" Caleb asked.

"Oh," said Jardine, "we could sort that out if the time comes."

"Thanks for the offer, Mr. Jardine," Caleb said, "but these are early days. I want to find out what there is in this being free."

"You do that," Jardine said. "I'll leave you now, but before I do, I've got a little present for you." He reached inside his coat and pressed his small pistol into Caleb's hand. "Slip that in your pocket," he said, "and don't wave it about. You never know when it might come in handy. Just don't go shooting everybody who might happen to offend you, Mr. Rivers. Keep it in reserve."

"I will, Mr. Jardine," Caleb said, putting it into his waistband and feeling the small but solid bulk of the pistol against his hip.

"We can't just stand here," Jardine said. "Might get arrested. So I'll say good-bye. We've come a long way since that morning at Lynche's Landing, haven't we?"

"Sure have," Caleb said.

"I can honestly say, Mr. Rivers, that it's been a pleasure. You take care of yourself."

"You, too, Mr. Jardine," he said, "and thank you for seeing me up here. You were right. I'd never have made it without you."

"My pleasure," Jardine said. When Jardine didn't start to move away, Caleb waited. After a long silence, Jardine finally spoke.

"Since we're unlikely to meet again this side of the grave," Jardine said, "there's something you ought to know. I've been meaning to tell you for a long time, but somehow, as your master, I couldn't find a way to do it." Again, Caleb waited.

"The fact is," Jardine said haltingly, "I know what really happened the night that Miss—that Nancy died. Old Doc Hollander didn't mean to let it out—I know he didn't—but finally, without naming names, he told someone, who told someone, who told me. At first I was angry at being deceived, but then I realized I had no right to be. What I ought to have been—and what I am—is grateful to you."

Jardine held out his hand. "I want to thank you, Caleb, for saving my son's life. Nancy wanted that baby more than anything. I can't think of anyone who would have—could have—done what you did that night, and I owe you thanks."

Caleb took his hand, and they shook for a long time without speaking. There didn't seem to be anything more to say. Then, letting go of Caleb's hand, Jardine turned away. He walked down the platform toward the carriage ranks.

Caleb stood and watched him go without an idea of what to do next.

— *45* —

When a policeman came wandering down the platform with his eyes on him, Caleb knew it was time to move on. At the exit of the station, a small boy, shouting incoherently, waved a newspaper in his face. Digging into his pocket for the remains of his food money, Caleb bought a paper. Spotting a coffee stall, he slipped onto a stool and looked at the newspaper. The headline screamed: "IT'S WAR! SHOTS FIRED: Rebels Capture Fort Sumter, War Cabinet Meets Urgently."

There wasn't really much more than that in the extra edition, but Caleb had a feeling that Jardine would not be hanging around New York City very long, not once he saw the papers and the details that would surely follow.

"May I have a cup of coffee?" Caleb asked the stall proprietor, a fat man wearing a dingy white apron. The man looked at him unblinkingly. Caleb repeated, "May I have a cup of coffee?"

"I don't serve niggers," the man finally said without expression.

Caleb thought of the pistol in his coat pocket and wondered how the man would react if he found it pointed between his eyes. But then he remembered Jardine's words. "Thank you kindly," he said and got down off the stool. As he turned to walk away, Caleb caught sight of his reflection in a window. There stood the most ragtag creature Caleb had ever seen: filthy outsized clothes that had obviously been slept in for days, a bedraggled hat that you wouldn't put on a dying mule, and four days' growth of beard. A man like that, Caleb thought, ought to be arrested on general principles. No wonder the stall keeper wouldn't serve him.

Outside the train station among the rushing people, Caleb wondered what to do next. He could wait for a cup of coffee, but if he was going to survive for the next twenty-four hours, he needed to find a place to sleep, eat, bathe, and get decent. But where?

"Excuse me, ma'am," Caleb said to a kindly looking woman carrying bundles of flowers, "can you tell me—" but she looked straight through him and kept walking. Then Caleb spotted a black face over the way. It belonged to a slim mulatto in a tight plaid suit, a bowler hat, and yellow patent-leather shoes. Caleb didn't like the looks of him or his clothes, but he had to start somewhere.

"Excuse me," Caleb said, "can you tell me where I can find a room? And a bath?"

The mulatto turned his pale brown eyes on Caleb in a combination of amusement and calculation. "Well, hello, cousin," he said. "You just hit town?"

"Yes," said Caleb, "and I'm looking for a place to stay for a few days. Is there a hotel here that takes blacks?"

"You got money?"

"Yeah," Caleb said, "I got money, but you're not going to get any of it. I may have just got off a train looking like a goddamned fool in this outfit, but there's no straw in my hair. Do you know where I can get a room or not?"

"Sure, sure," said the mulatto in a different tone of voice. "Go down to that corner. Turn left and walk north about five blocks, then turn right and just keep walking until you start seeing black faces. Ask anybody for the Rosemont Arms. They've got what you need. Tell the man at the desk Roy sent you. If he's got a squinty eye, that'll be Elmore. And don't let him charge you more than two dollars a night. Some tricky people in this city."

"Thanks, Roy," Caleb said. "I'll keep that in mind." He held out his hand. "I'm Caleb." Though a bit surprised, Roy shook it.

When he let go of it, Roy said, "From the calluses on your hand, Caleb, I'd say you were a working man."

"I was," said Caleb, "but no more. Thanks for your help."

"Don't mention it," Roy said. "I be here most days. If you need any more advice or maybe you're looking for a small poker game, just find me here. Roy knows where things are in the city."

"I'll keep that in mind," Caleb said and walked in the direction Roy had indicated.

After Caleb saw the sixth black face in a single block, he asked for the Rosemont Arms and found that it was right across the street. It was a squat, dirty brick building that had once been a family home. Only a tiny sign indicated what it was now. When he got a look at Caleb, Elmore the desk clerk, a short, chunky man with the squint that Roy had described, tried to charge him five dollars a night, offered to keep Caleb's money in the hotel safe, and told him that his cousin Verena had a thing about country boys. Caleb pointed out that Roy had a different view of the room prices, declined the kindly offer to hold his money, and said he'd let Elmore know about Verena. At this, Elmore adopted a businesslike manner, took a week's rent, gave him a key, and told him that the bath was at the end of the hall. Plenty of hot water this time of day.

"Enjoy your stay," he said.

"Oh, I will," Caleb said as he walked up the stairs.

The room was small and dark and could have been cleaner, but Elmore was right about the hot water, and Caleb soaked luxuriously until someone started banging on the door. Then he shaved, got dressed in the best clothes he had, and went back downstairs with most of his money still in his belt and Jardine's pistol in his coat pocket.

"Tell me, Elmore," he asked, "where could a man get a decent meal without goin' broke?"

Elmore considered him admiringly. "Are you sure you're the same man who went upstairs a little while ago?"

"I think so."

Elmore told him where to get a good, cheap meal and then added, "I would not like to criticize your dress, but allow me to point out that that six-shooter in your right-side pocket is not doing a thing for the fit of your jacket. If you're going to carry it, may I suggest a belt holster? I can get you one. Cheap."

"You do that, Elmore," Caleb said. "See you later."

After a good meal in a tiny, smoky, but fairly clean restaurant, Caleb settled back with his second cup of coffee to think about the possibilities. If he were careful, he would have enough money to live for more than six months, but he had no intention of watching his capital dwindle to nothing. After resting up a bit and exploring the big city, Caleb would have to line up some sort of a job and get a regular life. He thought about Drusilla at Three Rivers doing his job and trying to train that fool Caesar. He even thought about Missy, wherever the hell she was. He wouldn't mind finding a job like he had at Three Rivers and a woman like Missy. Not at all.

For the next couple of weeks, Caleb stayed up until all hours, slept late, and learned a little about the black man's life in New York City. There were no visible fences, but Caleb found that whenever he strayed too far from the area around the Rosemont Arms, he met a wall of hard looks and closed faces. He also invariably attracted the attention of a policeman, who would ask, "Are you looking for something?" and just as invariably point him back the direction he had come. It seemed to Caleb that although they didn't have packs of hounds up here in the North, they were just as good at keeping their blacks where they wanted them.

When Caleb became a bit bored, Roy steered him to a poker game over a cigar store, but it took only two hands to convince Caleb that he was out of his league. The first hand was promising, and Caleb dragged in a nice little pot as if this were nature's way. The second hand started out good, too. Caleb watched with admiration as he was dealt three beautiful kings. On the draw, he got two jacks. This did not displease him, either. With a high full house, Caleb was settling in happily to go with the betting, which had suddenly accelerated, when he caught a glance between the dealer and the man on his left, who'd introduced himself as a stranger just in from Philadelphia. There was something about that glance that Caleb didn't like, and when the Philadelphian bumped the bet up to two hundred dollars, Caleb folded his hand and said, "No thanks." He threw in that full house like a man abandoning his only son.

"What!" exclaimed the dealer. "You throwing—" but caught himself before he could reveal that he knew what he had dealt Caleb. Caleb's hand stayed among the discards. On the very next bet, the Philadelphian also lost confidence in his hand and folded, and the hand was won by a pair of tens, queen high on the dealer's right. When the next deal began, Caleb stood up and said, "I'm cashing in."

The dealer stood up, too, and glowered at Caleb. "Are you suggesting—"

"I'm suggesting nothing," Caleb said, pulling the right side of his coat back to reveal his revolver in the little holster that Elmore had sold him. "I'm just cashing in."

"Don't come back," growled the dealer as Caleb left the room.

"No danger of that," said Caleb, closing the door. He walked carefully down the stairs, occasionally glancing back.

The next day, Roy asked Caleb how he'd enjoyed the game.

"Oh, very much," Caleb said. "It reminded me of something they do down where I just came from."

"What's that?" asked Roy.

"Well, when they want to catch an alligator, they go out in a boat, dragging a live chicken on a line behind. When the gator rises to grab the chicken, they shoot the gator."

"You've lost me, cousin," said Roy.

"Well," said Caleb, "last night I felt a whole lot like that chicken. It made me nervous."

"But I heard you won a little," said Roy.

"That's only because for a little while I outswam those gators," Caleb said. "I don't believe I would want to make a career of it."

"I hope you don't think that I—" Roy began.

"Of course, not, Roy. Of course not," said Caleb soothingly.

After two weeks of celibacy, Caleb finally took Elmore up on his suggestion to visit Verena up on the top floor. She turned out to be a slim mulatto girl with no great family resemblance to Elmore, but a great deal of gaiety and a nice little body. Her room was much like Caleb's, but it was lit by a whole lot of candles, and the walls were draped with cheap but colorful scarves. There was a musky smell in the air that Caleb reckoned had to be incense. He had a good time and happily paid the agreed sum. But he resisted booking a return visit and turned down her offer to go on a shopping trip the next day to look at some lovely bracelets.

"Well?" Elmore asked when Caleb next came by the desk. "Did I lie?"

"Oh, no," Caleb said. "You have every reason to be proud of little Verena. Except for that disease she has."

"Disease?" Elmore said indignantly. "I don't know of any—"

"I'm sorry to be the one to tell you, your cousin has one of the worst cases of the *gotta haves* I've ever seen."

"Go on, man," said Elmore. "You're pulling my leg. That girl mighty keen on you."

"And I feel likewise," Caleb said.

After local inquiries for employment turned up only jobs giving out handbills or sweeping the streets, Caleb visited an employment agency on a nearby street. When he told the elderly white proprietor about his experience in Boston and at Three Rivers, the man gave Caleb a card to go see a Mrs. Holroyd over on Park Avenue at Thirty-Third Street, an area he'd never before visited.

Mrs. Holroyd's house was a mansion on a corner. A little brass plaque pointed down a narrow alley to the servants' entrance.

Caleb didn't actually see Mrs. Holroyd. Miss Jenkins, the housekeeper, was called down to interview him in the kitchen. A slim white woman with her hair tightly pulled back from her forehead, she sat at the kitchen table, looking at Caleb with bright, all-seeing eyes.

"Did you have an accident?" she asked.

"Ma'am?"

"That scar on your face. It's most—"

"Oh, yes, ma'am," Caleb said. "An overseer down in Virginia mistook my face for the back end of a horse and hit it with his whip."

"You must have done something." The mental picture that Caleb presented did not please her.

"Well, at that particular moment, ma'am, I fell down and expressed a certain amount of pain."

"No. I mean you must have done something *before* he hit you."

"Yes, ma'am. I failed to get out of his way fast enough. The overseer was suffering from a hangover at the time."

"Are you being facetious?"

"No, ma'am."

"I hope not. Tell me about your experience as a household servant."

Caleb told her the same thing he'd told the man at the employment agency.

Miss Jenkins showed no sign that she'd heard anything Caleb said. "Well," she said, "we're looking for a boy who can do the heavy work in this household. You look strong. Are you?"

"Yes, ma'am."

"You would have to be." She described a job that started at four in the morning, ended at ten in the evening, and seemed to involve endless humping of heavy objects up and down the stairs of the four-story house.

She concluded, "Your pay will be twenty-five dollars a month, and you will have every Sunday afternoon and two evenings a month off. Other than that, you would be expected to be on call. Do you understand what I have said?"

"Yes, ma'am."

"Would you like to see your room?"

"No, ma'am."

"I beg your pardon?" Miss Jenkins's tight little mouth formed a perfect *O* of surprise.

"I wouldn't want to waste your time," Caleb said. "Or mine. To tell you the truth, Miss Jenkins, I recently made considerable personal effort to break out of slavery, and I am not in a hurry to get back into it. The position you offer does not suit me. But thank you for your time, all the same."

"You do realize, don't you," Miss Jenkins asked, "that we are just entering upon a war to free your people?"

"So I understand, ma'am. And if I were still a slave, I'd be very grateful. But since I freed myself, I have to consider your efforts a little bit late."

"You are most ungrateful."

"Yes, ma'am."

Miss Jenkins reached over and pushed a button on the wall. There was a jangling overhead and a few moments later the sound of feet on the stairs. A slim brown man with carefully combed hair came through the door. He was wearing an apron over a white shirt and a neat dark tie. His sleeves were rolled up. He looked at Caleb with apprehension.

"Mr. Purvis," Miss Jenkins said severely, "this boy has been rude and impudent. I want you to thrash him." The apprehension on Purvis's face edged toward alarm.

"Madam?"

"You heard me. We cannot allow these people to come up here, rely upon our good nature and generosity, and then abuse us."

"May I suggest, Mr. Purvis," Caleb said, "that you might want to thrash me outside, rather than risk damage to this very nice kitchen?"

"Don't make it worse on yourself, boy," said Miss Jenkins.

"I won't, ma'am," Caleb said. "Thank you for your time."

"That'll be enough out of you," said Purvis, taking heart. "Let's go!"

"Yes, sir," said Caleb submissively. As they were walking out the back door to a little courtyard totally surrounded by brick walls, Miss Jenkins disappeared upstairs.

"I hope you appreciate my position, son," Purvis said.

"Oh, I do," Caleb said. "Do you think I made a mistake not taking the job Miss Jenkins so kindly offered?"

"Can you do anything else?" Purvis asked in a whisper.

"I think so."

"Then do it."

The two stood just inside the gate leading to the alley to Fifth Avenue. "Well, Mr. Purvis," Caleb said, "I guess you'd better get on with the thrashing. Are you a classic thrasher or sort of creative?"

"Son, strangely enough, that question has never come up before," said Purvis.

"Okay," said Caleb. "Let's do her quick and easy." He shrieked, "Oh, please, sir! Don't! Don't!" Then, with his open hand, he delivered several noisy but harmless blows to his own shoulder and upper arm. "Please!"

Caleb lowered his voice. "Shouldn't you be saying something, Mr. Purvis?"

"Oh, yes," said Purvis. "Thank you." Raising his voice to a rather reedy tremolo, he exclaimed, "Let that be a lesson to you, and don't you ever come back here again."

Caleb opened the gate and closed it again loudly. "Well thrashed, sir," he said to Purvis and held out his hand.

"My pleasure," said Purvis, shaking it.

"One last thing, Mr. Purvis," said Caleb before going through the gate, "I think you should show some signs of having delivered a severe thrashing. Excuse me." He reached out and mussed Purvis's carefully combed hair and pulled his discreet tie out over the front of his apron. "Now you look the perfect thrasher. Do I look thrashed?"

"Not that much, to be honest," said Purvis.

"Oh well. I'll slink away quickly so Miss Jerkins doesn't see me. Good luck, Mr. Purvis."

"You too, son."

— *46* —

After leaving Caleb at the train station, Jardine bought the same newspaper that Caleb did and checked into a hotel. He asked to be woken up at seven that evening, took a bath, and immediately went to bed. Lying there in comfort, Jardine tried to quell his racing mind, and finally fatigue overtook him.

"What!" Jardine, snatched from a bottomless pit of sleep, shouted at the loud knocking on the door.

"It's just gone seven o'clock, sir," came a muffled voice.

"Thanks," said Jardine, getting out of bed regretfully. Within half an hour, he had discovered that there was a train south at nine that night and checked out of the hotel. In another hour and a half, he had eaten the biggest steak he could find in Manhattan, bought some sandwiches and bottles of beer, and was waiting on the platform for the Dixie Special to start his journey home. He wondered what Caleb was doing and whether he'd seen the paper. At least he wouldn't have to worry about him on the return trip.

Jardine felt restless on the first leg of his journey home. At every stop, he bought a newspaper, and the seriousness of the situation became ever more evident. The action at Fort Sumter clearly would slide into war between the slave states and the North. As the train rolled through Pennsylvania headed for Philadelphia,

Jardine looked up from his paper to find a couple of soldiers in new uniforms staring meaningfully at him from across the aisle. He let his eyes flick across them and went back to reading. But his concentration was soon disturbed by muttering, and Jardine looked across the aisle to find them still staring at him. He lowered his newspaper.

"Can I help you gentlemen in any way?" he inquired softly.

"Huh? Whatcha mean?" asked the larger of the two.

"You seemed to be paying such a lot of attention to me," Jardine said. "I thought perhaps you had something to say. Do you?"

"No!" said the larger one. "Why should we?"

"No reason," said Jardine, fixing his eyes on the other one. "How about you?"

"N-no," the other soldier said. "I—"

"Then I suggest that we all mind our own business, and we'll get along just fine." Jardine again raised his newspaper, and the soldiers got off in Philadelphia with no more than ritual grumbling.

As Jardine headed southward, the newspapers presented a different view on the events at Fort Sumter. As the accents softened and deepened, an almost partylike atmosphere prevailed on the trains, and strangers shared their perceptions and analysis of the current situation. The duration of the war was a constant topic. A couple of Yankee commercial travelers trapped on the last train Jardine took huddled nervously until several flasks were produced and declarations of lack of personal enmity were made.

At Great Falls, while waiting for the boat home, Jardine met up with several friends who gave him the local angle on the situation. One said that there had been a small uprising on a remote plantation on Little Lynches River. A few of the boys had put it down without much trouble and with no loss of white life. Jardine also learned that Rafe Bentley was raising a squadron of Kershaw County dragoons and had been asking when he was going to get back.

When Jardine pulled off the turnpike onto the track leading to Three Rivers late the next afternoon, nothing seemed to have changed. He hallooed a work gang in the cotton field, and they hallooed him back. He spotted Big Mose's distinctive tall black hat among them. As Jardine drove up to the house, Drusilla, Caesar, and the house girls were waiting to meet him. Rose held Little Boyd up for his inspection, and Jardine was convinced that the boy had grown. William took the wagon and horses to the barn, and Jardine followed Drusilla up to the porch, where a small table was laid with whiskey, water, and chunks of ice in a covered bowl.

Sitting down, Jardine took a deep drink and listened as Drusilla gave him a short report of happenings at Three Rivers in his absence. Jardine wished he could ask her to sit down, as he used to ask Caleb to do. Drusilla said that Rafe Bentley had been over twice while he was away.

"Thank you, Drusilla," Jardine said. "I suppose there's some hot water?"

"Yes, Massa."

"Well, good. I think I will use a whole lot of it," Jardine said. "I'll have dinner at about the usual time. Why don't you let Caesar wait on me this evening so I can see how he's coming along?"

Drusilla's expression said that she was not keen on this idea, but her mouth said, "Yes, Massa."

Caesar's performance was not as bad as Drusilla had feared. He didn't actually drop anything, but under his nervous hand the dishes and cutlery seemed to have a life of their own. They set up a cacophony of clattering that was hard to ignore. Drusilla hovered in the background, looking as if at any minute she was going to leap in, strangle Caesar, and finish serving dinner herself. Her knuckles were pale from clenching her fists in restraint.

Finally, Jardine thanked Caesar, who was still shaking with nerves and running with sweat, for his sincere efforts and sent him back into the kitchen to collapse. Then he said to Drusilla, "I suppose you are wondering how Caleb made out?"

"I am, Massa."

"Well," said Jardine, "he had a rather difficult trip north. Our transportation system is not yet equipped to accommodate free blacks, and his progress was not without problems. Up in Virginia, some slave catchers got him confused with another feller, but he made it to New York City, all right." Drusilla relaxed visibly. "When I last saw him at the station, Caleb still looked like a scarecrow in a high wind, but he was savoring the glories of freedom. Since I wasn't in New York long myself, I can't report on his further progress, but I think he will be all right."

"Thank you, Massa," Drusilla said. "Where will you have coffee?"

"In my study, I think," said Jardine, "but bring it yourself. I've had enough of young Caesar and his unique style of service for one evening."

When Drusilla brought the coffee, Jardine was looking through the thick stack of newspapers he had collected on the journey from New York City. Jardine looked up. "I don't suppose that you would like a look at these newspapers when I've finished with them," he said.

"Yes, Massa."

"All right, but only on the condition that you are not teaching Caesar to read and write. You're not, are you?"

"No, sir. I've got enough problems teachin' Caesar the difference between left and right just now," said Drusilla.

"That's a relief. Between you and me, Drusilla, some hard times are coming, and we are going to have our hands full without the added menace of a semiliterate Caesar rampaging all over the place. That will be all."

"Thank you, Massa."

Jardine sat long into the night poring over the newspapers and trying to look into the future. He couldn't even see past the next day.

The next morning, Jardine rode over to Bellevue and found Bentley and half a dozen neighbors talking war. To hear them tell it, Kershaw County was the key to defending the South from the coming Yankee invasion.

"About time you got back," Bentley greeted him as Jardine tied up his bay. "We were beginning to wonder whether you hadn't turned your coat and decided to stay north. What kept you so long?"

Luke Bradford, a transplanted Yankee who had come south as a boy fifteen years before, asked, "For that matter, what were you doing up there at a time like this? You were lucky to get back."

"I had a delivery to make," said Jardine.

"Yes," said Bentley, "I noticed when I rode over to your place to try to root you out that your man Caleb seemed to be missing. I nearly got the hounds out."

"Is he really free in New York City?" asked another neighbor.

"He really is," Jardine said. "Next time you see him will probably be on the delivering end of a Yankee bayonet. There was a piece in one of the Yankee papers suggesting raising some nigger regiments."

"I'm looking forward to that," said Bradford.

"Maybe we ought to do the same," suggested Bentley. "Our niggers could shoot their niggers, and we could stay home in bed."

"You arm your darkies if you want to," said a farmer from downriver. "I'll sleep easier if mine stick to their hoes and mattocks. Those sharp implements make me nervous enough as it is."

"Too bad you didn't get back sooner, Boyd," Bentley said. "Staffing of the squadron is just about complete. I'm the major, of course, but I'm afraid all I've got left to offer you is either assistant bugler or pastry cook. How are your doughnuts?"

"Lethal at ten yards," said Jardine.

"You're hired," said Bentley.

But after lunch, when the others were smoking cigars and drinking brandy, Bentley took Jardine off to the side.

"Damn you, Boyd, you've caused me no end of staffing problems. I had you down for my executive officer, but that fool Calhoun, being the richest man in the county, had to have it. That clown has never buckled on a sword."

"Neither have I, Rafe," Jardine said, "except on a parade ground at the Citadel."

"Yes, maybe," Bentley said, "but at least you know which end of a sword to hold and can manage to stay in the saddle."

"He'll come along," Jardine said. "And besides, he looks good. Is that one of the new uniforms he's buying?"

"The executive version," Bentley said. "The rank and file will be wearing something less gaudy. I managed to talk him out of capes and plumed hats."

"What about umbrellas?"

"Damned near bought them, too," Rafe said. "But damn it, Boyd, I'm serious. All the captaincies have gone, too. If these fools had their way, they'd *all* be captains. All I've got left for you is a lieutenancy as commander of a troop. Will that do you?"

"That'll do me," Jardine said. "Can I pick my own NCOs?"

"Sure," said Bentley, "and look on the bright side. Most of these brass-mad fools will get themselves killed in training, not to mention in battle. You'll soon be up there where you belong."

"That gives me something to look forward to," Jardine said. "The imminent demise of my friends and neighbors."

"You know what I mean."

"I know what you mean, Rafe. But I'll be the happiest lieutenant in your squadron."

Before the meeting broke up, they all agreed that recruiting would start immediately, with training beginning in a month. Each would arrange management of his plantation so that he could fully devote himself to the dragoons. There was no telling when they'd be called up to fight the Yankees. Nobody voiced any doubt that they would be.

All the way back to Three Rivers, Jardine pondered what to do about the plantation. Little Boyd was no problem. He could go to one of Jardine's cousins inland from Charleston. That ought to be safe enough. But what about Three Rivers? Could Drusilla and Big Mose manage it without an overseer? What would happen if the fighting came as far south as Kershaw County and he was serving elsewhere? Jardine realized that in a war, one could not always defend his own little patch of ground.

At Three Rivers, Jardine retreated to his study and did some more serious thinking aided by a bottle of brandy. He found himself wishing that Caleb were there. Not that he would have the answer, but at least he would be someone to talk to. Damn free blacks, anyway. What the hell was freedom when the future of Three Rivers was at stake?

— *47* —

Caleb kept looking for work, but nothing tempted him enough to leave the comfortable life at the Rosemont Arms and the little community around it. There was too much to look at in New York City to ever see it all. Caleb even figured out a way to gain entrance to every part of the city. He wrapped a small box carefully and neatly wrote on a label the name "Mr. Boyd Jardine" and an address in the area he wanted to see. This invariably got him through the legion of policemen, doormen, and other uniformed functionaries who seemed to have no other purpose in life but to keep him within half a mile of the Rosemont Arms. As an extra touch, Caleb neatly penciled "By Hand" on the package. Sometimes Caleb would even seek out a policeman and thrust the package before his eyes with a suppliant "Suh?" Invariably, the officer would point an imperious arm in the right direction. To get back home, Caleb would readdress the package to a location not far from the Rosemont. And he always carried, safe in an inner pocket, his freedom paper from Jardine. He'd heard of gangs of slave catchers working the city streets.

In this way, Caleb saw much of New York City. In his travels, he began to notice soldiers parading on the streets in the days and weeks after the surrender of Fort Sumter. In all parts of town, local militia and new units of volunteers blossomed with banners, drums, and brand-new uniforms, usually flourishing antiquated weapons. The Chelsea Volunteers, the Hunter College Dragoons, the Lexington Heights Zouaves, with their colorful, Arabian-looking uniforms, all flaunted their willingness to march south and conquer the stronghold of King Cotton.

Caleb had plenty of time to follow the progress of the war in the papers he read every day. He looked eagerly for mention of South Carolina, but saw none after the confrontation at Fort Sumter that started the whole thing. The battles started small, with relatively few casualties, but then in July at a place in Virginia called Bull Run came a major collision of the blue and the gray that resulted in over 4,800 casualties. Close to two-thirds of them were Union troops. It was the North's greatest defeat of the war thus far. This was followed by battles at Hatteras Inlet, Ball's Bluff, and Belmont, which resulted in the loss of more young lives but didn't lead to a resolution. Lincoln juggled his generals, but failed to get the knockout punch he was looking for. The best thing you could call the war so far was a stalemate.

Restless and rootless, Caleb—his money dwindling—took a job as a stevedore unloading ships all night at docks on the Hudson River. This eased his financial situation and at the same time kept him off the streets, which were becoming even more unfriendly to a black face. Some New Yorkers who had lost loved ones in the war didn't hesitate to blame the blacks. Several blacks were attacked by drunken groups of young men and boys. New York didn't seem so safe to Caleb anymore, so he worked all night, slept all day, and was very careful in the evenings and on the weekends when he left the area around the Rosemont.

The remainder of 1861 passed seamlessly for Caleb. His work at the docks helped him grow stronger every day, but he had little use for his strength.

The new year started much the same, but then one Saturday near Washington Square, Caleb saw something he'd never seen before: a black man in an army uniform.

He was only a private, not very big and wearing a new blue uniform that did not fit, but he was definitely black, and the spectacle stopped Caleb cold.

"What are you looking at?" demanded the object of his attention.

"You," said Caleb. "What are you supposed to be?"

"I'm not supposed to be anything," the soldier said indignantly. "I *am* something. I'm a private in the Thirty-Ninth New York Black Volunteer Infantry. We're quartered in that armory down there." He pointed in the direction of a huge, grimy dark-brick building that looked like a medieval fortress.

"Tell me something, Mr. Private," Caleb asked, "do army rules allow you to drink beer?"

"Is it Saturday? Yep, especially on Saturdays."

"And is there any place near here that would sell a black man and his soldier friend a beer?"

"I think I can take you to one," said the soldier.

The private, who turned out to be called Henry Todd, told Caleb that even before the war was very old, there had been talk that free blacks ought to play a part in liberating their subjugated brethren. Although there was some uneasiness about putting weapons in the hands of blacks, Negro units had tentatively begun to be recruited. Henry, who had previously held a position much like that offered to him by Miss Jenkins, although in a humbler establishment, was one of the first in Manhattan to step forward.

"They even gave us these uniforms," Henry said once they were seated in a dungeonlike cellar room at a long wooden table. He wiped beer from his lips with a blue sleeve. "Of course, our rifles right now are old, but we're going to get new ones soon. And they're talkin' about teaching the illiterate to read and write."

"But you read, of course," said Caleb.

"And write," said Henry, taking another swallow of beer. "*And* cipher. Two and two is four."

"So I have heard," said Caleb.

"You know," said Henry to his new friend, "you ought to think about joining up. You're a big fella, not like most of us. You can see for yourself the uniform. The food's okay, and the pay's not bad for what you do." He leaned confidentially toward Caleb. "Tell you God's honest truth, Caleb, we don't do much."

"I'll think about it," said Caleb.

When they parted a couple of beers later, Todd suggested casually, "If you do sign up, mention my name. They know me in that office and it won't hurt your chances." And he told Caleb about the five-dollar bounty he would receive for recruiting Caleb.

"You can count on it," said Caleb.

After another couple of days of thinking it over, Caleb walked down to the armory Henry had pointed out. The white sentry looked at him.

"What do you want, Sambo?"

Caleb ignored the insult. "Fellow named Henry told me you were looking for black soldiers."

"You're no soldier," sneered the sentry.

"I might be," said Caleb.

Reluctantly, the sentry allowed Caleb through the gate and pointed him toward an orderly room just off the brick parade ground that made up the core of the armory. On the parade ground, white noncommissioned officers were drilling platoons of black soldiers. Shrill voices and the stamping of heavy boots echoed in the vast space.

In the orderly room, another white soldier told Caleb to sit down, pointing at a rough wooden chair near the window. Caleb sat and thought about the army's welcoming manner until a portly middle-aged man with three stripes on his blue sleeve came into the office, brushing crumbs from his impressive mustache.

"Sarge," said the soldier, "this fella says he wants to sign up."

The sergeant looked at Caleb with flat, appraising eyes.

"Papers?" he demanded.

"What kind of papers, sir?" Caleb asked.

"What kind of papers have you got?" the sergeant asked. "You can't sign up without papers."

"I've got a paper saying that I bought my freedom," Caleb said. "Will that do?"

"Let's see it."

Caleb brought the precious document from its hiding place. The sergeant snatched it from his hand, whirled, and started walking into an inner office. But before he could get to the door, Caleb was in front of him blocking it.

"What do you want?" the sergeant demanded, looking up into Caleb's determined face.

"Sergeant," Caleb said quietly, "where that paper goes, I go. I don't let it out of my sight."

The sergeant tried to force Caleb out of his way but lacked the weight necessary. Caleb did not budge.

"Damn your black—" the sergeant exclaimed, backing off and raising a fist. When Caleb neither flinched nor moved, he lowered his arm and said over his shoulder, "Private, call the guard."

"What seems to be the problem here, Sergeant?" asked a calm voice.

Caleb and the sergeant looked toward an officer just coming in from the parade ground. He was slim and soldierly, with a long mustache that curved on each side and an empty right coat sleeve neatly pinned up to the elbow.

"Major, this recruit is making difficulties," said the sergeant. "He won't—"

"I'm not a recruit yet, sir," said Caleb. "And that piece of paper is precious. I don't know where the sergeant was going with it, but if I lost it—"

The major looked Caleb over carefully, from his scarred face to the firm set of his feet on the rough planked floor. He listened to the Boston inflection in his voice. After a moment, he extended a hand. "I'll take care of this matter, Sergeant Garrison."

Garrison reluctantly surrendered the paper, raked Caleb with a look that had more promise than threat in it, and marched stiffly into an inner room.

"I'm Major Rogers," the officer told Caleb, extending his left hand. "If you will come with me"—Rogers looked at Caleb's paper—"Mr. Rivers. We can have a talk in private." He led Caleb through a maze of dark hallways and finally into a room with a barred window looking out over the parade ground. The commands of the drill sergeants were just audible. "Won't you have a seat," Rogers said, directing Caleb to one of a pair of chairs on either side of a small, round table. When Caleb was settled, the major seated himself and shouted for an orderly.

Major Rogers ordered two coffees from a white soldier and then turned to Caleb. "So, you want to be a soldier, Mr. Rivers?"

"Not very much, to be honest, sir," said Caleb. "But there doesn't seem to be much worth doing for a free black man in this city. I have to do something other than unload cargo ships all night."

"Don't you want to get revenge on those rebels who enslaved you?" the major asked.

"I was first a slave up in Boston," Caleb pointed out. "They call it indentured servitude there, but it adds up to the same thing. Down south, they just carried on the good work. I was freed in the South."

"So I see," said Rogers, surveying Caleb's precious paper. "I also see that you paid Mr. Jardine the impressive sum of five hundred and fifty dollars for your freedom. Do you mind if I ask how a slave accumulated that amount of money?"

"No," Caleb said. He told the major briefly about the summer he'd spent prizefighting in the boxing shows and fairs of Kershaw County. He didn't mention the poker game with Jardine.

"Most impressive," said the major with a smile once Caleb had finished. "Did you always win?"

"More than I lost," Caleb said modestly, "but it wasn't the prize money that counted, but the side bets made by Mr. Jardine."

"Mr. Jardine sounds like he was an excellent owner," said the major.

"He improved as he went along," said Caleb.

The orderly brought the coffee, and Major Rogers drank his in a quick gulp. "I've got to inspect the troops very soon, so time is short. Let's get down to business."

"All right," said Caleb a bit warily.

"My job," continued Rogers, "is to build one of the army's first-ever combat-ready black units to fight this war. A lot depends on my success. So far, I'm not setting the world on fire. These New Yorkers, frankly, are not impressive. For a start, most of them stand about five foot nothing and weigh even less. And there's not a whole lot of fighting spirit here that I've noticed." The major slammed his palm down on the little table, jolting the coffee cups. "No, Mr. Rivers, I need young men like you to build a fighting unit to be proud of."

He gestured toward his empty sleeve. "I'm not a whole lot of good as a fighter myself. I left this at Buena Vista. And I was right-handed, too," he added ruefully. "But that doesn't mean that I can't build an outfit able to disprove the general opinion that free blacks can't or won't fight. Do you see my problem?"

"Yes, sir," said Caleb.

"From what you tell me, it sounds like you can fight. Can you ride?"

"Some."

"Shoot?"

"Some."

"It's a long gamble," Rogers said, "but have you had any experience with a saber?"

"Some," said Caleb.

"By God," said the major, pounding the table again, "I've got to have you, Mr. Rivers. What will convince you?"

"I don't rightly know, sir," said Caleb. He knew that once he signed up, he belonged to them. He feared that the army might be a bit like slavery. "How long would I have to sign up for?"

"We're looking for three-year volunteers, but Lord only knows how long this damned war will last. Personally, I had a very snug little job out in Ohio when this blew up, but I doubt that I'll ever get back to it." He paused and looked at Caleb. "Damn, I'd conscript you if I could, but instead I have to convince you. I'll tell you one thing, Mr. Rivers, if you sign up, you won't need this anymore." He waved Caleb's paper at him.

"I have to keep it," Caleb said hurriedly.

"Of course you do," Rogers said. "If I were you, I'd have it framed. But you won't *need* it." He reached awkwardly into the inside pocket of his many-buttoned jacket, delved into a wallet, and then threw a small printed card onto the table between them. "That's my army identification card. Once you have one of *these*, nobody in this man's world is going to question your free status again. It would take a very brave and foolish slave catcher to even look cross-eyed at you once he saw one of these."

Caleb looked at the card and thought that the major was probably right.

"I can't make any guarantees," Rogers said hastily, "but from what I've seen of you, you're going to make a splendid soldier, and if there is anything I—and the Union army—need right now, it's more of them. You'll train right here until the unit is fully formed, and then you could go anywhere and do anything. Hell," Rogers laughed, "once you learn to read and write you might even become a sergeant."

"I can read and write," Caleb said, trying not to sound boastful.

"Can you, by damn?" Rogers looked at Caleb as if he'd found a diamond in his breakfast oats. "Can you? Then you *have* to join up. Damn it, Mr. Rivers, your country needs you. And if that doesn't get you, do it for your own benefit. I don't think there's a chance in hell that the rebs can beat us, but where do you think you would be if they did?"

"Back on the plantation," Caleb said.

"The odds are strong," said the major. "What do you say?"

Caleb ran everything through his head and made a decision. "I'll do it, sir." He held out his hand.

The major clasped it awkwardly. His grip was unusually strong. "Done!" he said. "You won't regret it, Mr. Rivers. I swear it."

Just then, a corporal knocked on the door frame and stepped into the office. "Formation, sir," he said.

"I'm on my way," Rogers said.

Rogers and Caleb got up. "I'll walk you to the orderly room on my way to inspect those rascals," said Rogers. "When can you report?"

"Next Monday morning?" Caleb said.

"Fine. Bright and early," Rogers said as they walked. "Treat yourself to a good breakfast somewhere. The food here is appalling." He caught himself. "I didn't tell you about that, did I?" He laughed. "Well, you have to remember, I *am* recruiting. You don't cook, by the way, do you?"

"Some," said Caleb, "but I don't plan to."

"I don't blame you. Filthy job. I suppose that's why the food is so bad."

At the orderly room, Rogers led Caleb to Garrison's tiny office, where the sergeant was struggling with a stack of paperwork. Garrison jumped to attention.

"At ease," Rogers said easily. "Sergeant Garrison, this man has agreed to enlist for three years. He will report ready for duty next Monday morning. He will be assigned to C Company under Sergeant Henkins. I've checked his paperwork, and all is perfectly in order. Do you have any questions?"

Garrison looked at Caleb and then at the major. "No, sir," he said.

"I'll leave him in your capable hands then," Rogers said. The blare of a bugle split the air outside. "I hear someone calling me." He offered his hand to Caleb again. "Good luck."

"Thank you, sir," said Caleb.

When Rogers was gone, the sergeant glared at Caleb. "So, you've *agreed* to join us, have you?"

"I'm joining," said Caleb shortly.

"And we're damned grateful," the sergeant said.

Caleb did not answer. His expression was calm and unchallenging.

Breaking off his penetrating stare, Garrison pushed the stack of paperwork to one side and took out a blank form. "Well, you'd better sit down then," he said. "Name?"

"Caleb."

"Family name?"

Though it should not have, the question once again caught Caleb by surprise. He hesitated for a moment.

"Come on," said Garrison. "I haven't got all morning. The war will be over if we don't get a move on."

Caleb made up his mind.

"Jardine," he said. "Caleb Jardine."

— *48* —

Boyd Jardine had selected his NCOs and nearly recruited all of his troops when, after a few days away in Camden, he returned to Three Rivers with someone sitting beside him in the gig. The visitor was a tall, lean man with a full, biblical beard. He walked with a pronounced limp, but his broad shoulders suggested strength, and his dark, penetrating eyes revealed determination. The two men toured most of the plantation during the morning, and after lunch, Jardine called Drusilla and Big Mose into his study, where he and his visitor were drinking whiskey.

"This," Jardine told his two most-trusted slaves, "is Captain Plunkett. He has come to Three Rivers with a view to acting as my overseer while I am away serving the Confederacy. I'll likely be at home for some time to come, but my duties with the county dragoons will increasingly take up my time. Captain Plunkett, this is Drusilla, who runs the house, and this is Big Mose, my chief field hand. He—"

"We know Captain Plunkett, Massa." Drusilla spoke determinedly with her eyes fixed on the visitor. "At least we know what people say about him. And we don't like what we hear."

"Why, you black bitch—" Plunkett started from his chair, but Jardine cut him off.

"Are you aware, Drusilla," Jardine asked calmly but icily, "that you are speaking disrespectfully of a white man and a guest at Three Rivers?"

"I am, Massa," Drusilla said, meeting his gaze. "May I speak directly?"

"Go ahead."

"If Captain Plunkett comes to Three Rivers, I will not work in this house. I will return to the fields or ask to be sold."

At this, Plunkett jumped from his chair and advanced menacingly on Drusilla with his fist raised, but she did not flinch. Before Plunkett could reach her, Big Mose moved to put his impressive bulk between them. His mild eyes were on Plunkett's face.

But he spoke to Jardine. "Massa," he said, "I feels the same. No disrespect to you, suh, but Captain Plunkett comes to Three Rivers, I can't work for him."

"I can see, Jardine," Captain Plunkett said, getting control of himself, "that there's a big job to be done here."

"Thank you, Captain Plunkett," Jardine said coolly, but he addressed Drusilla. "I assume that you have been discussing this with the people?"

"Yes, Massa," she said firmly, "we have."

"And can you tell me the basis of your objections to Captain Plunkett?"

"Yes," she said. "Captain Plunkett is known in the county as a slave beater and a slave murderer. And we know it is true."

"See here!" Captain Plunkett exclaimed. "I won't have some goddamned slave wench blackening my name." He would have struck her, but Big Mose remained steadfastly in his way.

"I beg your pardon, Captain," Jardine said, "for the rudeness of my people. If you will finish your whiskey, I'll drive you to the landing to catch the next boat. I am sorry to have wasted your time."

The men rode to the landing in stony silence, and Jardine's mood was not much improved on his return. He disappeared into his study and was not seen again until dinner. He ate in silence, waited on by Drusilla and Caesar. When Caesar had gone to the kitchen with a tray load of dishes, Jardine said to Drusilla, "Tell Caesar that he will not be needed anymore today, and bring two coffees to my study."

When Drusilla came into the study with a tray, Jardine told her to sit down in the chair where Caleb used to sit. Drusilla sat down uneasily and ignored the second cup of coffee. After a long silence during which he lit a cigar, Jardine said, "Might as well drink that cup of coffee, Drusilla. That's what it is for." As she sipped warily, he continued, "Don't think that I underestimate what you did today. Though it angered me, I recognize that it took real courage. Mose wouldn't have done it without your lead, and I don't believe that Caleb would have done it, either. Not that he lacked the courage, but it just wasn't his style. You are a remarkable woman, Drusilla."

When she did not respond, Jardine went on. "But now that you have chased Captain Plunkett away—oh, don't deny it," Jardine said when Drusilla opened her mouth to protest. "You did it as surely as if you had chased him down to the turnpike with a broom. At this very moment he is probably telling all of Camden what a lily-livered slavelover I am and how you rule me with a combination of womanly wiles and obeah. Thanks to you and Mose, my reputation in this county is about shot."

When Drusilla again said nothing, Jardine asked, "Aren't you even going to deny it?"

"No, sir," Drusilla said. "But even white people know what that man is."

"Yes, they probably do," Jardine admitted. "I must admit that he does not come without reputation. But damn it, Drusilla, I'm on call from week to week. This time next month, I could be in the field with my troop, far from Three Rivers. Do you really think that you and Mose can run this place without me?"

"Yes, Massa," Drusilla said.

"Well, Drusilla," Jardine said, "that's not very flattering, but my ego is not the important thing here. You read all those newspapers I gave you?"

"Yes, sir."

"Then you know that the Yankees are serious about bringing us back into the Union. Unlike some of our neighbors, I don't underestimate their chances. The North is very powerful. If they win this war, you and all of the rest of the people on this farm will probably be freed. The Yankees, most of them, anyway, probably don't want to do it, but events seem to have got ahead of common sense. And, in the meantime, this place has to be held together or none of us will have a home once the war is over. Do you understand?"

"Yes, Massa."

"Well, you're one up on me then, but I won't try to bring in another white overseer. I've always had my own doubts about the species, and I'll have to trust you and Mose. But mostly you, Drusilla. Are you aware that you will probably be the only black woman in charge of a plantation in this county, if not the entire South?"

"Yes, Massa."

"And you're not worried?"

"Yes, Massa," Drusilla admitted. "I am. But we can do it."

— *49* —

Dressed in his best and freed of the dead weight of the revolver, but not of the reassuring presence of his money belt, Caleb said good-bye to Elmore at seven o'clock on Monday morning. Then, mindful of the major's advice, he ate the best steak he could find at that hour and headed for the West Side Armory. Everything he owned was in the worn carpetbag. He was sitting in the outer office when Sergeant Garrison passed by him on his way to the orderly room, picking his teeth.

"You," said Garrison without halting.

Caleb didn't say anything. He'd already learned at this early stage in his army career that the less you said, the better.

He was still waiting half an hour later when a small, worried-looking private came out of the orderly room and said, "Sarge wants you." Caleb followed him in.

Garrison did not look up. "That precious paper of yours," he said, holding out his hand. Caleb gave him a true copy of the paper he'd had made the week before. Garrison got up and ostentatiously walked out of the office with the paper. Caleb just stood there.

When he came back into the office, Garrison said, "This is not the original."

"No, sir."

Garrison looked at him for a long moment and then sat down, pulled a form out of a desk drawer, and silently began writing. In a few moments, he stopped, turned the paper around, handed Caleb a dipped pen, and said, "Put your mark there at the bottom." He pointed at the spot with a tobacco-stained finger.

Caleb took the pen. "I believe, sir," he said, "that there is a five-dollar bounty for the soldier who recommended that I enlist."

"So?"

"I'd like to be sure that he gets the money," Caleb said.

"I'll take care of that." Garrison jabbed the form with his finger. "Make your mark."

"His name is Private Henry Todd," said Caleb.

"I'll fill it in later."

"I believe that's T-o-d-d," said Caleb.

"I know how to spell his goddamned name, Private," Garrison bellowed. When Caleb again did not respond, Garrison shifted his finger up to another part of the form.

"Okay, if you want Todd to get the money, *you* write his name."

Caleb quickly found the blank line and printed "Henry Todd." He then signed "Caleb Jardine" at the bottom of the form, as he had practiced the night before, handed Garrison the pen, and sat back.

Garrison didn't waste any time being astonished that Caleb could write. Neither was he pleased. "Orderly!" he shouted and, grabbing a piece of paper, scrawled a note. When the panting orderly arrived, he said, "Take him to Sergeant Henkins, C Company, and give the sergeant this."

"Yes, Sarge," said the orderly. "Follow me," he added to Caleb. Caleb could feel Garrison's eyes on his back as they left the office.

"You didn't make any friend there," the orderly said to Caleb as they walked across the parade ground.

Sergeant Henkins, a white-haired old man who had been yanked out of happy retirement by the declaration of war, looked at Garrison's note and then at Caleb.

"You're late," he said simply. "You've missed breakfast."

"Yes, sir," said Caleb.

Initially, Henkins had planned to follow Garrison's advice to make Caleb's life miserable, but in practice this turned out to be hard to do. Aside from looming over most of the rest of the recruits like a cypress tree in a swamp and being in superb physical condition, Caleb followed orders, learned quickly, seldom spoke unless spoken to, and showed all the signs of becoming an excellent soldier. However, one morning Garrison was watching C Company drill. He'd dropped a reminder in Henkins's ear at the sergeant's mess the night before, and Henkins thought he had better put on a show.

"Jardine!" his old voice shouted.

"Sir!"

"Fall out!"

Caleb stepped out of ranks.

"Give Jardine a rifle." McMann, his fat, lazy corporal, went to the rack, selected one of the heavy old muskets used for training, and thrust it into Caleb's arms.

"Port arms," Henkins commanded, and Caleb brought the ancient weapon up, its muzzle at the height of his left shoulder, its butt at his right hip. "Forward march!" Caleb began moving. "Double time, march!" Just before Caleb ran into the high black-stained brick wall, Henkins shouted, "Column left!" and Caleb found himself running all by himself just inside the wall while Henkins stood in the middle of the parade ground shouting orders. The rest of the training units watched, feeling very grateful that they weren't Caleb.

For five, ten, fifteen minutes, Caleb ran mindlessly. The musket was beginning to weigh seriously on his arms, but other than that he felt very little pain. To pass the time, he imagined that he was ahead of a pack of Kershaw County hounds, running for his life. Caleb could see out of the corner of his eye that Garrison was enjoying the spectacle and made up his mind that he would not give the sergeant the satisfaction of seeing him stop running before the order came.

There's no way of telling how long Henkins would have made Caleb run if he hadn't looked up and seen Major Rogers watching from his window. Then Henkins recalled that Rogers, the battalion's executive officer, had made it clear that he would be keeping a close personal watch on Caleb's training and progress. The next time that Caleb came around, Henkins halted him, relieved him of the rifle, and ordered him to fall back in ranks.

"What was that all about?" whispered Hellewell, a scrawny recruit from Pennsylvania.

"You tell me," said Caleb.

"Silence in the ranks!" ordered Henkins and went back to drilling his company.

About a month after Caleb enlisted, things started looking up. The company was coming to the end of basic training, and Henkins had the men out drilling as usual when a brawny cavalry sergeant came striding onto the parade ground carrying a pair of blunt-edged training sabers. Henkins turned the company over to the visitor, who faced the trainees.

"My name is Sergeant Blanchard," he told them, speaking slowly as though to a group of foreigners. He held the sabers at arm's length. "Does anyone know what these are?"

No one answered.

"Are you deaf?" he roared.

"No, sir," came the ragged response. Blanchard surveyed them with disgust. His eye caught on Caleb.

"You—Big Boy," he shouted, pointing a saber at Caleb. "Do *you* know what this is?"

"Yes, sir," said Caleb. "It's a saber."

"Now we're getting somewhere," said Blanchard sarcastically. "In fact, it *was* a forty-two-inch scimitar type known popularly as a 'wrist breaker.' That's why we cut it down to thirty-six inches. Get your black butt out here." A sigh of relief went up from the other recruits.

Caleb stepped out of ranks and approached the sergeant, who looked him up and down.

"What's your name, boy?"

"Jardine, sir. Caleb Jardine."

Caleb had at least two inches on the sergeant. "Big as you are, Jardine," Blanchard said, "you might be excused for mistaking this for a razor." The recruits laughed, as they were expected to. Suddenly, Blanchard threw one of the blunt training sabers at Caleb, who caught it by the hilt.

Without a pause, Blanchard followed up with a broad stroke that Caleb parried noisily with the side of his blade. Instead of waiting for the sergeant's next move, Caleb let the force of Blanchard's thrust spin him halfway around and took advantage of the momentum to launch a chopping blow that caught Blanchard's saber solidly just above the hilt. The sound of steel on steel rang out over the parade ground. Blanchard clutched his right hand in his left and waited for the pain to subside. Caleb stood at the alert.

The recruits held their breath as they waited for Blanchard's reaction. Instead of exploding, he looked at Caleb and said, "Now that you've got that out of your system, why don't we show these boys what a saber is for."

For fifteen minutes, he and Caleb showed the recruits the variety of thrusts, blows, blocks, and parries available to the skilled *sabreur*. Finally, both running with sweat, they stopped, and

Blanchard told the recruits, "Though it can be used on foot, the saber is essentially meant to be employed on horseback."

Raising two fingers to his mouth, he gave a shrill whistle. There was a whistle in response, and a corporal of cavalry came galloping onto the parade ground leading a big bay. He dismounted and handed the reins of the second horse to Blanchard.

Pointing with his saber at Caleb, the sergeant said, "Pritchard, lend your mount to this recruit." Though clearly not happy, the corporal obeyed. Without even inquiring whether Caleb could ride, Blanchard swung aboard the big bay and rode thirty yards to the front left of the formation. Caleb mounted and rode thirty yards in the opposite direction. Then he wheeled the dappled gray around so he was facing Blanchard. The saber was in his right hand, its blade vertical and resting lightly on his right shoulder.

Holding his saber high overhead, Blanchard bellowed at the recruits, "Your friend Private Jardine and I will now demonstrate some of the basic equestrian tactics with the saber. Since I am a sergeant in the United States Army, for the purposes of this demonstration, Jardine will represent the rebel cavalry. He looks pretty fierce, does he not?" The recruits laughed. "However, do not expect him to win this engagement. Johnny Reb never wins." Extending his arm and saber fully toward Caleb, Blanchard spurred his horse into a trot. So did Caleb.

"On this first pass," shouted Blanchard, "I shall thrust, and Private Jardine will parry my thrust." He spurred the bay into a canter. Caleb did the same. As the two horsemen converged, Blanchard hit the bay hard with his spurs, causing it to cannon toward Caleb. At the same time he thrust the blunt saber directly at Caleb's chest.

Patiently, Caleb maneuvered the gray at a slight angle from the charge of the bay and waited for the thrust, his saber close to and across his body, right to left. His eyes never left Blanchard's face. At the last moment, Caleb spurred the gray, meeting the bay's charge shoulder to shoulder and checking Blanchard's progress. Leaning to the left, he let the sergeant's saber pass his body and then immediately swept his own saber across his body and tied up Blanchard's sword arm. The two horsemen remained locked like this for perhaps twenty seconds, a tableau of frustrated energy. Blanchard struggled—he hoped not too obviously—to free his sword arm but could not. Finally, he relaxed and so did Caleb. The two horses danced apart with a clatter of metal and a groan of leather.

"You see," Blanchard told the recruits. "Jardine managed to successfully parry my thrust and tie me up long enough for an infantryman to shoot us both. There is a lesson in that. The cavalry saber is a shock weapon. Once the horseman loses forward momentum, its value is greatly decreased."

The recruits—and Sergeant Henkins—tried to look as though they understood this.

"And now," Blanchard shouted, spurring his horse, "we will reverse that last exercise. Jardine will thrust, and I will parry." The two again rode thirty yards in opposite directions and wheeled to face each other. "In your own time, recruit," Blanchard shouted.

Caleb patted the neck of the nervous gray and imitated the horse-settling noise he had often heard Jardine make. He gathered the gray under him as Blanchard waited impatiently. Then, wishing that he were wearing spurs, Caleb used his heavy army boots to viciously jolt the gray in the ribs on both sides. The shocked horse rocketed toward Blanchard, eyes flaring and tail streaming straight out. Caught sitting back in the saddle, Blanchard barely had time to raise his saber halfway before Caleb's blade knocked it aside and passed between the sergeant's left arm and body. As Caleb's shoulder hit his chest, Blanchard rocked back in the saddle, and for a minute it looked as though he would fall to the dusty brick parade ground.

Finally, Caleb reined back, and Blanchard regained his balance. The two horses backed off. "As the result of that charge, gentlemen," Blanchard told the recruits with a forced smile, "I am officially what we in the cavalry call *dead*. Your friend Jardine has killed me. You see what I meant when I said that the cavalry saber is a shock weapon. That marks the end of today's demonstration. They're all yours, Sergeant—except Private Jardine."

Henkins marched the dazed troops away, and the corporal rushed up to see what damage had been done to his horse.

Blanchard whirled around. "What the hell do you think you were doing?"

"Shock tactics, sir," said Caleb.

"You could have killed me," Blanchard said.

"Yes, sir," Caleb said, "if I'd wanted to."

"Get off that horse," Blanchard ordered.

"Yes, sir," Caleb said, dismounting easily and giving the gray a pat on the neck by way of apology. The corporal grabbed the reins from Caleb's hand and for a moment considered throwing a punch at him. Once he took in the size of the recruit, however, the urge passed quickly.

Blanchard also dismounted and threw the reins of the bay to Pritchard. "Cool 'em off and rub them down and see if this madman has done any harm to Ben," he told the corporal. He turned to Caleb. "You, follow me."

Caleb followed the sergeant's broad back into the castlelike headquarters and through the gloomy corridors to Major Rogers's outer office. Rogers's orderly looked up at Blanchard affably.

"I want to see the major," Blanchard told him.

"I'll see if he's in," said the orderly.

"I know damn well he's in," Blanchard said.

"I'll see if he is in to *you*," said the orderly.

In a minute, the orderly was back. "The major will see you now," he told Blanchard.

"You sit down," Blanchard told Caleb.

"The major will see you *both* now," the orderly told him. "His orders."

Without another glance at Caleb, Blanchard marched stiffly into Rogers's office and saluted with an unnecessarily forceful stamp of his right boot.

Rogers returned his salute. "At ease, Sergeant. What can I do for you?" Caleb remained at attention. He might as well not have been there.

"Sir," Blanchard began, "this man—"

"I know, Sergeant," the major interrupted. "I saw it all."

"Then you know, sir, that this recruit disrupted a demonstration of equestrian saber techniques, abused a US Army horse, endangered my life as well as his own, and violated army discipline," said Blanchard.

"That's about what it looked like to me, too," Rogers said easily. "He also deeply embarrassed a noncommissioned officer of the US Army in the course of his official duty." Rogers swiveled toward Caleb. "What do you have to say for yourself, Recruit Jardine?"

"Nothing, sir," Caleb said.

"Well, then," Rogers said. "It looks like an open and shut case to me. What would you like me to do with this man?"

"I want you to give him to me, sir," Blanchard said. "We're forming the first unit of black cavalry, and I need men who can ride and fight. I don't have time to turn your webfeet into horse soldiers. I reckon this one"—he nodded toward Caleb—"is crazy, but then you have to be crazy to be in the cavalry anyway. I think I can tame him."

"I don't know, Sergeant," Rogers said as if Caleb weren't there, "I had plans for Recruit Jardine myself. When his draft finishes training, I was thinking of keeping him on to help train new levies."

"Sir," Blanchard said, "begging your pardon, but that would be a waste of a natural cavalryman. If he can shoot like he can ride and handle a saber—"

"I know," Rogers said, "I know. And I do not want to impede the war effort, but there are other considerations. I was going to make Recruit Jardine a corporal, the first black noncommissioned officer in this command. What has your unit got to offer Jardine besides hard work, horse shit, and certain death? I assume that the officers and NCOs of this new black unit will be white."

"Of course, sir," said Blanchard, taken aback. "Our blacks are all privates."

"That's a shame," Rogers said. "Now, if I thought that within, say, three months, given continuing progress on Recruit Jardine's part, he could be wearing corporal's stripes, that might go a long way toward loosening my hold on him, which, at the current time, is a death grip. I don't like to lose a good soldier."

"Sir, as you well know, I can promise nothing," said Blanchard. "In the cavalry, sergeants do not hand out corporal's stripes."

"Oh, I know," Rogers said with a smile, "but in my experience they have an awful lot of influence on their commanders. Who is yours, by the way?"

"Colonel Surridge," Blanchard said.

"Iron Pants Surridge?"

"I have heard the expression," Blanchard said neutrally.

Rogers thought and tugged on his long mustache. "I'll tell you what I'll do. If Recruit Jardine wants to die in the saddle, you can take him with you. But I'm going to be writing Colonel Surridge about our little discussion and your promise to make Jardine a corporal within three months."

"Sir," Blanchard protested, "I—" but Rogers was turning to Caleb.

"Recruit Jardine," he said, "are you crazy enough to join the cavalry?"

"Yes, sir," said Caleb.

— *50* —

For his first two weeks with the cavalry, Caleb cleaned the stables. He could see some justice in this because of the way he'd abused that corporal's gray gelding, and he made special efforts to be nice to Ben, sneaking him sugar cubes and carrots from the mess hall. But toward the end of the second week, horse shit and wet straw had begun to pall.

"Tell me, Zeke," he complained to another black recruit one day in the stables, "does a black man in this troop ever get to handle anything more dangerous than a pitchfork?"

"You may be eager to get your ass shot off," Zeke said, "but not me. I still can't explain why I raised my hand when they asked could anybody ride a horse. I'm happy in this nice, warm stable. I'm in no hurry to get killed."

"You're a smart boy, Zeke," said the first sergeant, who had just walked into the area between the stalls. "You may live to see this war finished." The first sergeant, a big man with an outsized head, opened the door to the stall where they were working. "As for you, Jardine, report to the parade ground with your unit tomorrow morning, and we'll see how dangerous you are with a bayonet. In the meantime, get this shit hole cleaned up. The horses are starting to complain."

Caleb found it hard to get to sleep that night. He knew why he'd spent two weeks shoveling shit, and he knew that he would be a target the next morning. Sergeant Blanchard, when he noticed Caleb at all, still shot him surly looks when they passed in the squadron area. In the black barracks, which not so long before had been stables and still smelled like it, the other recruits stared curiously at Caleb, both in awe of what they had heard of him and glad that they were not getting the attention he was.

The next morning dawned cool and misty. On the parade ground, the black recruits were issued old bayonets to fix onto their even older rifles. "Now, listen, meatheads," the corporal, an old infantryman, shouted, "whatever you do, do not remove the scabbard from your bayonets. You are here this morning to learn, not kill each other. Now, fall in, and let's get at it."

The corporal marched them to a remote corner of the training area, where bales of straw stacked three high and draped with crudely drawn Confederate flags served as the targets for bayonet practice. "Now," he said, "just because the bayonet is an infantry weapon and you will be the high and mighty cavalry, do not think that it is beneath you to learn how to use it. When you come off those beautiful ponies in battle—and you will—you will be damned glad that you know what to do with a bayonet. Now, form lines facing those stacks of hay bales, and when I say 'Charge!' I want you to tear those bales apart. Don't be shy. You don't need an introduction. And remember, I want to hear some noise when you attack. If you can't kill the rebs with the bayonet, maybe you can scare them to death."

Caleb purposely got himself third in line to attack one of the targets. Back at the armory, Sergeant Henkins had given them some basic bayonet drills. Caleb had a pretty good idea of what to do, but he wanted to see how the other recruits did it before he tried.

"Recruits! Attention. Fix bayonets. Present bayonets! Charge!" the corporal shouted, and the first half-dozen recruits started forward in a ragged line, none wanting to be the first to attack the bales. "No, no, no, no!" screamed the corporal before they got halfway to the bales. The recruits straggled to an embarrassed halt and stood awkwardly, like passengers waiting for a trolley. "It's not a goddamn dance," the corporal said. "You're fighting for your life. It's kill or be killed. Does anybody here have any idea how it's supposed to be done?"

They were all silent, but then Caleb raised his hand. The other recruits backed away from him as if he had smallpox.

"What's your name?" the corporal demanded.

"Jardine, sir."

"Well, Jardine, step forward. Recruits, Mr. Jardine here believes he is an expert on this weapon. In fact, he is a bayoneting fool. He will now show you the approved method of attacking and killing the enemy." The other recruits laughed and jostled each other. "Recruit Jardine," the corporal screamed. "Attention. Fix bayonet! Present bayonet! Charge!"

Before the final word left the corporal's mouth, Caleb sprang forward with a blood-curdling howl of rage and in three long steps was upon the targets. Using his sheathed bayonet more as a blunt instrument than a blade, he speared the central bale of hay in the first stack, got his weight under it, and then threw it back high over his head, knocking down one recruit and scattering the rest. Then, continuing to scream like a madman, Caleb whirled and attacked the other stacks of bales, leveling them with a sweep of his bayonet and jabbing them viciously when they were on the ground. When his bayonet stuck in one bale, Caleb kicked it to pieces with his heavy boots.

The other recruits just gaped, but the corporal, once he was over his surprise, started shouting, "Well done, Jardine! That's the way! Enough, Jardine, enough! For Christ's sake—"

But not until the sixth and final stack had been laid low did Caleb, running with sweat and festooned with bits of straw, stop and come to attention, his eyes staring straight ahead. He tried to control his gasping breaths.

"That, boys, is a bit more like it," said the corporal.

Drawn to the area by Caleb's howls, Colonel Surridge and his adjutant rode their horses to about fifty yards away, and then the adjutant stood in the stirrups and shouted, "Corporal!"

Spotting his commanding officer, the corporal said, "Jardine. Get those stacks rebuilt and see if you can inspire these dummies." As he ran toward the colonel, he heard Caleb say, "All right, let's get them back up!"

When he got to the two officers, the corporal snapped a salute. "Sir!"

"Corporal," said Surridge, "who was that recruit imitating a madman?"

"Recruit Jardine, Caleb," said the corporal.

The adjutant murmured to the colonel, "You may recall getting a letter about Jardine last week, from Major Rogers of the training command. Rogers said he reckoned him highly. Thinks Jardine ought to be wearing corporal's stripes."

Colonel Surridge looked over to where Caleb was supervising rebuilding of the bayoneting targets. "Perhaps, Greenaway," the colonel told the adjutant, "or perhaps a straitjacket. Send that man to my office directly after lunch. And tell him to get some of that straw off of him first. That will be all, Corporal."

Colonel Surridge had just reined his horse around to return to his office when a sudden burst of screams went up from the direction of the bayonet training. Turning his horse around again, Surridge saw that, under Caleb's direction, the black recruits were attacking the haystack targets with noise and gusto. Caleb patrolled behind them shouting, "Stick 'em, boys, stick 'em!"

"Greenaway, didn't I hear you say that free blacks have no spunk?" Surridge asked.

Colonel Surridge looked up from his paperwork when the orderly knocked and entered.

"He's here, sir," said the orderly.

"Who's here?"

"The madman."

"And which madman would that be?" the colonel asked.

"Recruit Jardine, sir."

"Send him in."

Caleb entered the room, saluted, and said, "Recruit Jardine reporting as ordered, sir." He stood at attention.

"At ease, recruit," the colonel said, indicating a heavy wooden chair in front of his desk. "Sit down."

Once Caleb was seated, the colonel asked, "Jardine, are you mad?"

"No, sir."

"Then how do you explain that display you put on today at bayoneting training?"

"Well, sir, nobody seemed to want to come to grips with the enemy, so—"

"The enemy?" the colonel inquired.

"The bales of hay, sir. So I thought that by exaggerating a bit, I could give them the idea and stir things up a bit. I was getting bored."

"Bored?"

"Yes, sir."

"Well, we wouldn't want that," the colonel said drily. "Jardine, how long have you been in the army?"

"Just over six weeks, sir."

"I've seen from Sergeant Henkins's report that you are an excellent shot. Do you think you can encourage that ability in recruits?"

"Yes, sir."

Surridge looked down at a sheet of paper on his desk. "Major Rogers speaks highly of you. He didn't want to lose you."

"I owe a lot to Major Rogers, sir," Caleb said. "It was his idea that I enlist. I was just curious."

"Well, Jardine," said Surridge, "I'm not going to take Major Rogers's advice. I'm not going to promote you to corporal. Ordinarily I would, but I'm not." He paused.

"Sir?"

"Jardine," the colonel said decisively, "go get that jacket hanging next to my long coat."

"This one, sir?" Caleb asked, laying his hand on a narrow-waisted blue jacket.

"That's the one. Put it on."

Jardine was puzzled, but he obeyed. He pulled the jacket over his work shirt and stood looking at the colonel.

"Do you see what is on the sleeves of that jacket, Jardine?"

"Yes, sir. Sergeant's stripes."

"They're yours. Sit down, Sergeant Jardine, and I'll explain a few things."

When Jardine, still wearing the jacket, was seated, Surridge continued, "According to regulations, Sergeant Jardine, you shouldn't even be a corporal, much less a sergeant. But I'm trying to build possibly the first black cavalry squadron here, and I haven't got a hell of a lot of time. I need a black sergeant to inspire these men, to make them believe that they can be crack cavalrymen. You're that sergeant. I'm giving you a squad in D Troop starting immediately. But don't forget two things: One, if you let me down, those stripes will come off as fast as they went on. And two, you are going to catch hell from the white sergeants and corporals. Most of them think you should be up in a tree in Africa eating bananas. Do you think you can handle it?"

"Yes, sir," said Caleb. "Being a slave's a hard life, but it teaches you to survive."

"I hope so," Surridge said. "I will back you as much as I can, but you're going to have to do most of it yourself."

"I will, sir."

Surridge stood up and extended his hand. "Now, get out there, Sergeant, and prove that I'm not out of my mind."

Jardine stood up, shook the colonel's hand, backed up a step, and saluted. "Yes, sir." He started to take off the jacket.

"No," said Surridge. "It's yours. It looks a little big, but I think you'll grow into it. Report to Lieutenant Padgett at D Troop barracks. He'll assign your duties."

"Sir." Caleb saluted again and left the office.

Caleb hadn't gone ten steps from headquarters when the corporal in charge of the stables, who until the day before had been his boss, saw him and roared, "Jardine! Where the hell did you get that jacket?"

"From Colonel Surridge, Corporal," Caleb replied. They both turned and saw Surridge at his second-floor window, arms crossed over his chest, looking down at them. "Any other questions?"

— 51 —

Caleb's unexpected and speedy transition from shit shoveler to sergeant was not without complications. Although Lieutenant Padgett, commander of D Troop, had been informed about his new black sergeant in advance, he looked at him with a combination of alarm and doubt. Showing Caleb the small cadre room where he would sleep, Padgett said, "Noncommissioned officers meeting in the orderly room in thirty minutes. Don't be late." He hurried away.

Caleb was sitting on the metal springs of his new bed wondering what the hell to do next when he heard a loud rap on the door, and a man with a pale-white freckled face stuck his head in the room.

"Jardine?" said the man.

"Yes," said Caleb, startled.

"Can I come in, then?" His voice had a foreign-sounding lilt to it.

"Yes," said Caleb, and in walked a large man wearing sergeant's stripes.

"I'm O'Neill," he said, holding out his hand, "B Troop. Colonel Surridge said you might be sitting here wondering which end is up."

"He was right," said Caleb.

"O'Neill is here," the stranger said, "to see that all becomes clear. As an Irishman and a Fenian to boot, I'm considered by many in this squadron the next thing to a black, so it is poetic justice that I should look after you."

"What's a Fenian?"

"Don't start me on that," O'Neill said, "or we'll never get there and back."

"Get where?"

"To the supply room, of course. The most important thing about this sergeant business is looking like one." He took a step back and surveyed Caleb from top to toe. "That jacket will do— barely. But the rest of your gear, especially those clodhopping boots, will have to go. Let's get moving. Wee Padgett gets very vexed if anyone is late for his meetings."

Twenty-five minutes later, when Caleb and O'Neill walked into the orderly room, the lieutenant was looking at his pocket watch. Everyone else in the room was looking at Caleb with surprise. Snapping shut the cover on his watch, Padgett announced that the meeting had started. "As you can see, we have a new sergeant—Jardine," he told the assembled NCOs. "He will handle the third squad, assisted by Corporal Whitmore. Now—"

Before Padgett could continue, Whitmore, a rangy dark-haired man with a hatchet face, stood up. "I'm no rebel, sir," he said with a pronounced drawl, "but I did not come up here from western Virginia to work under no nigger."

"Sit down, Corporal," Padgett said coldly and stared at Whitmore until he obeyed. "Nobody is going to force you to work under Sergeant Jardine, Whitmore. But the word from Colonel Surridge is that anyone who cannot live with his staffing decisions can leave his stripes in my office after this meeting. Now, let's continue." He raked over the NCOs with his eyes. "We have only a few more weeks to turn this rabble into a fair approximation of mounted riflemen, and we will do it. As of now, all leaves and passes are canceled until we do. First Sergeant Dixon will distribute the schedule for the next three weeks, starting at 0600 hours tomorrow morning. Any questions?"

When none of the NCOs spoke, Padgett said, "Meeting dismissed."

Dixon's command of "Attention!" brought the sergeants and corporals to their feet, and Padgett left the room. All was silent, and Caleb and O'Neill waited until the rest had filed out of the office. No one looked at Caleb.

"Well, son," said O'Neill after they had left, "you survived your first ordeal, but don't worry, you have plenty to come."

"Do you think Whitmore will quit?" Caleb asked.

"Not that boyo," O'Neill said. "He loves those stripes too much. But you'll doubtless have to fight him. Now, let's have a quick drink."

Over a small whiskey in his room, O'Neill did his best to fill Caleb in on some of the details about being an NCO that Caleb would ideally have had months, if not years, to learn.

"First thing you have to know," O'Neill said, "is that a sergeant is someone who acts like a sergeant. It's as simple as that. Second is that the corporals do all the work. That's how they become sergeants. I know you can whip Whitmore, but you'll be better off using him. He's a good corporal, even if he is poor white trash from Virginia. He's never owned slaves—couldn't afford them—but that doesn't mean he loves niggers. Does that word bother you?"

"Nope," Caleb said. "I'm used to it."

"Get used to it some more. You're going to hear a lot of it. Now," said O'Neill, draining his glass, "get over to your barracks, go over that training schedule with Whitmore, and kick some arses."

"Whose?"

"It don't matter. Just kick some."

Caleb

Back at his barracks, Caleb found Whitmore and told him to muster the troops. Whitmore looked at him hard, but five minutes later Caleb's squad was assembled outside the barracks with Whitmore standing in front of them.

Caleb looked them over for a couple of minutes. They did the same to him. He wasn't impressed. Though they seemed slightly more like soldiers than the recruits back at the armory, and they stood at a version of attention, they didn't look a lot like cavalry. Caleb wasn't pleased, and he thought that he'd better let them know it from the beginning.

"I am Sergeant Jardine," he told them. "Corporal Whitmore and I are your noncommissioned officers. It is our job to make you into a fighting unit. This is going to involve a lot of hard work, starting right now. Are there any questions? Speak up if there are."

A big private in the first rank raised his hand.

"Yes?" said Caleb, stepping in front of him.

"Were you a slave, Sergeant?"

"Yes I was, until last spring," Caleb said. "Why do you ask?"

"I was born free, right here in New York," the private said, "and I ain't taking orders from a slave."

Caleb didn't speak, but his fist shot out and caught the man on the jaw. The private fell forward from the ranks like a sack of flour.

Ignoring him, Caleb asked, "Any more questions?"

No one else spoke from the ranks, but Whitmore said under his breath, "I've been wanting to do that since that boy arrived."

"Detail a man to get a bucket of water, Corporal," Caleb said. "In the meantime, I want to see how these troops drill. Carry on."

That evening, when Caleb and O'Neill walked into the noncommissioned officers' mess and sat down, about thirty sergeants and corporals got up, left their dinners, and stalked out. The two ordered and started eating as if nothing had happened.

"It's started," said Caleb.

"Yes," O'Neill said, "but let's see how long it lasts. What they don't know is that Surridge has closed the NCO club and sealed the post. That means they won't be able to buy any dinner tonight. We'll see what a little hunger does for their tolerance."

The next morning, only half a dozen NCOs walked out. "They're learning," said O'Neill. At dinner that night, Caleb was still eating alone with O'Neill and getting hostile looks, but nobody left the mess without eating.

"It's working," said O'Neill. "Are you the sociable type?"

"Not usually. Why?"

"Well, if I were you, I'd steer clear of the NCO bar until one of the white sergeants invites you. Those poor fellows need somewhere to talk about niggers with stripes."

"That suits me," said Caleb. "I'm going to be pretty busy for the next six weeks."

At the next muster of his squad, Caleb looked over his men. "How's your jaw, Carter?" he asked.

"Still a bit sore, Sergeant," Carter said.

"Learn from it," Caleb said. "Now listen, all of you. Corporal Whitmore and I are trying to do the impossible: turn you into some sort of cavalrymen in a very short time. But we are going to do our best, and *you* are going to do your best or perish. You were chosen for this unit because you can ride, and you will be the best riders in this squadron." He drew his saber and brandished it overhead.

"You may not become as good with your saber as you should be, but—Corporal!" Whitmore threw him a carbine, and Caleb raised it high in his other hand. "You will become expert with this. It is a Sharps 1851 single-shot .52 caliber carbine. You will fire it from horseback at a gallop, and your accuracy will be outstanding. I can guarantee you that you will be the best mounted rifles the rebs have ever seen. They will not believe their eyes."

He turned to Whitmore. "Dismiss the squad, Corporal. I want them back here with their carbines and their mounts fully saddled in fifteen minutes."

After a meeting of his officers at the end of that week, Colonel Surridge asked Lieutenant Padgett how Sergeant Jardine was doing.

"Well, sir," said Padgett, "Corporal Whitmore despises him and the men hate him."

Surridge waited for the rest with a sick feeling in his stomach.

"But he's a natural sergeant. In less than a week, Jardine's got them working their butts off. They hate every minute of it, but he's taken the worst squad in my troop, and damned if I don't think he's going to turn it into one of the best. That is, if one of them doesn't shoot him first. Do you know he had them out riding an obstacle course in full field packs until eleven o'clock last night?"

"Lose any men or horses?" Surridge asked.

"Not that I know of," said Padgett.

At the end of training, Colonel Surridge scheduled a parade and a war game on a big enclosed field just outside the camp. The parade was intended to show just how well his blacks had learned to handle their mounts.

The war game was something special, a long-standing tradition of the camp. At the center of the large close-cropped field was a flat-topped mound some thirty feet in diameter with sharply sloping sides that were eight feet high. At dead center of the mound was a tall wooden flagpole. Fixed to the top of the flagpole that morning would be the colors of a nearby white infantry training regiment. Surridge had invited the regiment to defend the mound from his men. After their display of equestrian skills, Surridge's mounted rifles would have fifteen minutes to capture those colors or lose the game.

Along with Surridge and the colonel commanding the infantry battalion, a number of invited guests—including two brigadier generals and the divisional commander—stood on the reviewing stand, looking on doubtfully as Surridge's squadrons formed on the field.

"You claim these troops can ride some, Surridge?" asked one of the brigadier generals, striking the leg of his high boot with a riding crop.

"We'll see very soon, sir," Surridge said ambiguously.

"Tell you what, Surridge," suggested the infantry colonel, a West Point man, "to make this more interesting, I'll bet you fifty dollars that your blacks don't capture our colors."

"I hate to sully military matters with filthy lucre, Colonel," Surridge said, "but I'll stake our colors against yours. Winner gets to keep the other's colors until the next war game. What do you say? I've got a spot for yours all picked out in our mess hall."

"Top that bet up with three barrels of beer," said the infantry colonel, "and it's a deal."

"Done!" said Surridge, trying to look more confident than he felt.

A blare of bugles announced that Surridge's squadron had formed on the field. His officers rode to the front of the reviewing stand to salute their colonel and the visitors.

"Carry on, Major," Surridge said, and the officers, including Padgett, wheeled their mounts around and returned to their respective troops. The squadron band began to play "Garry Owen," and Surridge's squadron began a standard display of equestrian skills. In ranks around the edge of the field stood the white infantrymen waiting impatiently for their part in the day's activities.

Carefully, and with only slightly ragged precision, the mounted blacks answered their sergeants' commands. Forming first two columns, then four, then eight, the riders guided their mounts through a series of drills designed to show their ability to control the horses. Then a bugle sounded "Charge!" and the troopers, on a thirty-horse front, galloped across the parade ground, sabers glinting in the bright sunlight.

"I don't believe it," sang out a voice from the ranks of the visiting white battalion, "niggers on horseback."

"Maybe they're really minstrels," called out another, but their sergeants quickly scowled them into silence.

At the end of the display, Colonel Surridge's officers saluted him, then returned to their units. Surridge was surprised that neither Caleb nor Corporal Whitmore were among the NCOs. He made a mental note to find out why.

"My congratulations, Surridge," said the divisional commander. "For only eight weeks' training, your mounted rifles ride remarkably well. I'm impressed. It generally takes two years to fully train a cavalryman."

"Thank you, sir," said Surridge. "They're hardly fully trained cavalrymen, but my officers and NCOs worked very hard to get results. I'm proud of them."

"Ah, now comes the most interesting part of the program, sir," said the infantry colonel confidently. At a signal, his bugler sounded "Assemble," and the white infantry battalion, banners flying but without their weapons, began to march in formation toward the mound in the middle of the field. Shouting sergeants formed them into a square around the mound, and twenty of the largest trainees climbed to the top of the mound as a last line of defense should Surridge's blacks breach the square.

Then, as the bugles blared again, the infantry ranks parted in the middle of the square to admit a squad led by a sergeant carrying the infantry battalion's colors. The color sergeant scrambled up the slope of the mound with as much dignity as possible, and both the host squadron and their guests saluted as he stood on the shoulders of a tall recruit and fixed the colors high up on the flagpole.

As the color sergeant jumped down, Surridge signaled, and the boom of a cannon announced the beginning of the war game.

"Now we'll see something," said the infantry colonel.

"We certainly shall," agreed Surridge.

The two colonels consulted their watches to ensure that they showed the same time, and at Surridge's cue, his squadrons began to move. At first their maneuvers looked much like the display they had just completed. With as much precision as they could muster, the black troopers rode two by two at a trot around the periphery of the infantry square as if looking for a weakness, an opportunity to attack. They trotted their horses as close to the front rank of foot soldiers as possible. Instinctively, the infantry recruits squeezed together and backed away from the horses as their NCOs shouted, "Hold the line! Hold the line!" The infantry trainees stood shoulder to shoulder, five deep around the mound in a seemingly impenetrable phalanx. The infantrymen shouted ribald remarks and catcalls, but the mounted soldiers rode in total silence, their NCOs maintaining tight discipline.

Then, at a signal from the adjutant, the mounted rifles broke off their circling maneuver and formed a mass of four troops—eight horses wide and thirty horses deep—in front of a wide gate at the right perimeter of the field facing the mound. The mounted blacks straightened their lines and then sat looking directly ahead at the foe. Their faces were expressionless.

"That's five minutes," said the infantry colonel to Surridge. "What the hell are your people doing?" A murmur of impatience went up from the other officers on the reviewing stand. "That's a good question," said Surridge. He was wondering the same thing.

But then the bugles sounded again. To the measured beat of drums, the mass of horsemen began moving slowly toward the mound. Their movement was so measured, so nearly funereal, that spectators on the reviewing stand broke out in laughter. The waiting infantrymen began to lean forward in anticipation, but the advancing cavalry did not alter its pace.

The divisional commander turned to Surridge and whispered, "I've never seen this before, Colonel. What's it called?"

"Damned if I know, sir," said Surridge.

"Are they giving up, Surridge?" whispered the infantry colonel.

"I don't think so."

"Ten minutes," the infantry colonel said to Surridge, but his words were nearly drowned out as the mounted rifles' bugles suddenly blared, and the black troopers spurred their horses to a trot, then a canter, then a full gallop, aiming dead straight at the infantry square. As they rode, their guidons snapping in the breeze, they began shouting, screaming, and howling, producing a cacophony of noise. As the racing horses grew nearer to the infantry square, the noise turned to an uproar. It looked as though they were going to ride right into the infantry ranks.

"Jesus Christ!" said the infantry colonel, and all three general officers looked at Surridge with wonder. Surridge kept his eyes straight ahead, although he could hardly believe what he was seeing.

The howling horsemen thundered closer and closer until, fifty yards from the nervous square, they broke off in fours to the left and the right, finally revealing the very last rank of horses, which, the observers noted with astonishment, seemed to be riderless. This final rank continued full tilt toward the infantry square, and as it grew closer, the middle of the rank surged forward until it formed a sharp inverted *V*, at which point the riders swung up from the sides of their horses where they had been clinging.

A collective gasp went up from the spectators. The riders were naked to the waist, and their faces and bodies were painted with red, white, and blue symbols. Sitting behind the large rider of the leading horse was what seemed to be a black child, who was also stripped to the waist and painted with bright patterns. In their right hands the bizarre horsemen brandished short staffs streaming with yellow ribbons. As the eight horsemen closed in on the infantry recruits, their formation grew ever sharper.

The divisional commander leaned over to Surridge and remarked, "This is better than a circus, Colonel, even if it doesn't work."

When the horsemen had almost reached the infantry square, their leader thought he detected a slight wavering in the infantry ranks and rode straight for it, his painted face grim with determination. At the last moment, the infantrymen at the point of the attack broke formation and scattered. The two horsemen in the lead broke through the infantry ranks and, with only a slight hesitation as they hit the slope of the mound, burst to the top, dispersing the inner guard. The lead horseman rode straight toward the flagpole. Suddenly the small figure behind him was standing on the saddle with his hands on the rider's shoulders. Then, just as it seemed that the horse would collide with the pole, the little man vaulted to the shoulders of the rider and then to the flagpole, scrambling upward toward the infantry's colors.

As the small man climbed, the lead rider wheeled his mount tightly around the base of the flagpole, and the second horseman rode in a larger circle around the edge of the mound to discourage defenders who might try to regain the summit. Quickly, the small soldier reached the colors, yanked them free, and, with a shrill whistle, slid down the pole, landing once again behind the lead rider. The two horsemen rode a celebratory circuit around the edge of the mound, plunged back into the infantry ranks, burst free, and rejoined their squadron. The cavalrymen had regrouped and were riding in a wide circle around the mound, whooping and shouting. As they rode, the cannon boomed, announcing that the colors had been captured and the war game was over.

The black mounted rifles formed a long column of twos and slowly and decorously rode toward the reviewing stand. At the front of the column were the eight shirtless, painted riders. Caleb and Whitmore, chevrons painted on their arms, rode in front, holding aloft between them the infantry regiment's colors. Behind Caleb rode Eldon "Monkey" Higgins, the smallest trooper in the squadron, formerly a racetrack exercise boy. When they got to within a few yards of the reviewing stand, Caleb and Whitmore dismounted, folded the infantry colors into a neat triangle, and handed them to Higgins. Advancing to the stand, Higgins saluted smartly and presented the colors to Colonel Surridge while the rest of the spectators gaped. Then the three men remounted and led their squadron in a lap of honor around the field, where the disorganized infantry recruits were milling about.

Colonel Surridge turned to salute the two-star divisional commander, who returned his salute and said, "Highly unorthodox tactics, Colonel, but they worked."

— *52* —

Orders for the Eleventh Volunteer Mounted Rifles (Colored) came the following week. The Union had suffered a serious defeat in the Battle of Bull Run in northeastern Virginia the summer before, and General Pope needed all of the men he could muster for what looked like a repeat engagement.

After meeting with his officers, Surridge had an extra word with Lieutenant Padgett.

"Do you think your boys are ready?" he asked.

"No, sir," said Padgett, "but they'll do their best. I've never seen such rapid improvement in a group of recruits."

"What about Jardine?" the colonel asked. "I'd really like to keep him here to help train the next intake of recruits."

"In an ideal world, sir, I'd agree," Padgett said, "but without him, I wouldn't take any bets on D Troop. Jardine is the glue that holds them together. Without him, they're half-trained, undisciplined, black rabble."

"I know," said Surridge. "I suppose the only question that remains now is who will shoot Jardine first—our side or the rebs."

It was a sultry, rainy day when the squadron rode through the streets to the railway yard to entrain for Virginia, and their guidons hung limp. The small, sullen crowd that had turned out to see them off looked on with wonder. A loud voice called, "Good riddance to black rubbish!" A few stones and dirt clods flew out of the crowd and ricocheted off the men and horses

When the ranks of D Troop began to waver, Caleb called out, "Steady! Eyes front! Steady the troop!" A small stone struck his shoulder, but he ignored it.

At the freight yard, Caleb and the men loaded their horses into several boxcars and settled themselves in another. Then they settled in—saddles for pillows, horse blankets for covers—for a long ride.

"Do you suppose," Monkey Higgins called out, "there's a dining car on this train?"

They arrived at Gainesville, the nearest railhead to Bull Run, in an early morning mist. As Lieutenant Padgett was supervising the unloading of the horses, a weary transportation major approached him wonderingly. "What the hell are those?" he demanded, staring at the black cavalrymen.

"Eleventh Mounted Rifles," Padgett responded, saluting as smartly as he could, considering the hour.

"But they're black!"

"Yes, sir," said Padgett.

"But I thought blacks were afraid of horses."

"These aren't, sir."

Because no one knew quite when the next battle would begin or what to do with the black squadron, they were stuck away in the corner of a fenced pasture on the outskirts of Stone Bridge to await orders. This suited both the men, who were not keen to get shot at, and their officers, who knew how badly they needed more training in the field. Once the tents were set up, latrines dug, and a cookhouse established, Caleb and the other NCOs began a furious training program of skirmishing tactics, rifle practice from horse-back, and group discipline.

Troops from white units in the area with nothing better to do began to line a long fence on one side of the pasture, enjoying the novelty of watching armed blacks in uniform. Some of them had seen black soldiers before, but none carrying anything more deadly than a broom. Soon the white soldiers began to bring their rations along with them, and a carnival atmosphere sprang up. As they watched the black horsemen train, white soldiers cheered, whooped, and called out witticisms.

"Hey, darkie," called one to a trumpet corporal, "where's your banjo?"

Another shouted, "Does that shoe polish come off?"

Cautioned by their officers and NCOs, the black soldiers ignored the raillery until finally, after nearly a week, it began to interfere with training. Ordering the men to take a break, the squadron's officers and sergeants gathered in a corner of the pasture.

"Does anyone besides me think this is becoming more than a joke?" the adjutant asked.

A loud chorus of assent broke out.

"Well, what are we going to do about it?" the adjutant asked. "I tried talking to their commander, but he thinks we're just as big a joke as his troops do."

"We could open fire on them," suggested Corporal Whitmore.

"A tempting solution, Whitmore," said Lieutenant Padgett, "but perhaps a bit drastic. Any other suggestions?"

"I have an idea, sir," said Sergeant O'Neill.

A little later, the black cavalrymen were ordered to mount up. Leading their troops to the far side of the pasture, the officers and NCOs ordered them to form a single long line opposite the jeering white soldiers. The black cavalrymen sat silently in their saddles, staring at their tormenters. On either end of the line, color sergeants unfurled their guidons.

"Oh, goody," called a white sergeant, "they're going to parade. I love a parade!" The onlookers laughed.

Then the officers and the NCOs of the Eleventh rode out and spaced themselves in front of their troops. Turning back in his saddle, the adjutant unsheathed his saber and held it high in the direction of the white troops.

"Squadron!" he called out. "Atten—shun! Present sabers!" Two hundred and fifty blades flashed in the morning sunshine, accompanied by the creaking of leather and clanking of metal as the horses strained against the reins. "Buglers, sound the charge!" the adjutant ordered. Then, as the bugles blared, he turned and leveled his saber toward the far fence and bellowed, "Charge!"

As one, the long line of black cavalrymen surged forward, gathering speed as they rode.

At first, laughter went up from the watching white soldiers, but as the thundering line of horses came closer and gathered speed, a nervous tremor went up and down the rail fence. Several soldiers dropped their food, and one called out, "I don't think they're kidding!" At that, a soldier bolted, and others joined him. The retreat from the fence became a rout as the soldiers ran for their lives. The smart ones stayed where they were, cowering beneath the rails of the fence.

First the officers cleared the fence, then the NCOs, followed by a long rippling line of black cavalrymen whose momentum carried them among the fleeing white troops, knocking down several. Some did not get up.

Reassembling his mounted troops in a long line facing the pasture, with many of the white troops still trapped between them and the fence, the adjutant once again raised his sword and called out, "Present sabers!" Again a flash of steel ran along the line. "Buglers," began the adjutant, "sound the—" But at this, the remaining white troops began to hurriedly pick up their equipment and wounded. Within minutes, the area along the fence was clear of all but the debris that had been dropped in the rout.

Looking along the fence with satisfaction, the adjutant lowered his sword and shouted, "Sheathe your sabers! Right wheel, forward!" The black cavalrymen slowly rode double file back into the pasture to continue training.

When the commander of the white unit complained about the injuries to several of his troops, Colonel Snaith, the Eleventh's new CO, suggested that if the white soldiers trained more and gawked less, they'd be better prepared to fight the rebels.

One day while the mounted rifles were still awaiting deployment, Caleb was passing corps headquarters when his eye caught on a diagram on a notice board. It showed the names and locations of the units gathered for the coming battle. Running his finger down the list, he saw the name Seventh Boston Rifles. Determining that their bivouac was not far away, Caleb rode in that direction. As he rode he ignored the curious glances of white soldiers and the hurried salutes returned by officers.

When Caleb got to the Seventh's area, he approached a private standing guard next to the gate.

"Excuse me," Caleb began. The soldier jumped as if he'd seen a ghost.

"What the hell are you pretending to be?" he demanded.

"I'm not pretending to be anything," Caleb said fiercely. "I *am* a sergeant in the US cavalry, Private, and I'm addressing a question to you. Do you have any doubts about that?"

"I suppose not," said the guard, equally bemused and intimidated.

"Well," Caleb continued, "what I want to know is whether you have an officer called Brent Staunton in the Seventh."

Now the guard looked even more confused. "Well," he said. "We've got a Brent Staunton." He waved his arm in the direction of the biggest tent in the compound. "Just ask over there," he said. He added "Sergeant" as an afterthought.

Caleb rode over to the big, round tent and tied his horse to a post. As he was walking over to the tent, two privates wearing white aprons came out carrying a large cooking pot between them.

"Excuse me," said Caleb. "I'm looking for Staunton. Brent Staunton."

The two men gaped at Caleb and then put down the big pot. One of them called into the tent, "Staunton! A *gentleman* to see you!" Then he dashed back to the pot, and he and the other soldier disappeared, giggling, with their load.

Caleb waited patiently until a few minutes later a soldier in a work uniform with his sleeves rolled up over his elbows came out into the bright summer sunshine, blinking after the dim interior of the tent. He was thin, slightly bent, and badly needed a shave. Despite his youth, there was something worn and weary in his attitude. He, too, was wearing a cook's apron. He looked at Caleb, but did not really take him in.

"Yes?" he said. "I'm Staunton. Are you looking for me?"

"Hello, Brent," said Caleb, holding out his hand. "How are you doing?"

Staunton stared at this apparition, this big black cavalry sergeant with the scarred face and hair cut short. "I'm sorry," he started to say in a cultured Boston accent, but then recognition entered his pale eyes. "Caleb?" he asked. "Caleb, is that you?"

"Nobody else," said Caleb, his hand still extended.

"My God," said Staunton, grabbing the hand and shaking it. "I can't believe it. I simply cannot believe it. I thought you were dead."

"Not quite," said Caleb. "Can you spare a minute? I mean, you haven't got anything burning in there?"

"No, no," said Staunton. "Nothing so glorious. They've got me washing dishes. Wait right here. I've got a break coming. Wait, all right?"

"All right," said Caleb.

In a moment Staunton was back, stripped of his apron and lighting a cigarette. "Come on," he said. They walked over to a bench made of roughly cut branches and sat down in the morning sunshine.

"Jesus," said Staunton, taking a deep drag on his cigarette and looking at Caleb. "How long has it been—seven years?"

"Something like," Caleb said. "Ever since—"

Staunton looked pensive. "Yes, since I sold you. I'm really sorry about that, Caleb. I had no choice. Those gamblers really had me. I hope you're not still harboring hard feelings."

"Tell you the truth, Brent," Caleb said, "I hated you for a long time. I thought we were like brothers. But you taught me not to trust anyone. If I'd met you two or three years ago, I'd probably have killed you. I went through some hard times down south. But that was a long time ago, and things have changed since then."

Staunton didn't seem to know what to say. Then he cleared his throat and looked at Caleb's yellow stripes. "Sergeant Caleb Staunton. At least we've got one military success in the family."

"No," Caleb corrected him. "Sergeant Caleb *Jardine*. I took the name of the farmer who bought me a few years ago down in South Carolina and who sold me my freedom toward the end of '60."

"Jardine," said Staunton thoughtfully. "I guess I don't blame you. Not a bit. But I do wish there was a Staunton going some-where in this damned army. I suppose you volunteered?"

"Yes," said Caleb. "I arrived in New York City the same day they fired on Fort Sumter. I hadn't planned to join any army, but to tell you the truth, there didn't seem to be a lot of opportunities for free blacks in New York. When did you volunteer?"

"May," said Staunton, "if you can call it that. You remember when—when we last saw each other—I had just started at Harvard?"

"Yes," said Caleb. "How did that work out?"

"It didn't. At the end of my third term, they said that either I had to do some studying or hit the road. Well, I hit the road. That would have been about '57 or so. I lived in the house until it had to be sold to pay my debts. And then I lived on what little was left— and a bit of luck gambling—until this spring. The luck and the last of my money seemed to vanish together, and I really didn't have much choice. It was either enlist or end up in the gutter."

"That bad?" asked Caleb.

"No," said Brent. "Worse." He smiled ruefully. "But things have gotten better. Believe it or not, I like the army. I'm not the success you are, but I've applied for a commission. If Harvard hasn't forgotten that I did *any* work during those three terms, I may get one—or at least a chance at officer candidate school. Which will get me out of this hole. Have you heard anything about what's going on?"

"Meeting I just came out of, they seemed about as confused as we are," said Caleb. "I'm just going to go back to my squadron to continue training those poor devils and wait for orders. If that battle that's promised around here is anything like they say, they're going to need some mounted rifles even if they are black." Caleb started to get up. "I'd better be getting back to our bivouac before they post me as a deserter."

Staunton got up, too. "Caleb," he said, "it's been a real pleasure. You've been heavy on what's left of my conscience." He held out his hand. "I hope you don't hate me anymore."

"Not anymore, Brent," Caleb said, taking his hand. "Those days are long gone. Maybe we'll meet again."

"I hope so, Caleb," Staunton said, and he watched as Caleb swung up on his horse, waved good-bye, and rode toward the camp exit. Staunton stood looking long after Caleb had disappeared from sight.

— *53* —

For the next few days, all was calm. Then McDowell's corps suddenly discovered that it had such a thing as the Eleventh Mounted Rifles. The squadron spent days in the saddle and nights on the ground wherever dark found them, foraging for food wherever they smelled cooking. Otherwise they lived on hard biscuits, stream water, and whatever small furred or feathered things they could kill and cook. For a time, they moved together. Then troop by troop they were drawn off to support units that had already moved on by the time the cavalrymen reached their destinations.

For five days, Padgett's troop was put to work digging trenches for white troops, who lay back and enjoyed having servants. Just as the black troops were about to mutiny, they were ordered to relieve white troops in another sector of the ever-changing front. There, they were set to work digging their own trenches. Once they were getting comfortable, orders came to move, and they reluctantly left their new homes for others to inherit.

Throughout these confusing days and dark nights, the talk was constantly of the rebels. Encouraged by his victory, Confederate General Longstreet had decided to push hard on General McClellan's battered Union forces to see if he could encourage the Yankees to go home and leave the South alone. The distant sound of cannons and rifle fire kept everyone in the Eleventh alert to the point of nervousness, but they seldom if ever saw anything they could identify as the enemy. Occasionally, under the orders of almost anyone wearing brass, they were ordered to stop, dismount, find what cover they could, and blaze away at an invisible enemy. Once, they were lined up with a couple of troops of white cavalry and sent, rifles blazing, on a futile charge across a small brook where they found nothing more threatening than an encampment of slaves who had scattered when their plantation was overrun. Several of the slaves were killed by wild fire, and one member of Caleb's troop died of a broken neck when his mount tried to go through, rather than over, a fallen tree.

Once ordered to join General Porter's forces at Groveton, Padgett's troop—being black and riding horses—had been commandeered by Kearny's division as messengers. No longer working as a unit, they found themselves dispersed all over the Bull Run area. When one of the Eleventh Mounted Rifles delivered his message, he often found himself recommandeered by another unit. Almost everywhere they went, they were viewed with a combination of welcome and suspicion. Many of the Union troops they encountered could not believe that there was such a thing as a black Federal soldier. Some thought they were runaway slaves who had taken uniforms off the dead. Once, when Monkey Higgins had been sent with a dispatch to a light artillery unit near New Market, he was himself amazed to find that the unit was composed of black volunteers from Pittsburgh and that he knew a couple of them from a local racetrack.

Reduced by a shortage of men to delivering messages himself, Caleb arrived at General Sigel's headquarters, handed over his dispatch, and prepared to mount up to go back where he'd come from. But then the adjutant, a lieutenant colonel who'd hardly noticed him, looked up and said, "Hold on a minute, soldier. Are you a *real* sergeant?"

Not knowing how else to answer, Caleb saluted and said, "Sergeant Caleb Jardine, Eleventh Mounted Rifles, sir."

"Are you a fighting man?"

"Yes, sir."

"Then why are you delivering dispatches?"

"A major told me to, sir."

"Well," said the officer, "*I'm* a colonel telling you that I need a sergeant. Hell, last time I looked, I needed a lieutenant and *several* sergeants. And we're expecting another visit from Johnny Reb any time now. Welcome to Sigel Country."

"But, sir—" Caleb began.

But the colonel was already calling to someone outside the tent. "Baker! Get your raggedy ass in here."

A weary-looking corporal in filthy clothes came in and saluted limply. "Sir?"

"Take this sergeant and give him to Captain Lockhart of Company B. And tell the captain that he owes me a very big favor. Now get out of here—both of you."

"What's happening here?" Caleb asked the corporal as they walked through a small copse of trees toward a distant hill.

"We're getting the shit shot out of us," said the corporal. "I hope you're good at digging holes. All we seem to do is get new troops, use them up, and bury them."

Reporting to Captain Lockhart, who had made his headquarters under a live oak tree, the corporal saluted and said, "Colonel Benning's compliments, sir. This here sergeant belongs to you now. Colonel says you owe him."

"Well, this is something new." Lockhart laughed. "I had an Irish piper last week and six Germans who couldn't speak a word of English, but never before a black sergeant. Thank the colonel, Baker, and tell him that I will return the favor one of these times." When the corporal had saluted and turned away, the captain looked up at Caleb. "No offense, Sergeant," he said. "I'm getting demented from lack of sleep, but I am very glad to see you. I've got three platoons without a sergeant between them. You have your choice. Any preferences?"

"Sir, I'd prefer one with men who won't fall over in a faint at the sight of a black face."

"All right," said Lockhart, "I'll give you to Lieutenant Alleyne of the Third Platoon. Unless he's kidding me, he's from Barbados, and I think they have some blacks there. Welcome to Fox Company." He looked back down at the paperwork on his little collapsible table.

While Caleb was trying to find Alleyne and the Third Platoon, half a mile away, on the other side of an unnamed creek, Boyd Jardine had his own problems. As Rafe Bentley had predicted, a vacancy for captain had opened up quickly when Philip Poindexter had turned out to have more dash than ability. He joined the family cemetery plot without ever seeing anyone more hostile than members of his own troop.

Bentley had been wrong about something else, though. His leisurely prediction of three months to get their troops trained and fully operational had telescoped into a little over a month. Jardine barely had enough time to say good-bye to Boyd Junior and send him to a cousin's house not far from Charleston, hide as many valuables as possible, and hand over the keys to Three Rivers to Drusilla and Mose.

"I wish that I could go with you, Marse," Caesar said as the house staff gathered to see Jardine off.

"Caesar," Jardine said, "I wish that you could go instead of me." Halfway down to the gate, he turned in his saddle and saw them still waving. The last thing he saw of Three Rivers was Mose waving his big black hat.

After that it was all motion, if very little action, for the Kershaw County Dragoons. By boat, train, and horse, they wandered generally northward, never settling and never seeing much action until they fetched up nearly a year later at Henry House Hill as part of General Longstreet's reserves at what the Confederates called the Second Battle of Manassas. They might have stayed there for the duration of the war—Longstreet had little regard for home-grown militia—but demands for more troops toward the middle of August got them pushed forward to fill a hole on the south side of an unnamed creek while waiting for a Yankee counterattack.

And then they waited for the rest of that hot, dry August for the counterattack that seemed like it was never going to come. Except for the exchange of a few ritual shots across the creek, Jardine's men had little to do but dig in, wait, and worry about those they'd left at home. Benjy Pitman had ended up hiring Captain Plunkett to look after Bienville and was getting reports that Plunkett's heavy hand and whip had the plantation in near revolt. Jardine did not bother to tell Pitman that his own slaves had chased the captain away.

One morning, as Jardine was making up his guard roster, he got word that Corporal Parsons in the observation platform, high in an elm tree, wanted him to see something. When Jardine climbed up to the platform, Parsons handed him the binoculars.

"Captain, you are not going to believe this."

"Believe what?" Jardine asked, adjusting the glasses to bring the tree-shaded area across the creek into focus. "I don't see anything but trees."

"Be patient, sir," Parsons said. "He'll be back. They got a nigger sergeant over there."

"A sergeant?" Jardine asked.

"Big as life," Parsons said, "and twice as ugly. I never saw him before this morning. I nearly fell out of this goddamned tree."

"Look, Parsons, I don't have all day to—"

"I swear I saw him, sir," Parsons said. "He'll be back." He gestured toward a sniper with a German hunting rifle higher up in a nearby beech. "Shall I tell Smokey to see if he can pick that black bastard off? It's a long shot, but there's not much wind this morning."

"No," said Jardine firmly. "We are not wasting bullets on niggers, sergeants or not. You remind Smokey that he is not to snipe at anyone under the rank of major without my express order. You got that?"

"Yes, sir."

Caleb had found Lieutenant Alleyne asleep in the shade of a blackberry bush and woke him as gently as possible.

"Sergeant Jardine reporting, sir," Caleb said. "Captain Lockhart says you're short a sergeant, and now I belong to you."

"Can't be, Sergeant," said Alleyne, a slight man with dark-honey skin and tightly curled sun-bleached hair. "We outlawed slavery nigh thirty years ago where I come from." He held out his hand. "Help me up, will you?" He looked at the big man standing in front of him. "Where the hell did Lockhart find you?"

"I found *him*, sir," said Caleb. "I started out this morning as a messenger from corps to your headquarters when a colonel commandeered me. He sent me to Captain Lockhart and Captain Lockhart sent me to you."

"Well, God bless the chain of command, Sergeant," Alleyne said, yawning. "I was just dreaming that someone had sent me a big, ugly sergeant to terrify my men into a semblance of order."

"You're not going to send me on, then?" Caleb asked.

"Not on your life," said Alleyne. "As soon as I get the branding iron smoking, you are going to officially belong to Third Platoon, Fox Company, the finest collection of odds and ends in the Union army."

"How do you suppose they are going to react to a black sergeant?" Caleb asked.

"They are going to love you like a brother, or rather, a father," Alleyne said. "I'll tell them that you are one of my cousins from the—where are you from, Sergeant?"

"Boston, sir."

"From the Boston branch of the Alleyne family. You ever been to Barbados?"

"No, sir. Not that I recall."

"You wouldn't have forgotten it," Alleyne said. "Most beautiful place on earth. And you would have learned that there are probably more black Alleynes on the island than white ones." He lowered his voice and leaned toward Caleb. "You may have noticed that I, myself, am not the whitest person you will ever meet, though if you suggested that back in Bridgetown, I'd have to call you out." He held out his hand. "Richie Alleyne at your service, Sergeant."

Caleb took the hand. "Caleb Jardine at yours, sir," he said.

"Welcome aboard, Caleb," Alleyne said. "Between the two of us, we are going to get this outfit into some kind of shape."

Caleb and Alleyne had barely begun that monumental task, and Jardine had scarcely climbed down from the observation platform, when General Lee gave the order to begin what was to become known as the Second Battle of Bull Run or Second Manassas, depending on whose side you were on. And it was to begin on the little arc of territory nominally held by the Kershaw County Dragoons.

Rafe Bentley hurriedly called his officers together. "Unless this is another of those goddamned false alarms, boys," he told them, "you have just about enough time to give your troops a cold feed, issue them as much ammunition as you have, and get them saddled up. Soon as the big guns start up in the rear, we are going to storm across that crick and reclaim that little patch of heaven for the Confederacy."

"What do we do when we get to the other side, Colonel?" asked a young lieutenant.

"Assuming you are still alive, son," Bentley said, "kill everything that resists, capture anything that doesn't, and dig in for a counterattack. I'll try to think of something for you to do then. Now, get to your men."

On the other side of the creek, Caleb was patiently trying to explain to his new command that those distant figures on the other side of the creek might finally decide to do something active and deadly. He'd hoped to have a month or so for this task, but scarcely a week later the roar of Confederate guns announced that the time had indeed come.

"Get to your dugouts," he told his men, "and shoot at anything that comes up that slope. Don't stop shooting until they're not coming anymore." The soldiers, numb with the knowledge that the battle was finally about to begin, ran to their trenches. In the distance, they could hear the Confederate bugles and a first ragged salvo of rifle shots.

Swinging aboard his horse, Caleb rode the length of the Third Platoon sector, checking that the men were pointed in the right direction and looking for Alleyne, who had been called to headquarters. He found Alleyne and his aide standing at the edge of Third Platoon country trying to regain their breath.

"Christ!" exclaimed Alleyne. "We had to run all the way back. Did you order this attack, Sergeant?"

"No, sir," said Caleb. "Not that I remember, anyway."

"Well, you'd better get off that goddamned horse. I won't have a sergeant presenting a better target than I do. It challenges my authority. Are all the troops on the line?"

"Yes, sir. And most of them seem to be pointing toward the enemy."

"Praise the Lord!" said Alleyne. "It's a miracle. Well, let's see if we can inspire them a little." He turned to his aide. "Smithers, haven't you got a rifle somewhere?"

"Yes, sir."

"Well, get it. I want you to shoot me if I look like I am going to do anything heroic. Now," he said to Caleb, "you take the left side of our sector, and I'll take the right. Those bastards shall not get through, right?"

"Right, sir," said Caleb.

Back on the left side of the Third Platoon line, Caleb worked his way from dugout to dugout, checking ammunition, tapping canteens to see whether they were full, and trying to keep the troops from panicking. The new, barely trained volunteers were nervous. A shot was fired two dugouts away, and Caleb hurried over there in a rage. "What are you shooting at?" he demanded. He looked down the slope but could see nothing except the thin covering of trees hiding the creek.

"Nothing, sir," said a very small private from New Hampshire. "My finger slipped."

"Keep it on the trigger guard for now," Caleb said. "You'll want that cartridge in a little while when the rebs are charging."

"Sergeant," asked one of the soldiers, "is it true that you used to be a slave?"

"Yes," said Caleb.

"What was it like?"

"Better than this," Caleb said. Moving to the back of the line, he shouted, "Now hold steady, keep your eyes on those trees, and don't fire until I give you the signal. When you start firing, don't stop until you get an order or you're out of ammunition. Aim low. Even if you only hit a man in the foot, that's enough to stop him. If you can't hit the men, shoot the horses; they're a bigger target. Now, I want to hear some noise from you men— Hurrah!"

The men's response was a feeble noise closer to a murmur than a shout.

"Damn it," Caleb screamed. "Do it again, and this time mean it! On three: One! Two! Three! HURRAH!"

This time, the men's response was more respectable.

"That's better," said Caleb, "now—"

The distant rifle fire was suddenly louder, and one of Caleb's men shouted, "Here they come!" and another shot was fired.

"Hold your fire," Caleb shouted. "You can't hit anything at this distance!" Down the slope, tiny figures were just entering the woods. "Pick out a target," said Caleb, "and when I give you the signal, hit it. Then choose another. Keep your eyes open and don't waste a shot."

The mounted figures got closer and closer, and Caleb could sense the tension building in his men. "Slowly, slowly," he called out. "Plenty of time. Pick a target. Pick a target."

When he found that he could begin to make out the features on the faces of the attackers, Caleb drew his saber and waved it over his head.

"Fire!"

The resulting volley was ragged, but down the slope some horsemen fell, and the advance seemed to waver a bit.

"Fire again!" Caleb shouted. "Fire at will!" He drew the .36 caliber Colt Navy revolver that Alleyne had found for him and leveled it at the oncoming horsemen more for the effect than in hopes of hitting anyone. One by one, he squeezed off the six rounds and was gratified to see a cavalryman fall from his horse with both hands to his throat. As the rebs grew closer, bullets began to thud into the earth in front of the dugouts and whip through the trees above.

The next volley from Caleb's men was less ragged, and the men began to see its effect on the attackers. Staying low, Caleb worked his way behind the dugouts, both to encourage the men and check on casualties. By the time he got to the left end of the line, only three had been killed and another two wounded. Signaling to the orderlies, he had the wounded men pulled back behind the line. He urged the remaining riflemen to take their dead comrades' ammunition and keep firing.

When the fire from the dugouts caused the charging cavalrymen to begin to turn back, Caleb told his corporal to keep the men firing. Then, he retrieved his horse from the copse behind the dugouts and rode toward the other half of the Third Platoon's lines. Here, things weren't going so well. Though the attackers had been unable to carry the dugouts, they'd lain down halfway down the slope and were riddling the line with deadly fire. Everywhere Caleb looked he saw dead soldiers slumped over the front of their dugouts. The noise was deafening.

"Where's Lieutenant Alleyne?" Caleb shouted at a shocked-looking private, but the man just waved a hand toward the right of the line. Caleb soon found Alleyne lying on his face just in front of a dugout. Turning him over, he saw a neat round hole in the middle of Alleyne's forehead. A trickle of blood ran from it into his right eye. Alleyne's mouth was open wide, as if he'd been shouting when he was hit.

— *54* —

Pulling the lieutenant's body back into an empty gun pit, Caleb looked around and saw most of Alleyne's surviving men lying on their bellies behind the dugouts. They'd clearly started to bolt for the rear and then discovered that this, too, was dangerous. Some had their hands over their heads, as if this would stop a bullet. Running over to them, Caleb began kicking wildly at the men and shouting.

"Get into those dugouts. Go! Go!"

Rather than be kicked to death, the men started crawling back into the dugouts. One soldier did not move, and Caleb found that he'd been kicking a dead corporal. Another cried out, too badly injured to move. "Sorry," Caleb said, but he soon had all the survivors who were able to move back in their dugouts. Crawling along behind them, he ordered them to recover their rifles and recommence firing. Soon, they'd resumed firing, and the approach of the rebels ground to a halt.

Satisfied that he had done about all he could, Caleb was about to go back to check on the other end of the line, when a major rode up from the trees behind the dugouts and hurriedly dismounted.

"Where's your officer?" he shouted, crouching beside Caleb.

"Dead, sir," Caleb said, pointing to Alleyne's body in the dugout.

"Who are you?"

"Sergeant Jardine, sir," Caleb said. "Eleventh Mounted Rifles, now Lieutenant Alleyne's platoon sergeant."

"Are you in charge here?"

"I don't see anybody else, sir."

"Well, Sergeant," the major said. "Things look bad. I don't think we're going to be able to hold this position much longer. How's the other end of your line?"

"Last time I saw them they were doing better than this end," said Caleb.

"How's your ammunition?"

"Getting low."

"I'll try to get some up to you," the major said. "In the meantime, you hold on here as long as you can. If we're going to withdraw, I'll send you a messenger. Be prepared either way."

"Yes, sir."

The major crawled toward his nervous horse, swung into the saddle heavily, and rode back into the trees.

Looking around at the soldiers in the dugouts, Caleb saw one, a thin, pale-faced man with a light growth of beard, who seemed to be firing more steadily and methodically than the others. Crawling over to him, Caleb asked, "What's your name?"

"Crawford," said the man, still firing.

"You're in charge here, Crawford," Caleb said. "Keep these men firing. I have to go check on the other end of the line. If a messenger comes, send someone to get me."

"Okay, Sarge."

Pausing to relieve Alleyne of his cartridge belt and sidearm, the twin of his own, Caleb strapped them on and began crawling toward his horse.

Once his troop was safely across the creek, Boyd Jardine ordered them to dismount at a sheltered spot where the sharply uphill slope of the ground toward the Union positions offered some cover. Ordering his sergeant to keep the men there and check their ammunition and equipment, he and his corporal crept up the slope until they could see over to a less steep section of terrain. There, they saw the infantry unit that had preceded them pinned down by light-arms fire from the dugouts on the other side of the woods.

Continuing to creep toward the infantry unit, Jardine came upon a lieutenant who was directing fire at the dugouts and urging his men to move forward without much success.

"Where's your captain?" Jardine asked the lieutenant.

"Dead, sir," said the lieutenant, gesturing ahead. "Caught a bullet smack in the throat."

"Can you take those dugouts?"

"Doesn't look like it right now," said the lieutenant, "but we're trying."

"Well," said Jardine, "I've got a troop of cavalry down the slope that's eager to give you a hand. Do you think you can keep the Yanks' heads down and give us a chance to get close enough to do some good?"

"We'll do our best, sir."

"All right," Jardine said. "I'm going to be bringing them up right quiet like in a few minutes. When you hear our bugles, we'd appreciate it if you'd give those bastards a bit of hell, and maybe between us we can get this one over."

"Will do, sir," said the lieutenant as Jardine and his corporal started crawling back down the slope.

Caleb was approaching the left side of the line from the trees at the rear when he heard a bugle call, and the volume of small-arms fire coming toward them suddenly increased. Spurring his horse, he rode out of the woods to see rebel cavalry charging up the slope some two hundred yards from the dugouts. They were closing rapidly and their sabers flashed in the sunlight. Several fired pistols as they rode through the infantry who were providing them with covering fire.

The rifle fire from the troops in the dugout, who had never before faced cavalry, faltered, and Caleb saw several of them half turn as if to scramble from the dugout. Digging his spurs into his mount's sides, Caleb surged forward.

"Fire! Fire! Damn you! Hold the line! Shoot! Shoot!" As he rode, he put the reins into his mouth and drew both pistols, leveling them at the charging cavalry as his horse reached the dugout.

Caleb felt his horse rising under him as it soared over the dugout. It landed on the other side, caught its balance, and galloped toward the approaching line of gray-clad horsemen. Realizing that he had no other choice now, Caleb blazed away at the leading horseman, an officer, with both pistols until he was clicking on empty cylinders.

Caleb thought that he had missed, but the officer stiffened in the saddle, rocked back, half turned to the left, and tumbled to the ground headfirst. His mount, also hit, screamed and veered to the left, colliding with one side of the line of horsemen who had been following their officer. Momentum broken and suffering casualties, that side of the charge wobbled and then broke. Riders checked and half turned in their saddles to see where the others were. Some began to turn back. On the right side of the charge, three lone Confederate horsemen carried on toward the dugout, but at the last minute—finding themselves alone and exposed— they veered off under heavy fire.

Holstering his pistols, Caleb drew his saber and rode directly toward the hesitating left side of the charge, screaming at the top of his lungs. The apparition of a giant black man brandishing a saber further confounded the hesitant horsemen, and soon the charge was totally broken. Its remnants were riding back down the slope, abandoning their casualties and some riderless horses. The infantry, at first slowly and then more rapidly, began to join the rout. A cheer went up from the dugout behind Caleb.

Realizing both that he was in command of the field and that it could not last forever, Caleb loaded his pistols and checked the fallen horsemen to make sure that none were shamming and still dangerous. Then he rode over to where the fallen officer's mount, bleeding from a flesh wound, was grazing quietly by the body of his rider lying face down in the short grass. Caleb dismounted and stood looking down at the body. There was a bloody hole in the back of the dead man's long gray jacket where Caleb's shot had gone clear through his body.

Kneeling down, Caleb turned the body over and found himself looking at Boyd Jardine's unmarked and expressionless face. The first words he had ever spoken to Jardine suddenly flashed into Caleb's mind: "You don't want to buy me. I'll kill the man who buys me." That seemed a lifetime ago.

Caleb felt a sharp stab of regret. "I'm sorry," he told the man who had been his master, his enemy, and finally, his friend. He reached down and closed Jardine's eyes.

Caleb was staring down at the face of his dead former master when he heard shouting from the dugouts. He looked up to see a lieutenant standing on top of a dugout and shouting at him, "Sergeant! We've got to get out of here. Big attack coming. We can't hold out. Come on!" The lieutenant turned to the troops and began to shoo them from the dugouts as if they were a flock of chickens.

Caleb started to mount his horse. But then he stopped and turned back to Jardine's body. Kneeling again, he wrapped his arms around Jardine and rose to his feet.

"Steady, steady," he murmured and, with great effort, laid the body across the saddle of Jardine's horse. He then mounted his own horse and led Jardine's burdened animal toward the nearly empty dugouts. As Caleb threaded his way through the retreating

Union troops, some looked with curiosity at the black sergeant leading a horse with a dead body on it, but none questioned him.

Half an hour later, when they crossed the strong Union line near Centreville, Captain Lockhart, trying to organize and account for the remnants of Company B, spotted Caleb.

"Sergeant Jardine!"

Caleb stopped and turned toward the captain, who was coming at him with hand extended. "It's a relief to see you, Sergeant," Lockhart said, shaking his hand. "I thought that you'd stopped one, like poor Alleyne. I'm glad to see you haven't. Unscratched, eh?"

"Yes, sir," said Caleb.

"The lucky survive," said the captain, "and sometimes the brave. I've heard what you did with Alleyne's platoon, Sergeant, and it won't be forgotten."

"Thank you, sir."

Lockhart suddenly seemed to notice the load on the horse Caleb was leading. "If you don't mind me asking, what have you got there?"

"Prisoner, sir," said Caleb. "But he died on me."

"An officer?" asked Lockhart.

"Yes, sir," Caleb said. "He was."

"There's a wagon somewhere around here," Lockhart said vaguely, "picking up the dead."

"I'll find it, sir," said Caleb.

"All right, Sergeant," Lockhart said. "And after you do, report to Lieutenant Fergus over by that red barn. He's got the Third Platoon now, and he'll be glad to see you."

"Yes, sir," Caleb said, saluting and beginning to lead his horse away.

But instead of looking for the wagon for the dead, Caleb borrowed a spade from a puzzled corporal. Beside a small brook he stopped at a spot that he thought he could find again. Caleb tied both horses to a tree, lowered Jardine's body to the ground, and began to dig a grave. Two days later, a report appeared on the front page of the *New York Times*.

"Union Suffers Another Defeat at Second Battle of Bull Run," the headline read. "Stanton vows command changes as Confederates repeat victory in northeast Virginia."

Toward the end of the report were two brief paragraphs. One, headed "Among the Slain," listed Boyd Jardine: Captain, CSA, Kershaw County Dragoons.

The other, under the heading "Conspicuous During the Action," reported that Sergeant Caleb Jardine of the Eleventh Mounted Rifles had been mentioned in dispatches for conspicuous gallantry and was brevetted Second Lieutenant of Volunteers (Colored), effective immediately.

About the Author

Charles Alverson was born in California and, after living in England and Wales, now lives as a confirmed expatriate in Serbia. He has been writing novels since 1971 across a range of genres: thriller, detective, young adult, humor, and popular fiction. He has also written children's books, short plays, and nonfiction, and he worked as a reporter for the *Wall Street Journal* and *Rolling Stone*. Alverson also cowrote the screenplays for the films *Jabberwocky* and *Brazil*. *Caleb* is his first historical novel, but not his last.